JOSEY WALES

Two Westerns by Forrest Carter

GONE TO TEXAS
&
THE VENGEANCE TRAIL
OF JOSEY WALES

Afterword by Lawrence Clayton

University of New Mexico Press
Albuquerque

Gone to Texas was first published in 1973
under the title *The Rebel Outlaw: Josey Wales.*
The Vengeance Trail of Josey Wales
was first published in 1976.

Library of Congress Cataloging-in-Publication Data

Carter, Forrest.
[Rebel outlaw]
Josey Wales : two westerns / by Forrest Carter.
p.   cm.
Contents: Gone to Texas—The vengeance trail of Josey Wales.
ISBN 0-8263-1168-7
1. Wales, Josey (Fictitious character)—Fiction.
2. Western stories.
I. Carter, Forrest.
Vengeance trail of Josey Wales. 1989.   II. Title.
PS3553.A777J6   1989
813'.54—dc20   89-16587 CIP

This volume contains the complete texts
of the Delacorte Press editions
of *Gone to Texas* and *The Vengeance Trail of Josey Wales.*

Contents

GONE TO TEXAS

For Ten Bears

Preface

Missouri is called the "Mother of Outlaws." She acquired her title in the aftermath of the Civil War, when bitter men who had fought without benefit of rules in the Border War (a war within a War) could find no place for themselves in a society of old enmities and Reconstruction government. They rode and lived aimlessly, in the vicious circle of reprisal, robbery, and shoot-out that led to nowhere. The Cause was gone, and all that remained was personal feud, retribution . . . and survival. Many of them drifted to Texas.

If Missouri was the Mother, then Texas was the Father . . . the refuge, with boundless terrain and bloody frontier, where a proficient pistolman could find reason for existence and room to ride. The initials

"GTT," hurriedly carved on the doorpost of a Southern shack, was message enough to relatives and friends that the carver was in "law trouble," and Gone To Texas.

In those days they weren't called "gunfighters"; that came in the 1880's from the dime noveleers. They were called "pistolmen," and they referred to their weapon as a "pistol," or by the make . . . a "Colts' .44." The Missouri guerrilla was the first expert pistolman. According to U.S. Army dispatches, the guerrillas used this "new" war weapon with devastating results.

This is the story of one of those outlaws.

The outlaws . . . and the Indians . . . are real . . . they lived; lived in a time when the meaning of "good" or "bad" depended mostly on the jasper who was saying it. There were too many wrongs mixed in with what we thought were the "rights"; so we shall not try to judge them here . . . but simply, to the best of our ability, to "tell it like it is" . . . or was.

The men . . . white and red . . . and the times that produced them . . . and how they lived it out . . . to finish the course.

Part 1

Chapter 1

The dispatch was filed December 8, 1866:

FROM: Central Missouri Military District. Major Thomas Bacon, 8th Kansas Cavalry, Commanding.

TO: Headquarters, Texas Military District, Galveston, Texas. Major General Charles Griffin, Commanding.

Dispatch filed with: General Philip Sheridan, Southwest Military District, New Orleans, Louisiana.

DAYLIGHT ROBBERY OF MITCHELL BANK, LEXINGTON, LAFAYETTE COUNTY, MISSOURI DECEMBER 4 THIS INSTANT. BANDITS ESCAPING WITH EIGHT THOUSAND DOLLARS, U.S. ARMY PAYROLL: NEW-MINTED TWENTY-DOLLAR GOLD PIECES. PURSUIT TOWARD INDIAN

3

NATIONS TERRITORY. BELIEVED HEADED SOUTH TO
TEXAS. ONE BANDIT SEVERELY WOUNDED. ONE IDENTI-
FIED. DESCRIPTION FOLLOWS:
JOSEY WALES, AGE 32. 5 FEET 9 INCHES. WEIGHT 160
POUNDS. BLACK EYES, BROWN HAIR, MEDIUM MUS-
TACHE. HEAVY BULLET SCAR HORIZONTAL RIGHT CHEEK-
BONE, DEEP KNIFE SCAR LEFT CORNER MOUTH. PREVI-
OUSLY LISTED WANTED BY U.S. MILITARY AS EX-
GUERRILLA LIEUTENANT SERVING WITH CAPT. WILLIAM
"BLOODY BILL" ANDERSON. WALES REFUSED AMNESTY-
SURRENDER, 1865. IN ADDITION TO CRIMINAL ACTIVITY,
MUST BE REGARDED AS INSURRECTIONIST REBEL.
ARMED AND DANGEROUS. THREE-THOUSAND-DOLLAR RE-
WARD OFFERED BY U.S. MILITARY, MISSOURI DISTRICT.
DEAD OR ALIVE.

It was cold. The wind whipped the wet pines into
mournful sighing and sped the rain like bullets. It
caused the campfires to jump and flicker and the soldiers around them to curse commanding officers and
the mothers who gave them birth.

The campfires were arranged in a curious half-
moon, forming a flickering chain that closed about
these foothills of the Ozark Mountains. In the dark,
cloud-scudding night the bright dots looked like a net
determined to hold back the mountains from advancing into the Neosho River Basin, Indian Nations, just
beyond.

Josey Wales knew the meaning of the net. He squatted, two hundred yards back in the hollow of heavy
pine growth, and watched . . . and chewed with slow
contemplation at a wad of tobacco. In nearly eight
years of riding, how many times had he seen the cir-
cle-net of Yankee Cavalry thrown out around him?

It seemed a hundred years ago, that day in 1858. A

young farmer, Josey Wales, following the heavy turning plow in the creek bottoms of Cass County, Missouri. It would be a two-mule crop this year, a big undertaking for a mountain man, and Josey Wales was mountain. ALL the way back through his great-grandfolk of the past in the blue ridges of Virginia; the looming, smoke-haze peaks of Tennessee and into the broken beauty of the Ozarks; always it had been the mountains. The mountains were a way of life; independence and sanctuary, a philosophy that lent the peculiar code to the mountain man. "Where the soil's thin, the blood's thick," was their clannishness. To rectify a wrong carried the same obligation as being beholden to a favor. It was a religion that went beyond thought but rather was marrowed in the bone that lived or died with the man.

Josey Wales, with his young wife and baby boy, had come to Cass County. That first year he "obligated" himself for forty acres of flatland. He had built the house with his own hands and raised a crop . . . and now this year he had obligated for forty more acres that took in the creek bottom. Josey Wales was "gittin' ahead." He hitched his mules to the turning plow in the dark of morning and waited in the fields, rested on his plow stock, for the first dim light that would allow him to plow.

It was a long time before Josey saw the smoke rising, that spring morning of 1858. The creek bottom was new ground, and the plow jerked at the roots, and Josey had to gee-haw the mules around the stumps. He hadn't looked up until he heard the shots. It was then he saw the smoke. It rose black-gray over the ridge. It could only be the house. He had left the mules, running barefoot, overalls flapping against his skinny legs; wildly, through the briars and sumac, across the rocky gullies. There had been little left when he fell, exhausted, into the swept clearing. The timbers of the cabin had fallen in. The fire was a guttering smoke that had already filled its appetite. He ran, fell, ran again . . . around and around the ruin, screaming his wife's name, calling the baby boy, until his voice hoarsened into a whisper.

He had found them there in what had been the kitchen. They had fallen near the door, and the blackened skeleton arms of the baby boy were clinging to his mother's neck. Numbly, mechanically, Josey had gotten two sacks from the barn and rolled up the charred figures in them. He dug their single grave beneath the big water oak at the edge of the yard, and as darkness fell and moonlight silvered over the ruins, he tried to render the Christian burial.

But his Bible remembering would only come in snatches. "Ashes to ashes . . . dust to dust," he had mumbled through his blackened face. "The Lord gives and the Lord takes away." "Ye're fer me 'er agin' me, said Jesus." And finally, "An eye fer an eye . . . a tooth fer a tooth."

Great tears rolled down the smoked face of Josey Wales there in the moonlight. A tremble shook his body with uncontrollable fierceness that chattered his teeth and jerked his head. It was the last time Josey Wales would cry.

Chapter 2

Though raiding had taken place back and forth across the Missouri-Kansas Border since 1855, the burning of Josey Wales' cabin was the first of the Kansas "Redleg" raids to hit Cass County. The names of Jim Lane, Doc Jennison, and James Montgomery were already becoming infamous as they led looting armies of pillagers into Missouri. Beneath a thinly disguised "cause" they set the Border aflame.

Josey Wales had "taken to the brush," and there he found others. They were guerrilla veterans, these young farmers, by the time the War between the States began. The formalities of governments in conflict only meant an occupying army that drove them deeper into the brush. They already had their War. It was not a formal conflict with rules and courtesy, battles that began and ended . . . and rest behind the lines. There were no lines. There were no rules. Theirs was a war to the knife, of burned barn and ravaged countryside, of looted home and outraged womenfolk. It was a blood feud. The Black Flag became a flag of honorable warning: "We ask no quarter, we give none." And they didn't.

When Union General Ewing issued General Order Eleven to arrest the womenfolk, to burn the homes, to depopulate the Missouri counties along the Border of Kansas, the guerrilla ranks swelled with more riders. Quantrill, Bloody Bill Anderson, whose sister was killed in a Union prison, George Todd, Dave Pool, Fletcher Taylor, Josey Wales; the names grew in infamy in Kansas and Union territory, but they were the "boys" to the folks.

Union raiders launching the infamous "Night of Blood" in Clay County bombed a farmhouse that tore off the arm of a mother, killed her young son, and sent two more sons to the ranks of the guerrillas. They were Frank and Jesse James.

Revolvers were their weapons. They were the first to perfect pistol work. With reins in teeth, a Colts' pistol in each hand, their charges were a fury in suicidal mania. Where they struck became names in bloody history. Lawrence, Centralia, Fayette, and Pea Ridge. In 1862 Union General Halleck issued General Order Two: "Exterminate the guerrillas of Missouri; shoot them down like animals, hang all prisoners." And so it was like animals they became, hunted, turning viciously to strike their adversaries when it was to their advantage. Jennison's Redlegs sacked and burned Dayton, Missouri, and the "boys" retaliated by burning Aubry, Kansas, to the ground, fighting Union patrols all the way back to the Missouri mountains. They slept in their saddles or rolled up under bushes with reins in their hands. With muffled horses' hooves, they would slip through Union lines to cross the Indian Nations on their way to Texas to lick their wounds and regroup. But always they came back.

As the tide of the Confederacy ebbed toward defeat, the blue uniforms multiplied along the Border. The ranks of the "boys" began to thin. On October 26, 1864, Bloody Bill died with two smoking pistols in his hands. Hop Wood, George Todd, Noah Webster, Frank Shepard, Bill Quantrill . . . the list grew longer . . . the ranks thinner. The peace was signed at Appomattox, and word began to filter into the brush that amnesty-pardons were to be granted to the guerrillas. It was little Dave Pool who had brought the word to eighty-two of the hardened riders. Around the campfire of an Ozark mountain hollow he explained it to them that spring evening.

"All a feller has to do is ride in to the Union post, raise his right hand, and swear sich as he'll be loyal to the United States. Then," said Dave, "he kin taken up his hoss . . . and go home."

Boots scuffed the ground, but the men said nothing. Josey Wales, his big hat pulled low to his eyes, squatted back from the fire. He still held the reins of his horse . . . as if he had only paused here for the moment. Dave Pool kicked a pine knot into the fire, and it popped and skittered with smoke.

"Guess I'll be ridin' in, boys," he said quietly and moved to his horse. Almost as one the men rose and walked to their horses. They were a savage-looking crew. The heavy pistols sagged in holsters from their waists. Some of them wore shoulder pistols as well, and here and there long knives at their belts picked up a twinkle from the campfire. They had been accused of many things, of most of which they were guilty, but cowardice was not one of them. As they swung to their mounts they looked back across the campfire and saw the lone figure still squatting. The horses stomped impatiently, but the riders held them. Pool advanced his horse toward the fire.

"Air ye' goin', Josey?" he asked.

There was a long silence. Josey Wales did not lift his eyes from the fire. "I reckin not," he said.

Dave Pool turned his horse. "Good luck, Josey," he called and lifted his hand in half salute.

Other hands were lifted, and the calls of " 'Luck" drifted back . . . and they were gone.

All except one. After a long moment the rider slowly walked his horse into the circle of firelight. Young Jamie Burns stepped from his mount and looked across the fire at Josey. "Why, Josey? Why don't ye go?"

Josey looked at the boy. Eighteen years old, rail-thin, with hollowed cheeks and blond hair that spilled to his shoulders beneath the slouch hat. "Ye'd best make haste and ketch up with 'em, boy," Josey said, almost tenderly. "A lone rider won't never make it."

The boy smoothed the ground with a toe of his heavy boot. "I've rid with ye near 'bout two year now, Josey . . ." he paused, "I was . . . jest wonderin' why."

Josey stood and walked to the fire, leading his horse. He gazed intently into the flames. "Well," he said quietly, "I jest cain't . . . anyhow, there ain't nowheres to go."

If Josey Wales had understood all the reasons, which he did not, he still could not have explained them to the boy. There was, in truth, no place for Josey Wales to go. The fierce mountain clan code would have deemed it a sin for him to take up life. His loyalty was there, in the grave with his wife and baby. His obligation was to the feud. And despite the cool cunning he had learned, the animal quickness and the deliberate arts of killing with pistol and knife, beneath it all there still rose the black rage of the mountain man. His family had been wronged. His wife and boy murdered. No people, no government, no king, could ever repay. He did not think these thoughts. He only felt the feeling of generations of the code handed down from the Welsh and Scot clans and burned into his being. If there was nowhere to go, it did not mean emptiness in the life of Josey Wales. That emptiness was filled with a cold hatred and a bitterness that showed when his black eyes turned mean.

Jamie Burns sat down on a log. "I ain't got nowheres to go neither," he said.

A mockingbird suddenly set up song from a honeysuckle vine. A wood thrush chuckled for night nesting.

"Have ye got a chaw?" Jamie asked.

Josey pulled a green-black twist from his pocket and handed it across the fire. The man and the boy were partners.

Chapter 3

Josey Wales and Jamie Burns "took to the brush."
The following month Jesse James tried to surrender
under a flag of truce and was shot through the lungs,
barely escaping. When the news reached Josey his
opinion of the enemy's treachery was reinforced, and
he smiled coldly as he gave Jamie the news, "I could've
told little Dingus,*" he said.

There were others like them. In February, 1866,
Josey and Jamie joined Bud and Donnie Pence, Jim
Wilkerson, Frank Gregg, and Oliver Shephard in a
daylight robbery of the Clay County Savings Bank at
Liberty. Outlawry exploded over Missouri. A Missouri
Pacific train was held up at Otterville. Federal Troops
were reinforced, and the Governor ordered out militia
and cavalry.

* "Dingus" was the nickname given Jesse James by his
comrades.

But now the old haunts were gone. Twice they barely escaped capture or death through betrayal. The riding was growing more treacherous. They began to talk of Texas. Josey had ridden the trail five times, but Jamie had never. As fall brought its golden haze of melancholy to the Ozarks and the hint of cold wind from the north, Josey announced to the boy over a morning campfire, "After Lexington we're goin' to Texas." The bank at Lexington was a legitimate "target" for guerrillas. "Carpetbag bank, Yank Army payroll," Josey said. But they had gone against the rules, without a third man outside of the bank.

Jamie, with his flat gray eyes, coolly manned the door while Josey took the payroll. They had hit, guerrilla-style, bold and open, in the afternoon. When they came out, jerking the slipknot of their reins from the hitch rack, it was Jamie first up and riding his little mare. As Josey jerked his reins loose he had dropped the money bag, and as he stooped to retrieve it the reins had slipped from his hand. At that moment a shot rang out from the bank. The big roan had bolted, and Josey, instead of chasing the horse, had crouched, the money bag at his feet, and with a Colts' .44 in each hand poured a staccato roar of gunfire at the bank. He would have died there, for his instinct was not that of the criminal to run and save his loot, but that of the guerrilla, to turn on his hated enemies.

As people crowded out of the stores and blue uniforms poured out of the courthouse, Jamie whirled his horse and drummed back up the street, the little mare stretching out. He grabbed the trailing reins of the roan and while Josey turned the big .44's toward the scattering crowd he calmly led the roan at a canter back to the lone figure in the street.

Josey had holstered his pistols, grabbed up the bag,

and swung on the horse Indian-fashion as it broke into a dead run. Down the street they had come, the horses side by side, straight at the blue uniforms. The soldiers scattered, but as the horses came near to a scope of woods just ahead, the soldiers, kneeling, opened up with carbines. Josey heard the hard splat of the bullet and brought the big roan close to Jamie . . . or the boy would have fallen from the saddle.

Josey slowed the horses, holding the arm of Jamie as they came down into the brakes of the Missouri River. Turning northeast along the river, Josey brought the horses to a walk in the heavy willow growth and finally halted them. Far off in the distance he could hear men shouting back and forth as they worked their way into the brakes.

Jamie Burns had been hit hard. Josey swung down from his horse and lifted the jacket of the boy. The heavy rifle slug had entered his back, just missing the spine, but had emerged through his lower chest. Dark blood was caked over his trousers and saddle, and lighter blood still spurted from his wound. Jamie gripped the saddle horn with both hands.

"It's right bad, ain't it, Josey?" he asked with surprising calm.

Josey's answer was a quick nod as he pulled two shirts from Jamie's saddlebags and tore them into strips. He worked quickly making heavy pads and placed them on the open wounds, front and back, and then wound the stripping tightly around the boy. As Josey finished his work Jamie looked down at him from beneath the old slouch hat.

"I ain't gittin' off this hoss, Josey. I kin make it. Me and you seen fellers in lot worse shape make it, ain't we, Josey?"

Josey rested his hand over the tightly gripped hands

of the boy. He made the gesture in a rough, careless way . . . but Jamie felt the meaning. "Thet we have, Jamie," Josey looked steadily up at him, "and we'll make it by a long-tailed mile."

The sounds of horses breaking willows made Josey swing up on his horse. He turned in his saddle and said quietly to Jamie, "Jest hold on and let thet little mare follow me."

"Where to?" Jamie whispered.

A rare smile crossed the scarred face of the outlaw.

"Why, we're goin' where all good brush fighters go . . . where we ain't expected," he drawled. "We're doubling back to Lexington, nat'uly."

The dusk of evening was bringing on a quick darkness as they came out of the brakes. Josey set their course a few hundred yards north of the trail they had taken out of town, but angling so that it appeared they were headed for Lexington, though their direction would take them slightly north of the settlement. He never broke the horses into a trot but kept them walking steadily. The sounds of the shouting men on the river bank grew fainter and w re finally lost behind them.

Josey knew the posse of militia and cavalry were searching for their crossing of the Missouri River. He pulled his horse back alongside the mare. Jamie's mouth was set in a grim line of pain, but he appeared steady in the saddle.

"Thet posse figures us fer Clay County," Josey said, "where little Dingus and Frank is stompin' around at."

Jamie tried to speak, but a quick jolt of pain cut his breath into a half shriek. He nodded his head that he understood.

As they rode, Josey reloaded the Colts and checked

the loads of the two pistols in his saddle holsters. With quick glances over his shoulder, he betrayed his anxiety for Jamie. Once, with the icy calm of the seasoned guerrilla, he held the horses on a wooded knoll while a score of possemen galloped past on their way to the river. Even as the horses thundered close, not fifty yards from their concealment, Josey was down off his mount and checking the bandages under Jamie's shirt.

"Look down at me, boy," he said. "Iff'n you look at 'em they might git a feelin'."

There was dried blood on the tight bandages, and Josey grunted with satisfaction. "We're in good shape, Jamie. The bleeding has stopped."

Josey swung aboard the roan and clucked the horses forward. He turned in the saddle to Jamie, "We'll jest keep walkin' 'til we walk slap out of Missouri."

The lights of Lexington showed on their right and then slowly receded behind them. West of Lexington there were Kansas City and Fort Leavenworth with a large contingent of soldiers; Richmond was north with a cavalry detachment of Missouri Militia; to the east were Fayette and Glasgow with more cavalry. Josey turned the horses south. All the way to the Blackwater River there was nothing except scattered farms. True, Warrensburg was just across the river, but first they had to put miles between themselves and Lexington.

Boldly, Josey turned onto the Warrensburg road. He pulled the mare up beside him, for he knew that Jamie was weakening and he feared the boy would fall from his horse. The hours and miles fell behind them. The road, though dangerous to travel, presented no obstacles to the horses, and the tough animals were accustomed to long forced marches.

As the first gray light streaked the clouds to the east, Josey jerked the horses to a standstill. For a moment he sat, listening. "Riders," he said tersely, "coming from behind us." Quickly he pulled the horses off the road and had barely made the heavy brush when a large group of blue-clad riders swept past them. Jamie sat erect in the saddle and watched with burning eyes. The drawn, tight lines of his face showed that only the pain had kept him conscious.

"Josey, them fellers ride like the Second Colorado."

"Well," Josey drawled, "yore eyes is fine. Them boys is right pert fighters, but they couldn't track a litter of pigs 'crost a kitchen floor." He searched the boy's face as he spoke and was rewarded with a tight grin. "But," he added, "jest in case they can, we're leavin' the road. That line of woods means the Blackwater, and we're goin' to take a rest."

As he spoke, Josey turned the horses toward the river. With a casual joke he had hidden from the boy their alarming position. One look at Jamie in the light showed his weakness. He had to have rest, if nothing more. The horses were too tired to run if they were jumped, and the appearance of soldiers from the north meant the alarm was to be spread south. They figured him for heading to the Nations. This time they figured him right.

Chapter 4

The heavy timbered approaches to the Blackwater afforded a welcome refuge from the open rolling prairie over which they had come. Josey found a shallow stream that ran toward the river and guided the horses down it, knee-deep in water. Fifty yards back from the sluggish Blackwater he brought the horses up the bank of the stream and pushed through heavy sumac vines until he found a small glade sunken between banks lined with elm and gum trees. He helped Jamie from the saddle, but the boy's legs buckled under him. Josey carried him in his arms to a place where the bank overhung the glade. There he lay blankets and stretched Jamie out on his back. He pulled the saddles from the horses and picketed them with lariats on the lush grass of the marshy ravine. When he returned, Jamie was sleeping, his face flushed with the beginning of fever.

It was high noon when Jamie wakened. The pain washed over him in heavy throbs that tore at his chest. He saw Josey hunched over a tiny fire, feeding the fire with one hand as he maneuvered a heavy tin cup over the flame with the other. Seeing Jamie awake, he came to him with the cup, and cradling the boy's head in his arms, he pressed the cup to his lips. "A little Tennessee rifle-ball tonic, Jamie," he said.

Jamie swallowed and coughed, "Tastes like you made it with rifle balls," and he managed a weak grin.

Josey tilted more of the hot liquid down his throat. "Sass'fras and iron root, with a dab of side meat . . . we ain't got no beef," he said and eased the boy's head back on the blanket. "Yonder, in Tennessee, every time there was a shootin' scrape, Gran'ma commenced to boil up tonic. She'd send me to the hollers to dig sass'-fras and iron root. Reckin I dug enough roots to loosen all the ground in Carter County. Re'clect that oncet Pa been coughin' fit to kill fer a month of Sundays. Everybody said as how he had lung fever. Gran'ma commenced to feedin' him tonic ever' mornin'. Then one night Pa had a fit of coughin' and spit up a rifle ball on the pillarcase . . . next mornin' he felt goodern' a boar hawg chasin' a sow. Gran'ma said was the tonic done it."

Jamie's eyes closed, and he breathed with heavy, broken rhythm. Josey eased the tangled blond head down on the blanket. For the first time he noticed the long, almost girlish eyelashes, the smooth face.

"Grit an' sand, by God," he muttered. There was tenderness in the gesture as he smoothed the tousled hair with a rough hand. Josey sat back on his heels and looked thoughtfully into the cup. He frowned. The liquid was pink . . . blood, lung blood.

Josey watched the horses cropping grass without seeing them. He was thinking of Jamie. Too many times, in a hundred fights, he had seen men choke on their blood from pierced lungs. The nearest help was the Nations. He had been through the Cherokee's land several times on the trail to Texas and back. Once he had met General Stand Watie, the Cherokee General of the Confederacy. He knew many of the warriors well and once had joined with them as outriders to General Jo Shelby's Cavalry when Shelby raided north along the Kansas Border. The bone-handled knife that protruded from the top of his left boot had been given him by the Cherokee. On its handle was inscribed the Wanton mark that only proven braves could wear. He trusted the Cherokee, and he trusted his medicine.

Although he had heard that the Federals were moving in on the Cherokee's land because of their siding with the Confederates, he knew the Indian would not be easily moved and that he still controlled most of the territory. Jamie had to be gotten to the Cherokee. There was no other help. In his mind Josey sketched the map of the country he knew so well. There were sixty miles of broken, rolling prairie between him and the Grand River. Beyond the Grand was the haven of the Ozarks that could be skirted but was always near at hand for safety . . . all the way to the border of the Nations.

Gathering clouds had moved over the sun. Where it had been warm, a brisk wind picked up from the north and brought a chill. Josey was reluctant to wake the boy, who was still sleeping. He decided to wait another hour, bringing them closer to the dusk of evening. It was pleasant in the glade. The light wash of the river was constant in the distance. A redheaded woodpecker set to hammering on an elm, and brush wrens chattered, gathering grass seeds in the ravine.

Josey rose and stretched his arms. He knelt to pull the blanket higher around Jamie, and in that split instant the chill warning of silence ran cold over him. The brush wrens flew up in a brown cloud. The woodpecker disappeared around the tree. He moved his hand toward the holstered right pistol as he turned his head upward to the opposite bank and looked into the barrels of rifles held by two bearded men.

"Now you jest do that, cousin," the taller one spoke. He had the rifle to shoulder and was sighting down the barrel. "You bring that ol' pistol right out."

Josey looked at them steadily but didn't move. They weren't soldiers. Both wore dirty overalls and nondescript jackets. The tall one had mean eyes that burned down the rifle barrel at Josey. The shorter of the two held his rifle more loosely.

"This here is him, Abe," the short one spoke. "That's Josey Wales. I seen him at Lone Jack with Bloody Bill. He's meaner'n a rattler and twicet as fast with them pistols."

"Yore a real tush hawg, ain't ye, Wales?" Abe said sarcastically. "What's the matter with that'n laying down?"

Josey didn't answer but gazed steadily back at the two. He watched the wind flutter a red bandanna around the throat of Abe.

"Tell you what, Mr. Wales," Abe said, "you put yore hands top of yore head and stand up facin' me."

Josey clasped his hands on top of his hat, stood slowly, and squared about to face the men. His right knee trembled slightly.

"Watch him, Abe," the short man half yelled, "I seen him. . . ."

"Shut up, Lige," Abe said roughly. "Now, Mr. Wales, I'd as soon shoot ye now, 'ceptin' it'll be harder to drag ye through the brush to where's we can git our pound price fer ye. Move yore left hand down and unbuckle that pistol belt. Make it slow 'nough I kin count the hairs on yer hand."

As Josey slowly lowered his hand to the belt buckle, his left shoulder moved imperceptibly beneath the buckskin jacket. The movement tilted forward the .36 Navy Colt beneath his arm. The gun belt fell. From the corner of his eye Josey saw Jamie, still sleeping beneath the blanket.

Abe sighed in relief. "There, ye see, Lige, when ye pull his teeth he's tame as a heel hound. I always wanted to face out one of these big pistol fighters they raise all the fuss about. It's all in the way ye handle 'em. Now ye call up Benny back there on the horse."

Lige half turned, his eyes still darting back at Josey. With his free hand he cupped his mouth, "Bennnnny! Come up . . . we got 'em." In the distance a horse crashed through the undergrowth, moving toward them.

Josey felt the looseness come over him that marks the fighter, natural born. He coolly measured the distance while his brain toted up the chances for a pistolman. He was past the first tense moment. His adversaries had relaxed; there was a third coming up. This caused a slight distraction, but he needed another before the third man arrived. For the first time he spoke . . . so suddenly that Abe jumped. "Listen, Mister," he said in a half-whining, placating tone, "there's gold in them saddlebags . . ." he brought his right hand easily from his head to point at the saddles, "and you can . . ."

In midsentence he rolled his body with the quickness of a cat. His right hand was already snaking out the Navy as his body flipped over down the bank. The rifle shot dug the ground where he had been. It was the only shot Abe made. The Navy was spitting flame from a rolling, dodging target. Once, twice, three times . . . faster than a man could count, Josey fanned the hammer. The glade was filled with a solid roar of sound. Abe pitched forward, down the bank. Lige staggered backward into a tree and sat down. Blood spurted like a fountain from his chest. He never got off a shot.

Out of the roll, Josey came to his feet, running up the bank and into the undergrowth; but the frightened horseman had wheeled his mount and fled. Returning, Josey rolled the facedown Abe over on his back. He noted with satisfaction the two neat holes made by the Navy, less than an inch apart in the center of Abe's chest. Lige sat against the tree, his face frozen in startled surprise. His left eye stared blankly at the treetops, and where his right eye had been, there was a round, bloody cavern.

"Caught 'em a mite high," Josey grunted and then noticed the gaping hole in Lige's chest. He turned. Halfway down the opposite bank, Jamie lay prone on his stomach, a .44 Colt in his right hand. He grinned weakly back at Josey.

"I knowed ye'd go fer the big 'un first, Josey. I shaded ye by a hair on that 'un."

Josey came across the glade and looked down at the boy. "If ye've started them holes in ye to leakin' agin, I'm goin' to whup ye with a knotted plow line."

"They ain't, Josey, honest. I feel pert as a ruttin'

buck." Jamie tried to rise, and his knees buckled under him. He sat down. Josey walked to the saddlebags and brought back a small bag. He handed the bag to Jamie.

"Jaw on this side meat and 'pone while 1 saddle the horses," he commanded. "We got to ride, boy. Thet feller rode out'n here won't let his shirttail hit his back 'til he's got mobs after us all over hell and Sunday." Josey was moving as he talked, cinching saddles, checking the horses, retrieving his holstered pistols, and finally reloading the .36 Navy.

"We got near fifty mile to the South Grand. Most of it is open with no more'n a gully ever' ten mile to hide a hoss. Them Colorado boys rode south . . . spreadin' word and roustin' out all the jaspers after reeward money. Now," he said grimly, "they'll know fer sure, we're headed south."

A fit of coughing seized Jamie as Josey lifted him into the saddle, and Josey watched with alarm as blood tinted his lips. He swung on his horse beside the boy.

"Ye know, Jamie," he said, "I know a feller lives in a cabin at the fork of the Grand and Osage. Ye'd be safe there and ye could lay out awhile. I could show m'self back upcountry and . . ."

"I reckin not," Jamie interrupted. His voice was weak, but there was no mistaking the dogged stubbornness.

"Ye damn little fool," Josey exploded, "I ain't totin' ye all over hell's creation and ye dribblin' blood over half Missouri. I got better things to do. . . ." Josey's voice trailed off. Anxiety in his tone had crept past his seeming outrage.

Jamie knew. "I tote my end of the log," he said weakly, "an' I'm stickin', slap to Texas."

Josey snatched the reins of the mare and started the horses toward the river. As they passed the sprawled figure of Abe, Jamie said, "Wisht we had time to bury them fellers."

"To hell with them fellers," Josey snarled. He spat a stream of tobacco juice into Abe's upturned face, "Buzzards got to eat, same as worms."

Chapter 5

They followed the river bank downstream, away from Warrensburg, and crossed at a shallows belly-deep to the horses. Coming out of the river, they pushed at a walk through a half mile of thick bottom growth before they came up to thinning timber. It was two hours until sundown, and before them lay the open prairie broken only by rolling mounds. To their right was Warrensburg with the Clinton road running south; a road they couldn't use now.

Josey pulled the horses up in the last shelter of trees. He scanned the sky. Rain would help. It always helped to drive undisciplined mobs and posses back indoors. Although the clouds were thickening, there was no immediate promise of rain. The wind was brisking stronger out of the north, cold and sharp, bending the waist-high bushes across the prairie.

Still they sat their horses. Josey watched a dust cloud in the distance and followed it until it petered out . . . it was the wind. He studied the rolls of mounds and came back to study them again . . . giving time for any horsemen to come into view who might have been hidden. All the way to the horizon . . . there were no riders. Josey untied a blanket from behind his saddle and brought it around the hunched shoulders of Jamie. He tugged the cavalry hat lower to his eyes.

"Let's ride," he said tersely and moved the roan out. The little mare fell in behind. The horses were rested and strong. Josey had to hold the roan down to a walk to prevent the shorter-legged mare from breaking into a trot.

Jamie urged the mare up alongside Josey. "Don't hold back 'count of me, Josey," he yelled weakly against the wind, "I kin ride."

Josey pulled the horses up. "I ain't holdin' back 'count of you, ye thickheaded grasshopper," he said evenly. "Fust place, if we run these hosses, we'll kick up dust, second place they's enough posses in south Missouri after us to start another war, and in the third place, ye try runnin' 'stead of thinkin' and they'll swing us on a rope by dark. We got to wolf our way through."

A half hour of steady pace brought them to a deep wash that split their path and ran westward. Choked with thick brush and stunted cedar, it afforded good cover, but Josey guided the horses directly across and up onto the prairie again. "They'll curry-comb them washes . . . anyways, that'n ain't goin' in our direction," he remarked dryly.

A hundred yards farther and he stopped the horses.

Stepping down, he retrieved a brush top from the ground and retraced their steps back to the wash. Carefully as a housewife, he backed, sweeping away the hoofprints in the loose soil. "Iff'n they pick up our trail, and they're dumb enough . . . they could lose two hours in thet wash," he told Jamie as he swung the horses forward again.

Another hour, steadily southward. Jamie no longer lifted his head to scan the horizon. Jolting, searing pain filled his body. He could feel the swelling of his flesh over the tightly wrapped bandage. The clouds were lowering, heavier and darker, and the wind carried a distinct taste of moistness. Dusk of evening lent an eerie light to the wind-whipped prairie brush that made the landscape look alive.

Suddenly Josey halted the horses. "Riders," he said tersely, "comin' from behind us." Jamie listened, but he heard nothing . . . then, a faint drumming of hooves. Far ahead, perhaps five or six miles, there was a knoll of thick woods. Too far. There was no other cover offered.

Josey stepped down. "A dozen, maybe more, but they ain't fanned out . . . they're bunched and headin' fer them woods yonder."

Carefully, with unhurried calm, he lifted Jamie from the saddle and sat him spraddle-legged on the ground. Leading the roan close to the boy, he seized the horse's nose with his left hand, and throwing his right arm over its head, he grabbed the roan's ear. He twisted viciously. The roan's knees trembled and buckled . . . and he rolled to the ground. Josey extended a hand to Jamie and pulled the boy to the horse's head. "Lay 'crost his neck, Jamie, and hold his nose."

Leaping to his feet, Josey grabbed the head of the mare. But she fought him, backing and kicking, swinging him off the ground. Her eyes rolling, and frothing at the mouth, she almost bolted loose from his grip. Once, he reached for the boot knife but had to quickly renew his hold to prevent the horse from breaking away. The hoofbeats of the posse were now distinct and growing in sound. Desperately, Josey swung his feet off the ground. Still holding the mare's head, he locked his legs around her neck and pulled his body downward on her head. Her nose dragged into the dirt. She tried to plunge, lost her footing, and fell heavily on her side.

Josey lay as he had fallen, his legs wrapped around the mare's neck, holding her head tightly against his chest. He had fallen not three feet from Jamie. Facing the boy, he could see the white face and feverish eyes as he lay chest-down over the roan's neck. The drumming beat of the posse's horses now made the ground vibrate.

"Can ye hear me, boy?" Josey's whisper was hoarse.

Jamie's white face nodded.

"Listen, now . . . listen. Iff'n ye see me jump up, ye stay down. I'll take the mare . . . but ye stay down 'til ye hear shootin' and runnin' back toward the river. Then ye lay back on thet roan. He'll git up with ye. Ye ride south. Ye hear me, boy?"

The feverish eyes stared back at him. The thin face set in stubborn lines. Josey cursed softly under his breath.

The riders came on. The horses were being cantered, their hooves beating rhythmically on the ground. Now Josey could hear the creak of saddle leather, and from his prone position he saw the body of horsemen loom into view. They passed not a dozen yards from the flattened horses. Josey could see their hats . . . their shoulders, silhouetted against the lighter horizon.

Jamie coughed. Josey looked at the boy and slipped the thong from a Colt and held the pistol in his hand across the head of the mare. Blood trickled from the mouth of Jamie, and Josey saw him heave to cough again. Then he watched as the boy lowered his head; he was biting into the roan's neck. Still the riders came by in a maddening eternity. Blood was dripping now from the nose of Jamie as his body heaved for air.

"Turn loose, Jamie," Josey whispered, "turn loose, damn ye, or ye'll die." Still the boy held on. The last of the riders moved from view, and the hoofbeats of their horses faded. Josey stretched to his full length and hit Jamie a brutal blow against his head. The boy rolled on his side and his chest expanded with air. He was unconscious.

Rising to his feet, Josey brought the mare up where she stood, head down and trembling. He pulled Jamie from the roan, and the big horse rose, snorted, and shook himself. He bent over the boy and wiped the blood from his face and neck. Lifting his shirt, he saw a mass of horribly discolored flesh bulging over the tight wrappings. He loosened the bandages and from his canteen he patted cold water over Jamie's face.

The boy opened his eyes. He grinned tightly up at Josey and from behind set teeth he whispered, "Whupped 'em agin, didn't we, Josey?"

"Yeah," Josey said softly, "we whupped 'em agin."

He rolled a blanket and placed it under Jamie's head and stood facing southward. The posse had disappeared into the closing darkness. Still he watched. After a long time he was rewarded with the flickering of campfires from the woods to the southwest. The posse was encamping for the night.

Had he been alone, Josey would have drifted back toward the Blackwater and with the morning followed the posse south. But Josey had seen mortification in wounded men before. It always killed. He figured a hundred miles to the Cherokee's medicine lodge.

Jamie was sitting up, and Josey lifted him onto the mare. They continued southward, passing the lights of the posse's camp on their right.

Though the sky was dark with clouds Josey calculated midnight when he brought the horses to a halt. Though conscious, Jamie swayed in the saddle, and Josey lashed his feet in the stirrups, bringing the rope under the horse's belly to secure the boy.

"Jamie," he said, "the mare's got a smooth single-foot gait. Nearly smooth as a walk. We got to make more time. Can ye handle it, boy?"

"I can handle it." The voice came weak but confident. Josey lifted the roan into a slow, mile-eating canter, and the little mare stayed with him. The undulating prairie slowly changed character . . . a small, tree-bunched hillock showed here and there. Before dawn they had reached the Grand River. Searching its banks for a ford, Josey picked a well-traveled trail to cross and then pushed on across open ground toward the Osage.

They nooned on the banks of the Osage River. Josey grained the horses from the corn in Jamie's saddlebags. Now, to the south and east, they could see the foothills of the wild Ozark Mountains with the tangled ravines and uncountable ridges that long had served the outlaw on the run. They were close, but the Osage was too deep and too wide.

Over a tiny flame Josey steamed broth for Jamie. For himself, he wolfed down half-cooked salt pork and corn pone. Jamie rested on the ground; the broth had brought color to his cheeks.

"How we goin' to cross, Josey?"

"There's a ferry 'bout five mile down, at Osceola crossing," Josey answered as he cinched the saddles on the horses.

"How in thunderation we goin' to git acrost on a ferry?" Jamie asked incredulously.

Josey lifted the boy into the saddle. "Well," he drawled, "ye jest git on it and ride, I reckin."

Heavy timber laced with persimmon and stunted cedar bushes shielded them from the clearing. The ferry was secured to pilings on the bank. Back from the river there were two log structures, one of which appeared to be a store. Josey could see the Clinton road snaking north for a half mile until it disappeared over a rolling rise and reappeared in the distance.

Light wood smoke drifted from the chimneys of both the store and the dwelling, but there were no signs of life except an old man seated on a stump near the ferry. Josey watched him for a long time. The old man was weaving a wire fish basket. He looked up constantly from his work to peer back toward the Clinton road.

"Old man acts nervous," Josey muttered, "and this here would be a likely place."

Jamie slumped beside him on the mare. "Likely fer . . . reckin things ain't right?"

"I'd give a yaller-wheeled red waggin to see on the other side of them cabins," Josey said . . . then, "Come on." With the practiced audacity of the guerrilla, he walked his horse from the brush straight toward the old man.

Chapter 6

For nearly ten years old man Carstairs had run the ferry. He owned it . . . the store and the house, bought with his own scrimped-up savings, by God. For all of that time old man Carstairs had walked a tightrope. Ferrying Kansas Redleg, Missouri guerrilla, Union Cavalry . . . once he had even ferried a contingent of Jo Shelby's famous Confederate riders. He could whistle "Battle Hymn of the Republic" or "Dixie" with equal enthusiasm, depending upon present company. Morning and night these many years, he had berated the old lady, "Them regular army ones ain't so bad. But them Redlegs and guerrillas is mad dogs . . . ye hear! Mad dogs! Ye look sidewise at 'em . . . they'll kill us all . . . burn us out."

With cunning he had survived. Once he had seen

Quantrill, Joe Hardin, and Frank James. They and seventy-five guerrillas were dressed in Yankee uniforms. They had questioned him as to his sympathies, but the old man's crafty eyes had spotted a "guerrilla shirt" under the open blue blouse of one of the men . . . and he had cursed the Union. He had never seen Bloody Bill or Jesse James . . . or Josey Wales, and the men that rode with them, but their reputations transcended Quantrill's in Missouri.

Only this morning he had ferried across two separate posses of horsemen who were searching for Wales and another outlaw. They had said he was in this area and all south Missouri was up in arms. Three thousand dollars! A lot of money . . . but they could have it . . . fer the likes of a gunslingin' killer sich as Wales. That is . . . unless . . .

Cavalry would be coming down the road any minute now. Carstairs looked around. It was then he saw the horsemen approaching. They had come out of the brush along the river bank, an alarming fact in itself. But the appearance of the lead horseman was even more alarming to Carstairs. He was astride a huge roan stallion that looked half wild. He approached to within ten feet and stopped. High top boots, fringed buckskin, the man was lean and had an air of wolfish hunger about him. He wore two holstered .44's, and the guns were tied down. Several days' growth of black beard stubbled his face below the mustache, and a gray cavalry hat was pulled low over the hardest black eyes old man Carstairs had ever seen. The old man shuddered as from a chill and sat frozen, the fish basket suspended outward in his hands . . . as though he were offering it as a gift.

"Howdy," the horseman said easily.

"Well, how . . . howdy," Carstairs fumbled. He felt numb. He watched, fascinated, as the horseman slid a long knife from his boot top, cut a wad of tobacco from a twist, and fed it into his mouth.

"Figgered we might give ye a mite of ferryin' business," the horseman said slowly past the chew.

"Why shore, shore." Old man Carstairs stood up.

"But . . . " the horseman caught him short, in the act of rising, "so's there won't be nothin' mistooken, I'm Josey Wales . . . and this here's my partner. We're jest a hair pushed fer time and we need a tad of things first."

"Why, Mr. Wales." Carstairs rose. His lips trembled uncontrollably, so that the forced smile appeared alternately as a sneer and a laugh. Inwardly he cursed his trembling. Dropping the fish basket, he managed to step toward the horse, extending his hand. "My name's Carstairs, Sim Carstairs. I've heard tell of ye, Mr. Wales. Bill Quantrill was a good friend of mine . . . mighty good friend, we'uns. . . ."

"T'ain't a sociable visit, Mr. Carstairs," Josey said flatly, "who all ye got hereabouts?"

"Why nobody," Carstairs was eager, "thet is 'cept the old lady there in the house and Lemuel, my hired hand. He ain't right bright, Mr. Wales . . . runs his mouth and sich . . . he's there, in the store."

"Tell ye what," Josey said as he pitched five bright double eagles at the feet of Carstairs, "me and you will amble on up to the house and the store. I got a tech of cramp . . . so I'll ride. When we git there, ye don't go inside . . . but ye step to the door and tell the missus that we got to have CLEAN bandages . . . lots of 'em. We got to have a boiled-up poultice fer a bullet wound . . . and hurry."

The old man looked askance at Josey, and receiving a nod he quickly gathered the gold coins out of the dust and moved at a half trot toward the house.

Josey turned to Jamie behind him, "You stay here and keep the corners of them buildings under eyes." He put the roan on the heels of the old man. Stopping the horse at the porch of the log cabin, he listened while Carstairs shouted instructions through the open door of the cabin. Then as the old man turned from the door, "Let's step over to the store, Mr. Carstairs. Tell yore feller in there we want a half side of bacon, ten pound of beef jerky, and twenty pound of horse grain."

Carstairs returned with the bags, and Josey had just settled the grain behind his saddle when a tiny white-haired woman stepped through the door of the cabin. She held a pipe in her mouth and extended a clean pillowcase stuffed with the bandages toward Josey.

Moving his horse to the edge of the porch, Josey tipped his hat. "Howdy, ma'am," he said quietly, and reaching for the pillowcase he placed two twenty-dollar gold coins in her small hand. "I thank ye kindly, ma'am," he said.

Sharp blue eyes quickened in the wrinkled face. She took the pipe from her mouth. "Ye'll be Josey Wales, I reckin."

"Yes, ma'am, I'm Josey Wales."

"Well," the old lady held him with her eyes, "them poultices be laced with feather moss and mustard root. Mind ye, drap water on 'em occasional to keep 'em damp." Then without pause she continued, "Reckin ye know they're a-goin' to heel and hide ye to a barn door."

A faint smile lifted the scar on Josey's face. "I've heard tell of sich talk, ma'am."

He touched his hat . . . whirled the roan and followed the old man to the ferry. As they walked their horses aboard the flat, he looked back. She was still standing . . . and he thought she gave a secret wave of her hand . . . but she could have pushed a strand of hair back from her face.

Old man Carstairs felt bold enough to grumble as he walked the couple cable from bow to stern on the ferry. "Usually have Lem here to help. This here is heavy work fer one old man."

But he moved the ferry on out across the river. To the north a distinct rumble of thunder rolled across the darkening clouds. As the current caught the ferry they moved more swiftly on a downward angle; and half an hour later, Josey was leading the horses onto the opposite bank and into the trees.

It was Jamie who saw them first. His shout startled Carstairs, who was resting against a piling, and made Josey whirl in his tracks. Jamie was pointing back across the river. There, from the bank they had just left, was a large body of Union Cavalry, blue uniforms standing out against the horizon. They were waving their arms frantically.

Josey grinned, "Well, I'll be a suck-aig hound."

Jamie laughed . . . coughed and laughed again, "Whupped 'em agin, Josey," he said jubilantly . . . "We whupped 'em agin."

Carstairs didn't share in the enthusiasm. He scrambled up the bank to Josey. "They're hollerin' fer me to come over . . . I got to go . . . I cain't hold up." A gleam touched his eyes . . . "but I'll hold up 'til ya'll are out of sight . . . even longer. I'll make do somethin's wrong. You fellers git goin', quick."

Josey nodded and headed the horses up through the

trees. Only a short distance, and undergrowth blocked their view of the river. Here he halted the horses.

"Thet feller ain't goin' to hold up thet ferry . . . he's goin' to bring that cavalry over," Jamie said.

Josey looked up at the lowering clouds. "I know," he said, "wants hisself a piece of the reeward." He brought the horses about . . . back to the river.

Carstairs had already moved the ferry from the bank. Walking the cable at a half trot, he was making rapid time toward midstream. Across the river a blue-clad knot of men were pulling on the ferry's cable.

Josey dismounted. From a saddlebag he pulled nose bags for the horses, poured grain into them, and fastened them over the mouths of the horses. The big roan stomped his hooves in satisfaction. Jamie watched the ferry as it neared the opposite bank . . . the shouts of the men came faintly to their ears as fully half of the cavalry present boarded the ferry.

"They're comin'," Jamie said.

Josey was busying himself checking the hooves of the munching horses, lifting first one and then another foot. "From the tracks, t'other side, I'd cal'clate forty, fifty hosses was brought acrost this mornin'," he said, "and they're ahead of us. Reckin we need to space a little time 'twixt them and us."

Jamie watched the ferry moving toward them. Soldiers were walking the cable. " 'Pears to me we're goin' to be needin' a little space behint us too," he said bleakly.

Josey straightened to look. The ferry was almost to midstream, and as they watched, the current began to catch, pulling the cable in a taut curve. Josey slid the .56 Sharps from the saddle boot.

"Hold Big Red," he said as he handed the horse's

reins to Jamie. For a long time he sighted down the barrel . . . then . . . BOOM! The heavy rifle reverberated in echo across the river. All activity stopped on the ferry. The men stood motionless, frozen in motion. The cable parted from the pilings with a snap of telegraphic *zing* of sound. For a moment the ferry in the middle of the river floated motionless, suspended. Slowly it began to swing downstream. Faster and faster, as the current picked up its load of men and horses. Now there was shouting . . . men dashed first to one end and then the other in confusion. Two horses jumped over the side and swam about in a circle.

"Godalmighty!" Jamie breathed.

The confused tangle of shouting men and pitching horses was carried at locomotive speed . . . farther and farther . . . until they disappeared around the trees of the river bend.

"That there," Josey grinned, "is called a Missouri boat ride."

Still they waited, letting the horses finish the grain. Across river they saw a mad dash of blue cavalrymen head south down the river bank.

From the Osage Josey turned the horses southwest along the banks of the Sac River. Across the Sac was more open prairie, but on their left was the comforting wilderness of the Ozarks. Once, in late afternoon, they sighted a large body of horsemen heading southwest, across the river, and they held their horses until the drumming hoofbeats had died in the distance. North of Stockton they forded the Sac, and nightfall caught them on the banks of Horse Creek, north of Jericho Springs.

Josey guided the horses up a shallow spring that fed the creek, into a tangled ravine. One mile, two, he traveled, halting only when the ravine narrowed to a thin slash in the side of the mountain. High above them trees whipped in a fierce wind, but here there was a calmness broken only by the gurgling of water over rocks.

The narrow gorge was choked with brush and scuppernong vines. Elm, oak, hickory, and cedar grew profusely. It was in a sheltered clump of thick cedar that he threw blankets and Jamie, lying in the warm quietness, fell asleep. Josey unsaddled the horses, grained and picketed them near the spring. Then close to Jamie he dug an "outlaw's oven," a foot-deep hole in the ground with flat stones edged over the top. Three feet from the fire no light was visible, but the heated stones and flames beneath quickly cooked the pan of side meat and boiled the jerky broth.

As he worked he attuned his ears to the new sounds of the ravine. Without looking, he knew there was a nest of cardinals in the persimmon bushes across the branch; a flicker grutted from the trunk of an elm and the brush wrens whispered in the undergrowth. Farther back, up the hollow, a screech owl had taken up its precisely timed woman's wail of anguish. These were the rhythms he placed in his subconscious. The high wind whining above him . . . the feathery whisper of breeze through the cedars . . . this was the melody. But if the rhythm broke . . . the birds were his sentinels.

He had eaten and fed Jamie the broth. Now he heated water and wet the poultices. When he took the old bandages from around Jamie, the big hole in his chest was blotched with blue flesh turning black. "Proud" flesh speckled the wound in puffy whiteness. The boy kept his eyes from the mangled chest, looking steadily up to Josey's face.

"It ain't bad, is it, Josey?" he asked quietly.

Josey was cleaning the wound with hot rags. "It's bad," he said evenly.

"Josey?"

"Yeah."

"Back there, on the Grand . . . thet was the fastest shootin' I ever seed. I never shaded ye. Na'ar bit."

Josey didn't answer as he placed the poultices and wrapped the bandages around the boy.

"Iff'n I don't make it, Josey," Jamie hesitated, "I want ye to know I'm prouder'n a game rooster to have rid with ye."

"Ye are a game rooster, son," Josey said roughly, "now shet up."

Jamie grinned. He closed his eyes, and the shadows quickly softened the hollowed cheeks. In sleep he was a little boy.

Josey felt the heavy drag of exhaustion. In three days he had slept only in brief dozes in the saddle. His eyes had begun to play tricks on him, seeing the "gray wolves" that weren't there . . . and hearing the sounds that couldn't be. Time to hole up. He knew the feeling well. As he rolled into his blankets, back in the brush, away from Jamie and the horses, he thought of the boy . . . and his mind wandered back to his own boyhood in the Tennessee mountains.

There was Pa, lean and mountain-learned, settin' on a stump. "Them as won't fight fer their own kind, ain't worth their sweat salt," he had said.

"I reckin," the little boy Josey had nodded.

And there was Pa, layin' a hand on his shoulder when he was a stripling . . . and Pa wa'ant give to show feelin's. He had stood up to the McCabes down at the settlement . . . and them with the sheriff on their side. Pa had looked at him, close and proud.

"Gittin' on to be a man," Pa had said. "Always re'clect to be proud of yer friends . . . but fight fer sich as ye kin be prouder of yer enemies." Proud, by God.

Well, Josey thought drowsily . . . the enemies was damn shore the right kind, and the friend . . . the boy . . . all sand grit and cucklebur. He slept.

A brief splatter of rain wakened him. There was the ghostly light of predawn made dimmer by dark clouds that rushed ahead of the wind. Light fog trapped in the ravine added to the ghostly air. It was colder. Josey could feel the chill through his blanket. Overhead the wind whined and beat the treetops. Josey rolled from his blanket. The horses were watering at the spring. He grained them and coaxed a flame alive in the fire hole. Kneeling beside Jamie with hot jerky broth, he shook the boy awake. But when his eyes opened, there was no recognition in them.

"I told Pa," the boy said weakly, "that yaller heifer would make the best milker in Arkansas. Four gallon if she gives a drap." He paused, listening intently . . . then, a chuckle of laughter. "Reckin that red bon's a cheater, Pa . . . done left the pack and jumped that ol' fox's trail."

Suddenly he sat up wildly, his eyes frightened. Josey placed a restraining hand on his shoulder. "Pa said it was Jennison, Ma. Jennison! A hunnert men!" Just as suddenly he collapsed back onto the blankets. Sobs racked him, and great tears ran down his cheeks. "Ma," he said brokenly, "Ma." And he was still . . . his eyes closed.

Josey looked down at the boy. He knew Jamie had come from Arkansas, but he had never discussed his reasons for joining the guerrillas. Nobody did. Doc Jennison! Josey knew he had carried his Redleg raids into Arkansas where he had looted and burned so many farmhouses that the lonely chimneys left standing became known as "Jennison Monuments." The hatred rose again inside him.

As he raised Jamie's head to feed him the broth the nightmare had passed, but he could feel that the boy was weaker as he lifted him into the saddle. Once more he lashed Jamie's feet to the stirrups. He figured sixty miles to the border of the Nations, and he knew that troops and posses were gathering in growing numbers to block his reckless ride.

"Reckin they figger me fer plumb loco," Josey muttered as he rode, "fer not takin' to the hills." But the hills meant sure death for Jamie. There was a narrow chance with the Cherokee.

His simple code of loyalty disallowed any thought of his own safety at the sacrifice of a friend. He could have turned into the mountains on the off chance that help could be found for the boy . . . and he himself would have been safe in the wildness. For men of a lesser code it would have been sufficient. The question never entered the outlaw's mind. For all their craft and guerrilla cunning, tacticians would consider this code as such men's greatest weakness . . . but on the other side of the coin the code accounted for their fierceness as warriors, their willingness to "charge hell with a bucket of water," as they were once described in Union Army reports.

The tactical weakness in Josey's case was apparent. The Union Army and posses knew his partner was desperately wounded. They knew he could get medical help only in the Nations. His mastery of the pistols, his cunning born of a hundred running fights, his guerrilla boldness and audacity, had carried him and Jamie through a roused countryside, but they also knew the code of these hardened pistol fighters. Where they could not divine the mind and tricks of the wolf, they knew his instinct. And so horsemen were pounding toward the border of the Nations to converge and meet him. They knew Josey Wales.

Chapter 7

The cold dawn found them riding across an open space of prairie ground, the mountains to their left. Before noon they forded Horse Creek and continued southwest, staying close to the timbered ridges, but Josey keeping the horses on dangerous open ground. Time was the enemy of Jamie Burns. Shortly after noon Josey rested the horses in thick timber. Placing strips of jerky beef in Jamie's mouth, he gruffly instructed, "Chaw on it, but don't swaller nothin' but juice."

The boy nodded but didn't speak. His face was beginning to take on a puffiness, and swelling enlarged his neck. Once, far to their right, they saw dust rising of many horses, but the riders never came into view.

By late afternoon they had forded Dry Fork and

were crossing, at an easy canter, a long roll of prairie. Josey pulled to a halt and pointed behind them. It appeared to be a full squad of cavalry. Although they were several miles away, the soldiers had apparently spotted the fugitives, for as Josey and Jamie watched, they spurred their horses into a gallop. Josey could easily have sought shelter in the wild mountains not a half mile on their left, but that would mean hard . . slow traveling, rather than the five miles of prairie they had before them. In the distance a tall spur of mountain extended before them over the prairie.

"We'll make fer that mountain straight ahead," Josey said. He brought his horse close to Jamie. "Now listen. Them fellers ain't shore yet who we are. I'm goin' to make 'em shore. When I shoot at 'em . . . you let that little mare canter . . . but ye hold 'er down. When ye hear me shoot agin . . . ye turn 'er loose. Ye understand?" Jamie nodded. "I want them soldier boys to run them horses into the ground," he added grimly as he slid the big Sharps from the saddle boot.

Without aiming, he fired. The echoes boomed back from the mountain. The effect was almost instantaneous on the loping cavalrymen. They lifted their arms, and their horses stretched out in a dead run. The mare set off in an easy canter that rapidly left Josey behind. The big roan sensed the excitement and wanted to run, but Josey held him down to a bone-jarring, high-step trot.

There was a distance of a half mile . . . now three-quarters . . . now a mile separating the cantering mare from him. Behind, he could hear the first faint beating of running horses. Still! he jogged. The drumming of hooves became louder; now he could hear the faint shouts of the men. Slipping the knife from his boot, he carefully cut a plug of tobacco from the twist. As he cheeked the wad the hoofbeats grew louder.

"Well, Red," he drawled, "ye been snortin' to go . . ." he slid a Colt from a holster and fired into the air, ". . . now RUN!" The roan leaped. Ahead of him, Josey saw the mare gather haunches and settle lower as she flew over the ground. She was fast, but the roan was already gaining.

There was never any doubt. The big horse bounded like a cat over shallow washes, never breaking stride. Josey leaned low in the saddle, feeling the great power of the roan as he flew over the ground, closing the gap on the mare. He was less than a hundred yards behind her when she made the heavy timber of the ridge. As Josey pulled back on the roan, he turned and saw the cavalrymen . . . they were walking their horses, fully two miles behind him. Their mounts had been "bottomed out."

Jamie had pulled up in the timber, and as Josey reached him the heavy clouds opened up. A blinding, whipping rain obscured the prairie behind them. Lightning touched a timbered ridge, cracked with a blue-white light, and the deep rumbling that followed caught up the echoes and merged with more lightning stabs that made the roar continuous. Josey pulled slickers from behind their cantles.

"A real frog-strangler," and he wrapped a slicker around Jamie. The boy was conscious, but his face was twisted and white, and his body rigid in an effort to cling to.the saddle.

Josey gripped his arm, "Fifteen, maybe twenty miles, Jamie, and we'll bed down in a warm lodge on the Neosho." He gently shook the boy. "We'll be in the Nations, another twenty miles . . . we'll have help."

Jamie nodded . . . but he did not speak. Josey pulled the reins of the mare from the clenched hands that held the saddle horn, and leading, moved the horses at a walk upward into the ridges.

The lightning flashes had stopped, but the rain still came, whipped into sheets by the wind. Darkness set in quickly, but Josey guided the roan with a sureness of familiarity with the mountains. The trails were dim now, that sought out the cuts between the ridges; that headed straight into a mountain only to turn and twist and find a hidden draw. They were still there . . . the trails he had followed with Anderson, going into and coming out of the Nations. The trails would carry him through the corner of Newton County and onto the river flats of the Neosho, out of Missouri.

The temperature fell. The rain lightened, and the breath of the horses made puffs of steam as they walked. It was after midnight before Josey called a halt to the steady pace. He saw the campfires below him . . . the half circle that hung like a necklace . . . enclosing the foothills of these mountains between him . . . and Jamie . . . and Neosho Basin a few miles away.

There was still some movement around the fires. As he squatted in the timber he could see an occasional figure outlined against the flame . . . and so he waited. Behind him the roan stamped an impatient foot, but the mare stood head down and tired. He dared not take Jamie from the saddle . . . there were only a few miles across the flats to the Nations . . . and a few more miles to the Neosho bottoms. There was a bitter-cold bite now in the wind, and the rain had almost stopped.

Patiently he watched, jaws slowly working at the tobacco. An hour passed, then another. Activity had died down around the campfires. There would be the pickets. Josey straightened and walked back to the horses. Jamie was slumped in the saddle, his chin resting on his chest. Josey clasped the boy's arm, "Jamie," but the moment his hand touched him, he knew. Jamie Burns was dead.

The realization of the boy's death came like a physical blow, so that his knees buckled and he actually staggered. He had known they would make it. The riding, the fighting against all odds . . . they HAD made it. They had whipped them all. Then for fate to snatch the boy from him. . . . Josey Wales cursed bitterly and long. He stretched his arms around the dead Jamie in the saddle . . . as if to warm him and bring him back . . . and he cursed at God until he choked on his own spittle.

His coughing brought back sanity, and he stood for a long time saying nothing. His bitterness subsided into thoughts of the boy who had stubbornly followed him with loyalty, who had died without a murmur. Josey removed his hat and stepping close to the mare placed his arm about the waist of Jamie. He looked up at the trees bending in the wind. "This here boy," he said gruffly, "was brung up in time of blood and dyin'. He never looked to question na'ar bit of it. Never turned his back on his folks 'ner his kind. He has rode with me, and I ain't got no complaints . . . " he paused, "Amen."

Moving with a sudden resolve, he untied the saddlebags from the mare and lashed them to his own saddle. He unbuckled the gunbelt from Jamie's waist and hung it over the roan's pommel. This done, he mounted the roan and led the mare, with the dead boy still in the saddle, down the ridge toward the campfires. At the bottom of the ridge he crossed a shallow creek and coming up from its bank found himself only fifty yards from the nearest campfire. There were pickets out, but they were dismounted, walking from fire to fire at a slow cadence.

Josey pulled the mare up beside the roan. He looped the reins back over the head of the horse and tied them tightly around the dead hands of Jamie that still gripped the saddle horn. Now he sidled the roan close, until his leg touched the leg of the boy.

"Bluebellies will give ye a better funeral, son," he said grimly, "anyways, we said we was goin' to the Nations . . . by God, one of us will git there."

Across the rump of the mare he laid a big Colt, so that when fired the powder burn would send her off. He took a deep breath, pulled his hat low, and fired the pistol.

The mare leaped from the burning pain and stampeded straight toward the nearest campfire. The reaction was almost instantaneous. Men ran toward the fires, rolling out of blankets, and hoarse, questioning shouts filled the air. Almost into the fire the mare ran, the grotesque figure on her back dipping and rolling with her motion . . . then she veered, still at a dead run, heading south along the creek bank. Men began to shoot, some kneeling with rifles, then rising to run on foot after the mare. Others mounted horses and dashed away down the creek.

Josey watched it all from the shadows. From far down the creek he heard more gunfire, followed by triumphant shouts. Only then did he walk the roan out of the trees, past the deserted campfires, and into the shadows that would carry him out of bloody Missouri.

And men would tell of this deed tonight around the campfires of the trail. They would save it for the last as they recounted the tales told of the outlaw Josey

Wales . . . using this deed to clinch the ruthlessness of the man. City men, who have no knowledge of such things, seeking only comfort and profit, would sneer in disgust to hide their fear. The cowboy, knowing the closeness of death, would gaze grimly into the camp-fire. The guerrilla would smile and nod his approval of audacity and stubbornness that carried a man through. And the Indian would understand.

Part 2

Part 2

Chapter 8

The cold air had brought heavy fog to the bottoms of the Neosho. Dawn was a pale light that ghosted through weird shapes of tree and brush, made unearthly in the gray thickness. There was no sun.

Lone Watie could hear the low rush of the river as it passed close by the rear of his cabin. The morning river sounds were routine and therefore good . . . the kingfisher and the bluejays that quarreled incessantly . . . the early caw of a crow-scout . . . once . . . that all was well. Lone Watie felt rather than thought of these things as he fried his breakfast of fish over a tiny flame in the big fireplace.

Like many of the Cherokees, he was tall, standing well over six feet in his boot moccasins that held, half tucked, the legs of buckskin breeches. At first glance he appeared emaciated, so spare was his frame . . . the doeskin shirt jacket flapping loosely about his body, the face bony and lacking in flesh, so that hollows of the cheeks added prominence to the bones and the hawk nose that separated intense black eyes capable of a cruel light. He squatted easily on haunches before the fire, turning the mealed fish in the pan with fluid movement, occasionally tossing back one of the black plaits of hair that hung to his shoulders.

The clear call of a nighthawk brought instant movement by the Indian. Nighthawks do not call in the light of day. He moved with silent litheness; taking his rifle, he glided to the rear door of the one-room cabin . . . dropped to belly and slid quickly into the brush. Again the call came, loud and clear.

As all mountain men know, the whippoorwill will not sing when the nighthawk is heard . . . and so now, from the brush, Lone answered with that whipping call.

Now there was silence. From his position in the brush Lone listened for the approach. Though only a few feet from the cabin he could scarcely see it. Sumac and dead honeysuckle vine had grown up the chimney and run over the roof. Brush and undergrowth had encroached almost to the walls. What once had been a trail had long since been covered over. One must know of this inaccessible hideout to whistle an approach.

The horse burst through the brush without warning. Lone was startled by the appearance of the big roan. He looked half wild with flaring nostrils and he stamped his feet as the rider reined him before the cabin door. He watched as the rider dismounted and casually turned his back to the cabin as he uncinched saddle and pulled it from the horse.

Lone's eyes ran over the man; the big, holstered

pistols, the boot knife, nor did he miss the slight bulge beneath the left shoulder. As the man turned he saw the white scar standing out of the black stubble and he noted the gray cavalry hat pulled low. Lone grunted with satisfaction; a fighting man who carried himself as a warrior should, with boldness and without fear.

The open buckskin jacket revealed something more that made Lone step confidently from the brush and approach him. It was the shirt; linsey-woolsey with a long open V that ended halfway down the waist with a rosette. It was the "guerrilla shirt," noted in U.S. Army dispatches as the only sure way to identify a Missouri guerrilla. Made by the wives, sweethearts, and womenfolk of the farms, it had become the uniform of the guerrilla. He always wore it . . . sometimes concealed . . . but always worn. Many of them bore fancy needlework and bright colors . . . this one was the plain color of butternut, trimmed in gray.

The man continued to rub down the roan, even as Lone walked toward him . . . and only turned when the Indian stopped silently, a yard away.

"Howdy," he said softly and extended his hand, "I'm Josey Wales."

"I have heard," Lone said simply, grasping the hand, "I am Lone Watie."

Josey looked sharply at the Indian. "I re'clect. I rode with ye oncet . . . and yer kinsman, General Stand Watie, 'crost the Osage and up into Kansas."

"I remember," Lone said, "it was a good fight" . . . and then . . . "I will stable your horse with mine down by the river. There is grain."

As he led the roan away Josey pulled his saddle and gear into the cabin. The floor was hard-packed dirt. The only furnishings were willows laid along the walls draped with blankets. Besides the cooking utensils there was nothing else, save the belt hanging by a peg that carried a Colt and long knife. The inevitable gray hat of the cavalry lay on a willow bed.

He remembered the cabin. After wintering at Mineral Creek, Texas, near Sherman, in '63, he had come back up the trail and had camped here. They had been told it was the farm of Lone Watie, but no one had been there . . . though there was evidence left of what had been a farm.

He knew something of the history of the Waties. They had lived in the mountains of north Georgia and Alabama. Stand Watie was a prominent Chief. Lone was a cousin. Dispossessed of their land by the U.S. government in the 1830's, they had walked with the Cherokee tribe on the "Trail of Tears" to the new land assigned them in the Nations. Nearly a third of the Cherokee had died on that long walk, and thousands of graves still marked the trail.

He had known the Cherokee as a small boy in the mountains of Tennessee. His father had befriended many of them who had hidden out, refusing to make the walk.

The mountain man did not have the "land hunger" of the flatlander who had instigated the government's action. He preferred the mountains to remain wild . . . free, unfettered by law and the irritating hypocrisy of organized society. His kinship, therefore, was closer to the Cherokee than to his racial brothers of the flatlands who strained mightily at placing the yoke of society upon their necks.

From the Cherokee he had learned how to hand-fish, easing his hands into the bank holes of the mountain streams and tickling the sides of trout and bass, that the gray fox runs in a figure eight and the red fox runs in a circle. How to track the bee to the honey hive, where the quail trap caught the most birds, and how curious was the buck deer.

He had eaten with them in their mountain lodge-pole cabins, and they had brought meat to his own family. Their code was the loyalty of the mountain man with all his clannishness, and therefore Lone Watie merited his trust. He was of his kind.

When the War between the States had burst over the nation, the Cherokee naturally sided with the Confederacy against the hated government that had deprived him of his mountain home. Some had joined General Sam Cooper, a few were in the elite brigade of Jo Shelby, but most had followed their leader General Stand Watie, the only Indian General of the Confederacy.

Lone returned to the cabin and squatted before the fire.

"Breakfast," he grunted as he extended the pan of fish to Josey. They ate with their hands while the Indian looked moodily into the fire. "There's been a lot of talk in the settlements. Ye been raising hell in Missouri, they say."

"I reckin," Josey said.

Lone dusted meal on the hearth of the fireplace and from a burlap extracted two cleaned catfish, which he rolled in the meal and placed over the fire.

"Where ye headin'?" he asked.

"Nowheres . . . in pa'ticular," Josey said around a mouthful of fish . . . and then, as if in explanation, "My partner is dead."

For a few harrowing days he had had somewhere to go. It had become an obsession with him, to bring Jamie out of Missouri, to bring him here. With the death of the boy the emptiness came back. As he had ridden through the night he had caught himself checking back . . . to see to Jamie. The brief purpose was gone.

Lone Watie asked no questions about the partner, but he nodded his head in understanding.

"I heard last year thet General Jo Shelby and his men refused to surrender," Lone said, " . . . heard they went to Mexico, some kind of fight down there. Ain't heard nothin' since, but some, I believe, left to join up with 'em." The Indian spoke flatly, but he shot a quick glance at Josey to find the effect.

Josey was surprised. "I didn't know there was other'n thet didn't surrender. I ain't never been farther into Texas than Fannin County. Mexico's a long way off."

Lone pushed the pan toward Josey. "It is somethin' to think about," he said. "Men sich as we are . . . our trade . . . ain't wanted around hereabouts . . . seems like."

"Something to think about," Josey agreed, and without further ceremony he walked to a willow bed and unbuckled his guns for the first time in many days. Placing his hat over his face, he stretched out and was in deep sleep in a moment. Lone received this unspoken confidence with implacable routine.

The days that followed slipped into weeks. There was no more talk of Mexico . . . but the thought worked at the mind of Josey. He asked no questions of Lone, nor did the Indian volunteer information about himself, but it was apparent that he was in hiding.

As the winter days passed, Josey relaxed his tensions and even enjoyed helping Lone make fish baskets, which he did with a skill equaling the Indian's. They set the baskets in the river with meal balls for bait. Food was plentiful; besides the fish they ate fat quail from cunningly set traps on the quail runs, rabbit, and turkey, all seasoned with the wild onion, skunk cabbage, garlic, and herbs Lone dug from the bottoms.

January, 1867, brought snow across the Nations. It swept in a great white storm out of the Cimarron flats, gathered fury over the central plateau, and banked its blanket against the Ozarks. It brought misery to the Plains Indian, the Kiowa, the Comanche, Arapaho, and Pottawatomie . . . short of winter food they were driven toward the settlements. The snow settled in four-foot drifts along the Neosho, but driftwood was plentiful and the cabin was snug. The confinement brought a restlessness to Josey Wales. He had noted the leanness of Lone's provisions. There was no ammunition for his pistol, and the horses were short of grain.

And so it was, as they sat silently around the fire of a bleak evening, Josey placed a fistful of gold pieces in Lone's hand.

"Yankee gold," he said laconically, "we'll be needin' grain . . . ammunition and sich."

Lone stared at the glittering coins in the firelight, and a wolfish smile touched his lips.

"The gold of the enemy, like his corn, is always bright. It'll cause some questions in the settlement, but," he added thoughtfully, "if I tell 'em the blue pony soldiers will take it away from them if they talk . . ."

Bright, crystal-blue days brought the sun's rays in an unseasonable warmth and melted away the snow in a few days and fed new life into the rivulets and streams. Lone brought his gray gelding to the cabin and prepared to leave. Josey carried Lone's saddle to the door, but the Indian shook his head.

"No saddle . . . also no hat . . . no shirt. I'll wear a

blanket and carry only the rifle. I'll be a dumb blanket buck, the soldiers think all Indians with a blanket are too stupid to question."

He left, riding along the river bank, where the marshy bottom would hide his tracks . . . a forlorn, hunched figure under his blanket.

Two days passed, and Josey felt the tenseness of listening for Lone's return. The feeling of the trailed outlaw returned, and the cabin became a trap. On the third day he moved his bedroll and guns to the brush and alternated his watch between river bank and cabin. He could never have been persuaded that Lone would betray him, but many things could have happened.

Lone could have been found out, backtracked by a patrol . . . many of them had Osage trackers. He had moved the roan from the stable and picketed him in the brush when on the afternoon of the fourth day he heard the clear call of the nighthawk. He answered and watched as Lone slipped silently up from the river bank, leading the gray. The Indian looked even more emaciated. Josey suddenly wondered at his age as he saw wrinkles that sagged the bony face. He was older . . . in a dispirited sense that had suckled away the sap from his physical body. As they unloaded the grain and supplies from the back of the horse the Indian said nothing . . . and Josey volunteered no questions.

Around the fireplace they ate a silent meal as both stared into the flames, and then Lone quietly spoke. "There is much talk of ye. Some say ye have killed thirty-five men, some say forty. Ye'll not live long, the soldiers say, for they've raised the price fer yer head. It's five thousand in gold. Many are searching fer ye, and I myself saw five different patrols. I was stopped two times as I returned. I hid the ammunition in the grain."

There was a touch of bitterness in Lone's laugh.

"They would've stolen the grain, but I told them I had gathered it from the leavings of the post . . . thrown out by the white man because it made the white man sick . . . and I was takin' it to my woman. They laughed . . . and said a damn Indian could eat anything. They thought it was poisoned."

Lone fell silent, watching the flames dance along the logs. Josey splattered one of the logs with a long stream of tobacco juice, and after a long time Lone continued. "The trails are patrolled . . . heavy . . . when the weather breaks, they'll begin beatin' the brush. They know ye are in the Nations . . . and they'll find ye."

Josey cut a plug of tobacco. "I reckin," he said easily, with the casual manner of one who had lived for years in the bosom of enemy patrols. He watched the firelight play across the Indian's face. He looked ancient, a haughty and forlorn expression that harked backward toward some wronged god who sat in grieved dignity and disappointment.

"I'm sixty years old," Lone said. "I was a young man with a fine woman and two sons. They died on the Trail of Tears when we left Alabama. Before we were forced to leave, the white man talked of the bad Indian . . . he beat his breast and told why the Indian must leave. Now he's doin' it again. Already the talk is everywhere. The thumpin' of the breast to justify the wrong that will come to the Indian. I have no woman . . . I have no sons. I would not sign the pardon paper. I will not stay and see it again. I would go with ye . . . if ye'll have me."

He had said it all simply, without rancor and with no emotion. But Josey knew what the Indian was saying. He knew of the heartache of lost woman and child . . . of a home that was no more. And he knew that Lone Watie, the Cherokee, in saying simply that he would go with him . . . meant much more . . . that he had chosen Josey as his people . . . a like warrior with a common cause, a common suffrage . . . a respect for courage. And as it was with such men as Josey Wales, he could not show these things he felt. Instead, he said, "They're payin' to see me dead. Ye could do a lot better by driftin' south on yer own."

Now he knew why Lone had refused to sign the pardon paper . . . why he had deliberately made an outcast of himself, hoping that the blame would be placed on such men as himself . . . rather than his people. On this trip he had become convinced that nothing would save the Nation of the Cherokee.

Lone took his gaze from the fire and looked across the hearth into the eyes of Josey. He spoke slowly. "It is good that a man's enemies want him dead, for it proves he has lived a life of worth. I am old but I will ride free as long as I live. I would ride with such a man."

Josey reached into a paper sack Lone had brought back with the supplies and drew forth a round ball of red, hard rock candy. He held it up to the light. "Jest like a damn Indian," he said, "always buying somethin' red, meant fer foolishness."

Lone's smile broadened into a deep-throated chuckle of relief. He knew he would ride with Josey Wales.

The bitterness of February slipped toward March as they made preparation for the trail. Grass would be greening farther south, and the longhorn herds, moving up from Texas on the Shawnee Trail for Sedalia, would hide their own movements south.

Mexico! The thought had lingered in Josey's mind. Once, wintering at Mineral Creek, an old Confederate cavalryman of General McCulloch's had visited their campfires, regaling the guerrillas with stories of his soldiering with General Zachary Taylor at Monterrey in 1847. He told tales of fiestas and balmy fragrant nights, of dancing and Spanish *señoritas*. There had been the thrilling recital of when the emissary of General Santa Anna had come down to inform Taylor that he was surrounded by twenty thousand troops and must surrender. How the Mexican military band, in the early morning light, had played the "Dequela," the no-quarter song, as the thousands of pennants fluttered in the breeze from the hills surrounding Taylor's men. And Old Zack had ridden down the line, mounted on "Whitey," bellering, "Double-shot yer guns and give 'em hell, damn 'em."

The stories had enthralled the Missouri pistol fighters, farm boys who had found nothing of the romantic in their dirty Border War. Josey had remembered the interlude around that Texas campfire. If a feller had nowheres in pa'ticlar to ride . . . well, why not Mexico!

They saddled up on a raw March morning. An icy wind sent showers of frost from the tree branches, and the ground was still frozen before dawn. The horses, grain-slick and eager, fought the bits in their mouths and crow-hopped against the saddles. Josey left the heading to Lone, and the Indian led away from the cabin, following the bank of the Neosho. Neither of them looked back.

Lone had discarded the blanket. The gray cavalry hat shaded his eyes. Around his waist he wore the

Colts' pistol, belted low. If he would ride with Josey Wales . . . then he would ride as boldly . . . for what he was . . . a companion Rebel. Only the hawk-bronze face, the plaited hair that dangled to his shoulders . . . the boot moccasins . . . marked him as Indian.

Their progress was slow. Traveling dim trails, often where no trail showed at all, they stayed with the crooks and turns of the river as it threaded south through the Cherokee Nation. The third day of riding found them just north of Fort Gibson, and they were forced to leave the river to circle that Army post. They did so at night, striking the Shawnee Trail and fording the Arkansas. At dawn they were out on rolling prairie and in the Creek Indian Nation.

It was nearing noon when the gelding pulled up lame. Lone dismounted and ran his hands around the leg, down to the hoof. The horse jumped as he pressed a tendon. "Pulled," he said, "too much damn stable time."

Josey scanned the horizon about them . . . there were no riders in sight, but they were exposed, with only one horse, and the humps in the prairie had a way of suddenly disclosing what had not been there a moment before. Josey swung a leg around the saddle horn and looked thoughtfully at the gelding. "Thet hoss won't ride fer a week."

Lone nodded gloomily. His face was a mask, but his heart sank. It was only right that he stay behind . . . he could not endanger Josey Wales.

Josey cut a wad of tobacco. "How fer to thet tradin' post on the Canadian?"

Lone straightened. "Four . . . maybe six mile. That would be Zukie Limmer's post . . . but patrols are comin' and goin' around there, Creek Indian police too."

Josey swung his foot into the stirrup. "They all ride hosses, and a hoss is what we need. Wait here." He jumped the roan into a run. As he topped a rise he looked back. Lone was on foot, running behind him, leading the limping gelding.

Chapter 9

The trading post was set back a mile from the Canadian on a barren flat of shale rock and brush. It was a one-story log structure that showed no sign of human life except the thin column of smoke that rose from a chimney. Behind the post was a half-rotted barn, obviously past use. Back of the barn a pole corral held horses.

From his position on the rise Josey counted the horses . . . thirty of them . . . but there were no saddles in sight . . . no harness. That meant trade horses . . . somebody had made a trade. For several minutes he watched. The hitch rack before the post was empty, and he could see no sign of movement anywhere in his range of vision. He eased the roan down the hill and circled the corral. Before he was halfway around, he saw the horse he wanted, a big black with deep chest and rounded barrel . . . nearly as big as his roan. He rode to the front of the post, and looping the reins of the roan on the hitch rack, strode to the heavy front door.

Zukie Limmer was nervous and frightened. He had reason. He held his trading post contract under auspices of the U.S. Army, which specifically forbade the sale of liquor. Zukie made more profit from his bootlegging than he did from all his trade goods cheating of the Creeks. Now he was frightened. The two men had brought the horses in yesterday and were waiting, they said, for the Army detachment from Fort Gibson to come and inspect them for buying. They had turned their own horses into the corral, and dragging their saddles and gear into the post, had slept on the dirt floor without so much as asking a leave to do so. He knew them only as Yoke and Al, but he knew they were dangerous, for they had about them the leering smiles of thinly disguised threat as they took whatever pleased them with the remark, "Put that on our bill," at which they both invariably burst into roars of laughter at a seemingly obvious joke. They claimed to have papers on the horses, but Zukie suspected the horse herd to be Comanch . . . the fruits of a Comanche raiding party on Texas ranches of the Southwest.

The evening before, the larger of the two, Yoke, had thrown a huge arm around the narrow shoulders of Zukie, drawing him close in an overbearing, confidential manner. He had blown the breath of his rotten teeth into Zukie's face while he assured him, "We got papers on them horses . . . good papers. Ain't we, Al?"

He had winked broadly at Al, and both had laughed uproariously. Zukie had scuttled back behind the heavy plank set on barrels that served as his bar. During the night he had moved his gold box back into the sloping lean-to shed where he slept. All day he had stayed behind the plank, first hoping for the Army patrol . . . now dreading it; for the men had broken into his whiskey barrel and had been liquoring up since midmorning.

Once, Zukie had almost forgotten his fear. When the Indian woman had brought out the noon meal and placed the beef platters before them on the rough table, they had grabbed her. She had stood passively while they ran rough hands over her thighs and buttocks and made obscene suggestions to each other.

"How much you take fer this squaw?" Al, the ferret-looking one, had asked as he stroked the woman's stomach.

"She ain't fer sale," Zukie had snapped . . . then, alarmed at his own brevity, a whine entered his tone . . . "That is . . . she ain't mine . . . I mean, she works here."

Yoke had winked knowingly at Al, "He could put 'er on the bill, Al." They had laughed at the remark until Yoke fell off the stool. The woman had escaped back into the kitchen.

Zukie was not outraged at their treatment of the woman; it was that he had anticipated her for himself. She had been there at the post just four days, and as was his way, Zukie Limmer never entered upon anything in a straight manner . . . he sidled his way, crablike, forward. Cunning was his nature; it made the prize better.

She had walked into the post from the west and had offered an old dirty blanket for sale. Zukie had sized her up immediately. She was an outcast. The heavy scar running the length of her right nostril was the punishment of some of the Plains tribes for unfaithful-ness. "One too many bucks," Zukie had snickered and repeated it. It was clever, and Zukie savored his humor. She was not unpretty. Maybe twenty-five or thirty, still slender, with pointed breasts and rounded thighs that pushed against the fringed doeskin. Her mocca-sins had been worn through and hung in tatters on swollen feet. Her bronze face, framed by plaited black hair, was stoical, but her eyes reflected the haunted look of a hurt animal.

Zukie had felt the saliva juices entering his mouth as he looked at her. He had run his hands over the firm roundness of her breasts and she had not moved. She was hungry . . . and helpless. He had put her to work . . . and he knew how to train Indians . . . especially Indian women. He had watched for the opportunity, and when she had fallen and overturned a nearly empty barrel of brine he had pushed her face into the floor with one hand while he had beaten her with a barrel stave until his arm was weary. She had stayed motionless under the beating, but he had felt the ani-mal strength in her. Sinewy, flat stomach, firm but-tocks and thighs . . . properly mastered; Zukie relished the thought. When he ate at his table he opened the back door of the lean-to and made the woman squat outside, with the half-starved hound, and he had tossed scraps to her to eat. She was about ready to be moved into his bed, and she wouldn't be uppity.

Now Yoke demanded more food, and the Indian woman came, bringing more beef and potatoes. As she reached the table Yoke encircled her waist with a big arm, lifted her from the floor, and slammed her length-wise on the tabletop. He pressed his huge body down on her breasts, and grabbing her hair, tried to hold her upturned face steady while he slobbered over her mouth. His voice was thick with lust and liquor. "We're gonna have us a little squaw . . . ain't we, Al?"

Al was caressing the thighs of the woman, his hands moved under her doeskin skirt. She kicked and twisted her face, not crying out . . . but she was helpless. The heavy door opened suddenly, and Josey Wales stepped through. Everybody froze in motion.

Zukie Limmer knew it was Josey Wales. The talk of the reward was everywhere. The description of the man was exact; the twin tied-down .44's, the buckskin jacket, the gray cavalry hat . . . the heavy white scar that jagged the cheeks. The man must be crazy! No, he must not care whether he lives or dies, to go about making no attempt to disguise himself.

Zukie had heard the stories of the outlaw. No man could feel safe in his presence, and Zukie felt the recklessness . . . the ruthlessness that emanated from the man. The threat of Yoke and Al faded as of naughty schoolboys. Zukie Limmer placed his hands on the plank . . . in plain sight . . . and a cold, dread fear convinced him his life hung balanced on the whim of this killer.

Josey Wales moved with a practiced quickness out of the door's silhouette and with the same fluid motion moved to the end of the bar so that he faced the door. He appeared not to notice the Indian woman and her tormentors. They still held her but watched, fascinated, as he leaned easily on the bar. Zukie turned to face him . . . keeping his hands tightly on the plank . . . and looked into black eyes that were cold and flat . . . and he physically shivered. Josey smiled. Perhaps it was meant to be friendly, but the smile only served to deepen and whiten the big scar so that his face took on an inexpressible cruelty. Zukie felt like a mouse before a big purring cat and so was impelled to make some offer.

"Have a whiskey, mister?" he heard himself squeaking.

Josey waited a long time. "Reckin not," he said dryly.

"I got some cold beer . . . good brewed-up Choc. It's . . . it's on the house," Zukie stammered.

Josey eased the hat back on his head. "Well now, that's right neighborly of ye, friend."

Zukie placed a huge tin cup before him and from a barrel dipped the dark liquid into it. He was encouraged by the action of Josey Wales drinking beer. It was, after all, a human act. Perhaps the man had some reasonable qualities about him. Surely he could think humanely . . . and sociably.

Josey wiped the beer from his mustache with the back of a hand. "Matter of fact," he said, "I'm lookin' to buy a hoss."

"A hoss . . . ah . . . a horse?" Zukie repeated stupidly.

Al had staggered to the bar. "Gimme a bucket of that Choc," he said thickly.

Zukie, still staring at Josey, dipped a tin bucket of the beer from the barrel and placed it on the bar. "The horses," he said, "belong to these gentlemen. They'll more than likely. . . that is . . . I'm sure they'll sell you one."

Al turned slowly to face Josey, holding the bucket of beer waist-high, and under it he held a pistol . . . the hammer already thumbed back. A sly, triumphant smile wreathed his face.

"Josey Wales," he breathed . . . and then chortled, "Josey Wales, by God! Five thousand gold simoleons walkin' right in. Mr. Chain Blue Lightening hisself, that ever'body's so scairt of. Well now, Mr. Lightening, you move a hair, twitch a finger . . . and I'll splatter yore guts agin the wall. Come over here, Yoke," he called aside to his partner.

Yoke shuffled forward, loosing the Indian woman. Zukie was terrified as he looked from Al to Josey. The outlaw was staring steadily into the eyes of Al . . . he hadn't moved. Confidence began to return to Zukie.

"Now look, Al," Zukie whined, "the man is in my place. I recognized him, and I'm due a even split. I . . ."

"Shet up," Al said viciously, without taking his eyes from Josey, "shet up, you goddamned nanny goat. I'm the one that got 'em."

Al was growing nervous from the strain. "Now," he said testily, "when I tell you to move, Mr. Lightening, you move slow, like 'lasses in the wintertime, or I drop the hammer. You ease yore hands down, take them guns out, butt first, and hold 'em out so Yoke can git 'em. You understand? Nod, damn you."

Josey nodded his head.

"Now," Al instructed, "ease the pistols out."

With painful slowness Josey pulled the Colts and extended them butt first toward Yoke. A finger of each hand was in the trigger guard. Yoke stepped forward and reached for the proffered handles. His hands were almost on the butts of the pistols when they spun on the fingers of Josey with the slightest flick of his wrists. As if by magic the pistols were reversed, barrels pointing at Al and Yoke . . . but Al never saw it.

The big right-hand .44 exploded with an ear splitting roar that lifted Al from the floor and arched his body backward. Yoke was dumbfounded. A full second ticked by before he clawed for the pistol at his hip. He knew he was making a futile effort, but he read death in the black eyes of Josey Wales. The left-hand Colt boomed, and the top of Yoke's head . . . and most of his brains . . . were splattered against a post.

"My God!" Zukie screamed. "My God!" And he sank sobbing to the floor. He had witnessed the pistol spin. A few years later the Texas gunfighter John Wesley Hardin would execute the same trick to disarm Wild Bill Hickok in Abilene. It would become known in the West as the "Border Roll," in honor of the Missouri Border pistol fighters who had invented it . . . but few would dare practice it, for it required a master pistoleer.

Acrid blue smoke filled the room. The Indian woman had not moved, nor did she now, but her eyes followed Josey Wales.

"Stand up, mister," Josey leaned over the plank and looked down at Zukie, who pulled himself to his feet. His hands were trembling as he watched the outlaw carefully cut a chew of tobacco and return the twist to his jacket. He chewed for a moment, looking thoughtfully at Zukie.

"Now, let's see," he said with studied contemplation, "ye say them hosses belong to these here pilgrims?" He designated the "pilgrims" by accurately hitting Al's upturned face with a stream of tobacco juice.

"Yes . . . Yes," Zukie was eagerly helpful, " . . . and Mr. Wales, I was only trying to throw them off . . . to help you . . . with that talk of the reward."

"I 'preciate thet kindly," Josey said dryly, "but gittin' back to the hosses, 'pears like these here pore pilgrims won't be in the need of them hosses no more . . . seein' as how they have passed on . . . so I reckin the hosses is more or less public property . . . wouldn't ye say?"

Zukie nodded vigorously, "Yes, I would say that . . . I would agree to that. It sounds fair and right to me."

"Fair'n fair and right as rain," Josey said with satisfaction. "Now me being a public citizen and sich as that," Josey continued, "I reckin I'll take along my part of the propitty, not havin' time to wait around fer the court to divide it all up."

"I think you should have all the horses," Zukie said generously. "They . . . that is, they really belong to you."

"I ain't a hawg," Josey said. "We got to think of the other public citizens. One hoss will do me fine. You git thet loop of rope hangin' yonder, and ye come on out, and we'll ketch up my propitty."

Zukie scurried out the door ahead of Josey and trotted to the corral. They caught up the big black. Josey rigged a halter and mounted the roan. From his saddle he looked down at Zukie, who nervously shifted his feet.

"Reckin ye can live, mister," and his voice was cold, "but a woman is a woman. I got friends in the Nations, and word gittin' to me of thet woman bein' mistreated would strike me unkindly."

Zukie bobbed his head, "I pledge to you, Mr. Wales . . . I give my solemn word, she will not be . . . again. I will . . ."

"I'll be seein' ye," and with that, Josey sank spurs to the roan and was off in a whirl of dust, leading the black behind him. The Indian woman watched him from where she crouched behind the lean-to.

As Josey topped the first rise he found Lone waiting with rifle trained on the trading post. Lone's eyes glistened as he looked at the black.

"A feller would have to sleep with thet hoss to keep his grandma from stealing him," he said admiringly.

"Yeah," Josey grinned. "Got him cheap too. But if

we ain't movin' on in a minute, the Army's most like to git 'em. A patrol is due any minute from Fort Gibson."

They worked fast, switching Lone's gear from the gray gelding to the black. The gelding moved off immediately, cropping grass.

"He'll be all right in a week . . . maybe he'll run free the rest of his life," Lone said wistfully.

"Let's move out," Josey said, and he swung the big roan down the hill, followed by Lone on the black. They were magnificently mounted now; the roan scarcely a hand higher than the strong black horse. Fording the Canadian, they moved toward the Seminole and the Choctaw Nations.

Less than an hour later, Zukie Limmer was pouring out his story to the Army patrol from Fort Gibson, and in three hours dispatches were alerting the state of Texas. Added to the dispatches were these words: SHOOT ON SIGHT. DO NOT ATTEMPT TO DISARM, REPEAT: DO NOT ATTEMPT TO DISARM. FIVE THOUSAND DOLLARS REWARD: DEAD.

The tale of the pistol spin fled southward, keeping pace with the dispatches. The story grew with each telling through the campfires of the drovers coming up the trail . . . and spread to the settlements. Violent Texas knew and talked of Josey Wales long before he was to reach her borders . . . the bloody ex-lieutenant of Bloody Bill; the pistol fighter with the lightning hands and stone nerves who mastered the macabre art of death from the barrels of Colt .44's.

Chapter 10

They rode far into the night. Josey left the trail heading to Lone and followed his lead. The Cherokee was a crafty trailsman, and with the threat of pursuit he brought all his craft into practice.

Once, for a mile, they rode down the middle of a shallow creek and brought their horses to the bank when Lone found loose shale rock that carried no print. For a distance of ten miles they boldly traveled the well-marked Shawnee Trail, mixing their tracks with the tracks of the trail. Each time they paused to rest the horses Lone drove a stick in the ground . . . grasping it with his teeth, he "listened," feeling for the vibrations of horses. Each time as he remounted he shook his head in puzzlement, "Very light sound . . . maybe one horse . . . but it's stayin' with us . . . we ain't shakin' it off."

Josey frowned, "I don't figger one hoss . . . maybe it's a damn buffalo . . . 'er a wild hoss follerin'."

It was after midnight when they rested. Rolled in blankets on the bank of a creek that meandered toward Pine Mountain, they slept with bridle reins wrapped about their wrists. They grained the horses but left the saddles on them, loosely cinched.

Up before dawn, they made a cold breakfast of jerky beef and biscuits and double-grained the horses for the hard riding. Lone suddenly placed his hand on the ground. He kneeled with ear pressed against the earth.

"It's a horse," he said quietly, "comin' down the creek." Now Josey could hear it crashing through the undergrowth. He tied the horses back behind a persimmon tree and stepped into the small clearing.

"I'll be bait man," he said calmly. Lone nodded and slipped the big knife from its scabbard. He placed it between his teeth and slid noiselessly into the brush toward the creek. Now Josey could see the horse. It was a spotted paint, and the rider was leaning from its back, studying the ground as he rode. Now he saw Josey but didn't pause, but instead lifted the paint into a trot. The horse was within twenty yards of Josey and he could see that the rider wore a heavy blanket over his head, falling around his shoulders.

Suddenly a figure leaped from the brush astride the paint and toppled the rider from the horse. It was Lone. He was over the rider, lying on the ground, and raised his knife for the downward death stroke. "Wait!" Josey shouted.

The blanket had fallen away from the rider. It was the Indian woman. Lone sat down on her in amazement. A vicious-looking hound was attacking one of his moccasined feet, and he kicked at the dog as he rose. The Indian woman calmly brushed her skirt and stood up. As Josey approached she pointed back up the creek.

"Pony soldiers," she said, "two hours." Lone stared at her.

"How in hell . . ." he said.

"She was at the trading post," Josey said, then to the woman, "How many pony soldiers?"

She shook her head, and Josey turned to Lone. "Ask her about the pony soldiers . . . try some kind of lingo."

"Sign," Lone said. "All Indians know sign talk, even tribes that cain't understand each other's spoke word."

He moved his hands and fingers through the air. The woman nodded vigorously and answered with her own hands.

"She says," Lone turned to Josey, "there are twenty pony soldiers, two . . . maybe three hours back . . . wait, she's talkin' agin."

The Indian woman's hands moved rapidly for a space of several minutes while Lone watched. He chuckled . . . laughed . . . then fell silent.

"What is it?" Josey asked. "Hell, man, cain't ye shet her up?"

Lone held his palm forward toward the woman and looked admiringly at Josey.

"She told me of the fight in the tradin' post . . . of your magic guns. She says ye are a great warrior and a great man. She is Cheyenne. Thet sign she give of cuttin' the wrist . . . thet's the sign of the Cheyenne . . . every Plains tribe has a sign that identifies them. The movin' of her hand forward, wigglin', is the sign of the snake . . . the Comanche sign. She said the two men ye killed were traders with the Comanch . . . called Comancheros . . . 'them that deals with Comanch.' She said she was violated by a buck of the Arapaho . . . their sign is the 'dirty nose' sign . . . when she held her nose with her fingers . . . and that the Cheyenne Chief, Moke-to-ve-to, or Black Kettle, believed she did not resist enough . . . she should have killed herself . . . so she was whupped, had her nose slit, and was cast out to die." Lone paused. "Her name, by the way, is Take-toha . . . means 'Little Moonlight'."

"She can shore talk," Josey said admiringly. He spat tobacco juice at the dog . . . and the hound snarled. "Tell her," Josey said, "to go back to the tradin' post. She will be treated better now. Tell her that many men want to kill us . . . that we gotta ride fast . . . thet there's too much danger fer a woman," Josey paused, "and tell her we 'preciate what she's done fer us."

Lone's hands moved rapidly again. He watched her solemnly as she answered. Finally he looked at Josey, and there was the pride of the Indian when he spoke. "She says she cannot go back. That she stole a rifle, supplies, and the hoss. She says she would not go back if she could . . . that she will foller in our tracks. Ye saved her life. She says she can cook, track, and fight. Our ways are her ways. She says she ain't got no-wheres else to go." Lone's face was expressionless, but his eyes looked askance at Josey. "She's shore pretty," he added with hopeful recommendation.

Josey spat, "Damn all conniption hell. Here we go, trailin' into Texas like a waggin train. Well . . . " he sighed as he turned to the horses, "she'll jest have to track if she falls back, and when she gits tired she can quit."

As they swung into their saddles Lone said, "She thinks I'm a Cherokee Chief."

"I wonder where she got thet idee," Josey remarked dryly. Little Moonlight picked up her rifle and blanket and swung expertly astride the paint. She waited humbly, eyes cast to the ground, for the men to take the trail.

"I wonder," Josey said as they walked the horses out of the brush.

"Wonder what?" Lone asked.

"I was jest wonderin'," he said, "I reckin that mangy red-bone hound ain't got nowheres to go neither."

Lone laughed and led the way, followed closely by Josey. At a respectful distance the blanketed Little Moonlight rode the paint, and at her heels the bony hound sniffed the trail.

They traveled south, then southwest, skirting Pine Mountain on their left and keeping generally to open prairie. More grass showed now on the land. Lone kept the black at a ground-eating canter, and the big roan easily stayed with him, but Little Moonlight fell farther and farther behind. By midafternoon Josey could just make out her bobbing head as she pushed the rough-riding paint nearly a mile behind. The soldiers had not come into sight, but late in the afternoon a party of half-naked Indians armed with rifles rode over a rise to their left and brought their ponies at an angle to intercept them.

Lone slowed the black.

"I count twelve," Josey said as he rode alongside.

Lone nodded. "They are Choctaws, riding down to meet the trail herds. They will ask payment fer crossing their lands . . . then they will cut out cattle . . . permission or not."

The Indians rode closer, but after they had inspected the two heavily armed men on the big horses . . . they veered off and slackened pace. They had ridden on for another quarter mile when Lone slid the black to a halt so suddenly that Josey almost ran his mount over him.

"Taketoha!" he shouted, "Little Moon . . . !" Simultaneously, they whirled their horses and set them running back over the trail. Coming to a rise they saw the Indians riding close, but not too close, to the paint horse. Little Moonlight was holding the rifle steady, and with it she swept the squad of Indians. The Choctaws saw Lone and Josey waiting on the rise and turned away from the Indian woman. They had gotten the message; that the squaw was, somehow, a member of this strange caravan that included two hard-appearing riders mounted on giant horses and a cadaverous-looking hound with long ears and bony flanks.

It was midnight when they camped on the banks of Clear Boggy Creek, less than a day's ride from the Red River and Texas. An hour later Little Moonlight jogged into camp on the paint.

Josey heard her slip silently around their blankets. He saw Lone rise and give grain to the paint. She rolled in a blanket a little distance from them and did not eat before she slept.

Her movements woke Josey before dawn, and he smelled cooking but saw no fire. Little Moonlight had dragged a hollow log close to them, carved a hole in its side, and placed a black pot over a captive, hidden fire.

Lone was already eating. "I'm gonna take up tepee livin' . . . if it's like this," he grinned. And as Josey stepped to feed the horses Lone said, "She's already grained 'em . . . and watered 'em . . . and rubbed 'em down . . . and cinched the saddles. Might as well set yore bottom down like a chief and eat."

Josey took a bowl from her and sat cross-legged by the log. "I see the Cherokee Chief is already eatin'," he said.

"Cherokee Chiefs have big appetites," Lone

grinned, belched, and stretched. The hound growled at the movement . . . he was chewing on a mangled rabbit. Josey watched the dog as he ate.

"I see ol' hound gits his own," he said. "Re'clects me of a red-bone we had back home in Tennessee. I went with Pa to tradin'. They had pretty blue ticks, julys, and sich, but Pa, he paid fifty cent and a jug o' white fer a old red-bone that had a broke tail, one eye out, and half a ear bit off. I ast Pa why, and he said minute he saw that ol' hound, he knowed he had sand . . . thet he'd been there and knowed what it was all about . . . made the best 'coon hound we ever had."

Lone looked at Little Moonlight as she packed gear on the paint. "It is so . . . and many times . . . with women. Yore Pa was a knowin' mountain man."

The wind held a smell of moist April as they rode south, still in the Choctaw Nation. At dusk they sighted the Red River, and by full dark the three of them had forded not far from the Shawnee Trail. They set foot on the violent ground of Texas.

Chapter 11

Texas in 1867 was in the iron grip of the Union General Phil Sheridan's military rule. He had removed Governor James W. Throckmorton from office and appointed his own Governor, E. M. Pease. Pease, a figurehead for the Northern Army under orders of radical politicians in Washington, would soon be succeeded by another Military Governor, E. J. Davis, but the conditions would remain the same.

Only those who took the "ironclad oath" could vote. Union soldiers stood in long lines at every ballot box. All Southern sympathizers had been thrown out of office. Judges, mayors, sheriffs were replaced by what Texans called "scalawags," if the turncoats were from the South, and "carpetbaggers," if they were from the North. Armed, blue-coated Militia, called "Regulators," imposed . . . or tried to . . . the will of the Governor, and mobs of Union Leaguers, half-controlled by the politicians, settled like locusts over the land.

The effects of the vulturous greed and manipulations of the politicians were everywhere, as they sought to confiscate property and home and line their pockets from levy and tax. The Regular Army, as usual, was caught in the middle and in the main stood aside or devoted their efforts to the often futile task of attempting to contain the raids of the bloody Comanche and Kiowa that encroached even into central Texas. These Tartars of the Plains were ferociously defending their last free domain that stretched from deep in Mexico to the Cimarron in the north.

The names of untamed Rebels were gaining bloody prominence; Cullen Baker, the heller from Louisiana, was becoming widely known. Captain Bob Lee, who had served under the incomparable Bedford Forrest in Tennessee, was waging a small war with the Union Leaguers headed by Lewis Peacock. Operating out of Fannin, Collins, and Hunt counties, Lee was setting northeast Texas aflame. There was already a price on his head. Bill Longley, the cold killer from Evergreen, was a wanted man, and farther south, around DeWitt and Gonzales counties, there was the Taylor clan. Headed by the ex-Confederate Captain Creed Taylor, there were brothers Josiah, Rufus, Pitkin, William, and Charlie . . . with sons Buck, Jim, and a whole army of a second generation.

Out of the Carolinas, Georgia, and Alabama, they fought under the orders of the Taylor family motto, marrowed in their blood from birth, "Whoever sheds a Taylor's blood, by a Taylor's hand must die." And they meant it. Entire towns were terrorized in the shootouts between the Taylors, their kith and kin . . . and the Regulators headed by Bill Sutton and his entourage. They were tough and mean; stubborn to defend their "propitty"; they had never been whupped, and they aimed to prove it.

Simp Dixon, a Taylor kinsman, died at Cotton Gin, Texas, his back to a wall . . . weighted down with lead . . . and both .44's blazing. He took five Regulators with him. The Clements brothers went "helling" through the carpetbag-controlled towns and periodically rode up the trail when the Texas heat got too unhealthy. The untended ranches of four years had loosed thousands of wild longhorns in the brush. The Northeast needed beef, and the Southern riders filled the trails as they "brush-popped" the cattle into herds and angled them north.

First up the Shawnee to Sedalia, Missouri . . . then the Chisholm to Abilene, Kansas . . . the Western Trail to Dodge City, as the rail lines moved west. Each spring and fall they turned the railhead cattle towns into "Little Texas" and brought a brand of wildness that forevermore would stamp the little villages in history.

It would be a year before a young lad, John Wesley Hardin, would begin his fantastically bloody career . . . but he would be only one of many. General Sherman said of the time and the place, "If I owned Texas and Hell, I would rent out Texas and live in Hell." Well, Sherman knowed where his fit company was at. For Texans . . . them as couldn't fork the bronc had best move out, preferably in a pine box.

And now word flew down the Trail. The Missouri Rebel and unequaled pistol fighter, Josey Wales, was Texas bound. It was enough to make a Texan stomp the ground in glee and spit into the wind. For the politician it brought frantic thoughts and feverish action. Both sides braced for the coming.

Campfires twinkled as far as the eye could see. Early herds, pushing for the top market dollar after a winter's beef-hungry span in the North, were stacked almost end to end. Longhorns bawled and scuffled as cowboys rounded them into a settling for the night. Josey, Lone, and Little Moonlight . . . riding close now . . . passed near the lead campfires, out of the light. The *plink-plank* of a five-string banjo sounded tinny against the cattle sounds, and a mournful voice rose in song:

> "They say I cain't take up my rifle
> and fight 'em now nor more,
> But I ain't a'gonna love 'em
> Now thet is certain shore.
> And I don't want no pardon
> Fer whut I was and am,
> And I won't be reconstructed,
> And I don't give a damn."

They dry-camped in a shallow gully, away from the herds. Unable to picket-graze the horses and with the added appetite of the paint horse, the grain was running low.

It was chuck time for the cowboys of the Gatling brothers' trail herd. There were three Gatling brothers and eleven riders pushing three thousand head of longhorns. It had been a rough day. Herds were strung out behind them, and immediately on their heels Mexican vaqueros with a smaller herd had pushed and shouted at them for more speed. Several fights had broken out through the day, and the riders were in an ugly mood. The longhorns were not yet "trail-broke," still wild as they were driven from the brush; and they had made charges, all day long, away from the main body, which had kept the cowboys busy. Ten of them squatted now, or sat cross-legged around the fire, wolfing beans and beef. Half their number would have to relieve the riders circling the herd and take up first night watch. They were in no hurry to climb back in the saddle. Rough-garbed, most of them wore the chapparal leather guards . . . the cowboys called them "chaps" . . . and heavy pistols hung from sagging belts about their waists.

The voice came clear, "Haaallooo, the camp." Every man stiffened. Four of them faded a few paces back from the fire into the darkness. They had "papers" on them, and though they were protected by the code of the trail . . . every rider of the trail herd would fight to the death in their defense . . . there was no sense borrern' trouble from a nosey lawman.

The trail boss, for a long moment, continued chewing his beef, giving them as needed it "scarcin' time." Then he stood up and bawled, "Come on in!" They heard the horse walking slowly . . . then into the fire-light. It was a huge black that snorted and skittered as the rider brought him close. He swung down and did not trust the black to rein-stand but tied him to the wheel of the chuck wagon. Without another word, he brought his tin plate and cup from a saddlebag, dipped huge portions of bean and beef from the pot, calmly poured black coffee into the cup, and squatted, eating, in the circle of riders. It was the custom. The chuck was open claim to any rider on the trail.

It was a fractious practice to ask questions in Texas. Whenever a man asked one, it was invariably preceded by "no offense meant" . . . unless, of course, he did mean offense . . . in which case he prepared to draw his pistol. There was no need for questions anyhow. Every cowboy present could "read." The rider wore moccasin boots, the long, plaited black hair. He was Indian. The gray cavalry hat meant Confederate. Confederate Cherokee. There was the tied-down .44 and knife. A fightin' man. He came from the Nations, to the north, and he was riding south . . . otherwise, if he had come from the south, he'd have chucked at the hind-end herd. The horse was too good for a regular Indian or cowboy, therefore he was on a fast run from somethin' when a feller had to have the best in horse-flesh. The "reading" required only a minute. They approved . . . and gave evidence of their approval by resuming their conversations.

"Onliest way they'll ever git Wales is from the back," a bearded cowpuncher opined as he sopped his beans with a biscuit.

Another rose and refilled his plate. "Whit rode with Bill Todd and Fletch Taylor in Missouri . . . he says he seen Wales oncet in '65, at Baxter Springs. Drawed on three Redlegs. . . . Whit says ye couldn't see his hands move . . . and na'ar Redleg cleared leather."

"Bluebellies cut his trail in the Nations," another said. "Say thar's another rider . . . maybe two with 'em now."

The trail boss spoke, "He was knowed to have friends 'mongst the Cherokees. . . . " His voice trailed off . . . he had spoken before he thought . . . and now there was an awkward silence. Eyes cut furtively toward the Indian, who appeared not to have heard. He was busying himself over his tin plate.

The trail boss cleared his throat and addressed himself to the Indian, "Stranger, we was wonderin' about trail conditions to the north. That is, if ye come from that d'rection, no offense."

Lone looked up casually and spoke around a mouthful of beef. "None taken," he said. "Grazin' ought to be good. Day t'other side of the Red, ye'll be pestered by Choctaws . . . little bunches of 'em, old rifles, muzzle load. Canadian ain't up . . . leastwise, it wa'ant few days ago. If ye're branchin' off on the Chisholm, ye'll strike the Arkansas west of the Neosho . . . ought not be runnin' high . . . but I never crossed that fer west. East, on the Shawnee . . . she's up a mite." He sopped the remains of the beans, washed his tin plate with sand, and downed the last of the coffee. "Lookin' to buy a little stock grain . . . iff'n ye got it to spare."

"We're grazin' our remuda . . . ain't totin' no grain," the trail boss said, "but fer jest the one hoss, mebbe. . ."

"Three hosses," Lone said.

The trail boss turned to the cook, "Give 'em the oats in the chuck," and to Lone, "Ain't much . . . no more'n fer a day 'er two . . . but we can eat corn fritters . . . cain't we, boys?"

The cowboys nodded their big hats in unison. They knew.

"I'd be obliged to pay," Lone said as he accepted the sack of oats from the cook.

"Not likely," a cowboy spoke clear and loud from the fire.

As Lone swung up on the black, the trail boss held his bridle briefly, "Union Leaguers, twenty-five . . . thirty of 'em . . . combed through the herds a day's ride back . . . headed west. Heerd tell Regulators was poppin' brush all through this here neck o' country." He loosed his hands from the bridle.

Lone looked down at the trail boss, and his eyes

glittered. "Obliged," he said quietly, whirled the black, and was gone.

"Good luck," the voices floated to him from the campfire.

Josey and Little Moonlight had waited in the shallow wash. He sat, holding the horses' reins, and Little Moonlight stood behind him, high on the bank, and watched for Lone's return. Before he heard Lone's approach, she touched him on the arm. "Hoss," she said.

Josey smiled in the dark, a Cheyenne squaw, talkin' like a leather-popper. He listened to Lone's report in silence. Somehow . . . he had taken it for granted . . . that Texas would be as it was when he had wintered here during the War; everything peaceful behind the Confederate lines . . . but now, the same treacheries were present that had plagued Missouri all the many long years.

His face hardened. It would be no leisurely ride to Mexico. He was surprised that his name was so well known, and the term "Regulators" was new to him. Lone watched and waited patiently for Josey to speak. Lone Watie was an expert trailsman. He had been a cavalryman of the first order, but he knew by instinct that this climate of Texas required the leadership of the master guerrilla.

"We'll night-ride," Josey said grimly, "lay out in the washes and tree cover by day. Farther south we git, better off we ought to be. Let's ride." They pointed the tired horses south, giving wide berth to the fires of the trail herds.

By the morning of the fourth day they sighted the Brazos and camped in a thick scope of cottonwoods a half mile back from the Towash road. Little Moonlight curled at the base of a tree and instantly was asleep.

There was no more horse grain, and Lone rope-picketed the horses on the sparse grass . . . and lay sprawled on the ground, his hat covering his face.

Josey Wales watched the Towash road. From where he sat, back to a cottonwood, he could see riders as they passed below him. A lot of riders, singly and in groups. Occasionally a wagon feathering up the powder-gray dust . . . and here and there a fancy hack. Toward the west he could see the town only dimly visible in the dust haze and a racetrack at the edge. Racing day; that meant a lot of people. Sometimes you could move 'mongst a lot of people and bear no notice at all.

Josey worked at a heavy tobacco cud and mused his thinking toward a plan. He saw no blue riders on the road. Mexico, that temporary goal for temporary men who had no world and no goal, was a long way off. They would grub supply in the town and turn south toward San Antonio and the border.

"Anyhow," he mused aloud, "iff'n Little Moonlight don't git a saddle . . . or a hoss . . . she'll bump her bottom off on thet paint." He would wake Lone at high noon.

Josey didn't know the name of the town. They were here by chance, having struck the old Dallas–Waco road after midnight and turned off as the first streaks of light hit the east.

The town was Towash, one of many of the racing and gambling centers of central Texas. There was Bryan to the southeast, which gained fame of a sort when Big King, owner of the Blue Wing saloon, lost that establishment on the turn of a card to Ben Thompson, the Austin gambler and ex-Confederate pistol heller. Brenham, Texas, farther south of the

Brazos, was another center for the hard-eyed gentry of card and pistol.

Towash was a ripsnorter. The town is gone now, with only a few crumbling stone chimneys to mark its passing . . . west of Whitney. But in 1867 Towash made big sign . . . Texas-style. It boasted the Boles racetrack, which attracted the sports and gamblers from as far away as Hot Springs, Arkansas. There was a hand ferry across the Brazos and close by a grist mill powered by a huge waterwheel. Dyer & Jenkins was the trading store. There was a barbershop that did very little business and six saloons that did a lot, dispensing red-eye . . . raw. Typical of many towns in the Texas of 1867, there was no law except that made by each man with his own "craw sand." Occasionally the Regulators out of Austin rode in . . . always in large groups . . . more for protection than law enforcement.

When this occurred, it was the custom of the bartenders to move down the bar, rag-wiping as they went, announcing sotto voce, "Blue bellies in town." This for the benefit of all the "papered" gentry present. Some faded, and some didn't. In such cases another Texan often died with his boots on . . . but took with him a numbered thinning of the ranks of the Regulators in the fierce undeclared war of Reconstruction Texas.

A light whistle brought Lone to his feet. Little Moonlight squatted beside him as Josey talked and with a stick drew their future trail in the dirt.

"Ye goin' in too?" Lone asked.

Josey nodded, "We're way south, last they heard tell of me was the Nations."

Lone shook his head in doubt, "The talk is everywhere, and yer looks is knowed."

Josey stood up and stretched, "Lots of fellers' looks

is knowed. I ain't goin' to spend the rest o' my life wallerin' 'round in the brush. Anyhow, we ain't comin' back thisaway."

They saddled up in the late afternoon and rode down off the hillock toward Towash. Little Moonlight and the red-bone trailed behind.

Chapter 12

Josey had not seen blue riders on the road because they were already in Towash. Led by "Lieutenant" Cann Tolly, twenty-four of them had quartered in two of the straggling log cabins that fronted the road on the edge of Towash. They were Regulators, and now they walked the street in groups of four and five, pushing their way with the arrogance of authority through the crowds and into the saloons. They were the same breed of men as their leader.

Cann Tolly had once tried to be a constable, wanting dominance over other men without the natural qualities that gave it to him. He had failed, miserably. When first called on to restore order in a saloon scuffle, he had been flooded with fear and had melted into a simpering, good-fellow attitude that brought laughter from the saloon toughs.

When the Civil War came, neither side held attraction for Cann Tolly. He affected a limp and as the War progressed he cadged drinks in saloons with tales of battles he had heard from others. He hated the returning Confederate veteran and the straight-backed Union cavalryman with equal ferocity. Most of all he hated the stubborn, tough Texans who had laughed at his cowardice.

Joining the Regulators gave him his badge of authority from the Governor, and he quickly toadied his way up in the ranks with the sadism that marks all men of fear . . . passing it off as "law" enforcement. Always backed by men and guns he tortured victims who showed fear in their eyes by insult and threat until the tortured men crawled lower than Cann Tolly crawled inside. Where he saw no fear he had them shot down with quick ferocity and so eliminated another "troublemaker." His was a false authority maintained by a false government. Lacking the true authority of respect by his fellow human beings, he enforced it with threat, terror, and brutality . . . and therefore . . . inevitably . . . must fall.

Lieutenant Tolly had spent the morning visiting those known peculiar dregs of the human race who take neither side of an issue but delight in ferreting out and betraying those who do. Clay Allison, the crippled pistoleer, had shot up Bryan three days ago and was believed headed this way. King Fisher had passed through town the day before, trailing back south . . . but had not stayed around for the fun . . . peculiar for a heller like Fisher, who loved games and action. But there would be enough to go around.

Late afternoon saw an end to the races, and the crowds poured back into Towash. The "boys," whoopin' it up, shot off their pistols and stampeded into the saloons to continue their betting urge at seven-up and five-card stud. The Regulators began looking them over.

It was into this confusion that Josey, Lone, and Little Moonlight rode their horses. Lone and Little Moonlight stayed mounted, as planned, across the street from the big sign that said "Dyer & Jenkins, Trade Goods." Josey rode to the hitch rack in front of the store, dismounted, and entered. To one side a crude bar stretched the length of the store, and jostling, laughing cowpunchers drank and talked. The trade-goods section was empty except for a clerk.

Josey called off his needs, and the clerk scurried to fill them. He would like to see the man gone as soon as possible. A man with two tied-down holsters was either a badman or a bluffer . . . and there weren't many bluffing men in Texas. Josey watched casually through the big window as blue uniforms sauntered down the boardwalks. Four of them paused across the street and looked curiously at the stoical Lone and then moved on. Two punchers circled the big black horse, admiring the fine points, and one of them said something to Little Moonlight. They laughed good-naturedly and walked into a saloon.

Josey selected a light saddle for the paint. He accepted the two sacks of supplies handed to him by the clerk and paid with double eagles. Now he moved slowly to the door and paused. Holding the saddle in one hand, he half dragged the two sacks with the other. With the easy air of a man checking the weather he looked up and down the boardwalk . . . there were no blue uniforms.

As he stepped to the walk he could see Lone start the black walking toward him . . . Little Moonlight behind . . . to take some of the supplies. He turned two paces up the boardwalk toward his horse and came face-to-face with Cann Tolly . . . and flanking him were three Regulators. At the same instant he had stepped from the store they had come out of the Iron Man saloon. Fifteen paces separated them from Josey.

The Regulators froze in their tracks, and Josey, with only the slightest hesitation, dipped his head and took another step.

"Josey Wales!" Cann Tolly yelled the name to alarm every Regulator in Towash. Josey dropped the saddle and the sacks and fixed a look of bleakness on the man who had shouted. The street became a clear distinctness in his eyes. From the side he saw Lone halt his horse. Men poured out of saloons and then fell back against the sides of buildings. The boardwalk emptied, and cowpunchers dived behind water troughs and some flattened themselves on the ground.

He saw a young woman, her eyes a startling blue, staring wild-eyed at him . . . her foot fixed on the hub of a wagon wheel. She had been about to mount to the seat, and an old woman held one of her hands. They were both motionless, like wax figures. The girl's straw-colored hair shone in the sun. The street was death-quiet in an instant.

The Regulators looked back at him . . . half surprise, half horror was on their faces. Another minute and the Regulators all over town would recover from the momentary shock and he would be surrounded.

Josey Wales slowly eased into the crouch. His voice shipped loud and flat in the silence . . . and it carried a snarl of insult.

"Ye gonna pull them pistols, 'er whistle 'Dixie'?"

The Regulator to his left moved first, his hand darting downward; Cann Tolly followed. Only the right hand of Josey moved. The big .44 belched as it cleared

leather in the fluid motion of rolled lightning. He
fanned the hammer with his left palm.

The first man to draw flipped backward as the slug
hit his chest. Cann Tolly spun sideways and made a
little circle, like a dog chasing his tail, and fell, half his
head blown off. The third was hit low, the big slug
kicking him forward, and he flopped on his face. The
fourth man was already dead from a smoking pistol
held in the hand of Lone Watie.

It had been a deafening, staccato roar . . . so fast
that a single shot could not be distinguished. The
Regulators had never cleared leather. The awesome
speed of the death-dealing outlaw ran through the
crowd like tremors of an earthquake. Bedlam broke
loose. Blue-clad figures ran across the street; people
jumped and ran . . . this way and that . . . like chickens
with a wolf among them.

Josey sprang to the back of the roan, and in an
instant the big horse was running, belly-down, and at
his saddle was the head of the black with Lone laying
forward on his neck.

They drummed west down the street and veered
north, away from the Brazos. They had to have distance, and there was no time to cross a river.

Regulators dashed for their hitch-racked horses,
which stood, all together, before a line of saloons. As
they were mounting, an Indian squaw, probably drunk,
lost control of her paint horse and dashed among
them, scattering men to right and left and stampeding
horses that bolted, reins trailing, down the street. A
Regulator finally struck her in the head with a swung
rifle butt and brought her crashing to the ground. The
riders mounted, rounded up the running horses, and
chased after the fleeing killers.

Behind them Little Moonlight lay motionless in the

dust, a bloody gash across her forehead, but one hand still holding the reins of a head-down paint . . . a gaunt red-bone hound whined and licked the trickling blood from her face. Near her the four Regulators lay untended, sprawled in violent death, their blood widening in a growing circle . . . soaking black in the gray soil of Texas.

Cowboys mounted their horses to depart for the far-flung ranches whence they came. Gamblers left on their high-stepping horses to return to the saloons of towns and villages that were haunts. With them they carried the story. The story that smacked of legend. The pistoleer without match in speed and nerve . . . the cold bracing of four armed Regulators strained the imagination with its audacity and boldness. The Missouri guerrilla, Josey Wales, had arrived in Texas.

When the news reached Austin, the Governor added twenty-five hundred dollars to the federal five thousand for the death of Josey Wales, and fifteen hundred dollars for the unnamed "renegade" Rebel Indian who had notched a Regulator at Towash. Politicians felt the threat as the shock waves of the story spread over the state. The hard-rock Texas Rebels chortled with glee. Texas had another son; tough enough to stand . . . mean enough; enough to walk 'em down, by God!

Two covered wagons rolled out of Towash that afternoon and crossed the ferry on the Brazos, headed southwest into the sparsely settled land of the Comanche. Grandpa Samuel Turner handled the reins of the Arkansas mules on the lead wagon, and Grandma Sarah sat beside him. Behind them their granddaughter Laura Lee rode with Daniel Turner, Grandpa's brother. Two old men, an old woman, and a young one, with nothing left behind in Arkansas and only the promise of an isolated ranch bequeathed by Grandma's War-dead brother. They had been warned of the land and the Comanche . . . but they felt lucky . . . they had somewhere to go.

It was Laura Lee, Josey had seen, straw hair and prim, high-collared dress, frozen in the act of mounting the wagon. Now she shuddered as she remembered the burning black eyes of the outlaw . . . the deadly snarl of his voice . . . the pistols shooting fire and thunder . . . and the blood. Josey Wales! She would never forget the name nor the picture of him in her mind. Bloody, violent Texas! She would not scoff again at the stories. Laura Lee Turner would become a Texan . . . but only after baptism in the blood of yet another of Texas' turbulent frontiers . . . the land of the Comanche!

Part 3

Chapter 13

Josey and Lone let the big horses out. Running with flared nostrils, they beat the dim trail into a thunder with their passing. One mile, two . . . three miles at a killing pace for lesser mounts. Froth circled their saddles when they pulled down into a slow canter. They had headed north, but the Brazos curved sharply back and forced them in a half-circle toward the northeast. There was no sound of pursuit.

"But they'll be comin'," Josey said grimly as they pulled up in a thicket of cedar and oak. Dismounting, they loosed the cinches of the saddles to blow the horses as they walked them, back and forth, under the shade. Josey ran his hands down the legs of the roan . . . there wasn't a tremble. He saw Lone doing the same with the black, and the Indian smiled, "Solid."

"They'll beat the brakes along the Brazos first," Josey said as he cut a chew of tobacco, "be looking fer a crossin' . . . cal'clate they'll be here in a hour." He rummaged in saddlebags, sliding caps on the nipples of the .44's and reloading charge and ball.

Lone followed his example. "Ain't got much loadin' to do," he said, "I was set to work on my end of the blues . . . but godamighty, I never seen sich greased pistol work. How'd ye know which one would go fer it first?" There was genuine awe and curiosity in Lone's voice.

Josey holstered his pistol and spat, "Well . . . the one third from my left had a flap holster and wa'ant of no itchin' hurry . . . one second from my left had scared eyes . . . knowed he couldn't make up his mind 'til somebody else done somethin'. The one on my left had the crazy eyes that would make him move when I said somethin'. I knowed where to start."

"How 'bout the one nearest me?" Lone asked curiously.

Josey grunted, "Never paid him no mind. I seen ye on the side."

Lone removed his hat and examined the gold tassels knotted on its band. "I could've missed," he said softly.

Josey turned and worked at cinching his saddle. The Indian knew . . . that for a death-splitting moment . . . Josey Wales had made a decision to place his life in Lone Watie's hands. He fussed with the leather . . . but he did not speak. The bond of brotherhood had grown close between him and the Cherokee. The words were not needed.

The sun set in a red haze behind the Brazos as Josey and Lone traveled east. They rode for an hour, walking the horses through stands of woods, cantering them across open spaces, then turned south. It was dark now, but a half-moon silvered the countryside. Coming out of trees onto an open stretch, they nearly bumped into a large body of horsemen emerging from a line of cedars. The posse saw them immediately. Men shouted, and a rifle cracked an echo. Josey whirled the roan, and followed by Lone, pounded back toward the north. They rode hard for a mile, chancing the uneven ground in the half-light and ripping through trees and brush. Josey pulled up. The thrashing behind them had faded, and in the far distance men's shouts were dim and faraway.

"These hosses won't take us out of another'n," Josey said grimly. "They got to have rest and graze . . . they're white-eyed." He turned west, back toward the Brazos. They stopped in the brakes of the river and under the shadows of the trees rope-grazed the horses with loose-cinched saddles.

"I could eat the south end of a northbound Missouri mule," Lone said wistfully as they watched the horses cropping grass.

Josey comfortably chewed at a wad of tobacco and knocked a cicada from his grass-stem perch with a stream of juice. "Proud I stuck this 'baccer in my pockets . . . leavin' all them supplies layin' in thet town. And Little Moonlight's saddle . . . " Josey's voice trailed off. Neither of them had mentioned the Indian woman . . . nor did they know of her dash into the horses that had delayed pursuit. Lone had anxiously marked their progress north and had felt relief when Josey had led back south. Little Moonlight would remember the trail, drawn with the stick on the ground, southwest out of Towash. She would take that trail.

As if echoing his thought, Josey said quietly, "We got to git south . . . somehow 'er 'nother . . . and quick." Lone felt a sudden warmth for the scar-faced outlaw who sat beside him . . . and whose thoughts wandered away from his own safety in concern for an outcast Indian squaw.

They took turns dozing under the trees. Two hours before dawn they crossed the Brazos and an hour later holed up in a ravine so choked with brush, vine, and mesquite that the close air and late April sun made an oven of the hideout. They had picked the ravine for its rock-hard ground approach that would carry no tracks. Half a mile into the ravine, where it narrowed to no more than a slit cleaving the ground, they found a cavelike opening under thick vines. Lone, on foot, went back along their path and moved the brush and vines back into place where they had passed. He returned, triumphantly holding aloft a sage hen. They cleaned the hen, but set no fire, eating it raw.

"Never knowed raw chicken could taste so good," Josey said as he wiped his hands with a bunch of vines. Lone was cracking the bones with his teeth and sucking out the marrow.

"Ye oughta try the bones," Lone said, "ye have to eat ALL of ever'thing when ye're hungry . . . now, the Cheyenne . . . they eat the entrails too. If Little Moonlight was here . . . " Both of them left the sentence hanging . . . and their thoughts brought a drowsy, light sleep . . . while the horses pulled at the vines.

Near noon they were aroused by the beating of horses' hooves approaching from the east. The riders stopped for a moment on the lip of the ravine above them, and as Josey and Lone held their horses by the nose . . . they heard the riders gallop south.

Sunset brought the welcome coolness of a breeze that shook the brush and brought out the evening grouse. Josey and Lone emerged cautiously onto the prairie. No riders were in sight.

"East of us," Josey said, as they surveyed the land, "it's too heavy settled . . . we got to go west . . . then turn south."

They headed the horses westward toward a gradual elevation of the land that brought them, as they traveled, to a prairie more sparse of vegetation, where the elements were more rugged and wild.

In 1867, if you drew a line from the Red River south through the little town of Comanche . . . and keeping the line straight . . . on to the Rio Grande, west of that line you would find few men. Here and there an outpost settlement . . . a daring or foolhardy rancher attracted by that unexplainable urge to move where no one else dare go . . . and desperate men, running from a noose. For west of that line the Comanche was king.

Two hours after daylight Josey and Lone sighted the squat village of Comanche and turned southwest . . . across the line. They nooned on Redman Creek, a small, sluggish stream that wandered aimlessly in the brush, and at midafternoon resumed their journey. The heat was more intense, sapping at the strength of the horses as it bounced back off a soil grown more loose and sandy. Boulders of rock began to appear and stunted cactus poked spiny arms up from the plain. At dusk they rested the horses and ate a rabbit Lone shot from the saddle. This time they chanced a fire . . . small and smokeless, from the twigs of bone-dry 'chollo brush. Coarse grass was bunched in thick patches that the horses cropped with relish.

Josey had lived in the saddle for years, but he felt the weariness, sapped by lack of food, and he could see the age showing on Lone's face. But the rail-thin

Cherokee was eager for pushing on, and they saddled up in the dark and walked the horses steadily southwest.

It was after midnight when Lone pointed at a red dot in the distance. So far, it looked like a star for a moment. But it jumped and flickered.

"Big fire," Lone said, "could be Comanches havin' a party, somebody in trouble, or . . . some damn fool who wants to die."

After an hour of steady traveling, the fire was plainly visible, leaping high in the air and crackling the dried brush. It appeared to be a signal, but approaching closer, they could see no sign of life in the circle of light, and Josey felt the hairs on his neck rise at the eeriness. Still out of the light, they circled the flames, straining eyes in the half-light of the prairie. Josey saw a white spot that picked up the moonlight, and they rode cautiously toward it. It was the paint horse, picketed to a mesquite tree, munching grass.

Josey and Lone dismounted and examined the ground around the horse. Without warning, a crouched figure sprang from the concealment of brush and leaped on the half-bent figure of Lone. The Cherokee fell backward to the ground, his hat flying from his head. It was Little Moonlight. She was holding Lone's neck, astride him on the ground . . . giggling and laughing, rubbing her face on his, and snuggling her head, like a playful puppy, into his chest. Josey watched them rolling on the ground.

"Ye damn crazy squaw . . . I come near blowin' yer head off." But there was relief in his voice. Lone struggled to his feet and lifted her far off the ground . . . and kissed her fiercely on the mouth. They moved to the fire, where Josey and Lone extinguished it with cupped hands of sand while Little Moonlight chattered around them like a child and once shyly clasped the arm of Josey to her body and rubbed her head against his shoulder. An ugly, deep gash ran the width of her forehead, and Lone examined it with tender fingers. "Ain't infected, but she could have shore stood sewing up a day er two ago . . . too late now."

"By the time that'n scars over," Josey observed, "she'll look like she stuck her haid in a wildcat's den . . . ast her how she got it."

Little Moonlight told the story with her moving hands, and as Lone repeated it to Josey, he listened, head down. She laughed and giggled at the confused Regulators, the running crowd, the stupefied people. Her own actions, which caused the hilarious scene of comedy, came out as an afterthought. She saw nothing extraordinary in what she had done . . . it was a natural action, as proper as pot-cooking for her man. When she had finished, Josey drew her to him and held her for a long moment, and Little Moonlight was silent . . . and moisture shone in the eyes of Lone Watie.

"We'd better git away from where this house fire was at," Josey said, and as they walked to the horses Little Moonlight excitedly ran to a brush heap and drug forth the new saddle that Josey had dropped in Towash.

"Supplies, by God!" Josey shouted, "she got the supplies."

Lone gestured to her and made motions of eating. "Eat," Lone urged. She ran and picked up a limp sack and from it extracted three shriveled, raw potatoes. "Eat?" Lone asked . . . and she shook her head. Lone turned to Josey, "Three 'taters, looks like that's it."

Josey sighed, "Well . . . reckin we can eat the damn saddle after Little Moonlight tenders it up . . . bumpin' her bottom agin it."

Only after an hour's riding was Josey satisfied with their distance from the fire . . . and they bedded down. Noon of the following day they crossed the Colorado and lingered there in the shade of cottonwoods until sundown. Sun heat was becoming more intense, and it was in the cool of dusk before they saddled and continued southwest.

Their southwest direction would not take them to San Antonio, but Josey knew that after Towash they must avoid the settlements.

Chapter 14

The Western outlaw usually faced high odds. Beyond their physical, practiced dexterity with the pistol and their courage, those who "done the thinkin' " were the ones who lasted longest. They always endeavored an "edge." Some, such as Hardin, stepped sideways, back and forth, in a pistol fight. They would draw their pistol in midsentence, catching their opponents napping. Most of them were masters of psychology and usually made good poker players. They concerned themselves with eye adjustment to light . . . or maneuvering to place the sun behind them. The audacious . . . the bold . . . the unexpected; the "edge," they called it.

To his reckless men Bloody Bill Anderson had been a master tutor of the "edge." Once he had told Josey,

"Iff'n I'm to face out and outlast another feller in the hot sun . . . all I want is a broom straw to hold over my head fer shade. A little edge, and I'll beat 'em." He had found his greatest student in the canny, mountain-bred Josey Wales, who had the same will to triumph as the wildcat of his native home.

So it was that Josey was concerned about the horses. They looked well enough, though lean. They ate the bunch grass and showed no lack of spirit. But too many times in the past years his survival had hung on the thread of his horse, and he knew that with two horses, given the same blood, breed, and bone, one would outlast the other in direct proportion to the amount of grain, rather than grass, that had been rationed to it. The wind stamina made the difference, and so gave the edge to the outlaw who grained his horse . . . if only a few handfuls a day. The "edge" was an obsession with Josey Wales, and this obsession extended to the horse.

When they crossed the wagon tracks in late afternoon of the following day Josey turned onto their trail. Lone examined the tracks, "Two wagons. Eight . . . maybe ten hours ago."

The tracks pointed west, off their course, but Lone was not surprised at Josey's leading them after the wagons. He had learned the outlaw's concerns and his ways, so that when Josey muttered an explanation, "We need grain . . . might be we could up-trade thet paint," Lone nodded without comment. They lifted the pace of the horses into a slow, rocking canter, and Little Moonlight alternately popped and creaked the new saddle as she bobbed behind them on the rugged little pony.

It was near midnight before Josey called a halt. They rolled in their blankets against the chill and were back in the saddles before the first red color touched the east. The elevation in the land was sharper since turning west, and by morning they were on the Great Plains of Texas. Where the wind had swept away loose soil, stark rock formations rose in brutal nakedness. Arroyos, choked with boulders, split the ground, and in the distance a bald mountain poked its barren back against the sky. As the sun rose higher, lizards scurried to the sparse shades of spiny cactus and a clutch of buzzards soared, high and circling, on their death-watch.

Heat rays began to lift off the baked ground, making the distant land ahead look liquid and unreal. Josey began to search for shade.

It was Lone who saw the horse tracks first. They angled from the southeast until they crossed the trail of the two wagons. Now they followed them.

Lone dismounted and walked down the trail, searching the ground. "Eight horses . . . unshod, probably Comanch," he called back to Josey. "But these big wide-wheel tracks . . . three sets of 'em . . . and they ain't wagons . . . they're two-wheel carts. I never heard of Comanches travelin' in two-wheel carts."

"I ain't never heard of anybody travelin' in two-wheel carts," Josey said laconically.

Little Moonlight had walked down the trail and now came back running. "Koh-mahn-chey-rohs!" she shouted, pointing at the track. "Koh-mahn-chey-rohs!"

"Comancheros!" Josey and Lone exclaimed together.

Little Moonlight moved her hands with such agitation that Lone motioned for her to go slower. When she had finished, Lone looked grimly up at Josey. "She says they steal . . . loot. They kill . . . murder the very old and the very young. They sell the women and strong men to the Comanche for the horses the Comanche takes in raids. They sell the fire stick . . . the gun to the Comanche. They have carts with wheels higher than a man. They sell the horses they get from the Comanches . . . like the two ye killed in the Nations. Some of 'em are Anglo . . . some Mexicano . . . some half-breed Indian."

Lone spread his hands and looked at the ground. "That's all she knows. She says she'll kill herself before she'll be taken . . . she says the Comanch will pay high price only for the unused woman and . . . her nose shows she has been used . . . that the Comanchero would . . . use her . . . rape her . . . many times before they sold her. That it would make no difference in her price." Lone's voice was hard.

Josey's jaws moved deliberately on a chew of tobacco. His eyes narrowed into black slits as he listened and watched the trail west. "Border trash," he spat, "knowed them two in the Nations was sich when I seen 'em. We'd best git along . . . them pore pilgrims in the waggins . . ."

Lone and Little Moonlight mounted, and in her passing, she touched the leg of Josey Wales; the touchstone of strength; the warrior with the magic guns.

The sun had slipped far to the west, picking up a red dust haze, when the tracks they were following suddenly cut to the left and dipped down behind a rise of rock outcroppings. Lone pointed silently at a thin trail of smoke that lifted, undisturbed, high into the air. They left the trail and walked the horses, slowly, toward the rocks. Dismounting, Josey motioned for Little Moonlight to stand and hold the horses while he and Lone stealthily walked, head down, to the top of the rise. As they neared the summit both bellied down and crawled hatless to the rim.

They weren't prepared for the scene a hundred yards below them. Three huge wooden carts were lined end to end in the arroyo. They were two-wheeled . . . solid wheels that rose high above the beds of the carts; and each was pulled by a yoke of oxen. Back of the carts were two covered wagons with mules standing in the traces. It was the scene twenty yards back of the wagons that brought low exclamations from Lone and Josey.

Two elderly men lay on their backs, arms and legs staked, spread-eagled on the ground. They were naked, and most of their withered bodies were smeared with dried blood. The smoke rising in the air came from fires built between their legs, at the crotch, and on their stomachs. The sick-sweet smell of burned human flesh was in the air. The old men were dead. A circle of men stood and squatted around the bodies on the ground. They wore sombreros, huge rounded hats that shaded their faces. Most of them were buckskin-trousered with the flaring chapparal leggings below the knees and fancy vests trimmed with silver conchos that picked up the sun with flashes of light. They all wore holstered pistols, and one man carried a rifle loosely in his hand.

As Josey and Lone watched, one of the men stepped from the circle, and sweeping the sombrero from his head, he revealed bright red hair and beard. He made an elaborate bow toward the corpse on the ground. The circle roared with laughter. Another kicked the bald head of a corpse while a slender, fancily dressed one jumped on the chest of a corpse and stomped his feet in imitation of a dance, to the accompaniment of loud hand-clapping.

"I make out eight of them animals," Josey gritted between clenched teeth.

Lone nodded. "There ought to be three more. There's eight hosses and three carts."

The Comancheros were leaving the mutilated figures on the ground and strolling with purpose toward the wagons. Josey looked ahead toward what drew their interest and for the first time saw the women in the shade of the last wagon.

An old woman was on her hands and knees, white hair loosened and streaming down about her face. She was vomiting on the ground. A younger woman supported her, holding her head and waist. She was kneeling, and long, straw-colored hair fell about her shoulders. Josey recognized her as the girl he had seen at Towash, the girl with the startling blue eyes, who had looked at him.

The Comancheros, a few feet from the women, broke into a rush that engulfed them. The girl was lifted off her feet as a Comanchero, his hand wrapped in her hair, twisted her head backward and down. The long dress was ripped from her body, and naked she was borne up and backward by the mob. Briefly, the large, firm mounds of her breasts arched in the air above the mob, pointing upward like white pyramids isolated above the melee until hands, brutally grabbing, pulled her down again. Several held her about the waist and were attempting to throw her to the ground. They howled and fought each other.

The old woman rose from her knees and flung herself at the mob and was knocked down. She came to her feet, swaying for an instant, then lowered her head like a tiny, frail bull and charged back into the mass, her fists flailing. The girl had not screamed, but she fought; her long, naked legs thrashed the air as she kicked.

Josey lifted a .44 and hesitated as he sought a clear

target. Lone touched his arm. "Wait," he said quietly and pointed. A huge Mexican had emerged from the front wagon. The sombrero pushed back from his head revealed thick, iron-gray hair. He wore silver conchos on his vest and down the sides of tight breeches.

"*Para!*" he shouted in a bull voice as he approached the struggling mob. "Stop!" And drawing a pistol, he fired into the air. The Comancheros immediately fell away from the girl, and she stood, naked and head down, her arms crossed over her breasts. The old woman was on her knees. The big Mexican crashed his pistol against the head of one man and sent him staggering backward. He stomped his foot, and his voice shook with rage as he pointed to the girl and turned to point at the horses. "He is tellin' 'em they'll lose twenty horses by rapin' the girl," Lone said, "and that they got plenty of women at camp to the northwest."

A burst of laughter floated up from the Comancheros. "He jest told 'em the old woman is worth a . . . donkey . . . and they can have her . . . if they think it's worth it," Lone added grimly.

"By God!" Josey breathed. "By God, I didn't know sich walked around on two legs."

The big leader drew a blanket from the wagon and threw it at the girl. The old woman rose to her feet, picked up the fallen blanket, and brought it around the younger woman, covering her. Orders were shouted back and forth; Comancheros leaped to the seats of the carts and wagons. Another bound the wrists of the two women with long rawhide rope and fastened the ends to the tailgate of the last wagon.

"Gittin' ready to leave," Josey said. He looked at the sun, almost on the rim of earth to the west. "They must be in a hurry to make it to thet camp. They're travelin' at night." He motioned Lone back from the rimrock. Pulling Jamie's pistol and belt from his saddlebags, he tossed them to Lone. "Ye'll need a extry pistol," he said and squatted on the ground before Lone and Little Moonlight and marked with his finger in the dust as he talked. "Put thet hat of yores on Little Moonlight, thet Indian haid of yores will confuse 'em. Ye circle on foot around behind. I'll give ye time . . . then I'll hit 'em, mounted from the front. What I don't git, I'll drive 'em into you. We got to get 'em ALL . . . one gits away . . . he'll bring back Comanch."

Lone squashed the big hat down over the ears of Little Moonlight, and she looked up, questions in her eyes, from under the wide brim. "Reh-wan," Lone said . . . revenge . . . and he drew a finger across his throat. It was the cutthroat sign of the Sioux . . . to kill . . . not for profit . . . not for horses . . . but for revenge . . . for a principle; therefore, all the enemy must die.

Little Moonlight nodded vigorously, flopping the big hat down over her eyes. She grinned and trotted to the paint and slid the old rifle from a bundle.

"No . . . No," Lone held her arm and signed for her to stay.

"Fer Gawd's sake," Josey sighed, "tell her to stay here and hold the hosses . . . and keep thet red-bone from chewing one of our laigs off." The hound had, throughout, made low, rumbling noises in his throat. Lone strapped the extra gunbelt around his waist.

"What if they don't run?" he asked casually.

"Them kind," Josey sneered, "always run . . . the ones thet can. They'll run . . . straight back'ards . . . they'll be trapped agin the walls of that there ditch."

Lone lifted his hand in half salute, and bent low, moved silently on moccasined feet out of sight around the rocks. Josey checked the caps and loads of his .44's and the .36 Navy under his arm. Twelve loads in the

.44's . . . there were eight horsemen . . . three cart drivers . . . that made eleven; his mind clicked. He had counted only nine; the leader and the eight men. He whirled to stop Lone, but the Indian was gone.

Where were the other two men? The "edge" could be on the other side. Josey cursed his carelessness; the upsetting sight of the women . . . but there were no excuses . . . Josey bitterly condemned himself. Little Moonlight sat down, still holding the reins of the horses, with the rifle cradled in her arms. Josey slipped back to the rimrock and counted off the minutes. The sun slid below the mountain to the west, and a dusky red glow illumined the sky.

Mounted horsemen dashed up and down the line of carts and wagons. The canvas on one of the carts was being lashed down by a half-naked breed, and Josey looked for the women. They were standing behind the last wagon, close together, their hands tied in front of them. Josey slid back from the rim. It was time.

A shout, louder than the others, caused him to scramble up for a look. He saw two Comancheros dragging a limp figure between them. Other men on horses and foot were running toward the men and their burden, and for a moment obstructed his view. They pointed excitedly toward the rocks, and some of the mounted men rode in that direction, while others pulled their burden toward the rear of the last wagon where the two women stood.

They dropped their burden to the ground. The long, plaited hair . . . buckskin-garbed. It was Lone Watie. Josey cursed beneath his breath. The two missing Comancheros he should have figured. As he watched, Lone sat up and shook his head. He looked around him as the leader of the Comancheros approached. The big Mexican jerked the Indian to his feet and talked rapidly, then struck him in the face. Lone staggered back against the wagon and stood, staring stoically straight ahead. Josey watched them down the barrels of both .44's. Had a Comanchero raised a gun or knife . . . he would not have used it.

The big Mexican was obviously in a hurry. He shouted orders, and two men leaped forward, lashed Lone's hands together, and secured the rawhide to the tailgate of the wagon with the women. As they did . . . Lone raised his arms and wigwagged his hands back and forth. He did not look upward toward the rocks where he knew Josey watched. The hand signal was the well-known message of the Confederate Cavalry, "All well here, reconnoiter your flanks!" Josey read the message, and the shock hit him; *his flanks! . . . the Comanchero horsemen who had raced for cover behind the wagons!*

Josey scrambled down the rocks and ran toward the horses. He motioned Little Moonlight to mount, and leading the black, they raced toward the only immediate cover, two huge boulders that stood fifty yards from the arroyo. They had barely rounded the boulders when four horsemen appeared over the top. They paused and scanned the prairie but did not approach far enough to see the tracks. Turning, they ran their horses in the direction from which the wagons had come and then disappeared back into the arroyo.

A horrendous squealing rent the air, and the horses jumped. It was the carts moving . . . their heavy wooden wheels screeching against ungreased axles. Little Moonlight moved her horse next to Josey.

"Lone," she said. Josey crossed his wrists in the sign of the captive and then sought to reassure the fear that flashed in her eyes. His scarred face creased in a half grin. He tapped his chest and the big pistol butts in their holsters and moved his hands forward, palm down, in the sign that all would be well. Little Moonlight still wore the big hat of Lone's, and now she nodded, flopping it comically on her head. Her eyes lost the fear; the warrior with the magic guns would free Lone. He would kill the enemies. He would make things as they were.

Josey listened to the squealing carts growing fainter in the distance. It was dark now, but a three-quarter yellow Texas moon was just lifting behind broken crags to the east. A soft golden haze made shadows of the boulders, and a cooling breeze stirred the sagebrush. Somewhere, far off, a coyote yipped in quick barks and ended it with a long tenor howl.

Little Moonlight brought a thin handful of jerky beef from her bundle and held it out to Josey. He shook his head and motioned for her to eat. Instead, he cut a fresh cud of tobacco from the twist, hooked a leg over his saddle horn, and slowly chewed.

"Iff'n I don't git but half of 'em, they'll kill Lone and them women," he said half aloud. "Iff'n they make it to thet camp, they're shore gonna sport thet Cherokee with a knife and fire coals."

Josey was startled from his musing. The hound had lifted his voice in a deep, lonesome howl that ended forlornly in a breaking series of sobs. The red-bone jumped sideways, barely escaping the stream of tobacco juice.

"Ye damn Tennessee red-bone . . . we ain't huntin' 'possum 'er 'coon. Shet up!" The hound retreated behind Little Moonlight's paint, and she laughed. It was a soft and melodious laughter that made Josey look at her. She pointed to the moon . . . and at the dog.

"Let's go," Josey said gruffly, and he spurred the roan toward the arroyo.

Chapter 15

Laura Lee Turner stumbled behind the wagon in the half-light of the moon. The high-button shoes were unsuitable for hiking, and she had already turned her ankles several times. The rough blanket tied around her shoulders irritated the burning skin where finger-nails had ripped away flesh on her back and stomach. Her breasts throbbed with excruciating pain, and her breath came short and hard. She had not spoken through her swollen lips since the attack . . . but that was not unusual for Laura Lee.

"Too quiet," Grandma Sarah had said when she came to live with her and Grandpa Samuel after her father and mother died of lung fever.

"Look, look, and whatta ye see, ain't right brite, Laura Lee," the children had sung around the log cabin schoolhouse, there in the Ozark Mountains . . .

when she was nine. She didn't go back to school. Kindly Grandma Sarah had shushed her when she'd say such things as, "Springtime's a'bornin' in this here thunderstorm," or "Clouds is like fluffy dreams a'floatin' crost a blue-sky mind."

Grandpa Samuel would look puzzled and remark, out of her hearing, "A leetle quare . . . but a good girl."

At fifteen, after taking her second box supper to a gathering in the settlement, she didn't go again. Grandpa Samuel had to buy hers . . . both times . . . in the embarrassment of the folks seeing one lone box left, and no boy would buy it.

"Ye'd ort to talk to 'em," Grandma Sarah would scold her. But she couldn't; while the other girls had chattered and giggled with the groups of boys, she had stood aside, dumb and stiff as a blackjack oak. She had large breasts, and her shoulders were square.

"Bones ain't delikit enough to attract these idjit whippersnappers," Grandma Sarah complained. The sturdy bones gave a ruggedness to her face that a preacher might charitably describe as "honest and open." The freckles across her nose didn't help any. Her waist was narrow enough, but she had a "heavy turn of ankle," and once when a backpack peddler had stopped by . . . and Grandpa had called her in for a shoe fitting, the peddler had laughed, "Got a fine pair of men's uppers will fit this here little lady." She had turned red and looked down at her twitching toes.

Grandma Sarah was practical, if disappointed . . . and resigned. She began preparing Laura Lee for the dismal destiny of unmarried maidenhood. Now, at twenty-two years of age, it was firmly settled; Laura Lee was an "old maid," and would so be, the rest of her life.

Grandma Sarah's bachelor brother Tom had sent the papers on his west Texas ranch, and when word reached them that he died at Shiloh, they made plans to leave the chert hill farm and take up the ranch. Laura Lee never questioned any thought of not going. There was nowhere else to go.

Now, stumbling behind the wagon, she had no doubt what awaited her. She accepted the fate without bitterness. She would fight . . . and then she would die. The wildness of this land called Texas had astonished her with its brutality. The picture of Towash flashed again in her mind; the picture of the scarred face, the searing black eyes of the killer, Josey Wales. He had looked deadly, spitting and snarling death . . . like the mountain lion she once saw . . . cornered against a rock face as men moved in upon it. She wondered if he were like these men into whose hands they had fallen.

Grandma Sarah stumbled along beside her. The long dress she wore cut her stride into short jerky steps, and sometimes she was forced to a half trot. Beside Grandma Sarah the captured savage walked easily. He was very tall and thin, but he strode with a lithe suppleness that denied the age of his wrinkled, oaken face, set in stoic calmness. He had said nothing. Even when the big Mexican had questioned and threatened him, he had remained silent . . . smiling, and then he had spat in the Mexican's face . . . and been struck backward.

She watched him now. Thirty yards behind them two horsemen rode, but she had seen the savage stealthily move the rawhide thong to his face twice before, and she was sure he chewed on it.

Dust boiled up in their faces from the squealing carts ahead, and a fit of coughing seized Grandma

Sarah. She stumbled and fell. Laura Lee moved to help her, but before she could reach the tiny figure the savage bent quickly and lifted her with surprising ease. He walked along, never breaking stride, as he held the little woman's tiny waist with his bound hands. He set her down and carefully kept his grip until Grandma Sarah had regained her stride. Grandma Sarah threw back her head to toss the long white hair back over her shoulders.

"Thank'ee," she mumbled.

"Ye're welcome," the savage said in a low, pleasant voice.

Laura Lee was stunned. The savage spoke English. She looked across at Lone, "You . . . that is . . . ye speak our language," she said haltingly, half afraid to address him.

"Yes, ma'am," he said, "reckin I take a swang at it."

Grandma Sarah, despite her jolting gait, was looking at him.

"But . . . " Laura Lee said, "ye're Indian . . . ain't ye?" She saw white teeth flash in the moonlight as the savage smiled.

"Yes, ma'am," he said, "full bred, I reckin . . . 'er so my pa told me. Don't reckon he had reason to lie about it."

Grandma Sarah couldn't contain any further silence. "Ye talk like . . . a . . . mountain . . . man," she jolted out the sentence from her half trot.

The Indian sounded surprised. "Why . . . reckin that's what I am, ma'am. Being Cherokee from the mountains of north Alabamer. Wound up in the Nations . . . leastwise, that is, 'til I wound up on the end of this here strang."

"Lord save us all," Grandma Sarah said grimly.

"Yes, ma'am," Lone answered, but Laura Lee noticed he had turned his head as he spoke and was scanning the prairie, as though he fully anticipated additional help besides the Lord's.

They lapsed into silence; the wagon was moving rapidly, and talking was difficult. The night wore on, and the moon passed its peak in the sky and dropped westward. It was cold, and Laura Lee could feel the chill as her naked legs opened the blanket with each stride. Once she felt the knot that held it loosening about her shoulders and she struggled futilely to hold it with her bound hands. She was surprised by the Indian suddenly walking close to her. He reached with his bound hands and silently retied the knot.

Grandma Sarah was stumbling more often now, and the Indian, each time, retrieved her and set her back in stride. He mumbled encouragement in her ear, "Won't be long, ma'am, before we stop." And once, when she seemed almost too weak to regain her legs, he had scolded her mildly, "Cain't quit, ma'am. They'll kill ye . . . ye cain't quit."

Grandma Sarah had a note of despair in her voice, "Pa's gone. 'Ceptin' Laura Lee, I'd be ready to go."

Laura Lee moved closer to the old woman and held her arm.

The moon hung palely suspended at the western rim when the streak of dawn crossed the big sky above them. Suddenly the wagon halted. Laura Lee could see a campfire kindled ahead and men gathering around it. Grandma Sarah sat down, and Laura Lee, sitting beside her, lifted her bound arms around the old woman and pulled her head down on her lap. She said nothing but clumsily stroked the wrinkled face and combed at the long white hair with her fingers.

Grandma Sarah opened her eyes. "Thank'ee, Laura Lee," she said weakly.

Lone stood beside them but he did not look toward the campfire ahead. Instead, he had his back to the wagon and gazed far off, along the way they had come. He stood like stone, transfixed in his concentration. After a long moment he was rewarded by catching the merest flicker of a shadow, perhaps an antelope . . . or a horse, as it dropped quickly over a roll in the plain. He watched more intently now and caught another shadow, moving more slowly, and curiously dotted with white, that followed the path of the first. His face cracked in a wolfish smile as he raised the rawhide to his teeth.

The sun rose higher . . . and hotter. The Comancheros were walking about now, stretching off the night's ride. The red-bearded man came around the wagon. Big Spanish spurs jingled as he walked. He carried a canteen in his hand and knelt beside Laura Lee and Grandma Sarah, and thrust the canteen into Laura Lee's hand.

"I'm gonna outbid the Comanch and breed you myself," he leered with a wide grin. Saliva and tobacco spittle ran down into his dirty beard. As he wiped his mouth on the back of one hand he slyly slid the other up her thigh. She struggled to rise, but he pressed himself down on her, one knee moving between her legs as he slipped a hand under the blanket and fondled her breasts. Lone plunged head down into the man with such force that he was knocked under the wagon. Laura Lee dropped the canteen. The Indian stood, implacable, as the red-bearded Comanchero cursed and thrashed his way to his feet. Without looking at Laura Lee, Lone said quietly, "Quick . . . the canteen . . . give water to Grandma . . . maybe her last chancet." She grabbed the canteen and tilted it to Grandma Sarah's lips as she heard the cracking thud of iron on bone, and the Indian fell beside her on the ground. He lay still, blood spurting over the coal-black hair.

Laura Lee was pouring water down Grandma Sarah. "Dadblame it, don't drown me, child," the old woman rose up, spluttering and choking.

The Comanchero grabbed the canteen, and Laura Lee fought him for it. She rose to her feet, twisting it from his grasp, and managed to splash water on the head of Lone. The Comanchero kicked her flat and retrieved the water. He was panting heavily. "You'll make a good lay when I bed you down," he spat. The scuffle had attracted more men toward the wagon . . . and he hurried away.

Laura Lee worked over the unconscious Lone. She turned him on his back and with the tail of her blanket clotted and stopped the blood flow. Grandma Sarah was up on her knees struggling with a string about her neck. She withdrew a small bag from the bosom of her dress. "Slap this asphitify bag under his nose," she instructed as she handed the bag to the girl.

Lone took one breath of the bag, twisted his head violently, and opened his eyes. "Beggin' yore pardon, ma'am," he said calmly, "but I never cottoned to rotted skunk."

Grandma Sarah's tone was weak but stern, "They'll shoot ye down iff'n ye cain't walk," she warned from her wobbly knees.

Lone rolled over on his stomach and brought himself to hands and knees. He stayed there a moment, swaying . . . then straightened up. "I'll walk," he grinned through caked blood, "not much more walkin' to do anyhow."

As he spoke, the wagon jerked, and Lone was forced to hold Grandma Sarah up by the seat of her underwear to straighten her legs and get her in stride.

There was no pause at noon; the caravan rolled steadily on, to the west. White alkali dust, mingled with sweat, caked their faces into unreal masks, and the sun heat sapped the strength from their legs. Now Lone held a steady grip on Grandma Sarah; her trembling legs made half motions of walking, but it was Lone who supported her weight.

The wagon began to drop downward as the caravan moved into a deep canyon. It was narrow, with sheer walls on either side, leveling off at the bottom. They were headed, now, directly into the sun. Laura Lee felt her legs trembling as she walked; she stumbled and fell but scrambled to her feet without help. Suddenly the wagons halted. She looked across at Lone. "I wonder why we've stopped?" Her voice sounded cracked and coarse in her ears.

There was a triumphant smile on the Indian's face ... she thought he had become crazed from the blow on his head. Finally, he answered her. "Iff'n I cal'clate right, we're facin' directly into thet sun. These walls hem us in. Thet would look like the thinkin' of a feller I know what figgers all the edge he can git. I ain't looked up ahead yet, but I'll bet my scalp a gent by the name of Josey Wales has stopped this here train."

"Josey Wales?" Laura Lee croaked the name.

Grandma Sarah, from her knees on the ground, whispered weakly, "Josey Wales? The killin' man we seen at Towash? Lord save us."

Lone eased around the tailgate of the wagon. Laura

Lee stood beside him. Fifty yards ahead of them, astride the giant roan, standing squarely in the middle of the sun, sat Josey Wales. Lone shaded his eyes, and he could see the slow, meditative working of the jaws.

"Chawin' his tobaccer, by God," Lone said. He saw Josey look to the side with musing contemplation.

"Now spit," Lone breathed. Josey spat a stream of tobacco juice that expertly knocked a bloom from sagebrush. The Comancheros looked aghast, riveted into statues at this strange figure who appeared before them and evidenced such nonchalant interest . . . in aiming and spitting at sagebrush blooms.

Lone chewed vigorously at the rawhide on his wrists. "Git ready, little lady," he muttered to Laura Lee, "hell is fixin' to hit the breakfast."

The riders at the rear of the wagons came past and joined the others at the front of the caravan. Laura Lee shaded her eyes against the white light of the sun. "You speak of him . . . Josey Wales . . . as though he were your friend," she said to Lone.

"He is more than my friend," Lone said simply.

Grandma Sarah, still sitting, pulled herself around the wagon wheel and watched. "Even fer a mean 'un like him, they're too many of 'em," she whispered, but she held the wagon wheel and watched.

They saw Josey straighten in the saddle and slowly . . . slowly, he lifted a stick, at the end of which was attached a white flag. He waved it back and forth at the Comancheros, all grouped together at the head of the caravan.

"That's a surrender flag!" Laura Lee gasped.

Lone grinned through the mask of dusky face, "I don't know what he's figgerin' to do, but surrender ain't one of 'em."

The Comancheros were excited. There was agitated

talk, and argument developed among them. The big Mexican leader, mounted on a dappled gray, rode among the men and pointed with his hand. He selected the man with the red beard, another particularly vicious-appearing Anglo with human scalps sewed into his shirt, and a long-haired Mexican with two tied-down holsters.

The four horsemen advanced in a line, walking their horses cautiously toward Josey Wales. As they began their advance, Josey, as slowly, brought the roan to meet them. Silence, disturbed only by a faint moan of wind in the canyon rocks, fell over the scene. To Laura Lee the horses moved painfully slowly, stepping gingerly as their riders held them in check. It seemed to her that Josey Wales moved his horse only slightly faster . . . not enough to cause notice . . . but nevertheless, when they came together, facing each other, the roan was much closer to the wagons. They stopped.

She saw the scarred face of the outlaw plainly now. The same burning black eyes from beneath the hat brim. He rose slowly, standing in the stirrups as though stretching his body, but the subtle movement brought the angle of his pistols directly under his hands.

Suddenly the flag fell. She didn't see Josey Wales move his hands, but she saw smoke spurt from his hips. The BOOMS! of the heavy-throated .44's bounced into solid sound off the canyon walls. Two saddles emptied . . . the Mexican with tied-down holsters somersaulted backward off his horse. The red-bearded man twisted and fell, one foot caught in a stirrup. The scalp-shirted horseman doubled and slumped, and as the big Mexican leader half whirled his horse in a frantic rearing, a mighty force tore the side of his face off.

The speed and sound of the happening was like a

sharp thunderclap, causing a scene of mass confusion. The grulla horse of the red-bearded man came stampeding back upon the wagons, dragging the dead man by one foot. The half-crazed horse of the Mexican leader had been jerked, by his death grip, into a yoke of oxen. Out of the tangle, riding directly at them, Laura Lee saw the giant roan.

Josey Wales had two pistols in his hands. The reins of the roan were in his teeth, and as he crashed into the remaining horsemen bunched by the wagon, she saw him firing . . . and the earsplitting .44's bounced and ricocheted sound all around them. One man screamed as he fell headlong from his bucking horse; yells and cursings, frightened horses dashing this way and that. In the middle of it all, Laura Lee heard a sound that began low and rose in pitch and volume until it climaxed in a bloodcurdling crescendo of broken screams that brought pimples to her skin. The sound came from the throat of Josey Wales . . . the Rebel yell of exultation in battle and blood . . . and death. The sound of the scream was as primitive as the man. He swept so close by the wagon that Laura Lee shrank from the hooves of the terrible roan thundering down on her. Whirling the big red horse almost in midair, he brought him around behind a cart driver, half-naked . . . running on foot, and shot him squarely between the shoulders.

A Comanchero, his sombrero lying on his back, dashed by on a running horse and disappeared down the canyon. Josey whirled the big roan after him, and the hooves of their horses echoed down the canyon and diminished in the distance.

A fancily dressed Comanchero lying near Laura Lee raised his head. Blood covered his chest, and he looked across the open ground directly into her eyes. "Water

. . ." he said weakly, and tried to crawl, but his arms would not support the weight, "please . . . water." Laura Lee watched horrified as he tried again to pull himself toward her.

An Indian rose from the rocks of the canyon. Long plaited hair and fringed buckskin, but wearing a huge, flopping gray hat. The figure trotted up to the bloody Comanchero and stopped a few feet from him. As he lifted his hand . . . the Indian raised an old rifle and shot him cleanly through the head. It was Little Moonlight, with the scrawny red-bone shuffling at her heels. Now she dropped the rifle and advanced on them, pulling a wicked-looking knife from her belt. "Injuns!" Grandma Sarah shouted from her seat by the wagon wheel. "Lord save us."

Lone laughed. He, like the women, had watched the juggernaut of death that hit the camp with something akin to fascination . . . now the sight of Little Moonlight released the tension. She cut the thongs from his wrists, wrapped her arms around him, and laid her head on his chest.

A pistol shot in the distance rolled a rumbling echo up the canyon. Around them was the aftermath of the storm. Men lay in the grotesque postures of death. Horses stood head down. The grulla, coming from the head of the caravan, alternately walked and stopped, dragging the limp corpse by a stirrup. Except for the moan of the wind, it was the only sound in the canyon.

They saw Josey walking the horses. He was leading a sorrel that carried a pistol belt and sombrero dangling from the horn of an empty saddle. Behind the sorrel was Lone's big black.

The roan was lathered white, and froth whipped from his mouth. Josey pulled the horses to a halt in the shade of the wagon and politely touched the brim of his hat to Laura Lee and Grandma Sarah. Laura Lee nodded dumbly at his gesture. She felt awkward in the blanket and ill at ease. How did anybody act so calm and have company manners, like this man, after such violent death. A few minutes before he had shot . . . and yelled . . . and killed. She watched him shift sideways in the saddle and hook a leg around the horn. He made no motion to dismount as he meticulously cut tobacco with a long knife and thrust the wad into his mouth.

"Proud to struck up with ye agin, Cherokee," he drawled at Lone, "I would've rode on to Mexico, but I had to come and git ye, so ye could make thet crazy squaw behave."

Lone grinned up at him, "Knowed that'd bring ye."

"Now," Josey drawled laconically, "iff'n ye can git it 'crost to her, more'n likely these here two ladies would cotton to gittin' cut loose, a dab of water . . . clothes and sich as thet."

Lone looked embarrassed. "Sorry, ma'am," he mumbled to Laura Lee.

Little Moonlight got two canteens of water from the wagons, and as Laura Lee splashed cool water over her face, Lone knelt with a canteen for Grandma Sarah.

Josey frowned. "I was wonderin' about grain fer the hosses."

"I knowed ye'd ask that," Lone said dryly. "As I was ambling along behind this here wagon, whistlin' and singin' in the moonlight, I says to myself, I've got to take time from my enjoyment to check about the grain in these here wagons. I know Mr. Wales will likely come ridin' by d'rectly and lift his hat . . . and fust thing . . . ast about the grain."

Laura Lee was startled by the laughter of the two

men. Bloody corpses lay all about them. They had all
narrowly escaped death. Now they laughed uproariously . . . but instinctively, beneath the laughter, she
sensed the grim humor and a deep bond between the
Indian and the outlaw.

As though reading her thoughts Josey dismounted,
opened the flaps of the wagon, and taking her by the
arm, helped her into the back. "Set there, ma'am," he
said. "We'll scuffle ye some clothes." Turning to
Grandma Sarah, he lifted her in his arms and carefully
placed her beside Laura Lee. "There now, ma'am," he
said.

Grandma Sarah looked keenly at him. "Ye shore
bushwhacked all of 'em, looks like . . . them as was
fightin' and them as was runnin'."

"Yes, ma'am," Josey said politely. "Pa always said a
feller ought to take pride in his trade." He didn't explain that the "running" Comancheros would most
surely bring back Indians.

"My God!" Grandma Sarah screamed. Josey and
Lone whirled in the direction she pointed.

Little Moonlight, a knife in one hand and two
bloody scalps in the other, was kneeling beside the
head of a third corpse on the ground. Laura Lee pushed
farther back in the wagon.

"She don't mean nothin' . . . bad, that is," Lone said.
"Little Moonlight is Cheyenne. It's part of her religion.
Ye see, ma'am, Cheyennes believe there ain't but two
ways ye can keep from goin' to the Huntin' Grounds—
that is to be hung, where yore soul cain't git out of
yore mouth, and the other is being scalped. Little
Moonlight is makin' shore thet our enemies don't git
there . . . then we'll have it . . . well, more easy, when
we git there. Kinda like," Lone grinned, "a Arkansas

preacher sendin' his enemies to hell. Indian believes they ain't but two sins . . . bein' a coward . . . and turnin' agin yer own kind."

"Well," Grandma Sarah said doubtfully, "I reckin that's one way of lookin' at it."

Laura Lee looked at Josey, "Does she keep . . . the . . . scalps?"

Josey looked startled. "Why . . . I don't reckin, thet is, I never seen her totin' none around. But don't ye worry about Little Moonlight, ma'am . . . she's . . . kin."

Lone and Josey mounted their horses and with lariats dragged the bodies of the Comancheros far down the canyon into the boulders and rolled rocks over them. They had stripped them of guns and piled the guns and saddles they took from the horses into the wagons.

In his scouting Josey had discovered a narrow cleft in the far wall of the canyon, and near it a rock tank held clear water. He and Lone rummaged the three big carts and found barrels of grain, salt pork, jerky beef, dried beans, and flour. There were rifles and ammunition. All this they piled into the wagons; and with the eight horses tethered behind, Lone and Little Moonlight drove the wagons to the cleft in the canyon, as Laura Lee and Grandma Sarah rode with them.

The ground dropped down as it met the canyon wall, almost hiding the wagons from the trail. It was cool in the shadows, and they made camp at dusk; the high wall and cleft at their backs, the wagons before them.

Josey and Lone watered the horses and mules at the tank, and after picketing the mules near the wall on bunch grass and graining the horses, they led the six oxen to water. Laura Lee, in the wagon, heard Josey speaking to Lone, "We'll butcher one of the oxen in the mornin' and turn the rest of 'em loose. Might as well leave them carts where they are . . . they's all kind of stuff in 'em . . . old watches . . . picture frames . . . I seen a baby's crib . . . looted from ranches, I reckin."

She thought of the terrible Comancheros. How many lonely cabins had they burned? How many of the helpless had they tortured and murdered? The wretched, hoarse screams of Grandpa Samuel echoed in her ears, and the laughter of his tormentors. She sobbed, and her body shook. Grandma Sarah, beside her, squeezed her hand, and great tears rolled silently down her wrinkled face.

A hand touched her shoulder. It was Josey Wales. The yellow moon had risen over the canyon rim, shadowing his face as he looked up to her in the wagon. Only the white scar stood out in the moonlight. "Pick up yer clothes, ma'am," he said softly, "and I'll carry ye up to the tank . . . ye can wash. I'll come back and git Grandma Sarah."

He swung her in his arms, and she felt the strength of him. Timidly, she slipped her arm about his neck, and as he walked upward to the tank, she felt an overwhelming weakness. The horror of the past hours, the terror; now the overpowering comfort in the arms of this strange man she should fear . . . but did not. The blanket fell away, but it didn't matter.

He placed her on a broad, flat rock beside the pool of water and in a moment returned, carrying the frail Grandma Sarah. He knelt beside them. "I'll have to cut them shoes off ya'alls feet. Reckin ye'll have to wear boot moccasins, it's all we got."

As he slid the knife along the leather, Laura Lee asked, "Where is . . . the Indian?"

"Lone? Him and Little Moonlight is down there

brushin' out our tracks," he chuckled softly with secret humor, "they done washed in the tank."

Their feet were swollen, puffy lumps, and ugly cuts slashed by the rawhide swelled their arms. Josey stood up and looked down at them. "They's a little wall spring trickles water in this here tank . . . feeds out'n the other end. Stays fresh and cold . . . ought to take the swellin' down. Tank ain't but three foot deep. I'll be close by . . . " and he pointed, "up there, in the rocks."

He disappeared into the shadows and in a moment reappeared, silhouetted against the moon, looking past them into the canyon.

Laura Lee helped Grandma Sarah into the tank. The water was cold, washing over her body like a refreshing tonic.

"I couldn't help cryin'," Grandma Sarah said as she sat in the water. "I cain't help worryin' about Pa and Dan'l, layin' back there on the prairie."

The voice of Josey Wales floated softly down to them, "They was buried, ma'am . . . proper." Did his ears catch everything? Laura Lee wondered.

"Thank'ee, son," Grandma Sarah spoke as softly . . . and her voice broke, "God bless ye."

Laura Lee looked up at the figure on the rock. He was slowly chewing tobacco, looking out toward the canyon . . . and with a ragged cloth he was cleaning his pistols.

Chapter 16

The morning broke red and hot and chased the chill from the canyon. Josey and Lone slaughtered an oxen and brought slabs of the meat to the smokeless fire Little Moonlight had built in a chimney crack of the canyon cleft. Laura Lee pushed a weakly protesting Grandma Sarah back on her blankets and walked to the fire on swollen feet.

"I can work," she announced flatly to Josey. Little Moonlight smiled and handed her a knife to slice the beef. Salting thin strips, they laid them on the flat rocks to cure in the sun, and it was late afternoon before they ate.

Laura Lee noticed that the two men never worked together. If one was working, the other watched the rim of the canyon. When she asked Josey why, he answered her shortly, "Comanche country, ma'am. This is their land . . . not our'n." And she saw that both he and Lone looked with studied concern at the spiral of circling buzzards that rose high in the air over the rocks that held the dead Comancheros.

They rested, filled with beef, in the dusk of shadows, against the canyon wall. Josey came to the blankets of Laura Lee and Grandma Sarah. He carried a small iron pot and knelt beside them.

"Taller and herbs Lone fixed. It'll take the swellin' down." He smoothed it on their feet and legs, and as Laura Lee blushed and timidly extended her leg, he looked up at her for a steady moment, "It don't matter none, ma'am. We do . . . what we have to do . . . to live. Ain't always purty . . . 'ner proper, I reckin. Necessary is what decides it."

Laura Lee lay back on the blankets and slept. She dreamed of a huge, charging red horse that bore down upon her, ridden by a terrible man with a scarred face who screamed and shot death from his guns. The deep howl of a wolf close by on the canyon rim awakened her. Grandma Sarah was sitting up, combing her hair. Close by in the shadows and facing her was Lone. Little Moonlight lay on the ground, her head on Lone's thigh. She didn't see Josey Wales. The soreness and swelling was gone from her feet.

"Is . . . where is Mr. Wales?" Laura Lee asked of Lone.

He looked toward the canyon valley flooded with the soft light of a nearly full moon. "He's here," he said softly, "somewhere in the rocks. He don't sleep much, reckin it's from years of brush ridin'."

Laura Lee hesitated, and her voice was timid, "I heard him say that he was kin to Little Moonlight . . . is he?"

Lone's laugh was low. "No, ma'am. Not like you mean. Where Josey come from . . . back in the mountains . . . the old folks meant different by thet word. If a feller told another'n thet he kin 'em . . . he meant he understands 'em. Iff'n he tells his woman that he kin 'er . . . which ain't often . . . he means he loves 'er." There was a moment of silence before Lone continued, "Ye see, ma'am, to the mountain man, it's the same thing . . . lovin' and understandin' . . . cain't have one without t'other'n. Little Moonlight here," and he laid his hand on her head, "Josey understands. Oh, he don't understand Cheyenne ways and sich . . . it's what's underneath, he understands . . . reckin loyalty and sich . . . and she understands them things . . . and well, they love thet in one 'nother. So ye see, they got a understandin' . . . a love fer one another . . . they're kin."

"You mean . . . ?" Laura Lee left the meaning in the question.

Lone chuckled, "No, I don't mean she's his woman . . . nothin' like thet. Reckin I cain't talk it like it is, ma'am . . . but Josey and Little Moonlight, either one would die flat in their track fer t'other'n."

"And you," Laura Lee said softly.

"And me," Lone said.

The night wind picked up a low sigh across the brush, and a coyote reminded them with his long howl of the distance and the loneliness of the desolate land. Laura Lee shivered, and Grandma Sarah placed a blanket around her shoulders. She had never asked questions . . . boldly of other people . . . but curiosity . . . and something more, overcame her reticence. "Why . . . I mean, how is it that he is . . . wanted?" she asked.

The silence was so long that she thought Lone

would not speak. Finally, his voice floated softly in the shadows, searching for words, "Iff'n I told ye that a lodge . . . a house was burnin' down, ye'd say thet was bad. Iff'n I told ye it was yore home thet was burnin' . . . and ye loved thet home, and them thet was in it, ye'd crawl . . . iff'n ye had to . . . to fight thet fire. Ye'd hate thet fire . . . but only jest as deep as ye loved thet home . . . not 'cause ye hate fire . . . but 'cause ye loved yer home. Deeper ye loved . . . deeper ye'd hate." The Indian's tone grew hard, "Bullies don't love, ma'am. They kill out'a fear and torture to watch men beg . . . tryin' to prove they's something low in men as they are. When they're faced with a fight . . . they cut and run. Thet's why Josey knowed he could whup them Comancheros. Josey is a great warrior. He loves deep . . . hates hard, ever'thing's that killed what he loves. All great warriors are sich men." Lone's voice softened, "It is so . . . and it will always be."

In the stillness Grandma Sarah felt for her hand and patted it. Laura Lee hadn't realized, but she was crying. She felt in Lone's words the loneliness of the outlaw; the bitterness of broken dreams and futile hopes; the ache of loved ones lost. She knew then what the heart of the implacable Indian squaw had always known, that true warriors are fierce . . . and tender . . . and lonely men.

It was early when she wakened. The sun was striking the top of the canyon rim, turning it red and moving its rays down the wall like a sundial. Little Moonlight was rolling blankets and packing gear into the wagons. Grandma Sarah, on her hands and knees over a big paper map spread on the ground, was pointing out to Josey and Lone, who squatted beside, different parts of the map. "It's in this valley, got a clear creek. See the mountains that's marked?" she was saying.

Josey looked at Lone, "What do ye say?"

Lone studied the map, "I say we're here," and he placed his finger on the map. "Here is the ranch she speaks of and the swayback mountain to its north."

"How fer?" Josey asked.

Lone shrugged, "Maybe sixty . . . maybe a hunnerd mile. I cain't tell. It's to the southwest . . . but we are goin' that way anyhow . . . to the border."

Josey was chewing on tobacco, and Laura Lee noticed his buckskins were clean and he was clean-shaven. He spat, "Reckin we'll take ya'll and the waggins, ma'am. Iff'n there's nobody there . . . we'll jest have to git ye up some riders . . . some'eres. Ye cain't stay, two womenfolk, by yerselves in this country."

"Look," Grandma Sarah said eagerly, "there's a town marked, called Eagle Pass . . . it's on this river . . . Rye-oh Grandee."

"That's Rio Grande, ma'am," Lone said, "and thet Eagle Pass is a long ways from yore ranch . . . this town here, Santo Rio, is closer . . . maybe some riders there."

As they talked, Laura Lee helped Little Moonlight load the wagons. She felt refreshed and strong, and the boot moccasins were soft on her feet. Little Moonlight was kneeling to gather utensils and smiled up at Laura Lee . . . the smile froze on her face, "Koh-manch," she said softly . . . then louder, so that Josey and Lone heard, "Koh-manch!"

Lone pushed Grandma Sarah roughly to the ground and fell on her. Josey took two swift strides and jerked Laura Lee backward as his body fell, full length, on hers. Little Moonlight was already stretched full length and head down.

The Comanche made no attempt to conceal himself. He was astride a white pony with the half-slump grace of the natural horseman. A rifle lay across his knees, and his black, plaited hair carried a single feather that waved in the wind. He was a half mile from them, silhouetted against the morning sun, but it was obvious that he saw and watched them.

Laura Lee felt the heavy breathing and the heartbeat of Josey. "He . . . has seen us," she whispered.

"I know," Josey said grimly, "but maybe he ain't been there long enough to count three women . . . and jest two men."

Suddenly the Comanche jerked his horse into a tight, two-footed spin and disappeared over the rim.

Lone ran for the mules and hitched them to the wagons. Josey pulled Laura Lee to her feet, "There's Comanchero clothes in the waggins . . . ye'll have to wear 'em . . . like menfolks," he said.

They put them on, big sombreros, flared chapparal pants. Laura Lee put on the largest shirt she could find; it was V'd at the neck, without buttons, and her large breasts seemed about to split the cloth. She blushed red . . . and still redder when she saw Little Moonlight changing clothes in the open.

"I reckin," Josey said hesitantly, "they'll have to do." There was a hint of awe in his voice. Grandma Sarah looked like a leprechaun under a toadstool, as the big sombrero flopped despairingly around her shoulders.

"Looks like a family of hawgs moved out'n the seat of these britches," she complained.

In spite of their predicament, Josey couldn't contain his laughter at the sight, and from a distance, Lone joined in, at the bunched, sagging trousers on the tiny figure.

"Sorry, ma'am," Josey said and burst into laughter again, "it's jest . . . thet ye're so little."

Grandma Sarah lifted the sombrero with both hands so she could better see her tormentors. "T'ain't the size of the dog in the fight, it's the size of the fight in the dog," she said fiercely.

"Reckin thet's right as rain, ma'am," Josey said soberly . . . and then, "Little Moonlight can drive one of the waggins," he said.

"I'll drive the other," Laura Lee heard herself saying . . . and Grandma Sarah looked at her sharply; she had never handled mules nor a wagon; and Grandma Sarah was torn between puzzle and pleasure at this growing boldness in what had been a shy Laura Lee.

Chapter 17

They brought the wagons down from the walls of the canyon and moved up onto the plain, turning southwest across an endless horizon. Lone, on the black, led the way, far ahead. Little Moonlight and Grandma Sarah sat the seat of the lead wagon, and Laura Lee drove the second, alone. Behind her the Comanchero horses, stretched out in a long line, each roped to the horse ahead, were tethered to the tailgate of her wagon. Huge skin waterbags flopped at their sides like misplaced camel humps.

Lone set the pace at a fast walk, suitable for the big mules. Josey rode at the sides of the wagons and ranged the roan out and back, watching the horizon. He knew in a moment that Laura Lee had never handled mules. She had begun by sawing the reins and alternately slackening and tightening her pull . . . but she was fast to learn, and he said nothing . . . anyway, there was too determined a set to Laura Lee's jaw to talk about it.

Twice Josey saw small dust clouds over the rise of plain, but they moved out of sight. They night-camped in the purple haze of dusk, placing the wagons in a V and rope-picketing the mules and horses close by on the buffalo grass.

Lone shook his head grimly when Josey spoke of the dust clouds, "No way of tellin'. We know that Comanch ain't travelin' by hisself . . . and there's Apache hereabouts. Don't know which one I'd ruther tangle with . . . both of 'em mean'ern cooter's hell."

Josey took the first watch, walking quietly among the horses. Any band of wandering warriors would want the horses first . . . women second. The moon was bright, bringing out a coyote's high bark, and from a long way off, the lone call of a buffalo wolf. The moon had tipped toward the west when he shook Lone out of his blankets . . . and found Little Moonlight with him. Josey squatted beside them. "Proud to see ya'll set up homesteadin'," he said and was rewarded by Lone's grin and Little Moonlight kicking him on the shin.

As he stretched beneath the wagon bed Josey felt a comfort from the gnawing concern he had felt for the aging Cherokee and the Indian woman. Lone and Little Moonlight had found a home, even if it was just an Indian blanket. Maybe . . . they would find a place . . . and a life . . . on the ranch of Grandma Sarah. He would ride to Mexico, alone.

They broke camp before dawn, and when the first light touched the eastern rim they were ready to roll the wagons.

"Ya'll had better strap these on," Josey extended belts and pistols to the women. He helped Grandma Sarah tighten the belt around her little waist and held up the big pistol for her, "Ye'll have to use two hands, I reckin, ma'am . . . but remember, don't shoot 'til yore target is close in . . . and this here weapon's got six bites in it . . . jest thumb the hammer." As he turned to help Laura Lee she wrapped a hand around the handle of the big pistol and pulled it easily from the holster. "Why, them's natural-born hands for a forty-four," Josey said admiringly.

Laura Lee looked at her hands as though they were new additions to her arms. Maybe too outsized for teacups and parties. Maybe all of her was . . . but seems like she fit this place called Texas. It was a hard . . . even mean land . . . but it was spacious and honest with its savagery, unlike the places where cruelty hid itself in the hypocrisy of social graces. Now she placed a foot on the hub of the wagon and sprang to the seat; picking up the reins of the mules, she sang out, "Git up, ye lop-eared Arkansas razorbacks." And Grandma Sarah, leaning far out to further witness this sudden growth of a lust for life in Laura Lee, nearly fell beneath a wagon wheel.

Steadily southwest. The sun angling on their right, and heat shimmering the distance. They dry-camped that night on the slope of a mesa and pushed early at dawn, walking the mules at a fast pace.

On the fifth day after leaving the canyon, they crossed a straggling stream, half alkali, and after filling their bags, they moved on. "Water brings riders," Lone said grimly.

Imperceptibly, the land changed. The buffalo grass grew thinner. Here and there a tall spike of the yucca burst a cloud of white balls at its top. Creosote and catclaw bushes were dotted with the yellow petals of the prickly pear and the savagely beautiful scarlet bloom of the cactus. Every plant carried spike or thorn, needle or claw . . . necessary for life in a harsh land. Even the buttes that rose in the distance were swept clean of softening lines, and their rock-edged silhouettes looked like gigantic teeth exposed for battle.

It was on the afternoon of this day that the Indian riders appeared. Suddenly they were there, riding single file, paralleling the wagons boldly, less than a hundred yards away. Ten of them; they matched the stride of their horses to the wagons and looked straight ahead as they rode.

Lone brought his horse back at an easy walk and fell in beside Josey. They rode together for a distance in silence, and Josey knew Laura Lee had seen the Indians, but she looked straight ahead, clucking to the mules like a veteran muleskinner.

"Comanches," Lone said and watched Josey cut a chew of tobacco.

He chewed and spat, "Seen any more of 'em anywheres?"

"Nope," Lone said, "that's all there is. Ye'll notice they got three pack horses packing antelope. They ain't got paint . . . they're dog soldiers . . . that's what the Comanch and Cheyenne calls their hunters . . . them as has to supply the meat. They've done all right, and they ain't a raidin' party . . . but a Comanch might have a little fun anytime. These here hosses look good to 'em . . . but they're checkin' how much it'll cost to git 'em."

They rode on for a while without speaking. "Ye stay close to the waggins," Josey said, defiling a cactus bloom with a stream of juice. He turned his horse toward the Indians, and Lone saw four holstered .44's strapped to his saddle, Missouri-guerrilla style. He put the roan at an angle toward them, only slightly increasing the horse's gait.

During the next quarter mile he edged closer to the Comanches. At first the warriors appeared not to notice, but as he came closer, a rider occasionally turned his head to look at the heavily armed rider on the big horse who looked frankly back at him, apparently eager to do battle.

Suddenly the leader lifted his rifle in the air with one hand . . . gave an earsplitting whoop, and cut his horse away from Josey and the wagons in a run. The warriors followed. Raising loud cries and waving their rifles, they disappeared as quickly as they had come.

As he drifted his horse back by the wagons, Grandma Sarah lifted her umbrella sombrero with both hands in salute . . . and Laura Lee smiled . . . broader than he had ever seen.

Lone wiped the sweat from his forehead, "Thet head Comanch come mighty close when he lifted thet rifle."

"I reckin," Josey said. "Will they be back?"

"No . . ." Lone said, a little uncertainly, "they're packin' heavy . . . means they're a ways from the main body . . . and they ain't travelin' in our direction. Onliest reason they won't be . . . it jest ain't convenient fer 'em . . . but they's plenty of Comanche to go 'round."

It was late afternoon when they raised the swayback mountain, part of a ragged chain of jumbled ridges and buttes that stumbled across the land, leaving wide gaps of desert between them. Grandma Sarah stared ahead at them, and as they camped in the red haze of sunset, she watched the mountain for a long time. By noon the following day they could see the mountain clearly. It was, close up, actually two mountains that peaked at opposite ends and ran their ridges downward parallel to each other, giving the appearance, at a distance, of a single mountain sagged downward in its center. Lone headed the wagons for the end of the near ridge, as it petered out in the desert.

It was not quite sunset when they rounded the ridge and were brought up short at the panorama. A valley ran between the mountains, and sparkling in the rays of late sun, a shallow creek, crystal clear, ran winding down the middle and led away into the desert. They turned up the valley, a contrasting oasis in a desert. Gamma grass was knee high to the horses; cottonwoods and live oak lined the creek banks. Spring flowers dappled the grass and carried their colors all the way to the naked buttes of the mountains that loomed on either side.

Antelope grazing on the far side of the creek lifted their heads as they passed, and coveys of quail scattered from ground nests. The valley alternately widened and narrowed between the mountains; sometimes a mile wide, and again narrowing to a width of fifty yards, creating semicircular parks through which they passed.

Longhorn cattle, big and fat, grazed the deep grass, and Josey, after a couple of hours traveling, guessed there were a thousand . . . and later, more and more of the huge beasts made him give up his estimate. They were wild, dashing at the sight of the wagons into the narrow arroyos that split the mountains on each side.

Josey saw rock partridge, ruff and sharp-tail grouse along the willows of the creek, and a short black bear, eating in a green berry patch, grunted at them and trotted away into the creek, scattering a herd of magnificent black-tailed deer.

They moved slowly up the valley, the weary, sun-heated, dusty desert travelers luxuriating in the cool abundance. The sun set, torching the sky behind the mountain an ember red that faded into purple, like paints spilled and mixing colors.

The coolness of the valley washed in their faces; not the sharp, penetrating cold of the desert, but the close, moist coolness of trees and water that refreshed and satisfied a thirst of weariness. The moon poked a near-full face over the canyon and chased shadows under the willows along the creek and against the canyon walls. The night birds came out and chatter-fussed and held long, trilling notes that haunted on the night breeze down the valley.

Lone stopped the wagons, and the horses cropped at the tall grass. "Maybe," he said almost in hushed tones, "we ought to night-camp."

Grandma Sarah stood up in the wagon seat. She had laid aside the sombrero and her white hair shone silver.

"It's jest like Tom writ it was," she said softly, "the house will be up yonder," and she pointed farther up the valley, "where the mountains come together. Cain't . . . cain't we go on?" Lone and Josey looked at each other and nodded . . . they moved on.

The moon was two hours higher when they saw the house, low and long, almost invisible from its sameness of adobe color with the buttes rising behind it. It was nestled snugly in a grove of cottonwoods, and as they pulled up beside it, they could see a barn, a low bunkhouse, and at the side, an adobe cook shack. Behind the barn there was a rail corral that backgated into what appeared to be a horse pasture circling back, enclosing a clear pool of water into which the creek waterfalled from a narrow arroyo. It was the end of the valley.

They inspected the house; the long, low-ceilinged front room with rawhide chairs and slate rock floor.

The kitchen had no stove, but a huge cooking fireplace with a Dutch oven set into its side. There was a rough comfort about the house; beds were made of timber poles, but stripped with springy rawhide, and long couches of the same material were swung low against the walls.

Unloading the wagons in the yard, in the shadows of the cottonwoods, Laura Lee impulsively squeezed the arm of Josey and whispered, "It's like a . . . a dream."

"It is that," Josey said solemnly . . . and he wondered how Tom Turner must have felt, stumbling across this mere slit of verdant growth in the middle of a thousand square miles of semiarid land. He judged the valley to be ten . . . maybe twelve miles long. With natural grass, water, and the hemming walls of the mountains, two, maybe three riders could handle it all, except for branding and trailing time, when extras could be picked up.

He was jarred from his reverie when he saw Lone and Little Moonlight walking close together toward the little house that set back in a grove of red cedars and cottonwood. The place had got hold of him . . . hell, fer a minute he was figurin' like it was home.

Laura Lee and Grandma Sarah were fidgeting about in the house. Nobody would sleep this night. He unhitched the mules and led them with the horses to the corral and pasture. Leaning on the rail of the corral, he watched them circle, kick their heels, and head for the water of the clear pool. The big mules rolled in the high grass. He brought the big roan last, unsaddled him, and lovingly rubbed him down. He turned him loose with the others . . . but first he fed him grain.

Laura Lee whipped up biscuits for their breakfast

and fried the jerky beef with beans in the tallow of the oxen. The women busied themselves flying dust and dirt out the windows and doors and bustling with all the mysterious doin's women do in new houses. Little Moonlight had clearly laid claim to the adobe in the cedars and appropriated blankets, pots, and pans, which she industriously trotted from the pile of belongings in the backyard. Lone and Josey carried water from the waterfall and filled the cedar water bins in the house. They patched the corral fences and cleaned the guns, stacking and hanging them in the rooms, in easy reach. Lone set traps on the creek bank, and they suppered on golden bass.

After supper Josey and Lone squatted in the shadows of the trees and watched the moon rise over the canyon rim. The murmur of talk drifted to them from the kitchen where Laura Lee and Grandma Sarah washed up the supper plates, and through the window the flicker of firelight took the edge off a light spring chill. Little Moonlight sat before the door of the 'dobe in the cedars and faintly hummed in an alto voice the haunting, wandering melody of the Cheyenne.

"It is her lodge," Lone said. "She's told me it's the first time she has a lodge of her own."

"Reckin it's her'n and yore'n," Josey said quietly.

Lone shifted uncomfortably, "The woman . . . I never thought, old as I am . . . this place is like when I was a boy . . . a young man . . . back there. . . . " His voice trailed off in a helpless apology.

"I know," Josey said. He knew what the Indian could not say. Back there, back beyond the Trail of Tears . . . back there in the mountains there had been such a place; the home . . . the woman. And now it was given to him again; but he fretted against what he felt was somehow . . . disloyalty to the outlaw. Josey spoke, and his voice was matter-of-fact and held no emotion, "Ye ain't knowed . . . by name. We'll git the riders, but I couldn't leave Laura Lee . . . the women-folks, without I knowed they was somebody to be trusted . . . to boss and look after. Ye must stay here . . . ye and Little Moonlight . . . she's near good as a man . . . better'n most. Ain't no other way. Besides, I'll be trailin' back this way and more'n likely need a place to hole up."

Lone touched the shoulder of Josey, "Maybe," he said, "maybe they'll fergit about ye, and . . ."

Josey cut a chew of tobacco and studied the valley below them. There was no use saying it . . . they both knew there would be no forgetting.

Chapter 18

Ten Bears trailed north from wintering in the land of the Mexicano, below the mysterious river that the pony soldiers refused to cross. Behind him rode five subchiefs, 250 battle-hardened warriors and over 400 squaws and children. Glutted with loot and scalps from raids on the villages and ranchos to the south, they had come back over the Rio Grande two days ago. They came back, as they had always done in the spring . . . as they always would do. The ways of the Comanche would not be shackled by the pony soldier, for the Comanche was the greatest horseman of the Plains and each of his warriors was equal to 100 of the bluecoats.

Ten Bears was the greatest of the war chiefs of the mighty Comanche. Even the great Red Cloud of the

Oglala Sioux, far to the north, called him a Brother Chief. There was no rivalry in all his subchiefs, for his place, his fame, was legend. He had led his warriors in hundreds of raids and battles and had tested his wisdom and courage a thousand times without blemish. He was eloquent in the speech of the white man, and last fall, as the buffalo grass turned brown, he had met General Sherman on the Llano Estacado and had told him the ways of the Comanche would not change. Ten Bears always kept his word.

When he had received the message that the bluecoat General wished to meet with him, he had at first refused. There had been four meetings in five years, and each time the white man offered his hand in friendship, while with the other hand he held the snake. At each meeting there was a new face of the bluecoat, but the words were always the same.

Finally he had agreed and selected the Llano Estacado as the meeting site . . . for this was the Staked Plain that the white man feared to cross; where the Comanche rode with impunity. It was a fit setting in the eyes of Ten Bears.

He had refused to sit, and while the bluecoat leader talked, he had stood, arms folded in stony silence. It was as he had suspected; much talk of friendship and goodwill for the Comanche . . . and orders for the Comanche to move farther toward the rim of the plain, where the sun died each day.

When the bluecoat had finished, Ten Bears had spoken in a voice choked with anger, "We have met many times before, and each time I have taken your hand, but when your shadow grew short upon the ground, the promises were broken like dried sticks beneath your heel. Your words change with the wind and die without meaning in the desert of your breast.

If we had not given up the lands you now hold, then we would have something to give for more of your crooked words. I know every water hole, every bush and antelope, from the land of the Mexicano to the land of the Sioux. I ride, free like the wind, and now I shall ride even until the breath that blows across this land breathes my dust into it. I shall meet you again only in battle, for there is iron in my heart."

He had stalked away from the meeting, and he and his warriors had burned and looted the ranches as they rode south through Texas into Mexico. Now he was returning, and hatred smoldered in his eyes . . . and in the eyes of the proud warriors who rode with him.

It was late on a Sunday afternoon when Ten Bears rounded the ridge of the mountains to make medicine in the cool valley . . . and saw the tracks of the wagons.

That same Sunday morning, the gathering for services took place in the shade of the cottonwoods that surrounded the ranch house. Grandma Sarah had announced it firmly at breakfast, "It's a Sunday, and we'all will observe the Lord's day."

Josey and Lone stood, awkwardly bareheaded; Little Moonlight between them. Laura Lee, still moccasined, but wearing a snow-white dress that accentuated the fullness of her figure, opened the Bible and read. It was a slow process. She moved her finger from word to word and bent her sun-browned face studiously over the pages: "Yea, though I walk through the valley of the shadow of death, I will fear no evil, for Thou art with me. Thy rod and Thy staff, they comfort me. . . ."

It took a long time, and Little Moonlight watched a house wren building a nest in a crack of the 'dobe.

With a great sigh of triumph, Laura Lee finished the Psalm, and Grandma Sarah looked sternly at her little congregation, expending a particularly lingering look at Little Moonlight. "Now we'll pray," she said, "and ever'body's got to hold hands."

Lone grasped the hand of Grandma Sarah and Little Moonlight; Josey took the right hand of Little Moonlight and extended his right to hold the hand of Laura Lee. He felt her tremble . . . and he thought he felt a squeeze. Little Moonlight perked up . . . there was more to the white man's ceremony.

"Bow yore heads," Grandma Sarah said, and Lone pushed Little Moonlight's head down.

"Lord," Grandma Sarah began in stentorian tones, "we're right sorry we ain't had time to observe and sich, but Ye've seen like it is. We ast Ye to look after Pa and Dan'l, they was . . . 'ceptin' a little liquorin' up, occasional . . . good men, better'n most, and they fit best they could agin that low-down, murderin' trash out o' hell that done 'em in. They died tol'able well, considerin', and," her voice broke, and she paused for a moment, ". . . and we thankee Ye seen fit to send one to bury 'em proper. We thankee fer this here place and ast Ye bless Tom's bones at Shiloh. We don't ast much, Lord . . . like them horned toads back East, wallerin' around in fine fittin's and the sin of Sodom. We be Texans now, fit'n to stand on our feet and fight fer what's our'n . . . with occasional help from Ye . . . Ye be willin'. We thankee fer these men . . . fer the Indian woman . . . " here, Grandma Sarah opened one eye and looked cannily at the bowed head of Josey Wales, ". . . and we thankee fer a good, strong, maidenly girl sich as Laura Lee . . . fit to raise strappin' sons and daughters to people this here land . . . iff'n she's give half a chancet. We thankee fer Josey Wales deliverin' us from the Philistines. Amen."

Grandma Sarah raised her head and sternly scanned

the circle. "Now," she said, "we'll end the service, ren-
derin' the song 'Sweet Bye and Bye.'" Lone and Josey
knew the song, and hesitantly at first, then joining
their voices with Laura Lee and Grandma Sarah, they
sang:

> "In the sweet bye and bye,
>   we shall meet on that beautiful shore,
> In the sweet bye and bye,
>   we shall meet on that beautiful shore."

They sang the chorus . . . and stumbled a bit over
the verses. Little Moonlight enjoyed this part of the
white man's ceremony most. She began a slow shuffle
of her feet that picked up tempo as she danced around
the circle; and though she didn't know the words, she
brought a peculiarly appealing harmony to it with an
alto moan. The red-bone flopped on his haunches and
began a gathering howl that added to the scene, growing in noise if not melody. Josey reached back a booted
toe to delicately, but viciously, kick him in the ribs.
The hound snarled.

It was . . . all in all . . . a satisfying morning, as
Grandma Sarah opined over a bounteous Sunday dinner; something they could all look forward to, each
and ev'ry Sunday morning.

Chapter 19

The scouts told him that only two of the horses were ridden, and Ten Bears knew the meaning of the wagons . . . white squaws. He ordered the camp set boldly in the open at the foot of the valley. Ten Bears took pride in the order of the tight, tidy circles of tepees that marked the strict, disciplined ways of the Comanche. They were not slovenly as had been the Tonkaways, and the Tonkaways lived no more; the Comanche had killed them all.

Ten Bears had hated and despised the Tonkaways. It had been rumored throughout the Comanche Nation, as well as the Kiowa and Apache, that the Tonkaways were human flesh eaters. Ten Bears knew that they were. As a young warrior, having just passed his test of manhood and inexperienced in the ways of the trail, he had been captured by them; he and Spotted Horse, another youthful brave.

They had been bound, and that night, as the Tonkaways sat around their fire, one of them rose and came to them. He had a long knife in his hand, and he had sliced a piece of flesh from Spotted Horse's thigh and carried it back and roasted it over the flames. Others had come with their knives and sliced the flesh from Spotted Horse; his legs and his groin, and in the friendliest manner had complimented him over the taste of his own flesh.

When they had hit the fountains of blood, they had brought firebrands to stop the flow . . . so to keep Spotted Horse alive longer. Ten Bears and Spotted Horse had cursed them . . . but Spotted Horse had not cried out in fear or pain, and as he grew weaker, he began his death song.

When the Tonkaways slept, Ten Bears had slipped his bonds, but instead of running he had used their own weapons to kill them. With the captured horses bearing the stripped skeleton of Spotted Horse and a dozen scalps, he had ridden, splattered with the blood of his enemies, back to the Comanche. He had not washed the blood from his body for a week, and the story chant of Spotted Horse and the courage of Ten Bears was sung in all the lodges of the Comanche. It had been the beginning of Ten Bears' rise to power and the beginning of the end for the Tonkaways.

Now, in the gathering dusk of evening, the sub-chiefs had their squaws set their separate fires along the cool creek. Their tepees blocked any entrance . . . or escape . . . from the valley.

Ten Bears knew of the white man's lodge at the end of the valley, where the canyon walls came together. He had settled there during the period of peace, after a meeting of Comanche and bluecoat, and more promises that would be broken. Ten Bears once had come to kill him and to kill his Mexicano riders . . . but when he and his warriors had ridden to the house, they had found no one.

Everything was still in order in the white man's lodge; the hard leaves from which the white man ate were set on his ceremonial table; the food was in the lodge, as were his blankets. True, the horses of the man and his Mexicano riders were gone, but the Comanches knew that no man would leave without his blankets and his food . . . and so they knew as certainly that the man and his riders had been snatched from the earth because of Ten Bears' displeasure. They had not disturbed the white man's lodge . . . it would be bad medicine.

Later, in the settlements, Ten Bears had learned that the man had gone to join the Gray Riders, who were fighting the bluecoats . . . but he had not told his warriors; they would have listened and accepted his words . . . but they had seen with their own eyes the evidence of mysterious disappearance. Besides . . . it added to the stature of Ten Bears' legend. Let them believe as they wished.

Ten Bears stood alone before his tepees as his women made food. He looked contemptuously at the medicine men as they began their chant. He had stopped the medicine dances when he found that the medicine men were accepting bribes of horses from braves who did not want to dance in the exhausting routine, the test of stamina that would decide if medicine was good or bad. Like religious leaders everywhere, they sought power and wealth, and so had become double-tongues, like the politicians. Ten Bears looked on them with the inborn disgust of the warrior.

He allowed them their chants and their prattlings of omen and signs, pomp, and ceremony . . . but he paid no attention to their advice nor their superstitions.

Now, with a few words and a wave of his arm, he sent riders along the rim of the canyon to station themselves and watch the lodge of the white men. There would be no escape in the morning.

Josey slept lightly in his bedroom across the hall from Laura Lee. He had not yet accustomed himself to the walls and roof . . . nor the silence away from the night sounds of the trails. Each night Laura Lee had heard him rise several times and walk softly down the stone-floored hall and then return.

She knew it was late when the low whistle wakened her. It had come from the thin, rifle-slot window of Josey's room, and she heard his walk, quick and soft, down the hall. She followed him on bare feet, a blanket wrapped around her nightgown, and stood in the shadows, out of the square of moon that shone on the kitchen floor. It was Lone who met Josey on the back porch . . . and she heard them talk.

"Comanches," Lone said, "all around us on the rims." His clothes were wet, and water dripped into little puddles on the rough boards.

"Where ye been?" Josey asked quietly.

"Down the creek, all the way. There's an army of 'em down there . . . maybe two, three hunnerd warriors . . . lot of squaws. It ain't no little war party. They're makin' medicine . . . so I stayed in the creek and got close to read sign. And listen to this . . ." Lone paused to give emphasis to his news . . . "ye know the sign on the Chief's tepee? . . . It's Ten Bears! Ten Bears, by God! The meanest hunk o' walkin' mad south of Red Cloud."

Laura Lee shivered in the darkness. She heard Josey ask,

"Why ain't they done hit us?"

"Well," Lone said, "thet moon is a Comanche moon all right . . . meanin' it's plenty light enough to raid . . . with plenty light fer the Happy Huntin' grounds if one of 'em died . . . but they're makin' medicine fer big things, probably ridin' north. They'll hit us in the mornin' . . . and that'll be it. There's too many of 'em."

There was a long pause before Josey asked, "Any way out?"

"No way . . ." Lone said, "sayin' we could slip by them that's on the rim . . . we'd have to go afoot up them walls, and they'd track us down in the mornin', out in the open, with no horses."

Again, a long period of silence. Laura Lee thought they had walked away and was about to peer around the door when she heard Josey.

"No way," he said.

"Git Little Moonlight," Josey ordered harshly and came back into the kitchen. He bumped full into Laura Lee standing there, and she impulsively threw her arms around his neck.

Slowly he embraced her, feeling the eagerness of her body against him. She trembled, and easily, naturally, their lips came together. Lone and Little Moonlight found them this way when they returned, standing in soft beams of the moon that filtered through the kitchen door. Josey's hat had fallen to the floor, and it was Little Moonlight who retrieved it and handed it to him.

"Git Grandma," he said to Laura Lee.

In the half-light of the kitchen Josey spoke in the cold, flat tone of the guerrilla chieftain. The blood drained from Grandma Sarah's face as their situation became clear, but she was tight-lipped and silent. Little Moonlight, holding a rifle in one hand, a knife in the other, stood by the kitchen door, looking toward the canyon rim.

"Iff'n I was lookin' fer a place fer a hole-up fight," he said, "I'd pick this 'un. Walls and roof is over two foot thick, all mud, and nothin' to burn. Jest two doors, front and back, and in sight of each other. These narrer crosses we call winders is fer rifle fire . . . up and down . . . and side to side, and cain't nobody come through 'em. The feller . . . Tom . . . thet built the house, ye'll notice, put these crossed winders all around, no blind spots; we got 'em right by each door. Little Moonlight will fire through that'n . . ." he pointed toward the heavy door that opened into the front of the house, "and Laura Lee will fire through this'n, by the back door."

Josey took a long step to stand in the wide space of floor that separated the kitchen from the living room. "Grandma will set here," he said, "with the buckets of powder, ball, and caps, and do the loadin' . . . can ye handle thet, Grandma?"

"I kin handle it," Grandma Sarah said tersely.

"Now Lone," Josey continued, "he'll fill in firing where at the rush is, and on towards the end, he'll be facin' thet hallway runs down by the bedrooms and keepin' fire directed thataway."

"Why?" Laura Lee asked quickly, "why would Lone be firing down the hall?"

" 'Cause," Josey said, "onliest blind spot is the roof. They'll finally git around to it. We cain't fire through the roof. Too thick. They'll dig a dozen holes to drop through back there in the bedrooms. That's why we're goin' to stack logs here at the door to the hall. All we're defendin' is these here two doors and space 'twixt 'em. When we git to thet part," he added grimly, "the fight will be 'bout over, one way or t'other'n. It'll be a last drive they'll make. Remember this . . . when things git plumb wuss . . . where it's liken to be ye cain't make it . . . thet means it's all goin' to be decided right quick . . . cain't last long. Then ye got to git mean . . . dirty mean . . . ye got to git plumb mad-dog mean . . . like a heller . . . and ye'll come through. Iff'n ye lose yore head and give up . . . ye're finished and ye ain't deservin' of winnin' ner livin'. Thet's the way it is."

Now he turned to Lone, who was leaning against the kitchen wall. "Use pistols short range . . . less reloadin', more firepower. We'll start a fire 'bout dawn in the fireplace and put iron on it . . . keep the iron red hot. Anybody gits hit . . . sing out . . . Lone'll slap the iron to it . . . ain't got time to stop blood no other way."

Josey looked at their faces. Tense, strained . . . but not a tear nor a whimper in the whole lot. Solid stuff, clear to the marrow.

They worked in the dark, bringing water to fill the bins and piling the pistols and rifles of the Comancheros on the kitchen table. There were twenty-two Colts' .44's and fourteen rifles. Lone checked the loads of the guns. They placed the kegs of powder, ball, and caps in the middle of the floor and stacked heavy logs, head high, with only room for a pistol barrel between them, at the door to the hall.

It was still dark when they rested . . . but the early morning twittering of birds had already begun. Grandma Sarah brought out cold biscuits and beef, and they ate in silence. When they had finished, Josey pulled off his buckskin jacket. The butternut-colored guerrilla shirt was loose fitting, almost like a woman's blouse. The .36 Navy Colt protruded from beneath his left shoulder.

He handed the jacket to Laura Lee, "Reckin I won't be needin' this," he said, " 'preciate it, iff'n ye'll keep it fer me." She took the jacket and nodded dumbly. Josey had turned to Lone and drawled, "Reckin I'll be saddlin' up now."

Lone nodded, and Josey was through the door and walking to the corral before Laura Lee and Grandma Sarah recovered the sense of what he had said.

"What . . . ?" Grandma Sarah said, startled. "Whar's he a-goin'?"

Laura Lee raced for the door, but Lone grabbed her by the shoulders and held her in a firm grip.

"Woman talk is no good fer him now," Lone said.

"Where's he goin' . . . what's happening?" she said frantically.

Lone pushed her back from the door and faced the women. "He knows he can do the best fer us on the back of a hoss. He's a guerrilla . . . they always figger to carry the fight to the enemy, and now he goes to do so again." Lone spoke slowly and carefully, "He is goin' into the valley to kill Ten Bears and many of his chiefs and warriors. When the Comanche comes to us . . . the head of the Comanche will be crushed . . . and his back broken. Josey Wales will do this, so thet . . . if we do as he has said we should do . . . we will live."

"Lord God Almighty!" Grandma Sarah said in hushed tones.

Laura Lee whispered, "He is goin' to the valley . . . to die."

Lone's teeth flashed in a grim smile, "He is goin' to the valley to fight. Death has been with him many years. He does not think of it." Lone's firm voice broke and shook with emotion, "Ten Bears is a great warrior.

He knows no fear. But today he will meet another great warrior, a privilege that comes to few men. They will know . . . when they face each other, Ten Bears and Josey Wales . . . and they will know their hatreds and their loves . . . but they will also know their brotherhood of courage, that the man of littleness will never know." Lone's voice had risen in an exultant thrill that was primitive and savage despite his carefully chosen words.

A thin hint of light touched the rim of the eastern canyon and silhouetted the Comanche warriors, slumped on their horses, dotting the light's edge above the ranch house. It was in this light that Josey Wales brought the big roan, frisking and prancing, to the rear of the house.

A sob tore from the throat of Laura Lee, and she rushed to the door. Lone caught and held her briefly. "He'll not like it, if ye cry," he whispered. She wiped her eyes and only stumbled once as she walked to the horse. She placed her hand on his leg, not trusting herself to speak, and looked up at him there in the saddle.

Slowly he placed his hand over hers, and the merest gleam of humor softened the hard black eyes. "Yore'er the purtiest gal in Texas, Laura Lee," he said softly, "iff'n Texas gits a queen, ye'll be it . . . fer ye fit the land . . . liken a good gun handle to a hand . . . 'er a hoss that's bred right. Ye re'clect what I'm sayin' now and mind it . . . fer it's true."

Tears welled up in her eyes, and she could not speak, and so she turned away, stumbling to the porch. Lone stood by the saddle and stretched his hand up to grasp Josey's. The grip was hard . . . the grip of brothers. He was stripped to the waist, and the wrinkled, bronze face had two streaks of white 'dobe across the cheeks and another on his forehead. It was the death face of the Cherokee . . . neither giving nor asking quarter of the enemy.

"We'll make it," Lone said to Josey, "but iff'n . . . it's otherwise . . . no women will live."

Josey nodded but didn't speak. He turned his horse away, toward the trail. As he passed, Little Moonlight touched his booted foot with the scalping knife . . . the tribute of the Cheyenne squaw, paid only to the mightiest warriors who go to their death.

As he passed from the yard, Grandma Sarah shouted . . . and her voice was clear and ringing, "Lord'll ride with ye, Josey Wales!" But if he heard, he didn't acknowledge the call . . . for he neither turned his head nor lifted his hand in farewell. The tears coursed unmindful down the withered face of Grandma Sarah, "I don't keer what they say 'bout 'em . . . reckin to me, he's twelve foot tall." She threw her apron over her face and turned back into the kitchen.

Laura Lee ran to the edge of the yard and watched him . . . the roan, held in check, stepping high and skittish as Josey Wales rode slowly down the valley by the creek and finally disappeared around the cleft of a protruding butte.

Chapter 20

Ten Bears woke in his tepee at dawn and kicked the naked, voluptuous young squaw from beneath his blankets. She was lazy. His other five women already had the fire going beneath the pot. Three of them were heavy with child. He hoped the newborn would be males . . . but secretly, he knew they would come too late to follow Ten Bears. They would grow and ride and fight in the legend of Ten Bears; but Ten Bears would be dead . . . fallen in battle. This he knew.

The only two sons he had possessed were dead at the hands of the bluecoats; one of them shot cowardly under the white talking flag that the bluecoats used. Ten Bears thought of this each morning. He brooded upon it and so rekindled the hatred and vengeance that the drug of sleep had softened in his mind . . . and in his heart.

The bitterness rose in his throat, and he could taste it in his mouth. Everything he loved . . . the free land . . . his sons . . . his womenfolk . . . all had been violated by the white man . . . most especially the bluecoat. He savagely tore at the meat with his teeth and swallowed big chunks in anger. Even the buffalo; once he had ridden onto a high plain, and as far as his eye could see lay the rotting, putrid carcasses of buffalo; killed by the white man; not for food, not for robes, but for some savage ceremony the white man called "sport."

Ten Bears rose and wiped the grease from his hands on his buckskin trousers. He reached two fingers into a pot and streaked the blue downward across his cheeks and across his forehead; the death face of the Comanche.

Now they would go to the white man's lodge. He wanted them alive, if possible; so that he could slowly burn the color from their eyes and make them scream their cowardice; so that he could strip the skin from their bodies and from their groins where life sprung from the male. The womenfolk would be turned over to the warriors . . . all of them . . . to be violated; and if they lived, they would be given to the ones who had captured them. The children . . . they would know that it was Ten Bears' wrath.

Shouts came from his warriors. They had leaped to their horses and were pointing up the valley. Ten Bears waved for his white horse, and as a squaw brought it forward, he sprang easily on its back and walked him to the center of the valley, before the gathering of chiefs and braves. The sun had broken over the eastern canyon rim and Ten Bears shaded his eyes. The moving figure was a horseman a mile away.

He came slowly, and Ten Bears moved out to meet him. Behind Ten Bears came the chiefs, their big war bonnets setting them apart; and behind the chiefs, strung out in a line that almost crossed the valley, rode over two hundred warriors.

Ten Bears wore no bonnet . . . only a single feather. He disdained the showy headdress. But there was no mistaking him; naked from the waist up, his rifle balanced across his big white horse, he rode ten paces ahead of his chiefs, and his bearing was of one born to command.

The many horses of the Comanches made an ominous hissing sound as they paced through the long grass, carrying the half-naked riders with hideously painted faces. Behind, from the tepees, a low, ominous war drum began its beat of death. Ten Bears checked the canyon rims as he rode, and saw his scouts coming back, flanking the course of the lone rider. They signaled . . . there was only one coming to meet him.

Now the eager hate in Ten Bears was tempered with puzzlement. The man did not carry the hated white flag, and yet he came on, casually, as though he rode without care . . . but Ten Bears noticed he kept the big horse headed directly toward his white one.

Less than a hundred yards now . . . and the horse! Fit for a Chief . . . taller, more powerful than his own white charger; it almost reared as it stepped high with power, nostrils flared at the excitement. Now he could see the man. There was no rifle, but Ten Bears saw the butts of many pistols holstered on the saddle, and that the man wore three pistols. A fighting man.

He wore the hat of the Gray Riders, and what Ten Bears had at first thought . . . with a shock . . . was war paint, became a great scar on the cheek as he came closer. Almost to a collision, he came so close, so that Ten Bears was the first to stop, and the big roan reared . . . and a murmur of approval for the horse ran through the ranks of Comanche braves.

Ten Bears looked into black eyes as hard and ruthless as his own. A shivering thrill of anticipation ran through the Chief's body . . . of combat with a great warrior to match his own mettle! The rider slid a long knife from his boot, and the chiefs behind Ten Bears moved forward with a low, threatening rumble. The rider appeared not to notice as he meticulously cut a big chunk of tobacco from a twist and shoved it into his mouth. Ten Bears had not flickered an eyelash, but there was a faint glint of admiration for the audacity of a bold warrior.

"Ye'll be Ten Bears," Josey drawled and spat tobacco juice between the legs of the white horse. He had not called him "Chief" . . . nor had he called him "great," as did all the bluecoats with whom Ten Bears had talked. There was the slightest touch of casual insult . . . but Ten Bears understood. It was the way of the warrior, not the double-tongues.

"I am Ten Bears," he said slowly.

"I'm Josey Wales," Josey said. The mind of Ten Bears raced back in search of the name . . . and he knew.

"You are of the Gray Riders and you will not make peace with the bluecoats. I have heard." Ten Bears half turned on his horse and waved his arm. The chiefs and braves behind him parted, leaving an open corridor.

"You may go in peace," he said. It was a magnificent gesture befitting a great Chief, and Ten Bears was proud of the majesty it afforded him. But Josey Wales made no motion to accept this grant of life.

"I reckin not," he drawled, "I wa'ant aimin' to leave nohow. Got nowheres to go."

The horses of the Comanche braves drew closer at his refusal. Ten Bears' voice shook with anger. "Then you will die."

"I reckin," Josey said, "I come here to die with ye, or live with ye. Dyin' ain't hard fer sich as ye and me, it's the livin' thet's hard." He paused to let the words carry their weight with Ten Bears . . . then he continued, "What ye and me cares about has been butchered . . . raped. It's been done by them lyin', double-tongued snakes thet run guv'mints. Guv'mints lie . . . promise . . . back-stab . . . eat in yore lodge and rape yore women and kill when ye sleep on their promises. Guv'mints don't live together . . . men live together. From guv'mints ye cain't git a fair word . . . ner a fair fight. I come to give ye either one . . . 'er to git either one from ye."

Ten Bears straightened on his horse. The vicious hatred of Josey Wales matched his own . . . hatred for those who had killed what each of them loved. He waited, without speaking, for the outlaw to continue.

"Back there," Josey jerked his thumb over his shoulder, "is my brother, an Indian who rode with the Gray Riders, and a Cheyenne squaw, who also is my kin. There's a old squaw and a young squaw thet belongs to me. Thet's all . . . but they're liken to me . . . iff'n it's worth fightin' about, it's worth dyin' about . . . 'er don't fight. They'll fight and die. I didn't come here under no lyin' white flag to git out from under yore killin'. I come here this way, so's ye'll know that my word of death is true . . . and thet my word of life . . . then, is true."

Josey slowly waved his hand across the valley, "The

bear lives here . . . with the Comanche; the wolf, the birds, the antelope . . . the coyote. So will we live. The iron stick won't dig the ground . . . thet is my word. The game will not be killed fer sport . . . only what we eat . . . as the Comanche does. Every spring, when the grass comes, and the Comanche rides north, he can rest here in peace, and butcher cattle and jerk beef fer his travel north . . . and when the grass of the north turns brown, the Comanche can do the same, as he goes to the land of the Mexicano. The sign of the Comanche," Josey moved his hand through the air, in the wiggling sign of the snake, "will be on all the cattle. It'll be placed on my lodge, and marked on trees and on horses. Thet's my word of life."

"And your word of death?" Ten Bears asked low and threatening.

"In my pistols," Josey said, "and in yer rifles . . . I'm here fer one or t'other," and he shrugged his shoulders.

"These things you say we will have," Ten Bears said, "we already have."

"Thet's right," Josey said, "I ain't promisin' nothin' extry . . . 'ceptin' givin' ye life and ye givin' me life. I'm sayin' men can live without butcherin' one 'nother and takin' more'n what's needin' fer livin' . . . share and share alike. Reckin it ain't much to talk trade about . . . but I ain't one fer big talk . . . ner big promises."

Ten Bears looked steadily into the burning eyes of Josey Wales. The horses stomped impatiently and snorted, and along the line of warriors a ripple of anticipation marked their movements as they sensed the ending of the talk.

Slowly Josey raised the reins of his horse and placed them in his teeth. Ten Bears watched the gesture with an implacable face, but admiration came to his heart.

It was the way of the Comanche warrior . . . true and sure. Josey Wales would talk no more.

Ten Bears spoke, "It is sad that governments are chiefed by the double-tongues. There is iron in your words of death for all the Comanche to see . . . and so there is iron in your word of life. No signed paper can hold the iron, it must come from men. The word of Ten Bears, all know, carries the same iron of death . . . and of life. It is good that warriors such as we meet in the struggle of death . . . or of life. It shall be life."

Ten Bears pulled a scalping knife from his belt and slashed the palm of his right hand. He held it high for all his chiefs and braves to see, as the blood coursed down his naked arm. Josey slid the knife from his boot and slashed across his own hand. They came close and placed their hands flat and palms together and held them high.

"So it will be," said Ten Bears.

"Kin, I reckin," said Josey Wales.

Ten Bears turned his horse back through the line of braves, and they followed him slowly down the valley toward the tepees. And the drums of death stopped, and out of the hush that followed, a male thrush sent his trilling call of life across the valley.

It was Lone who saw him coming, as he first appeared around the butte and walked the roan up the trail, nearly a mile away. It was Laura Lee who could not wait. She ran from the yard, down the trail, her blond hair streaming out behind her in the wind. Grandma Sarah, Little Moonlight, and Lone stood under the cottonwood tree and watched them as Josey held his arms wide and lifted Laura Lee to the saddle before him. As they came closer, Grandma Sarah could see, through watering eyes, that Josey held

Laura Lee in his arms and that both her arms were about his neck and her head lay on his breast.

Grandma Sarah's emotion could hold no bounds, and so she turned on Lone and snapped, "Now ye can warsh that heathern paint off'n yer face."

With one swoop, Lone swept Grandma Sarah from the ground and tossed her high in the air . . . and he laughed and shouted while Little Moonlight danced around them and whooped. Grandma Sarah yelled and fussed . . . but she was pleased, for when Lone set her down, she gave him a playful slap, straightened her skirts, and bustled into the kitchen. As Josey and Laura Lee rode into the yard, they all could hear it through the kitchen window; Grandma Sarah fixin' dinner . . . and a cracked voice singing: "In the sweet bye and bye . . ."

It was around the dinner table they talked of it. The brand would be the Crooked River Brand; the irons would be made by Lone, in the shape of Comanche sign.

"It'll cost ye a hunnerd head of beef every spring," Josey told Grandma Sarah, "and a hunnerd every fall, fer the Comanches of Ten Bears . . . so's we keep our word. But I figger three, maybe four thousand head in the valley . . . ye can still send a couple thousand up the trail ev'ry year, to keep yer grass balanced out."

"Fair 'nough," Grandma Sarah said, "iff'n it was five hunnerd a year . . . fair's fair. A word to share is a word to care."

"I'll have to git riders fer the brandin'," Josey said.

Lone studied the old map, "Santo Rio, to the south, is the closest town."

"Then I'll leave in the mornin'," Josey said.

Laura Lee came to him in his room that night, pale in the moon that made crosses of light through the windows and on the floor. She watched him lying there, for a long time, and seeing him awake, she whispered, "Did ye . . . did ye mean what ye said . . . about me being . . . like ye said?"

"I meant it, Laura Lee," Josey answered. She came to his bed, and after a long time she slept . . . but Josey Wales did not sleep. Deep inside, a faint hope had been born. It persisted with a promise of life . . . a rebirth he never believed could have been. In the cold light of dawn he was brought back to the reality of his position, but still, the hope was real . . . and before he left for Santo Rio, he kissed Laura Lee, secretly and long.

He rode down the valley, and the Comanche was gone; but staked at the mouth of the valley was a lance, and on it were the three feathers of peace . . . the iron word of Ten Bears. As he passed out of the valley's opening and headed south, he thought that if it could be . . . the life in this valley with Laura Lee . . . with Lone . . . with his kin . . . it would be the bloody hand of Ten Bears that gave it; the brutal, savage Ten Bears. But who could say what a savage was . . . maybe the double-tongues with their smooth manners and sly ways were the savages after all.

Part 4

Chapter 21

Kelly, the bartender, swatted bottle flies in the Lost Lady saloon. Sweat dripped from the end of his nose and down his pock-marked face. He cursed the stifling noontime heat; the blazing sun that blinded the eye outside the bat wings at the door . . . and the monotony of it all.

Ten Spot, frayed cuffs and pencil-dandy mustache, dealt five-card stud at the corner table, his only customers a rundown cowboy and a seedy Mex vaquero.

"Possible straight," Ten Spot monotoned as the cards slapped.

"Nickel ante," Kelly sneered under his breath and splattered a bottle-green fly lit on the bar.

"Goddamned tinhorn," he muttered loud enough for Ten Spot to hear . . . but the gambler didn't look up. Kelly had seen REAL gamblers in New Orleans . . . before he had to leave.

Rose came out of a bedroom at the back, yawning and snatching a comb through bed-frowzed hair.

"To hell with it," she said and tossed the comb on a table. She rapped the bar, and Kelly slid a glass and bottle of Red Dog expertly to her hand.

"How much'd he have?" Kelly asked.

Rose disdained the glass and took a huge swallow from the bottle. She shuddered. "Two dollars, twenty cents," and she slapped the money on the bar. Her eyes held the hard, shiny look of women fresh from the love bed, and her mouth was smeared and mottled.

"Crap," Kelly said as he retrieved the money and spat on the floor.

Rose poured a three-finger drink in the glass to sip more leisurely. "Well," she drawled philosophically, "I ain't a young heifer no more. I might ought to paid him." She looked dreamily at the bottles behind the bar. She wasn't . . . young, that is. Her hair was supposed to be red; the label on the bottle had proclaimed that desired result . . . but it was orange where it was not streaked with gray. Her face sagged from the years and sin, and her huge breasts were hung precariously in a mammoth halter. There was no competition in Santo Rio. The last stop for Rose.

Rose was like Santo Rio, dying in the sun; used only by desperate men or lost pilgrims stumbling quickly through; refugees from places they couldn't go back to . . . watching the clock tick away the time. The end of the line; a good horse jump over Texas ground to the Rio Grande.

Josey walked the roan past the Majestic Hotel, presumptuous in the name of a faded sign; a one-story 'dobe with a sagging wooden porch. There was a horse hitched in front, and he ran his eyes over its lines and its rigging. The sorrel was too good for the average cowboy, the lines too clean . . . legs too long. The rigging was light. There were only two other horses in town, and they stood, tails whipped between their legs by the wind, hitch-racked before the Lost Lady saloon.

He passed the General Merchandise store and slip-knotted the reins of the roan on the hitch rail beside the two horses. They were cow ponies, rigged with roping saddles. Nobody showed on the street. Santo Rio was a night town, if anything; a border town where the gentry did their moving by night.

When Josey Wales stepped into the Lost Lady, Rose moved instinctively farther back along the bar. She had seen Bill Longley and Jim Taylor, once, at Bryan, Texas . . . but they looked tame beside this'un. A lobo. Tied-down .44's and he stepped too quickly out of the door's sunlight behind him, scanned the room, then walked directly by Rose to a place at the bar's end, so that the room and door were in his line of vision.

Hat low as he passed, hard black eyes that briefly caught Rose with a flat look . . . and thunder! . . . that scar, brutal and deep across the cheek. Rose felt the hair on her neck rise stiff and tingly. The cowboy and the vaquero twisted in their chairs to watch him, then hastily turned back to their cards as Josey took his place.

Kelly signified his tolerance of all humanity by placing both hands on the bar. Ten Spot appeared not to notice . . . he was dealing.

"Whiskey?" Kelly asked.

"Beer, I reckin," Josey said casually, and Kelly drew

the beer, dark and foaming, and placed the schooner before him. Josey laid down a double eagle, and Kelly picked it up and turned it in his hand.

"The beer ain't but a nickel," he said apologetically.

"Well," Josey drawled, "reckin ye can give the boys at the table a couple bottles o' thet pizen . . . the lady here might want somethin', and have one ye'self."

"Well, now," Kelly's face brightened, "mighty decent of you, mister." The feller was high roller . . . added class, easy come, easy go . . . it was with them fellers.

"Thankee, mister," Rose murmured.

And from the card table the cowboy turned to wave a friendly thanks, and the vaquero touched his sombrero. "*Gracias, señor.*" Ten Spot flickered his eyes toward Josey and nodded.

Josey sipped the lukewarm beer, "I'm lookin' fer ropin' hands. I got a spread hunnerd miles north an' . . ."

The vaquero rose from his chair and walked to the bar. "*Señor,*" he said politely, "my *compadre,*" he indicated the cowboy who had stood up, "and myself are good with the cattle and we . . ." he laughed musically, white teeth flashing under the curling black mustache, "are a little . . . as you say, down on the luck." The vaquero extended his hand to Josey, "My name, *señor,* is Chato Olivares and this," he indicated the lean cowboy who came forward, "is *Señor* Travis Cobb."

Josey shook hands with first the vaquero and then the cowboy. "Proud t'strike up with ye," he said. He judged both of them to be in their middle forties, gray streaking the black hair of the Mexican and fading the bleached, sparse hair of the cowboy. Their clothes had seen hard wear, and their boots were heel-worn and scuffed. The faded gray eyes of Travis Cobb were inscrutable, as was the twinkling light of half humor in the black eyes of Chato.

They both wore a single pistol, sagging at the hip, but their hands were calloused from rope burns; working hands of cowboys. Josey made a snap decision.

"Fifty dollars a month and found," he said.

"Sold," drawled Travis Cobb, and his weathered face crinkled in a grin, "You could'a got me and Chato fer the found. Cain't wait to git my belly roundst some solid bunkhouse chow." He rubbed his hands in anticipation. Josey counted five double eagles on the bar.

"First month advance," he said. Chato and Travis stared unbelieving at the gold coins.

"*Hola!*" Chato breathed.

"Wal, now," Travis Cobb drawled, " 'fore I spend all of mine on sech foolishness as boots and britches, I'm a-goin' to buck the tiger agin."

Chato followed the cowboy back to the corner table . . . and Ten Spot shuffled the deck.

Kelly was in an expansive mood. He slid another schooner of beer, unasked, before Josey, and Rose moved closer to him at the bar. Kelly had noticed the scar-faced stranger had not given his name when he shook hands, but this was not unusual in Texas. It was accepted, and considered, to say the least, highly impolite to ask a gent his name.

"Well," Kelly said heartily, "rancher, huh, I'd never have thought . . ." he paused in midsentence. His eyes had strayed to a piece of paper on the shelf below the bar. He choked and his face turned red. His hands fluttered down for the paper, and he placed it on the bar.

"I ain't . . . it ain't none of my business, stranger. I

ain't never posted one of these things. Bounty hunter
. . . called hisself a special deputy . . . left it in here,
not an hour ago."

Josey looked down at the paper and saw himself
staring back from the picture. It was a good likeness
drawn by an artist's hand. The Confederate hat . . . the
black eyes and mustache . . . the deep scar; all made it
unmistakable. The print below the picture told his history and ended with: EXTREMELY QUICK AND ACCU-
RATE WITH PISTOLS. WILL NOT SURRENDER. DO NOT
ATTEMPT TO DISARM. WANTED DEAD: $7,500 REWARD.
The name JOSEY WALES stood out in bold letters.

Rose had moved close to read. Now she edged away
from the bar. Josey looked up. There was no mistaking the man who had stepped through the door. His
garb was dandy leather; tall and lean-hipped; and his
holster was tied low on his right leg. Josey took one
look and held it steady, locked in challenge with the
pale, almost colorless eyes. He was a professional pistolman . . . and he obviously knew his trade.

Josey took a half step from the bar, and his body
slid into the half crouch. Rose had stumbled backward
into a table, and she half leaned, half stood, in a frozen position. Kelly had his back against the bottles,
and Ten Spot, Chato, and Travis Cobb were turned,
motionless, in their chairs. The old Seth Thomas
clock, pride of Santo Rio, ticked loud in the room.
Wind whined around the corner of the building and
whipped a miniature dust cycle under the bat-wing
door. The bounty hunter's speech was expressionless.

"You'd be Josey Wales."

"I reckin," Josey's tone was deceptively casual.

"You're wanted, Wales," he said.

"Reckin I'm right popular," Josey's mouth twitched
with sardonic humor.

The silence fell on them again. The buzzing of a fly sounded huge in the room. The bounty hunter's eyes wavered before those of Josey Wales, and Josey almost whispered, "It ain't necessary, son, ye can leave . . . and ride."

The eyes wavered more wildly, and suddenly he whirled and bolted through the bat wings into the street.

Everyone came to life at once . . . except Josey Wales. He stood in the same position, as Kelly exclaimed and Rose plumped down in a chair and wiped her face with her skirts. The moment of relief came quickly to an end. The bounty hunter stepped back into the saloon. His face was ashen, and his eyes were bitter.

"I had to come back," he said with surprising calm.

"I know," Josey said. He knew, once a pistolman was broken, he was walking dead; the nerve gone and reputation shattered. He wouldn't last past the story of his breaking, which would always go ahead of him wherever he went.

Now the bounty hunter's hand swept for his holster, sure and fluid. He was fast. He cleared leather as a .44 slug caught him low in the chest, and he hammered two shots into the floor of the saloon. His body curved in, like a flower closing for the night, and he slid slowly to the floor.

Josey Wales stood, feet wide apart, smoke curling from the barrel of the pistol in his right hand. And in that smoke, he saw with bitter acceptance . . . there would be no new life for Josey Wales.

He left him there, face down on the floor, after arranging with Ten Spot and Kelly for his burial . . . and their split of the dead man's meager wealth in payment for the task. It was the rough decency and justice of Texas.

"I'll read over him," Ten Spot promised in his cold voice, and Josey, Chato, and Travis Cobb forked their broncs north, toward the Crooked River Ranch; past the spot where the bounty hunter would be buried, nameless; but with the simple cross to mark another violent death on the wild, windy plains of West Texas.

Chapter 22

Chato Olivares and Travis Cobb took to the Crooked River Ranch, as Lone said, "like wild hawgs to a swamp waller." They were good ropers and reckless riders . . . and enthusiastic eaters at Grandma Sarah's table. The two riders lived in the comfortable bunkhouse but took their meals in the kitchen of the main house with everybody else. Grandma Sarah was flustered, then pleased at the courtly, Old World manner of Chato Olivares. She thanked the Lord for it in one of her open Sunday prayer-sermons, adding that "sich manners brangs us to notice of civilization, which some othern's hereabouts might try doin'."

Josey and Lone rode with the cowboys, searching the cows out of brush-choked arroyos and back into the valley. It was hard, sweating work, rising before dawn and moving cattle until dark. They built a fan-shaped corral in one of the arroyos and narrowed down the high fencing until only a single cow could come through the chute. Here, in the chute, they slapped the Crooked River Brand of the Comanche sign to their hides and turned them loose, snorting and bawling, back into the valley.

Only yearlings and mavericks had to be roped and thrown, and Chato and Travis were experts with their long loops. They disdained "dallying"; the technique, after roping the cow, of whipping the rope in a tripping motion about the cow's legs. They were two expert, prideful workmen at their trade.

Josey lingered on through the long summer months. He knew he should have left already . . . before the men came riding for him; before those who loved him were forced into violence because of their loyalty. He silently cursed his own weakness in staying . . . but he put off the leaving . . . savoring the hard work, the lounging with the cowboys after the day's work ended; even the Sunday "services"; the peacefulness of summer Sunday afternoons, when he walked with Laura Lee on the banks of the creek and beside the waterfall. They kissed and held hands, and made love in the shadows of the willows, and Laura Lee's face shone with a happiness that bubbled in her eyes, and like all women . . . she made plans. Josey Wales grew quieter in his guilt; in his sin of staying where he should not stay. He could not tell her.

Josey gradually pushed Lone to the ramrod position of the ranch and took to riding more alone, leaving it to Lone to direct the work. He sent Travis Cobb east on a week's ride in search of border ranches for news of trail herding; where they might bunch their cattle with others . . . in the spring . . . for the drive north. Travis returned and brought good news of the Good-night-Loving Trail through New Mexico Territory that bypassed Kansas and ended at Denver.

Once, at supper, Josey had almost told them, when Grandma Sarah abruptly proposed, before everyone, that Josey accept a fourth interest in the ranch. "It ain't nothin' but right," she had said.

Josey had looked around the table and shook his head, "I'd ruther ye give any part of mine to Lone . . . he's gittin' old . . . maybe the ol' Cherokee needs a place to set in the sun."

Little Moonlight had laughed . . . she had under-stood . . . and stood up at the table and boldly ran her hand over a suspiciously growing mound of her shapely belly, "Old . . . Ha!" Everybody joined in the laughter except Grandma Sarah.

"They's goin' to be some marryin' up takin' place 'round here . . . with several folks I know."

Laura Lee had blushed red and shyly looked at Josey . . . and everybody laughed again.

Late summer faded softly, and the first cool nip touched the edge of the wind, putting the early glow of gold on the cottonwood trees along the creek. Josey Wales knew the word had gone back from the border . . . from Santo Rio . . . and he knew he had stayed too long.

It was Grandma Sarah who gave him the opening. At supper she complained of the need for supplies, and Josey said, too quickly, "I'll go." And across the glow of tallow candles his eyes met Lone's. The Cherokee knew . . . but he said nothing.

He saddled up in the early morning light, and the smell of fall was on the wind. He was taking Chato with him, and two packhorses . . . but only Chato and the horses would return. Lone came to the corral and watched him cinch the saddle down and place the heavy roll . . . a roll for long travel . . . behind the cantle.

Josey turned to the Indian and pressed a bag of gold coins in his hand. He passed it off lightly, "Thet ain't none o' mine . . . got mine right here," and he patted a saddlebag, "Thet there's yore'n, it was . . . Jamie's part, so . . . it's yore'n now. He'd a'wanted it used fer . . . the folks." They gripped hands in the dim light, and the tall Cherokee didn't speak.

"Tell Little Moonlight," Josey began, ". . . ah, hell, I'll be ridin' back this way and name thet young'un ye got comin'." They both knew he wouldn't, and Lone pulled away. He stumbled on his way to the 'dobe in the cedars.

Chato was mounted and leading the packhorses out of the yard when Josey saw Laura Lee. She came from the kitchen, shy in her nightgown, and shyer still, raised her face to him. He kissed her for a long time.

"This time," she whispered in his ear, "ye tell them in town to send the first preacher man up here thet comes ridin' through."

Josey looked down at her, "I'll tell 'em, Laura Lee."

He had ridden from the yard when he stopped and turned in the saddle. She was still standing as he had left her, the long hair about her shoulders. He called out, "Laura Lee, don't fergit what I told ye . . . thet time . . . about ye being the purtiest gal in Texas."

"I won't forget," she said softly.

Far down the trail of the valley he looked back and saw her still, at the edge of the yard, and the tiny figure of Grandma Sarah was close by her. On a knoll, off to the side, he saw Lone watching . . . the old cavalry hat on his head . . . and he thought he saw Little Moonlight, beside him, lift her hand and wave . . . but he couldn't be sure . . . the wind smarted his eyes and watered his vision so that he could see none of them anymore.

Chapter 23

Josey and Chato night-camped ten miles out of
Santo Rio and rode into town in late morning of the
following day. Chato had been subdued on the trip,
his usual good humor giving way to long periods of
silence that matched Josey's. They had not spoken of
Josey's leaving, but Chato knew the reputation of the
outlaw and was wise in the ways of the border. The
news of the Santo Rio killing could not have been kept
secret . . . there was nothing for a gunfighter to do but
move on. Chato dreaded the parting.

They hitched and loaded the supplies on the packhorses in front of the General Mercantile. Meal and
flour, sugar and coffee, bacon and beans . . . sacksful
of fancies. As they filled the last sack to be strapped on
the horse, Josey placed a lady's yellow straw hat with
flowing ribbon on top. He looked across the horse's

back at Chato, "It's fer Laura Lee. Ye tell her . . ." he let the sentence die.

Chato looked at the ground, "I understand, *señor*," he mumbled, "I shall tell her."

"Well," Josey said with an air of finality, "let's git a drink."

They left their horses before the store and walked to the Lost Lady. He would have the drink with Chato, and Chato would head north with the packhorses, back to the ranch. Josey Wales would cross the Rio Grande.

Ten Spot was playing solitaire at the corner table when they came in. Josey and Chato walked past two men at the bar having drinks and took up their places at the end. Rose was seated at a table, alone, and she cast a warning glance at Josey as he tossed her a greeting, "Mornin', Miss Rose . . .," and was instantly on his guard.

The atmosphere was strained and tense. Kelly brought the beer to them, but his face was white and drawn. He mopped the bar vigorously in front of Chato and Josey and under his breath he whispered, "Pinkerton man, and something called a Texas Ranger . . . lookin' for you." Chato stiffened and his smile faded. Josey lifted the schooner of beer to his lips, and over the rim he studied the two men.

They were talking together in low tones. Both were big men, but where the one wore a derby hat and Eastern suit, the other wore a battered cowboy hat that proved the quality of Mr. Stetson's work. His face was weathered by the wind, and his clothes were the garb of any cowboy. They both wore pistols on their hips, and a sawed-off shotgun was lying before them on the bar. They were professional policemen, though from two separate worlds.

Kelly was flicking specks from the bar, finding heretofore unseen spots and industriously rubbing the bar cloth at them. He was between the outlaw at one end of the bar and the lawmen at the other. Kelly didn't like his position. Now he scowled with a bleary look at a spot near Josey and attacked it with the cloth.

"Pinkerton man's federal," he whispered to Josey, "cowboy feller is Texas . . . fer Gawd's sake, man!" and he moved away, back up the bar, flicking dust from bottles. Chato slid a quick look at Josey as he sipped his beer. The men stopped their low talk and now looked down the bar, frankly and openly, at Josey and Chato.

The Ranger spoke into the heavy silence, and his tone was calm and drawling, "We're law officers, and we're looking for Josey Wales." There was no hint of fear in either of the lawmen's faces.

Chato, on Josey's left, stepped carefully away from the bar, and his tone was thinly polite, "The shotgun, *señores*, stays on the bar."

Josey didn't take his eyes from the men, but to Chato, in a voice that carried over the room, he said, "T'ain't yore call, Chato. Ye're paid to ride . . . reckin thet's what ye'd better be doin'."

The polite voice of Chato answered him, "*No comprendo*. I ride . . . and fight, for the brand. It is my honor, *señor*."

Not a breath was drawn, not a hand moved, except Ten Spot, who dealt his solitaire, seemingly oblivious of it all. Ten Spot laid a black eight on a black nine . . . it was the only way to beat the hand. From the corner table, his voice was thin and casual, as though remarking on the weather, "I seen Josey Wales shot down in Monterrey, seven . . . maybe eight weeks ago.

Me and Rose was takin' a little *paseo* down that way
. . . seen him take on five pistoleros. He got three of
'em before they cut him down. Ask Rose."

For the first time since he began speaking, Ten Spot
looked up and addressed himself to Josey, "I was in-
tending to tell you about it, Mr. Wells . . . next time
you came in. It was a real hoolihan . . ." and then to
the lawmen, "This is Mr. Wells, a rancher north of
here." Ten Spot broke the deck and started a new
shuffle.

Rose's voice was high and squeaky, "I was goin' to
tell you 'bout it, Mr. Wells, you remember, last time
you was in here, we was . . . uh, discussing that outlaw."

Behind the bar Kelly was nodding vigorously with
encouragement to the speakers. Neither Josey nor
Chato spoke . . . nor did they move. The lawmen
talked in low tones to each other. The Ranger looked
at Ten Spot, "Will you sign an affidavit to that?" he
asked.

"Yep," Ten Spot said and laid a red deuce on a red
trey.

"And you, Miss . . . er . . . Rose?" the Ranger looked
at Rose.

"Why shore," Rose said, "whatever that is," and she
took a healthy slug from a bottle of Red Dog.

The Pinkerton man took paper and pencil from his
coat and wrote vigorously at the bar.

"Here," he said and handed the pencil to Ten Spot,
who came forward and signed his name. The Pinkerton man looked at the signature and frowned, "Your
name is . . . Wilbur Beauregard Francis Willingham?"
he asked incredulously.

Ten Spot drew himself up to full height in his tattered frock coat. "It is, suh," he said stiffly, "of the Virginia Willinghams. I trust the name does not offend you, suh."

"Oh, no offense, no offense," the Pinkerton man said hastily.

Ten Spot, formally and stiffly, inclined his body in a slight bow. Rose took the pencil and brushed imaginary dust from the paper, hesitated, and brushed again, while her face reddened.

"The lady," Ten Spot said brusquely, "broke her reading glasses, unfortunately, while we were in Monterrey. Under the circumstances, if you will accept a simple mark from her, I will witness her signature."

"We'll accept it," the Ranger said dryly.

Rose laboriously made her mark and walked with whiskey dignity back to her table.

The Pinkerton man looked at the paper, folded it, and stuck it in his breast pocket. "Well . . ." he said uncertainly to the Ranger, "I guess that's it."

The Texas Ranger looked at the ceiling with a calculating eye, like he was counting the roof poles. "I reckon," he said, "there's about five thousand wanted men this year, in Texas. Cain't git 'em all . . . ner would want to. We jest come out of a War, and they's bound to be tore-up ground . . . and men . . . where a herd's stampeded. Way I figger it, what's GOOD, depends on whose a-sayin' it. What's good back east where them politicians is at . . . might not be good fer Texas. Texas is a-goin' to git straightened out . . . it'll take good men . . . Texas style o' good . . . meaning tough and straight . . . to do it. Takes iron to beat iron." He sighed as he turned toward the door, thinking of the long, dusty ride ahead.

"If yore're comin' back this way, stop in," Kelly invited.

The Ranger looked meaningfully, not at Kelly, but at Josey Wales. "Reckon we won't be back," he said, and with a wave of his hand he was gone.

For the first time in nine years Josey Wales was stunned. Where a moment before, his future was the grim, tedious trail of outlawry . . . of leaving those he had come to love . . . the valley he had so bitterly left behind; now it was life, a new life, that staggered his thinking and his emotions. Done, here in a saloon; in a run-down, sour-smelling saloon by people no one would look twice at on the streets of the cities; by men, among men . . . as Ten Bears had said.

Chato laughed and slapped him on the back. Kelly, completely contrary to his practice, set up the house. Ten Spot, thin smile and dead eyes, was shaking his hand, and Rose propped a heavy breast on his shoulder and kissed him enthusiastically.

Josey walked to the door, followed by the jingling spurs of Chato . . . like a man in a dream. He paused and looked back at these who would be judged as derelicts by those wont to judge. "My friends," he said, "when ye can find a preacher, bring 'em to the ranch. Miss Rose, ye'll stand up with my bride, and Ten Spot, ye and Kelly will stand with me. Ye'll come, 'er me and Chato will come and git ye."

Ten Spot, Rose, and Kelly watched from the saloon door as the two riders headed north. Suddenly they saw the riders spur their mounts. They whipped their pistols from holsters and shot into the air . . . and floating back came the wild yells of exuberant Texans . . . exuberance . . . and a lust for life.

"We'll git the padre from across the river," Kelly shouted. But the outlaw and the vaquero were too far away . . . and too noisy to hear.

Ten Spot slipped a sidelong glance at Rose, "I'll buy you a drink, Rose," he invited . . . and at her lifted eyebrow, he smiled, "No obligation . . . this one is for Texas."

Chapter 24

They came a week later; Ten Spot, Rose, and Kelly. They brought the padre; a fiddlin' man; two extra vaqueros, one of whom brought his guitar; and three sloe-eyed *señoritas*, who had come "good timin'" across the river. They came loaded down with Texas gifts, like a pair of boots for Laura Lee, bottles of red-eye, kegs of beer, and a ribbon for Grandma Sarah's hair. They came ready . . . rootin', tootin', Texas-style . . . for a wedding, and got two of them; Josey and Laura Lee, Lone and Little Moonlight.

Rose was resplendent as Maid of Honor in a sequined gold dress with tassels that shimmied as she walked. The padre frowned briefly at Little Moonlight's stomach, but he sighed and resigned himself; it was the way of Texas. Little Moonlight enjoyed the white man's ceremony immensely, and as instructed, shouted "Shore!" when asked to be Lone's wife.

The celebration lasted a number of days, in Texas tradition, until the fiddler's hands were too stiff to pull the bow . . . and the liquor ran out.

The wedding wasn't decently over and gone, before an almond-eyed girl was born to Little Moonlight . . . and Lone. Grandma Sarah fussed over the baby and rendered sermon-prayers to Laura Lee and Josey that sich was pleasing to the eyes of God.

The falls and the springs came, and Ten Bears rested and made medicine with his people, in their way. Until the autumn when Ten Bears and the Comanche came no more. The word of iron had been true. And Josey thought of it . . . what might have been . . . if men like the Ranger could have settled with Ten Bears . . . as he had. The thought came back mostly in the haunting, smoky haze of Indian Summer . . . each fall, when the gold and red touched the valley, in remembrance of the Comanche.

The firstborn to Josey and Laura Lee was a boy; blue-eyed and blond, and now Grandma Sarah relaxed to grow old in the contentment that the seed was replenished in the land. They did not name the baby boy after his father; Josey Wales insisted. And so they called him Jamie.

THE VENGEANCE TRAIL
OF JOSEY WALES

To the Apache

Chapter 1

Pablo Gonzales felt the change. That winter morning of
1868, he squatted against the adobe wall of the Lost Lady
Saloon and contemplated his bare feet, and waited out the
hours until sundown.

At sundown, Santo Rio reeled drunkenly alive, and men
came and drank and whored. In their leaving, sometimes
they tossed coins to this one-armed peon, who bowed and
smiled and swept his straw hat in the dust. Sometimes
they kicked him and laughed when he cowered on the
ground.

Pablo felt no bitterness. He had been born to peonage,
and now useless to grip the hoe or plow, he accepted his
position of scavenger without question.

But the sharpened instinct for survival still lived in Pablo Gonzales—nature's compensation to the unlanded peon.

And so he first felt the sound, rather than heard. He raised his eyes, past the Mexican children playing in the street, past the Majestic Hotel, and followed the rutted road where it dipped into the Rio Grande and dissipated aimlessly in the broken wastes of Mexico on the other side.

And now he heard it clearly, the measured tramp of many horses and the sound of saddles creaking, and the ominous jingling spurs that always accompanied the approach of Rurales.

The sun still shone, but the slanting rays turned metallic and steel-glinted to Pablo Gonzales. So it always shone on the presence of Rurales.

Pablo Gonzales' nostrils quivered at the musty smell of death. A woman's short laugh burst from the saloon. Pablo did not hear. He had vanished.

He did not seek the 'dobe hovels, but ran for open country with its mesquite and cholla brush. In his passing, he whistled a soft warning, and the children, old-cunning through their station of birth, disappeared. A dog tucked his tail, whimpering to his hiding.

The Texas border town of Santo Rio lay unsuspecting in its morning stupor as it received Capitan Jesus Escobedo and half a hundred of his Rurales.

Hard-drinking vaqueros had made a long night for Kelly, the bartender of the Lost Lady Saloon. He moved in sour silence, mopping the stinking puddles from tables, straightening the overturned chairs.

It was Rose, the lady-in-waiting, who had laughed, warmed by the first drink of the day and remembering the free-spending vaqueros.

The Rurales were hitching their horses when Kelly saw

them. The color drained from his face and left the pock-marks shadowing his whiteness.

"Rurales!" he whispered hoarsely. He turned to Rose at the bar. "Rurales!" he repeated dumbly.

Now they could hear them, shouting and laughing, flinging themselves from their horses in the peculiar wild abandon that marked their habits.

"God! Oh God!" Rose breathed.

Kelly stared stupidly at her. "Where's Ten Spot?"

"He's at the hotel," Rose whispered.

"Git," Kelly's whisper was hoarse, "git to the back room. Stay hid, tell Melina to stay hid. God's sake, stay hid."

Rose was already running on tiptoe, and closed the heavy door of the back room behind her.

They came jostling through the batwing doors of the Lost Lady, and their laughter died as they entered. Kelly placed himself behind the bar and smiled, a sickly slash of strained lips.

Still they came, circling to stand against the walls. Now they tore the batwings from the doorway and laughed with childish hysteria as they flung them across the saloon.

Some wore sombreros low, to the eyes; others pushed them back, dangling on cords behind hairy necks. They smiled fixedly at Kelly, as with a private joke they intended soon to reveal; brutish smiles, fanging teeth beneath drooping mustaches, matted beards.

Their short jackets and flared chaparrals were filthy with trail dust. Kelly felt a leap of horror at the dried blood on their clothing. Huge pistolas were shoved into belts; long knives hung on their hips, and on some, about their necks. They brought their rifles into the saloon with them.

Two rows deep, they stood around the wall and crowded to the bar. Then they parted for their Capitan.

His appearance brought a sudden rush of warmth to

Kelly, as one locked in a room with insane people might feel upon seeing a calm administrator of authority come to set matters right.

Capitan Jesus Escobedo wore the official army cap, which in itself spoke of order. He was cleanly shaved, with a thin mustache and stylish sideburns, and wore a saber buckled around a trim waist.

"Buenos dias, señor," he smiled politely over the bar at Kelly and extended his hand. Kelly grabbed it with enthusiasm.

"Bane-us dee-ass," Kelly fairly shouted, and felt only the slightest doubt at the glitter of the Capitan's eyes. But then Kelly did not know Captain Jesus Escobedo. The doubt grew uncomfortably with the ripple of giggles that circled the room.

Capitan Jesus Escobedo was an educated man. Beyond that, he was quite certain that his lineage was blooded with royal aristocracy. Perhaps that is why he had sided with Maximilian, the comic-tragic "Emperor of Mexico" appointed by Napoleon III.

Capitan Escobedo had served under the incredibly cruel Colonel François Achille Dupin, who relished warfare on the helpless and devised methods to satisfy his appetite.

"When you kill a Mexican, that is the end of him," Dupin had instructed his officers, "but when you cut off an arm or a leg, or blind his eyes with the hot iron, then he is thrown upon the charity of his friends. This requires more Mexicans to feed him. Those who raise corn cannot make soldiers. Maim or blind all prisoners." And so they did, leaving a monument of living carnage throughout all of northern Mexico.

Only last year, Maximilian had stupidly stood before the firing squad on El Cerro de las Campanas, The Hill of the Bells, and ended the dream of Napoleon the Little; but not that of Capitan Jesus Escobedo.

His uncle, General Mariano Escobedo, had served the Indian, Benito Juarez, and had in fact accepted the surrender of the foolish Austrian. And so Capitan Jesus Escobedo's promotion required a mere shrug of the shoulders: he was appointed to command a district; after all, aristocracy must take care of its own. What the little Indian in faraway Ciudad de Mexico did not know, of course, would cause him no ill.

In truth, Capitan Escobedo hated Benito Juarez, as he hated all Indians. He despised all peons and saw unthinkable chaos as a result of Juarez' announced plan to give land to them.

Through his service to Dupin, a slumbering sadism was awakened as he practiced the crippling art on screaming victims. It grew sharp-edged, as he became more imaginative. Capitan Jesus Escobedo was insane, but with a cunning and a polish of exquisite sadism that made him lend rationality to his acts, as it is with all such men of authority.

His half-wild Rurales riders were his absolute power over the district, and to control such power—he shrugged at the thought—it was necessary to "loosen the leashes . . . on occasion."

Now he pulled a handkerchief from his pocket and delicately dabbed at his forehead. Kelly watched him hungrily.

"My soldados," he said, "have ridden far, señor. Perhaps . . . ," he paused and looked around the room, "perhaps a drink for each of them before we resume our journey?" He smiled quickly with brilliant teeth. "We shall pay—in gold, of course."

"Why shore—shore!" Kelly said heartily, and set bottles of Red Dog on the bar. Eager hands passed the bottles to others around the room. Kelly turned and placed more bottles, and then hesitantly, still more. The hands reached for more. Kelly looked at the Capitan. He was still smiling.

"I am afraid, señor," he purred softly, "my riders are so like the niños, the children. They will require your benevolence. Por favor!"

Kelly emptied his shelves, but now his hands shook. He watched the brute faces upturning the raw liquor, and he shuddered while his mind raced ahead. Kelly had been in tight places before. The Capitan was pouring himself a drink.

"Well! Well!" Kelly exclaimed with false humor, "your boys drink like the U.S. Cavalry patrol boys that come by. They'll be glad to hear you boys paid a visit to the U.S.A." Kelly emphasized "U.S.A."

The Capitan raised an eyebrow as he poured another drink. His face furrowed in puzzlement: "Cavalry patrol?" he questioned politely. "But, mi amigo, you have no cavalry patrol on the border, and . . . ," a recovering smile broke his face, "in truth, Texas is not in the United States —so we have been officially informed. You are—is it not the Confederacy?" he asked politely.

"Oh no," Kelly laughed. "Ain't you heard? The war is over. Texas is back in the U.S.A. all right—yessir, the U.S.A."

The Capitan downed his drink and poured another. A chair crashed in the saloon and there was loud cursing. "Hola!" a Rurale shouted, "Musica!"

A rider leaped on a table and strummed a guitar. Booted feet stomped the floor and a bottle shattered against the wall. The Capitan seemed not to hear any of it. Mock doubt crossed his face as he looked at Kelly, "It's unthinkable, señor. No, I will not believe you, you are making the joke, señor." His tongue was thickening, and he wagged his head in remorse. "To make light of poor soldados who have been fighting the Apache . . ." The Capitan shook his head sadly.

"No!" Kelly said earnestly. He raised his voice to be heard above the growing noise, "No, really . . ."

Loud arguing and cursing rose above the din. Capitan Escobedo watched a bearded Rurale break a bottle in the face of another, sprawling him on the floor. There was uproarious laughter.

He turned to Kelly, "You comprendes, señor? My men are fretful, disappointed. The Apache camp had only the bitches, the women—and the bastardos, niños, the children. The bucks were not there. And while my superiors pay a hundred pesos for the scalp of the Apache buck, they pay only fifty for the bitch, twenty-five for the bastardos." The Capitan pointed toward the milling, stomping Rurales. "See, señor, the picayune hair at their belts; it is enough to disappoint the best soldado."

He leaned into Kelly's face and his eyes glittered with slyness. "Perhaps you have entertainment about, señor, for the temperamento of my poor soldados?"

Kelly was not a brave man. He saw the black hair bundles that dangled from the belts of the Rurales, the dark clots of bloodied ends where the scalp had been cut from the skull. They were from small heads—children's heads.

Kelly felt the strength drain downward, making his legs watery and uncontrollable. He knew quite suddenly that the Capitan was playing with him, and shortly would require more, much more amusement than the mere sight of Kelly withering in fear. If someone else could be the center of attention—not himself! Wildly, his mind raced; after all they *were* whores, Rose and Melina. His eyes sought the door to the back room.

The Capitan caught the movement of Kelly's eyes. "Ah!

amigo, you are a man of compassion." He clapped his hands and shouted, pointing to the door in the rear.

Kelly was overcome by his sin. He snatched bottles from beneath the bar and pushed them at the Capitan, "SEE!" he shouted, and stooped, coming up with more bottles, "SEE! LOOK!" He directed his shout toward the dozen Rurales rushing for the door. No one noticed him. They were almost to the door, when slowly, it opened.

It was Rose. She had dressed for the occasion, a scarlet dress with little glass sequins sewn on, picking up the light and flashing. It was tight-fitting, accentuating the broad full hips and rounding belly, the heavy breasts that pushed together in a huge snowy crevasse, straining over the low-cut front. It took attention away from the gray streaks in her orange dyed hair and the sag of jowls beneath the heavy make-up.

Silence dropped over the room. Rose calmly closed the door behind her. Her face was unnaturally white, but she smiled teasingly, threw her arms wide and walked on high heels toward the Capitan. Her large breasts bounced with a quivering promise as she walked and her buttocks fought the tight satin. Kelly groaned.

"Well, boys!" she shouted, and giggled, "Since I'm all there is, let's have a little drinkee and make fun."

The roar of the Rurales carried undertones of savage anticipation. Kelly saw a nerve jerk the face of Rose, but the smile stayed and there was no hesitation in her walk to the bar.

The Capitan pushed a bottle toward her. Rose tilted it for a long gulping drink. The Rurales crowded around, almost over her. One reached, and caressed the bareness of her breasts, running his hand down the deep cleavage, and gripping brutally.

"Grande!" he shouted, "grande mucho!" Rose shot a stream of Red Dog into his face. The Rurales roared.

"Un momento . . ." The Capitan looked archly at Rose. "What more might we find beyond your door, señorita?"

Rose raised the bottle again and spat whiskey into the Capitan's brilliant smile. He slapped her hard, bringing blood thinning from a corner of her mouth.

"The door!" he shouted. A mob of Rurales crashed the door.

She could not have been more than sixteen. Mexican-Indian peon, long black hair framing the little oval face and falling over the cheap white dress. She stumbled on high heels, whimpering as the hands pushed and pulled, wrapping in her hair, arching her body backward. A low "Ahhhhhhhhh!" swept the room.

"She jest stopped by!" Rose shouted. The Capitan threw back his head and laughed.

"She's the daughter of a *patrón*!" Rose screamed, but her voice carried no conviction.

"Música!" shouted the Capitan, and tilted his bottle. He was becoming drunk. The Rurales stomped their feet in slow cadence while a guitar picked up a rhythm.

Rose pushed away from the bar, but the Capitan signaled and two grinning Rurales wrapped their arms around her, pinning her between them. Pulling her large breasts from her dress, they laughed, bouncing them with their hands, twisting and squeezing while they watched Melina.

The slender girl made a valiant effort. First one and another grabbed her, jostling her in a wild dance around a circle of Rurales. The stomping thundered louder and faster.

She kept up the desperate dance, her small feet moving rapidly, even after the back of her dress had been torn away, and the front—and she danced entirely naked except for the stockings and the high-heeled dainty shoes.

Her body, small-tipped breasts turning upward, was lithe

and brown. She moved faster as the heavy boots picked up the rhythm. The circle became smaller. Her movements were a physical reflex to the sound. Her eyes were bright and hysterical.

The slender body rippled sensuously, perspiration sleeking the curves. The stomping became unbearable to the ear, and heavy breathing brought the air lustfully alive.

Her knees began to wobble. A huge Rurale snatched her from the grasp of another and jostled her furiously around the circle once, twice, lifting her in the air, gripping her body close, and he slid her down against his hardness. Her knees buckled.

He brought his big bulk down upon her, flattening her on the floor. "Ahhhhhhhh!" rose from the breathing. The circle closed in around them.

He moved his body in, between her legs. Pinning her hands to the floor, he brought his bearded face down and bit her mouth.

She twisted her slender hips left as he nakedly hunted for her. With a quick shove, he almost succeeded, but she twisted her hips to the right. With each movement a shout of "Ole!" went up. Again—and again.

She brought her knees up, placing her weight on her dainty feet and arching her hips in the air. Her eyes showed the desperation of her mistake as she felt him under her. The slender legs began to tremble as she tried to hold herself up; but slowly, slowly, she came down.

Suddenly the big hips of the Rurale plunged. She screamed, high-pitched, piercing the air, and her head flopped up from the floor, then back down, like a wounded animal. She screamed again . . . again; her body worked furiously in a frenzy of pain, twisting . . . up . . . down . . . arching . . . out of control as the Rurale plunged again, more rapidly now.

She was still screaming as he rolled from her and another plunged in his place—and another. The passion heat maddened the waiting Rurales. They argued and fought for position.

Now she lay limp, unconscious. First they twisted her arms to bring back movement to her body; after that, they touched lighted cigarillos to her to produce convulsive twitches at climactic moments . . . until the body would no longer twitch, as they held her in grotesque positions. The smell of burnt flesh hung in the air.

The Capitan watched, fascinated. Beads of sweat pimpled his face. Tears made thick trails in Rose's heavy make-up. She didn't sob. She didn't know she was crying. Kelly closed his eyes and sank to the floor behind the bar.

The flat bang of a small pistol split the closeness of the room, and the Rurales pushed back from one man, who staggered and fell.

Ten Spot stood in the door, a smoking derringer in his hand. He was hatless, neatly dressed in the black coat and ruffled shirt of a gambler. He saw the Capitan and coolly raised the ugly little pistol; but he never shot. A rifle cracked in the hands of a Rurale, knocking Ten Spot backward in a half flip. He spraddled in the doorway, legs jerking, and lay still.

Rose screamed. She lunged, grabbing a bottle and smashing it into the face of the nearest Rurale. Her mouth twisted maniacally. "You goddamned sonofabitches!" she screamed, and rushed at the Capitan, clawing his face.

They fell on her, angry dogs, mad with more than lust. But she fought. They dragged her to the middle of the room and ripped away the shiny satin dress. She screamed no more, but bit and kicked, and punched with her fists— and when her hands were pinned to the floor, she fought them with her feet. There was no laughter.

Her huge legs forced open, she took them, one by one, chewing at her breasts, as her body weakened. They kicked her face, smashed at her body until she lay unconscious. Her flesh no longer quivered.

The Capitan watched it all, intense, lips parted. He had them drag Kelly from behind the bar, and they shoved him down on the body of Rose.

"Perform for us, gringo!" The Capitan spat on him. Kelly cried. Tears rolled down the pouches of his face as he lay on Rose's naked body, his face inches from hers. His body shook with broken sobs.

Rose's left arm lay twisted unnaturally backward, almost pulled from its socket. She opened her eyes and looked into Kelly's. Her face, horribly mottled with blood, lips battered outward, broken teeth, twisted in the effort to speak.

"Rose . . . Rose . . . ," Kelly whispered brokenly, "I'm sorry, Rose . . . please . . . forgive me, Rose," and he buried his head in her breasts.

Rose raised a ponderous right arm and draped it uselessly around Kelly's neck. She whispered, "Pore Kelly . . . you didn't . . . deal it, podner . . . it jest . . . come up . . . busted flush . . ." Her eyes glazed and she sighed.

The Rurales had spent their passion. Now their thinking turned superstitiously on the death around them. A few crossed themselves. They grumbled and shuffled about, looking for whiskey, ready to quit and be gone.

The Capitan placed his boot on the chest of Ten Spot.

"This one breathes," he said. "Throw him over a horse. If he lives he must be executed."

Kelly stood dumbly in their midst and watched as they dragged Ten Spot to the horses.

"And now . . . ," the Capitan turned to face Kelly, once more the precise army officer, "we must see to you, mi amigo." He held his hand palm upward toward a Rurale, who placed a big pistola in his grip. He smiled and casually shot Kelly in the chest.

Kelly stumbled backward and sat down, his back against the bar. Blood spread over his shirt and small red bubbles puffed out from his lips. Then Kelly did a strange thing. He laughed. He laughed deep in his chest and brayed the laughter from his lips, and coughed, spewing a fog of pink mist, and laughed again.

The Capitan was astonished. He bent forward. "La Muerte, The Death—she is funny?"

Kelly shook his head and chuckled. "Naw," he coughed, "it ain't funny." He shook his head again, wobbling back and forth on his limp neck, and giggled at his secret joke. A red flood gushed over his chin. "Naw," he repeated, weaker now. The Capitan bent lower to hear. "But you are funny, my friend. I know . . . you see . . . yore hide is done measured. I ain't nothin', but . . . ," Kelly coughed, "but you . . . I'd ruther be right here where I am . . . than you. Ten Spot and Rose . . . they're friends of Josey Wales . . . JOSEY WALES!"

Kelly raised his eyes to the Capitan's and grinned horribly. "See ye in hell." And then, for once in his life, Kelly rose supremely to the occasion. He spat blood over the boots of the Capitan before he choked.

"Josey Wales?" the Capitan repeated. He watched his Rurales filing out to their mounts. Half a dozen rummaged behind the bar for whiskey. They brought out a box and turned it up on the bar, spilling the contents. It was all papers, and the papers were posters; the posters were all alike, of one man.

Capitan Escobedo looked down at the face staring up at him from the posters and felt the shock of vicious black eyes, glazed with hate, below the brim of a Confederate cavalry hat. A bone-deep bullet scar split the cheek above a black mustache. Beneath the picture he read:

JOSEY WALES: AGE 32, 5 FEET 9 INCHES, 160 POUNDS. BULLET SCAR HORIZONTAL RIGHT CHEEKBONE. DEEP KNIFE SCAR LEFT CORNER MOUTH.

PREVIOUSLY LISTED WANTED BY U.S. MILITARY AS EX-GUERRILLA LIEUTENANT SERVING WITH CAPTAIN WILLIAM "BLOODY BILL" ANDERSON IN MISSOURI.

WALES REFUSED AMNESTY AFTER THE SURRENDER, 1865. REGARD AS INSURRECTIONIST REBEL, BANK ROBBER, KNOWN KILLER OF AT LEAST 35 MEN.

ARMED AND DANGEROUS. EXTREMELY QUICK AND PROFICIENT WITH PISTOLS. DO NOT ATTEMPT TO DISARM. REPEAT, DO NOT ATTEMPT TO DISARM.

WANTED DEAD. REPEAT, WANTED DEAD. $7500 REWARD.

U.S. ARMY MILITARY DISTRICT: SOUTHWEST, GENERAL PHILIP SHERIDAN, COMMANDING.

The Capitan studied the posters for a long time. His Rurales were mounted, waiting.

The Missouri guerrillas were known to all military men, even in Mexico; the James boys, the Youngers, Bloody Bill Anderson, Josey Wales, Fletcher Taylor, Quantrill; unreal men of ferocious, blood-crazed reputations . . . unreal.

He rolled the posters together and folded them inside his coat, lifted a last drink from the bottle and led his riders, trailing dust, to the Rio Grande.

He shrugged. He could post the papers in the villages he passed on his way south. It would alert the known pistoleros; such a reward was dinero, mucho.

Still, as he crossed the Rio Grande, he could not restrain

the urge to look back over his shoulder. Curiously, the sun shone with a steel glint. The broken land behind him to the north harbored shadows, black and ominous.

Capitan Jesus Escobedo shivered unexpectedly and felt cold.

Chapter 2

The sun dropped in the west and streaked red ripples on the Rio Grande, blushing the cactus and mesquite, and fading them purple in the shadows. The first coyote yelped, far away. The wind pushed dust whirls spinning down the street of Santo Rio. No one ventured forth.

Inside the Lost Lady, Kelly sat piously dead, hands folded before him. His eyes stared at the twisted form of Melina. Even in death, she had a delicate grace, like a ballerina frozen in blood, head bowed in submission.

Pablo Gonzales came back. Like the dog that returns to where he has once been fed, Pablo came back to the Lost Lady. He hesitated on the threshold of this awesome death place, dropping his straw hat to cross himself. He almost fled.

But he was drawn to tiptoe past Kelly and Melina. To Rose.

Rose had put no price on her kindness to him, carelessly slipping the coins into his hand with a wink—or a curse—to hide the giving. And so Pablo came to stand above her, to beseech Our Lady of Guadalupe to speak in her behalf. He had no other gift.

He had been frightened. He should have warned her, and now he was ashamed. For the second time in her life, Rose, the whore, was asked for forgiveness.

Pablo prayed and looked down through the closing shadows at Rose's face. Her eyes were closed—beefy, beaten slits.

The eyes opened. Pablo stumbled backward, but the eyes burned at him, feverish, hypnotic, holding him. Her face twisted; then clearly, hoarsely, the whisper came. "Been holding out . . . Pablo. C'mere . . . close."

Pablo kneeled by her head. "Señorita . . ."

"Shut up!" she commanded. "Listen . . . I cain't hold . . . much longer. Go to Crooked River Ranch . . . Josey Wales . . . ye hear . . . Josey Wales?"

Pablo nodded, "Si, I hear, Señorita Rose."

Rose swallowed and closed her eyes for such a long time that Pablo thought her dead. The great body heaved. The eyes opened. "You tell Josey Wales . . . Ten Spot is alive . . . Ten Spot carried off by Capitan Jesus Escobedo . . . Escobedo . . . Ten Spot . . . ye hear?" She didn't wait for an answer. "Tell Josey I said . . . give you two hundred gold . . . ye'll git it . . . ye hear?"

"Si, but . . ."

She appeared not to listen. "Le' me hear you swear on some of them saints . . . you'll go . . . hurry up!"

Pablo hesitated. Her eyes fluttered open, fixing fiercely on his own. "Swear, goddammit!"

"Santo Pedro—Santo Juan—I will go," Pablo whispered hastily.

Rose sighed. "Tell Josey . . . ," her eyes closed, "tell Josey . . . I shore done tangled . . . the loop this time." Her big breasts quivered in a spasm that hardened the nipples. The spasm moved down her body in a wave, bunching and releasing her belly, jerking the bloody legs.

Pablo felt for the small wooden cross on the string about his neck and held it before her. Her eyes opened. She gazed at it for a long time. The understanding returned. Puffed lips tried to smile. "Thankee, son . . . but reckin . . . a snort of Red Dog . . . would do me more than likely . . . right smart more good." This time, the eyes did not close.

Pablo saw the life take leave, little flickers that grew weaker as it pulled away from the eyes, and left marbles staring at him. He felt her soul brush past him, hurrying, unleashed by the stubborn will. He heard it complain in the low moan of wind that cornered the building and whipped dust through the door. He ran.

He hid in the mule stables, far back behind the foulness of dung heaps. In the night he heard riders and much talk, but he did not move.

Pablo knew the bond of Rose and Ten Spot, and Josey Wales. He had seen him, big pistolas tied on his legs, the giant red horse.

Squatting beneath the batwing doors of the Lost Lady, he had heard Ten Spot the gambler and Rose the whore swear to the government hunters that they had seen Josey Wales killed in Mexico. They had signed the paper. This lie they gave to Josey Wales, as they gave Pablo the coins— for no reason. It was a great gift.

Bandido! The wise and learned clucked their tongues

and shook their heads in disgust. The stupid, plodding peons and their bandido heroes. Beyond comprehension.

But no national heroes for the peon. National meant government, and government meant the shifting, changing wars of politicians and generals. It was the peon who died. The peon who took his wife and children with him to the battlefields; they had nowhere else to go. The peon who died, or came back to the yoke and lived on short rations to pay for the war.

There were the hacendados, the patróns, who owned the land. But as with all men of wealth and power, they rode the tides unbattered, wiggling fish atop the currents. The hacendado paid his tithe to the victor.

For the soldados who crisscrossed his baronage, there were more fundamental appetites to appease. He offered the peons' women for fandangos. The green, unbudded Indian girls for the soldado who sought pain in others with his lust. The ripening, flowered bodies of older girls with their popping breasts and rounding hips for the connoisseur of pure pleasure. The hacendado kept his land.

There was the Church. But the priests and bishops of the Church bureaucracy ate and drank with the hacendados and the generals—and owned countless miles of land, farmed by the peon as tribute to the Church.

The Church had backed Maximilian against the little Indian, Benito Juarez; and the Church told the peon to expect his reward in heaven.

The peon attended the rituals. He sought the supreme unction at death and the blessing at birth; but he prayed, now, to the Santos, the Saints, not the priests, to intercede for his soul with God.

His strength was deceiving, was the peon's. The land he did not own, but farmed, and so loved it the more. Not with a possessive love, nor love of profit, but for what it was—his life.

And so his strength and stubbornness were the strength and stubbornness of the land. Yielding, but not yielding. Plowed and eroded, whipped by storms, but always there. Persisting by presence.

The peon had proved his courage behind the leadership of Benito Juarez. Sandal-footed, straw-sombreroed, with old musket and machete, he had whipped the Emperor's men, and the French, the ones who stayed behind. In truth, he had defeated the hacendados and the Church bureaucracy; but the wiggling fish remained as they were. Now they besieged the hands of Benito in Ciudad de Mexico and lashed the peon on the land, and in the silver mines. Pablo knew. He had carried a musket for Benito. He had lost his arm beneath the chopping hatchet of Dupin.

And so there was only God and the Santos; the land and the bandido.

The bandido was more reckless than the vaquero, wilder than the Rurales. He raided the hacendado and the government, and was damned by the Church, and so he had no soul. He dueled the wiggling fish, lived briefly and died quickly. And with each bandido's death, it was the stubborn, stoic peon who asked the Santos to intercede and return his soul. In this, the peon persisted, and the Church could not stop or dissuade him.

Pancho Morino, Ernesto "El Diablo" Chavez, Chico "Jungle" Patino, once they had been peons. As had the gringo bandido, Josey Wales.

Josey Wales. Pablo knew his life, as an aficionado of bullfights knows the life of a great toreador. Josey Wales had been a peon, a farmer, in a land called Missouri. Men called "Kansas Redlegs," part of the government no doubt, had killed his woman and his niño, and Josey Wales had joined guerrilleros to fight them.

When the revolution failed, Josey Wales would not surrender, as it is with all great bandidos. He had ridden into Texas with a compadre bandido, Lone Watie, of Cherokee Indian blood.

They had killed many men of government with their fast guns, and had taken women to wife and now ranched in the hidden valley to the northwest.

Pablo heard voices. Dawn had come, gray and pinked in the east. He came from behind the dung heaps, and through the stable door watched men digging graves behind the Majestic Hotel. They were burying Kelly and Melina and Rose. The sight brought back his oath. Pablo crept back to his hiding place. There was no one now to hide from; only the oath.

It was cool in the mule stables, but sweat rolled down his body. How far was it? A hundred miles? There was the Apache, the "Enemy," ever present, never relenting from his ghostly haunting of the plains, his horror. There was the Comanche, who never showed mercy. It was impossible.

Morning passed into afternoon, and Pablo crouched in the stable. Twice he walked to the door and came back. He had sworn to the Santos. At sundown, he stole a mule.

Vaguely he knew the Crooked River Ranch lay to the northwest. He headed the mule, old and shuffling, into the landscape of cactus and ocotillo.

The desert brings darkness as it does death, quickly and without warning. There was no moon, but the stars were brilliant in the black bowl. Pablo picked the brightest star to the right of the sun's setting and watched it between the ears of the mule.

Despite the desert night chill, he finally dozed, rocked by the slow plod. In snatches he came awake: when a wolf howled, close and threatening, answered by another; or when the mule stopped, questioning the insanity of carrying a sleeping peon to nowhere in the night. Each time Pablo kicked the mule and placed the star between its ears.

Light glowed in the east when he came to the arroyo. It was deep and narrow and carried the movement of sluggish water at its bottom. He dismounted and led the mule down. They both drank. Pablo squatted, watching the mule suck at the shallow stream, mostly mud. His head fell on his arm and he slept.

It was not the sun that wakened him. It was the sound of an impatient horse, not moving forth, but stomping at the ground. Before he opened his eyes, he knew he was dead.

They sat spotted ponies on the rim of the arroyo, perhaps a dozen. Hair dangled from reins here and there, with fresh pink skin tops that told of a recent raid. It accounted for the two riderless ponies.

Pablo stared, unblinking, and could not move. Without a word, they brought their horses down into the arroyo and dismounted. White and blue paint hideously distorted their faces, displacing the mouth, the chin, the cheek—but not the eyes. With cruel, naked hate, the eyes watched Pablo.

They wore breechclouts and moccasins, with a single feather in the hair. The hair was not loose like the Apache, but long and braided. Comanche!

They closed a circle tightly around Pablo, jerking the mule's rope roughly from him. A warrior wrapped his hand in Pablo's hair and yanked him to his feet, almost off the ground.

He held the hair aloft: "Bon-do-she!" And with a long knife, he lightly circled Pablo's head in a mock scalping motion. There was low laughter. It was not a happy laugh.

The warrior still held his hair, straining the scalp.

"Hablas español?" Pablo asked weakly.

A lean brave pushed his face close to Pablo's and grinned evilly. "Si—Mexicano?" he hissed.

"Si, señores . . . ," Pablo began. The warrior kicked him

between the legs. Pablo bent double, vomiting on the ground. A rifle butt smashed against his head, and he fell, dazed but not unconscious. His groin was swelling; throbbing darts of pain made him retch again.

The warriors left him. Dragging brush together and snapping sticks, they set a fire. Half of them gathered around the mule, and while two held its head, a third glided in to the mule's neck and circled it smoothly, deeply with his knife. The mule thrashed and kicked, but they twisted him to the ground.

While his legs still jerked, their knives moved down the backbone, pulling away the hide, as is the way of the Comanche. Skillfully they butchered and hung the meat, thonged with rawhide, on the back of a horse.

The liver and kidneys they sliced and roasted over the fire. Eating, squatting on their haunches, they paid no attention to Pablo. As they finished, licking the grease from their hands and the mule blood from their arms, their talk was low-toned. The talk was Comanche. Pablo could not understand them.

The sun tilted into the arroyo and lifted the stench of mule offal on the air. Pablo watched first one—three—now ten vultures, wheeling high with the languid patience of scavengers. He would soon join the offal.

Two warriors came; seizing him by the ankles, they dragged him to the fire. Moccasined feet pressed his shoulders to the ground, and they looked down at him while they jerked his pants down around his knees. Pablo watched a tall warrior slowly turning a knife blade over the flames. The horror struck him.

"Estuprador!" a warrior shouted down at him, and spat in his face.

"NO! no rapist, no estuprador!" Pablo shouted. "No. No, señores . . ."

The tall warrior stood over him now, the knife blade

red with heat. His face twisted evilly as he bent, kneeling between Pablo's legs. The faces looked down at him, waiting for the screams, the fear, the pain.

Pablo stopped struggling. He prayed aloud, surprisingly clear in the still air of the arroyo, "Santo Pedro, Santo Juan, take me quickly. I have tried—my oath—to reach Señor Josey Wales. It is not to be." Tears filled his eyes, blurring the warriors, who seemed to stand frozen, statue-like. Pablo waited. Nothing happened. No pain. The Santos had taken away the pain.

His eyes cleared. The warrior with the knife was bending curiously over him "Joh-seh Wales?" the tall warrior asked. Pablo was bewildered.

"Si," he said, "Josey Wales."

The feet were removed from his shoulders. "Joh-seh Wales!" the name was breathed by the warriors.

Excitement, hysteria seized Pablo. He leaped to his feet, pants falling to the ground. "Joh-seh Wales!" he shouted, leaping up and down, genitals flapping. "Joh-seh Wales!"

The warriors took up the shouting, jumping, grabbing Pablo and shaking him. "Joh-seh Wales!"

Pablo beat his breast with his fist and waved his hand in all directions. "Mi amigo! Joh-seh Wales! Vaya! Vamos Joh-seh Wales!" He snatched his pants from the ground, pulling them about his waist, and danced in a circle, wild-eyed.

The warriors lifted him on their shoulders and flung him on a pony. They leaped to their horses, and leading Pablo's among them, set off in a canter to the northwest.

The wind whipped Pablo's hair behind him. He was filled with exhilaration. A miracle! The Santos had wrought a miracle! He felt a destiny! A fate! A mission of the Santos! He was ordained.

Through noon heat and into the afternoon, the tireless Indian ponies cantered and trotted as the Comanche paced them, never stopping. They said nothing, keeping their eyes intently on the horizons around them.

The ground became broken. Jagged buttes rose against the skyline. The sun dropped in the west and died behind a naked mountain far away.

Suddenly the Comanche brought the ponies to a halt. They pulled Pablo's pony up beside the leading warrior. He placed the reins in Pablo's hand and pointed toward the mountain.

"Joh-seh Wales!" he announced, and whipped the rump of Pablo's pony viciously with a leather thong. The pony leaped into a dead run, almost unseating him.

Pablo fought the reins. After a long time he settled the pony into a bone-jarring trot. He looked around him for the Comanche. They were distant, to the south, loping their ponies. They did not look back.

Chapter 3

A deeper blackness than the sky, the mountain seemed to recede, and then began to grow: towering, naked with the broken teeth of butte rock, and then becoming two mountains, paralleling each other, sloping into the desert.

It was dawn when Pablo turned the slope of the nearest ridge. A clear creek ran down the valley between the mountains. At the entrance there was much sign of the Comanche, and as he walked the pony up the valley, the brand on trees carried the sign, the brand of the Crooked River Ranch—but also the wiggling snake sign of the Comanche.

The grass was knee-deep to the pony, and always the shallow clear creek ran in the center. There was cottonwood and live oak lining the banks of the creek. Pablo saw antelope, black-tail deer, quail and ruff grouse. The sweet virile smell of water, grass, trees, of life, set down between the mountains, shocked the senses of a rider coming from the desert.

Huge dim shapes of longhorn cattle lifted their magnificent heads at his coming, trotting warily away with warning snorts. The valley looked untouched, except for the crooked sign.

Pablo rode on, and the walls lifted higher on either side, coming almost together at places, making a narrow grass-floored arroyo, then opening out a half mile across. Now the light lifted the grayness of early dawn.

Instinctively Pablo looked behind him. A rider followed. He wore a Mexican sombrero and was short-jacketed, with the flared chaparrals of the vaquero. Pablo was afraid to speak or stop. He waved his hand, but the vaquero made no motion that he saw him. Pablo kicked his pony into a trot and heard the horse keep pace behind him.

Steadily he trotted the pony—an hour—two—between the winding sheer walls of the mountains. The longhorns and game were more plentiful, and as he twisted on the pony, looking about him, he saw the vaquero silently keeping pace.

Ahead, the mountains closed together to end the valley. Pablo saw the low adobe ranch house, set back in cottonwood and cedar. Around it were smaller adobes, and behind, a clear waterfall poured from a narrow cleft.

He was almost into the yard of the house when a loud whistle, "SKEEEEeeeeee!" came from the vaquero behind. It was the call of a Tennessee mountain nighthawk, and was instantly answered by a peculiar whipping whistle, the call of a whippoorwill. Both sounds were unfamiliar to Pablo.

But the figure was familiar, stepping casually before

him, blocking his way. Tall; a buckskin shirt hung loosely
on the gaunt frame, encircled by a belt holding a sagging
pistol. His copper face was bony and wrinkled, framed by
braided hair that hung like black whips over his shoulders.
He moved in boot moccasins, with a lithe grace that
belied his age. Pablo had seen him once in Santo Rio. It
was Lone Watie.

Holding the rein of Pablo's pony, he stared up at him,
black eyes beneath a gray cavalry hat of the Confederacy.

"Howdy," he said easily.

"Buenos dias, señor, Pablo answered, "I . . ."

"Hold on." Lone raised a hand. "If'n ye're a-goin' to
talk Mex, talk to Chato here." He jerked a thumb at the
vaquero, who had pulled up beside Pablo.

"No, señor," Pablo said hastily, "I speak inglés. I have
come of urgent need to see Señor Josey Wales."

Lone Watie's eyes narrowed to black slits, and the
vaquero moved his horse closer to Pablo.

"Josey Wales is dead," Lone said flatly.

"I know . . ." Pablo was uneasy. "That is, I know of
Señor Ten Spot, or Señorita Rose. It is from Señorita
Rose that I come."

A slow minute ticked away as Lone studied Pablo's
face. Morning brush wrens twittered in a tree, and far off
a cow bellowed for her calf. Pablo felt his scalp tighten.

Chato leaned from his saddle beside Pablo and placed a
hand on his shoulder. "You comprende, señor . . . ," his
voice was soft, "if you was to see Josey Wales, you would
die, mi amigo, unless acepcion by him—it is a necesidad."
White teeth flashed a wicked smile.

"I—must see him," Pablo answered stubbornly. Chato
Olivares shrugged his shoulders and looked at Lone. The
Cherokee turned without a word and led Pablo's pony to a
hitch rail at the rear of the house. They went through the

kitchen door, Lone leading, and Chato, spurs jingling, walking behind.

Pablo did not know what he would find beyond the door, but he was unprepared for what he saw.

A long table extended down the room; on it were platters of beef, sides of bacon, plates of beans and biscuits. The heavy smell of cooked food made juices in his mouth.

On one side of the table, a pretty Indian woman was eating, suckling an Indian baby at her shapely breast. Past her, a weathered Anglo cowboy was eating with head-down intentness. Across the table from them, a young blond woman, heavy-breasted, held an equally blond baby on her lap, and next to her, a Mexican vaquero was attacking a plate piled high with food.

At the far end of the table, Pablo saw him, and instinctively crossed himself for the bandido without a soul—Josey Wales!

He looked up at their entrance, black-haired and mustached, a brutal scar jagging his cheekbone. His eyes caught Pablo's, black as the Cherokee's, as hard, capable of cruel light. An old lady, tiny and white-haired, was placing more food on the table.

Lone and Chato tossed their hats on the floor and took seats at the table, Lone next to the Indian woman. She stopped eating and ran her arm around his waist, kissing him on the cheek.

Pablo stood, half bowed, and shuffled uncertainly. Chato, hugely filling his plate, did not look up, but tossed a thumb in Pablo's direction. "This is . . . ."

"Pablo Gonzales, señoras and señores," Pablo said politely.

". . . say he has to see you, Josey," Chato finished, and continued with his plate filling.

Josey Wales' hard eyes turned on Pablo. "Well?"

Before Pablo could answer, the old woman pointed to a place at the table and looked at Pablo. "Rat cheer," she said. Pablo looked nervously at the spot she had indicated, but saw no rats.

The blond woman smiled kindly at him. "She means for ye to sit right here," she said, and indicated the place.

"That's what I said," the old lady spoke indignantly.

"Señor?" Pablo asked, looking at Josey Wales.

"Set DOWN!" the old lady said loudly. Pablo sat.

Chato handed him plates of beans, biscuits and meat without looking up from his eating.

Their entrance had apparently interrupted a speech by the white-haired lady, for she began talking in mid-sentence, ". . . an' if'n we don't take some kind of damn mind about hit, Lord knows what this chere place is comin' to. Little Moonlight . . . ," she pointed a finger dramatically at the Indian woman, who was cutting meat from a platter with a wicked-looking knife, "has got ye all half the time tryin' to talk Cheyenne, 'cause *she* ain't got brains enough to learn how to talk. Well, I ain't a-goin' to talk *hit*! An' another thing—air ye listenin', Josey?"

Pablo stole a look at the outlaw. He was chewing tough beef while he ran a hand over the blond baby's head.

"Yes ma'am, Granma," he said without looking up, "I'm listening."

Everyone continued eating. Chato held up an empty platter and Granma took it, refilled it, and set it back on the table. She talked as she brought the food. "An' another thing—HEATHERNISM! Little Moonlight is continual a-hunchin' an' a-pumpin' up on Lone, ever'time the notion strikes her, *rat* out in the open. An' Lone, who was raised to know better, goes at hit with her like a damn boar coon—ye *hear* me, Lone?"

"Yes ma'am, Granma," Lone said humbly. He speared

two biscuits from a passing plate and ladled gravy over them.

"By God," Granma said, putting a plate of bacon beside Pablo's plate, "I don't know what would happen to the raisin' of these two pore young uns ifn hit wa'ant fer me." Suddenly she jabbed Pablo on the shoulder. "Air *you* saved, son?"

Pablo looked bewildered. "Religion," Chato mumbled at him around a mouthful of food.

"Oh, si, señora. I have been christened, I . . ."

"Ye see!" Granma said, "an' *he* ain't got but one arm!" Granma sniffed, looked closely at Pablo, and sniffed again. "But I'll tell ye, son, soon's ye finish eatin', I'll give ye some soft soap. Ye can git in the creek—damned if'n ye don't stink like a hawg—no offense meant, atall."

"Si, I will, señora," Pablo said. "I was held by Comanche and . . ." Everyone looked up from their eating.

Pablo told of the Comanche, how they captured him and butchered his mule, what they did when he used the name of Josey Wales.

"Josey met Ten Bears, a war chief," Granma said quietly, "in the valley. Told him sich as they both could die er live. That we wouldn't dis-spoil the land—they could use hit—we could use hit. When they come through, they make medicine, eat some o' the beef, there in the valley. Hit's a treaty of word, bein' bond. That's the reason they turned ye loose, son. Josey Wales abides his word. Don't ye fergit hit."

"Yes, si, señora, I will not forget," Pablo said, "I . . ." He was going to tell of Señorita Rose, but Granma interrupted, continuing her recitation of the decaying morality about her.

She looked meaningfully at Josey, who was sopping gravy with a biscuit. "Chato there," she pointed at the vaquero, "has total backslid. He might near cusses wuss than Lone. Ye hear me, Chato?"

"Yes ma'am, Granma," Chato mumbled as he chased his food with scalding coffee.

She didn't wait for his acknowledgment. "Travis there, and Miguel has took up tobaccer chewin' and spittin' ever'whares, which they taken from *you*, Josey. An' *yestiddy*," she pointed triumphantly at Little Moonlight, "*yestiddy* I seen *her* chewin' an' a-spittin'. By God, hit's got so a body has to leap like a grasshopper roundst here to keep from gittin' spit on!"

She bent, looking closely at the baby held by the blond woman. "Laura Lee, that young un looks plumb peak-ed. I told ye to give hit a spoon of calum root. C'mere, Jamie." She lifted the baby from Laura Lee's arms.

"Señorita Rose . . . she is dead," Pablo said in the silence. Granma froze, holding the baby in midair. Knives dropped on the table. Every head turned on Pablo.

"My God!" Granma breathed.

Chapter 4

Pablo told his story. He hesitated at the description of Rose and Melina. "Tell it all." The steel-soft voice was Josey Wales'. Pablo told it all. No one spoke when he finished.

The Indian baby whimpered in the silence, pulled from its tit and instinctively held tighter by Little Moonlight.

The stillness waited on Josey Wales, for the heat, the black rage, to fade, to die in his eyes. Slowly came the sane light of calm deliberation. It was almost physical. Granma sighed, "Damn!"

Josey motioned to Pablo. "Miguel, take him to the creek and git him some clothes." Miguel rose silently and ushered Pablo from the room. The men stood, pushing back their chairs in unison with Josey Wales. They followed him into the yard.

Beneath the cottonwoods, they sat on heels in a tight circle, shoulders hunched against the wind whining in the canyon: Chato Olivares, Lone Watie, Travis Cobb, and Josey Wales.

With a stick, Chato traced the map of Mexico on the ground. "We are here." He pricked the soil. "Below us, across Rio Grande, is the state of Chihuahua; to the west, Sonora; to the south, Durango. Capitan Escobedo would be of Chihuahua. It is a place—grande, Josey."

Josey Wales slid a long knife from the cavalry boot, cut a plug of tabacco and shoved it into his cheek. He chewed slowly and did not speak.

"Cain't figger it," Travis Cobb drawled, "blottin' ol' Kelly's brand and saddlin' Ten Spot—why not Ten Spot?"

Chato's smile glittered beneath the mustache. "Comprende Capitan Escobedo. He makes a little sport across the border; only putas, whores. He kills the witness, carries back a criminal who, he says, he was chasing. It justifies, if there are questions. Also, Ten Spot will make sport for the Rurales—example to scare the peons. Capitan Escobedo is not only a soldado, he is a politico. Esta uno bueno." Chato shrugged at the simplicity of it.

The men stood, watching Miguel return with Pablo. The peon wore chaparral leggings flared over the high-heeled boots of a vaquero, a tight-fitting jacket with one sleeve pinned to his shoulder, a leather sombrero.

Miguel grinned. "Vaya! El vaquero!" There was a trace of condescension in his laughter. Pablo shifted with embarrassment.

Josey Wales fixed him with a contemplative eye, and spat accurately in the map of Chihuahua.

"What do ye do, son, what's yer trade?" he drawled.

Pablo looked up. "I am—a beggar, señor."

"And before ye was a beggar?"

"I carried a rifle for General Benito Juarez, until . . ." He raised the arm stump. "Before—I was a farmer, señor."

A light flickered, and died, in the eyes of Josey Wales. "I was a farmer—oncet," he said. He was far away for a moment, listening to the wind-whine. The men shuffled awkwardly. Suddenly to Pablo, "How much did Rose promise ye to come here?" At Pablo's surprised look, he laughed shortly. "I know Rose."

"Two hundred gold pesos, señor," Pablo said, "but I will not take it."

"Why not?" Josey's tone was harsh.

"Because—I will not take it," Pablo repeated. Josey watched the stubborn set come to Pablo's jaw.

"Then why did ye come?" and his voice was softer. Pablo shifted uneasily. He felt he was on trial. Did the bandido kill all who did not satisfy his questions?

He shrugged his shoulders helplessly. "Because Señorita Rose was—kind to me." Expecting laughter, he glanced furtively at the men. There was none.

"What ye going to do now? Ye got a family?"

"I have no family, señor. I do not know."

Lone Watie watched the decision forming in Josey's eyes. He had sided the outlaw in gunfights, fled beside him ahead of posses, slept with him on the trail. He knew Josey Wales, beneath the hardness. Now he stepped to Josey's side, laying a hand on his shoulder. "Ye cain't think of takin' thet one-armed peon along. Ye got to have gun backin', Josey, *real* gun backin'."

"I've rid through Chihuahua," Travis Cobb drawled casually. "Know that neck o' Mexico. I . . ."

"Diantre! Hell!" Miguel spat. "It is me who knows Chihuahua, you damn gringo. You know nothing. It is . . ."

"You goddamned chili bean greaser," Travis snarled,

"me and Chato has stepped in every cowshit pile in Chihuahua. We pushed cows . . ."

Chato fixed Miguel with a cold stare of pity. "I was *born* in Chihuahua, you peon idiota! Like the back of my hand—every village, hacienda—I can find Escobedo as easily as mi pene. I . . ."

"Shet up," Josey said evenly. He chewed for a moment with measured meditation. "Fust off, we cain't take too many guns away from the womenfolk. They got to be *good* guns. Lone, ye'll stay, with Miguel and Travis."

There was no protest. The men studied the ground—except Chato, hitching his gun belt and watching Josey's face expectantly.

"I'll take Chato," Josey said, and tossed a nod at Pablo, "and this here farmer. Soon's he learns he ain't a yard hound—thet won't take long—he'll do."

He whirled on Pablo. "And I ain't no damn *see-norh*. It's *Josey*, ye understand?"

"Si, Sen—Josey," Pablo said hastily, "and I will go."

Chato looked at Pablo with disgust. "No one asked you —comprendes?"

"Ye know what to do," Josey said. "Git hosses fer Chato and Pablo that'll stay with mine. Hang a .44 on Pablo; he can handle it better'n a rifle. Vamoose!"

He walked away, into the house.

It wasn't easy, finding horses capable of staying with the big roan of Josey Wales. Each man carried a stiff looped lariat into the horse corral and made his own selection. They argued, pointing out weaknesses in the other's choices, but finally settled on a Morgan-chested gray for Chato, for Pablo a mean-looking grulla.

Rolled blankets, grub, and grain for the horses went behind the saddles.

Josey came from the house, holding Jamie, his arm around Laura Lee. As she took the baby from him, he kissed her long, full on the lips, and she whispered, "Ye'll take care, Josey."

"I will," he said. He pulled Little Moonlight close, her arms tightly about his neck, and squeezed Granma as she kissed his scarred cheek.

Granma was lifted from the ground by Chato as she hugged him. "Put me down, ye crazy Mexican," she protested. Chato laughed and slapped her narrow bottom. "By God!" Granma said, but she was pleased, and tears made her eyes twinkle.

The men shook hands silently, not forgetting Pablo. Lone Watie seized Josey's hand in the iron grip of a brother.

"If'n ye're not back quick, I'm comin'."

"I'll be back," Josey said, and swung into the saddle. Atop the giant roan, he looked a deadly figure. Twin-holstered .44's, leg-tied; a Navy .36 beneath the left arm, under the fringed jacket; strapped before him on the saddle were two holstered .44 pistols, and two were tied behind him.

It was the one-man dreadnaught style of the Missouri guerrilla.

Chato and Josey were mounted, their horses sidling in the wind. Pablo turned to mount the grulla. He was awkward in the high-heeled boots and missed the stirrup. The grulla skittered, snorting. Granma and Travis moved to help.

"Leave him be!" Josey's voice was harsh. They stopped. Pablo caught the horse and studied it for a moment. He held the reins in his hand and crossed the hand to the saddle horn. Sticking his toe in the stirrup, he lifted and swung, almost tossing himself over its back. He held on, teetering, as the grulla crow-hopped, and finally settled in the saddle, sombrero askew on his head.

Josey grunted, whirled the roan cat-like on powerful

haunches, and with a rush, led them out of the yard, down into the valley.

Looking back, Josey saw them bunched beneath the cottonwoods: Laura Lee and Little Moonlight, Granma and Miguel, Travis Cobb and Lone Watie. They were his life, found after the death in Missouri.

He saw them raise their hands and wave, like semaphore, back and forth, slowly; and he lifted the gray hat to signal his goodbye as he disappeared around the protruding butte.

Behind him, Chato waved his sombrero, before he too vanished. Pablo looked back. Still they waved. Timidly he raised his sombrero, then with a wide arc swept it over his head. Pablo had never waved goodbye before.

The question never rose among them: should lives be placed forfeit for a tinhorn gambler named Ten Spot? They were, all of them, swept up in the loyalty code of Josey Wales. The Mountain Code.

The Code was as necessary to survival on the lean soil of mountains, as it had been on the rock ground of Scotland and Wales. Clannish people. Outside governments erected by people of kindlier land, of wealth, of power, made no allowance for the scrabbler.

As a man had no coin, his coin was his word. His loyalty, his bond. He was the rebel of establishment, born in this environment. To injure one to whom he was obliged was personal; more, it was blasphemy. The Code, a religion without catechism, having no chronicler of words to explain or to offer apologia.

Bone-deep feuds were the result. War to the knife. Seldom if ever over land, or money, or possessions. But injury to the Code meant—WAR!

Marrowed in the bone, singing in the blood, the Code was brought to the mountains of Virginia and Tennessee and the Ozarks of Missouri. Instantaneously it could change a shy farm boy into a vicious killer, like a sailing hawk, quartering its wings in the death dive. It was the Code of the "Boys," the Missouri guerrillas that shocked a nation.

Josey Wales was conceived of the Highland Code, born of the Tennessee mountain feud, and washed in the blood of Missouri.

It all was puzzling to those who lived within a government cut from cloth to fit their comfort. Only those forced outside the pale could understand. The Indian—Cherokee, Comanche, Apache. The Jew.

The unspoken nature of Josey Wales was the clannish code. No common interest of business, politics, land or profit bound his people to him. It was unseen and therefore stronger than any of these. Rooted in human beings' most powerful urge—preservation. The unyielding, binding thong was loyalty. The trigger was obligation.

Kelly the bartender, schooled in human nature that whiskey reveals across the bar, recognized the Code, and so died content in his sure promise to Capitan Jesus Escobedo.

They rode. Josey leading, lifting the powerful roan into a slow lope across the desert. He did not lead them southeast, toward Santo Rio, but straight south, to the Rio Grande.

Cactus and mesquite straggled through the sagebrush. Spanish daggers and spiked ocotillo lent a fierceness to the dead land. The wind strummed a monotonous low chord.

They did not pause in the quick darkness after sunset; but Josey slowed pace in the uneven light of the stars.

It was after midnight when they waded their horses, stirrup-deep, across the Rio Grande, and entered the angry wound that was Mexico.

Mexico, 1868. Bleeding. Since Montezuma, Cuauahtome —Cortes. The wound never closed. Now contre-guerrillas, freshly loosed by their departed French masters, roamed the countryside. Armies of bandidos. Rurales, scalping, looting, raping, with fantastic orgasms of torture.

It was worth a man's life, taking his eyes from the horizon to pick a flower.

The gachupin, born in Spain, looked jealously down on the criollo—of Spanish blood, but born in Mexico. These were the hacendados, the hidalgos, who plotted against each other, against the peon, and held their baronages with cunning claws of tribute and death.

The criollo looked down on the mestizo, of mixed Spanish and Indian blood, but hired him to herd his cattle. At the bottom, the Indian peon, who hoed the corn.

Now. Por Dios! An Indian peon in the chair of El Presidente! The inscrutable Zapotec, Benito Juarez. Suspicion spread like a haunting shadow over Mexico. The Church bureaucracy deepened the shadow.

Juarez meant to confiscate the millions of Church-owned acres and give them to the peon. Juarez was a pagan. Bishops bribed generals to issue pronunciamentos against Juarez.

The hacendados bought scalps, as did the state governors, from Rurales, from bandidos. Any scalps. So long as the scalp was not their own. Death quieted unrest. People do not think of land when there is terror.

Comanches hit in whirlwind seasonal raids. There was the stealthy, never-ending horror of the Apache. Mexico was bleeding.

They pulled their saddles in a narrow arroyo. Hidden from eyes of the prairie, they rubbed the tired horses and grained them. Pablo clumsily, pulling the saddle, caring for the grulla. He was not helped.

They stretched, rolled in blankets on the ground, horses'

reins tied around their wrists. They did not eat. A war party—revenge, rescue, guerrilla-fashion.

It was cold in the first hint of dawn. Josey toed Pablo from his blanket. Chato was already saddling. Now Chato took the lead, turning southeast in a half loop, looking to cut a trail four days old, a trail of fifty horses. They ate jerked beef and cold biscuits as they rode.

Cortes described Mexico to the King of Spain by wadding a sheet of paper and tossing it before him. It was a good description. Jagged. Rocks rose bare-boned. Deep canyons cut suddenly across the prairie floor. Angular buttes. Jumbled boulders, bigger than houses, perched on the inclines of arroyos.

The morning passed, raising heat waves from the rocks, and baking the constant wind to an oven breath. They did not stop at noon.

Sometimes Chato was forced to leave their southeasterly course, searching for ways into and out of canyons and around insurmountable walls of bare butte.

It was late afternoon when they pulled up on the rim of canyon cleaving the prairie three hundred feet deep. Chato pointed to the narrow floor far below them.

"A trail, Josey," he said, "leading south."

Josey hooked a leg around his saddle horn and cut a tobacco plug. He chewed slowly, scanning the prairie. There was nothing. No sound in the late afternoon. Even the wind had diminished to a thin, whistling persistence. He spat over the canyon rim.

"Let's git down and see."

They turned south, a mile—two—and found a slope in the canyon wall. It was hot in the breathless canyon, working the horses slowly down the slope. They rested in the shadows on the floor.

Chato was first down, walking back, then forward on the trail.

"It is here, Josey," he said, "the tracks. Forty, maybe fifty horses, all shod. They are three—could be five days old. See the dung; it crumbles."

Josey did not dismount, but scanned the rim above them.

"Reckin it's Escobedo," he said quietly, "and gone south."

Chato was kneeling, studying the tracks. Now he came back and there was none of the reckless humor in his face. He looked soberly at Josey. "There are other tracks, following Escobedo. Maybe a day ahead of us."

"What kind be they?" Josey asked.

"They are not horse tracks. They are moccasin. Many of them," Chato said, "the track of the Apache."

Chapter 5

It was an old trail. Narrow and worn deep in the red rocks of the floor. Centuries of Indians had passed over it, a main artery leading south.

The guerrilla instinct of Josey Wales spaced their riding. He led, Chato fifty yards behind, Pablo in the rear. One does not bunch his riders in tight places.

He watched the rim high above them. The light died. Without reflected light from the prairie, the canyon was black, and Josey whistled Chato and Pablo closer. Alertness now depended upon ear. Separating the hollow echoes of the horses' hoofs, consigning that sound to routine, pushed back in the mind—leaving silence for the nerves to ponder.

It was the water sound that brought Josey to a halt. A light gurgle somewhere in the rocks. They found it in a slit arroyo breaking the canyon wall, a stream no bigger than a man's finger dribbling from the rocks. Pablo learned: horses come first.

Filling their hats, they watered the horses, unsaddled and rubbed them with blankets. While the horses ate grain from the nose bags, Josey carefully lifted their feet, feeling for pebbles that could lame.

Only then did the men eat, sparsely on salt bacon, jerked beef; and slept as before, with reins wrist-tied.

The canyon floor lifted as they rode in pre-dawn light. By the time sun tinged red on the rock faces, they were out on a treeless plateau. The tracks of the Rurales were closely bunched, meandering through chaparral and mesquite; beside them, the relentless moccasin prints.

Despite rising heat, they slow-loped across the plateau. Sweat ringed the saddle blankets and made rivulets in the dust on the horses' legs.

Once they stopped, at noontime, to blow their mounts.

"We are doubling their pace," Chato said, pointing to the tracks. "See, their horse tracks are flat, not heel-dug. They are walking. The Apache . . . ," he pointed to a moccasin print, "they are still running—the toe is dug heavy in the ground. They can outlast a horse—diablos on a trail."

With slow calculation, Josey looked at the trail. "Wonder why them Apache are hot-trailing Escobedo?"

Chato shrugged. "Quien sabe? Who knows? They love to kill."

It was midafternoon when the trail dipped over the plateau, leading into a shallow valley. A river coursed, twisting in the valley depth, and beside it, a town.

It was not a simple Indian village, but had a cathedral

spire, and was laid out plaza-style, ringed with adobes. The Apache tracks turned away from the trail.

They dismounted, squatting on the slope as they studied the town. Josey pointed. "The corral, back of that there building, is holding fifteen, maybe twenty hosses and mules. Escobedo ain't there, fer I see no more hosses about."

"The town is Saucillo," Chato said. "I have been there many times. The building is policia. There would be ten, maybe fifteen Rurales stationed there."

Josey straightened. "We'll ring the town, till we come behind a livery barn. The hosses need some cooling, rubbing down, watering and graining. We'll stay with the hosses till we put bottom back in 'em. Then we'll see what we can find out as to do with Mr. Escobedo."

They walked the horses, sloping to the town; and Pablo had just listened again to the guerrilla, who always seeks the edge: hosses first.

The wide aisle of the livery barn was cool and dim, refreshing to man and beast. The old wrangler was profuse with gracias and polite bows, accepting the gold double-eagle from Josey. He set the stable boys to work on the horses, and then nervously joined them.

Such horses! The roan, magnifico! No such horses could be owned, except by patróns, or politicos—or bandidos. These hombres were neither politicos nor patróns.

One, dressed fancily in black with the ivory-handled pistola, waited on haunches at the street door, smoking a cigarillo. He watched the street and the wrangler with cat eyes of suspicion.

At the other door, the one-armed Indian, dark—perhaps a Zapotec, or a Yaqui, the vicious kind—followed him with an even stare that showed nothing.

And the Anglo with the sombrero of the Rebel gringos and cruel scarred face, he paced the aisle, pistolas grandes swinging on his legs, and hovered over the horses, instructing the boys to wet blankets and rub the legs, the chests, the backs of the horses. Such care and preparacion!

The wrangler was filling grain sacks, feeling the gold coin in his pocket, when the realization suddenly struck his dull mind. He crossed himself. Then the greed began to nip.

Josey did not see him motion the ragged stable boy to his side and whisper; nor the boy slip out through the window.

And so they waited, ticking away minutes that were precious, letting the horses cool and rest. Finally they led the horses out onto the cobblestones of the plaza, walking three abreast.

The afternoon was late, bringing out señoritas who promenaded around the plaza under watchful eyes of duenas, gossiping on benches.

Through the plaza, walking, the horses' shoes ringing hollow on the stones, they turned down a street of shops and cantinas. The cantinas were coming to life in the soft dusk of evening.

They were not looking for them, and so missed the posters nailed at the corners of the plaza: the scar-face of Josey Wales. $7500 REWARD. DEAD. Nor had they any way of knowing that Captain Jesus Escobedo had left behind ten of his Santo Rio Rurales, taking the ten regulars of Saucillo with him.

They sought information on Escobedo; and the liquid, haunting guitar notes, floating through batwing doors, made them loop-tie their horses and stroll into the Cantina de Musica with scarcely a look behind them.

A single window faced the street and gave small light to the low-ceilinged room. A door to the side was curtained with stringed beads. Another door stood open at the back, where a mule was visible, cropping bunch grass. Flies buzzing over a dozen pulque-yeasted tables, the guitar notes, were the only sounds.

The cantinero behind the bar slop-sandaled forward to confront them. His face was fat, sullen, and he wiped the bar in the universal salute of bartenders.

He did not look up. "Tequila, mi amigo!" Chato shouted good-humoredly, and slapped the bar, flipping his sombrero back to hang by the thong about his neck.

Three bottles and glasses were set before them. The cantinero did not raise his eyes, and the outlaw senses of Josey Wales raised small hairs on his own neck. He looked keenly at the fat face as he spun a double-eagle on the bar.

"Escobedo?" he asked softly. The cantinero looked blankly at him and made no effort to answer.

Chato took a long swallow from the bottle. "Capitan de Rurales, Escobedo—sabes?"

"No . . . sé de Escobedo." The cantinero was placing silver change on the bar and did not look at Chato. The guitar notes died.

A woman came from behind the beaded curtain and laid a guitar on the bar next to Chato. She was full-blown. Breasts brown and ripe, hanging heavily. Crow-black hair brushed below the bare shoulders, and pock scars on her face gave a suggestive sensuality.

She knew her mark, and sided Chato without hesitation. Josey was pouring tequila into a glass. She slid a hand under Chato's shirt and rubbed his back.

"Tequila?" Chato asked politely, and shoved the bottle toward her.

"Si, caballero, si!" She seized the bottle by the neck, turned it up, then wiped her lips, wet, full, on Chato's cheek.

The slitted skirt revealed a strong thigh and olive hips. Chato slipped a hand under the slit and rubbed experimentally. Firm and muscled. She giggled. He turned to Josey with studied thoughtfulness. "You comprendes, Josey? The Rurales would have been here. They would have told her where they were going. Perhaps if I questioned her, alone, for a moment, I could discover . . ."

Josey downed the drink and sucked his teeth at the fiery liquid. "Yeah," he drawled, "I'm shore ye could. But don't take yer spurs off—ain't got the time."

Pablo blushed darkly and stared at the tequila he had poured into his glass.

Chato pulled again at the bottle and looked philosophical. "It is difficult to reason," he said. "I have been following the cows so long—always you follow them; and the lean-rumped cows are the culls—no bueno. The heavy-rumped cows are the unos buenos—perhaps that has made me what I have become, with confirmacion, a rump man."

"Yeah," Josey said drily, watching the cantinero move away to the end of the bar. "I kinder noticed that—ye and Travis—ye smell a little cowy too. I'll jest keep this here tequila. Git on with yer questioning."

Pablo downed the drink, like Josey, in one gulp. He wheezed, spat, coughed and bent double. Josey beat him on the back.

"Come, querida." Chato flung an arm about the neck of the woman and staggered only slightly as they passed through the beads.

Pablo was gasping. He leaned an unsteady elbow on the bar and tears ran down his face. "I—I am sorry, Josey," he said, and Josey watched the slight jerk of the cantinero's head at the name.

"That's all right, son," he drawled. "Drinking's the last thing ye got to learn." He didn't show the alarm racing through his mind. The bartender knew—knew the name, Josey Wales!

A steady squeak of bed springs came through the curtain beads, then short woman-cries.

"By God," Josey said, "I'm glad Granma ain't here."

"Me too," Pablo muttered. Pablo meant it.

They came without warning. Four through the front door, three in the back. Heavy pistols hanging on their hips. Some of them had not yet peddled the scalps. Hair hung from belts and vests. Rurales.

"Git away from me," Josey whispered venomously at Pablo. "Take a bottle. Git to a table at the side." Pablo grabbed a bottle and slipped quickly from their path.

They lined the bar on each side of Josey. The cantinero, without speaking, placed bottles before them. A stench filled the room, acrid in Josey's nostrils: dried blood, stinking bodies, horse sweat.

Easily, almost lazily, he took a bottle in one hand, a glass in the other, and casually moved from the bar, sauntering toward the shadowed center of the room.

The Rurales drank with gusto, smacking lips, watching Josey with canny eyes of triumph, wiping drooping mustaches and beards with the backs of their hands.

They did not notice being placed in the light of the two doors, the scar-face bandido in the center shadows; a very slight edge, but nevertheless an edge, for the professional pistolero.

The squeaking bed springs stopped. Pablo sat down at his table.

They turned, all as one, facing Josey. Smiling. Cunning smiles of double meaning, always reducing victims to quivering cowards. The leader, standing in their center, doffed his sombrero in mock politeness and held it before him. His smile grew broader, white teeth overbiting his lower lip. "Señor! We welcome you to our country. We . . ."

Josey Wales returned the smiles—it was meant to be a smile. They could not see his eyes, shadowed beneath the wide-brimmed hat; but the smile trenched the scar, deep and livid, giving a lynx effect of evil cruelty. The Rurales stiffened at the sight of such a man.

Josey spread his arms wide, holding the bottle and the glass. "See-norhs . . ." His voice carried the unmistakable whine of the frightened victim; the Rurales relaxed. "I ain't looking fer trouble. I was . . ."

The bottle and glass fell from his hands. Long before they touched the floor, a big Colt appeared magically. Josey Wales was fanning.

He shot the leader through the sombrero, dead center, the heavy .44 slug knocking him backward into the bar. The deep-throated pistol was fired staccato, so rapidly, it was solid sound. The face of a Rurale smashed, fountaining blood. Another twisted, head down in crazy floppings.

Josey dodged to his left, kicked against the 'dobe wall, like a ballet dancer, back toward the center of the room, fire belching from the barrel of a second Colt in his left hand as he moved.

One Rurale cleared leather, and flipped forward as he cleared, jolted by a low hit.

From behind the beaded curtain, another revolver opened up, rapid-fire. The room shook with the thunder. Smoke fogged the air. Pablo had jerked the pistol from his holster and was firing.

His first shot killed the unsuspecting mule behind the rear door, knocking it kicking in the sand. His second shattered bottles behind the bar. Getting the range, his third knocked the leg from under a Rurale.

Through it all, a wild scream rose, carrying upward, almost beyond the range of human voice, and fell, broken cries of inhuman exultation. The rebel yell of Josey Wales.

Two Rurales broke for the rear door. One made it, fleeing the sound and the blood-crazed killer. The second fell, his back blown out between the shoulders.

It was over in thirty seconds. Chato stood, naked from the waist down, outside the beaded curtain, pistol in hand.

Blood ran unnoticed from his side. Pablo, dangling the big pistol in his hand, looked dumbly at the carnage of bodies.

Josey Wales was over the bar, cat-quick, and yanked the cantinero to his feet. He shoved the barrel of a Colt into the fat throat. "Escobedo!" he snarled, and cocked the hammer.

The heavy face broke in sobs, "Por Dios! Por favor! He rides to Escalon! Escalon! Escalon!"

"He is speaking truthful." Chato spoke quietly, cold sober. "The woman, she say the same thing."

Josey crashed the pistol barrel across the head of the cantinero. He fell limp in the blood of his skull.

Josey inspected Chato's wound. " 'Tain't much," was his curt remark. He cut a tobacco plug. "Reckin we'd better be gittin' along." Chato hurriedly pulled on his pants and boots.

Josey was tilting bodies of Rurales with his toe. "Pablo," he called, "go through their pockets. Put everything on the bar."

Pablo holstered the pistol and bent, a little reluctantly, to the job. There were six of them, sprawled bloodied and smashed by the ponderous slugs of the .44's.

"This one," Pablo indicated a Rurale lying spread-eagle on his back, "is alive."

Josey walked to him and looked down. The Rurale was conscious. He had been hit in the stomach. The stench of torn intestines mingled with the sweetish odor of blood.

"Was ye at Santo Rio?" Josey asked quietly.

The Rurale grinned faintly. "SI!" he said boastfully, surprisingly strong. The grin twisted meanly. He reached a hand into the pocket of his leather jacket and drew forth a sparkling object. It dangled from his hand, swinging.

"Si . . . puta!" and he laughed, coughing. It was an earring, Rose's. The left-hand Colt slid easily upward in

Josey's grip, cocked as it cleared leather. He shot the Rurale between the eyes and watched him string-jerk with the sudden shock. He spat tobacco juice into the blank face.

Pablo had cleaned their pockets. A small mound of gold and silver coins lay on the bar.

"Halve it," Josey said, "you and Chato."

"But . . ." Pablo protested.

"It's gun law, son; onliest kind we can live by," Josey said evenly, "and ye done right well, son."

The vaquero and the peon halved the coins. Josey selected a double-eagle from the pile and flipped it to the naked woman, standing at the beaded curtain. Her face was impassive, stoic.

"That's fer the—question," he said, "and ye tell 'em Josey Wales and his friends done this—fer Santo Rio— understand?"

"Si, gracias," she answered, not smiling. She caught the coin and crossed herself quickly for the bandido who had no soul.

They rode, galloping through the cobblestoned plaza of Saucillo. Every door closed, windows shuttered.

To the south, they turned the horses, galloping, deliberately pacing.

Somewhere ahead of them, frightened horsemen were running their horses to death. Josey Wales! The blood-crazed bandido was riding wild in Mexico!

Chapter 6

In the twilight, deepening toward night, they galloped out of the river valley and up onto the vast Chihuahua plain. The southward trail toward Escalon drifted through cactus and mesquite.

Here, gamma grass grew in bunches so sparse it required forty acres to feed a cow, and many rancheros numbered their cattle in the tens of thousands; here, a Don measured his land not by acres, but how many days were required to cross it.

A neighbor's hacienda could be a hundred miles or more, and the cattle ran wild as the pumas, only occasionally rounded up by the vaqueros, who were wilder than the cattle.

It was the land of Chato Olivares, unbridled and reck-less, soaking its aimless existence into the soul of a man like an incense, until it owned him, and made him, and presented him to the towns as its spirit—the vaquero.

There was no moon. The night dropped its blanket and the wind turned cold. Chato led, slackening the pace, and it was he who whistled softly as he brought his horse to a halt. "There are not as many tracks, Josey," he said as Pablo and Josey reined in beside him. "It is dark, but some-where, they have turned aside. They are not on the trail to Escalon."

Josey's saddle creaked as he shifted weight. "Where? Where'd he be a-goin'?"

Chato shrugged in the darkness. "Maybe west to Coyamo, maybe northwest to Casa Grande. He is making a swing perhaps of his territory; but he is not going on the trail to Escalon. Quien sabe? It is too dark to tell."

Pablo's voice shook slightly. "But the riders, the Rurales who escaped, they will know. They are riding ahead. Capitan Escobedo will discover that we follow."

"Yeah, I know," Josey said; a faint touch of bitterness was in the words. He knew. Like it had been in Missouri and Kansas; always, the countryside up in arms. Where a man rode with his nerves tingling on his fingertips. Where he shot at the bush that did not wave as it should in the wind.

Now they would know. His stomach hardened, holding down the sickness of Missouri, tightening the nerves for the madness of the death game to come.

They sat their horses, stomping impatiently in the wind. Chato felt helpless, that somehow he had failed; but no one could fight the darkness.

It was Josey who broke the silence. "I figger," he said, "them yellers thet broke and run will tell tall tales to Escobedo. Might be it'll keep Escobedo running, and, if it's like ye say, Chato, Escobedo wants to put on a big show; maybe it'll buy some time fer Ten Spot . . ." His voice trailed away and he squinted his eyes at a star breaking the cloud cover. "We'll backtrack a mile er two; pull off the trail. Wait fer light."

Breathing hope into their hopelessness, he led them back up the trail and off it, into the brush. He unsaddled the roan, away from Chato and Pablo, haltering him to munch the gamma grass and tying the end of the tether to his saddle horn.

Pulling a Colt, he held it across his stomach as he stretched on the ground, head on saddle and hat tilted over his eyes. The eyes did not count now, only the ears and the ground-feel. The roan would snort at an undue presence. The sudden jerk of his head would pull the saddle.

Josey had not mentioned that Escobedo would now set up the ambuscades. Chato knew already; and Pablo—there was no need for his knowing.

He saw the wounded Rurale waving the earring of Rose tauntingly before him, and briefly, the picture flitted back to Missouri, of long ago—his smoldering cabin, the charred skeleton of his wife and his boy—this he had seen when he shot the Rurale between the eyes.

He swallowed the bitterness in his throat and drifted lightly into the restless sleep of the outlaw.

Chato and Pablo tethered their horses in the same manner, as Josey had told them, separate and apart. The night wind rose, and the cactus spines delicately played a light shrieking on the wind, as of spirits far away, agonizing in an ethereal chorus.

Pablo crawled close to Chato. "Chato," he said.

The vaquero did not lift the sombrero from his face, but he whispered, "If you would talk, niño, whisper, like the wind. Sound carries far on the plains of night."

Pablo crawled closer to where Chato lay. In the distance, a wolf mourned, long and quavering. "The wolf?" Pablo whispered.

"Si," Chato answered, "but it is also the cry used by the Apache; and the Apache crosses the plains only by night."

A coyote yipped a taunting reply.

"Chato?"

"Si?"

"Was it a necesidad—I mean, Señor Josey shooting the wounded Rurale, the taking from their pockets?" Pablo asked.

Chato laughed softly. "You will never comprendes, niño. The Rurale was a torturer. He loved to see the pain in others. Josey gave him the quick death. Their pockets? They are looters of the helpless. Justice is that one shall receive what one deserves, it is the only justice—good, or bad. It is the code of the bandido, Josey Wales. Would you leave the fillings of their pockets for the puta and the cantinero?"

"No," Pablo whispered hesitantly.

"Rest easy in your mind, Pablo," Chato whispered. "The coins that jingle your pockets are justice, and the prize of war. If Josey Wales could have hauled the Rurales before a judge, the judge would take the loot, and he would divide with his politicos, and they would buy new carriages with fringes on top, and their putas would wear new rings. And Josey Wales and Pablo and Chato Olivarés would be swinging from the gallows. That is their justice. Josey Wales? He has only the gun."

The silence was long and Pablo pondered the words. He began to crawl back to his saddle, for Chato was obviously asleep.

"Pablo?" the vaquero whispered.

Pablo stopped in his crawling. "Si?"

"Since you were a niño, you planted the maize, the corn, each spring in the ground. Verdad?"

"True," Pablo whispered.

"And you watched it grow, birthing with the rain from the womb of Mother Earth—and you helped, you hoed, you gathered, you savored the fruits of the kernel. Year following year. Verdad?"

"True," Pablo whispered.

"You effect the growing of the corn, but everything you effect, everything you do, has its effect upon you. The growing of the corn, and Mother Earth, have more effect on you, so that you are Pablo—a part of Her birthing and Her growing and Her fruiting, Her gentleness, Her everlasting life and living. You will live forever, Pablo. Be glad you no comprendes the storms that move across the currents above Mother Earth; for the storms come con fiero, with ferocity grande, but die quickly. They too are a necesidad, but they do not live long. So it is with Josey Wales."

"And you?" Pablo whispered after a long time. "What are you, Chato?"

The vaquero laughed softly. "Me? I am the tumbleweed that rolls with the wind. And, niño?"

"Yes?"

"If you do not sleep, and fall asleep tomorrow in the saddle when you are needed, Josey will shoot you. When I can see and count the spines on yonder cactus, we will ride."

Pablo crawled back to his saddle. He lay for a long time watching stars that winked between the scudding clouds. For the first time in his life, he was glad he was Pablo. The words of the vaquero stirred something backward through time, before his people had been yoked by the Spanish. He felt Indian.

Against his back Mother Earth felt alive. Her rains were holier than the water flicked upon him from the pot of the Spanish priest. Vaguely, drifting into sleep, he wondered if the vaquero was a pagan priest from long ago. He slept deep, and was not troubled.

Chato had been partly right in his guess of Escobedo's destination. Coyamo, to the west.

After leaving Saucillo with fifty riders at his back, Escobedo had shrugged off the peculiar haunting coldness left by the words of Kelly. Josey Wales—wild words and images spouted by a tequila-soaked cantinero. Superstition fit for a peon perhaps, but not for Capitan Jesus Escobedo.

He had not chosen Coyamo as his destination aimlessly. There was system, efficiency and ambition in the plans of Escobedo.

The rich silver mines dotted the land of this area, deep with their treasures; but the peons fled in the night; the better families would not settle the towns. Neither priest, nor prayer, nor sword could enlarge the sparse population. All for one reason. The Apache. The creeping death that raided, murdered, and used the wiles of El Diablo in their endless terror.

The Apache, like smoke in the hand; they would not stand and fight but ran for the Sierra Madre, but always, always, came back to strike again.

It was a source of great pain and embarrassment to the Governor of Chihuahua, as in all states of the north. It was of great issue in Ciudad de Mexico itself. Civilization had not only been halted by a handful of murderous animals; it was withering away.

The man of genius and planning, of action and foresight, had a future, becoming a colonel perhaps, even a general. With such power, he could share in the silver of the mines, play the game of land reform in Ciudad de Mexico with Benito Juarez, and with the other hand return the land to the Dons, and share also with them. From general to Don was not an impossible step. Don

General Jesus Escobedo! A rightful return of his name to the aristocracy to which it belonged.

There had been only two Apache bucks at the camp he and his Rurales had surprised. One had escaped. He had the other as a prisoner. Thirty-five bitches and bastardos put to the sword! He had one more Apache captive, a bitch, thirteen, maybe fourteen years of age. He had the gringo criminal.

His plan had the genius of simplicity. First, to hang the Apache buck in the town of Coyamo, to put spine in the Alcalde, the Mayor, and win praises from the mouth of the Alcalde and the Priest for his successful raid, praises that would reach the Governor and the bishops. It would demonstrate to the peons the power of his Rurales over the Apache.

From Coyamo he would travel further west to Aldamano and there, after his own private "questioning" of the Apache bitch, she would be hanged outside the town for all to see. The praises would come from Aldamano.

Then, leaving part of his force at Coyamo, part at Aldamano, he would travel with only ten Rurales to Escalon. There, before the military, closer to Ciudad de Mexico and the people of influence, he would recount his chase of the gringo who had killed a Mexican officer of the law. How he had pursued him to the haven of criminals, Santo Rio, fought a pitched battle with the bandidos there, and returned with the criminal.

Mexico! Demonstrating to the hated gringos of the north that the long arm of Mexican justice reached even to the Rio Grande, through, of course, the dedication of Capitan Escobedo. He would tell of the slain thirty-five Apache. The newspapers in the capital would acclaim his efforts. The bishops, who even now fretted at the dwindling tribute income from the peons, would bring pressure to give him more authority; and the mine owners, the Dons.

Perhaps from capitan to general—it had been done before. And with the power after that—why not?—El Presidente!

Wild dreams? Not in turbulent Mexico. Even more fantastic dreams had come true. The goal of Escobedo was possible, even probable, for he was not a dreamer alone. He was a man with the attributes necessary to carry out the dreams; no moral conscience blocked his actions. The plan would succeed.

Coyamo had been rebuilt by the Spanish from an old enjido, a communal Indian village. 'Dobe hovels crowded close behind the one main street of stores and cantinas. A church had been built to christianize the Indian; and a low 'dobe wall circled the town, one of the futile gestures against the Apache.

Escobedo brought his Rurales in at sundown, columns of twos, military-fashion. They were soldados now, and under pain of death to act otherwise.

Two paces behind, and at his side, rode Lieutenant Valdez; Escobedo had only slightly concealed his contempt for Valdez' mestizo blood.

Charging Valdez to quarter the Rurales near the stables and corrals, place guardias about the town, and throw the gringo and Apache buck in jail, he retired to the private quarters reserved for the Capitan of Policia. He had the Apache girl bound by her feet and hands and left in his quarters while he paid his respects to the Alcalde and the Priest.

The Alcalde's hacienda was set back, respectably, from the street, and pleasantly patioed, with an iron grill gate. It was in the patio they ate their meal; the Alcalde, his plump wife, and the Priest in attendance to the Capitan. Indian women served the courses, shuffling back and forth to the kitchen at sharp commands of the matrona.

For a mestizo, Escobedo thought, the Alcalde showed

some knowledge of manners. True, he was hasty in his eating, hurrying to get past the pleasantries.

How had been the Capitan's patrol? The health of his family? If he needed for his troops, only ask. The fat jowls of the Alcalde trembled in the candlelight. He waited impatiently for the cigars and wine, for the retirement of his wife, before presenting his case—the excuses for his lack of progress, which threatened to break his political career and send him back to the work of a menial bootlicker.

His voice rose in a whine: The peons brought in to work would not stay. They had even tried corralling them, like horses in a stockade, but they escaped and ran in the night. They were not rebellious. They were afraid. The Apache.

Some of the mines were only partially worked. Some had closed down. If the Capitan could relay his message to the south; could station more men ... if ... if ...

Escobedo had heard it all before. When was it? In 1760, the Governor of Chihuahua, answering the King of Spain's demand as to why he was not settling and progressing with his territory, offered the same excuse, as did the governors of Sonora and other states to the north. The Apache. In 1680, the same answer. The Apache.

How far back had it begun? How many political careers ruined? How many generals court-martialed? How many families of aristocracy disgraced and exiled to oblivion? The Apache.

Escobedo nodded his head in sympathy through the cigar smoke. He murmured his agreement with the waving hands of the Alcalde. He waited for the Priest to speak.

The Priest was a thin man, and wore his black robes with dignity. His face was white, esthetic, obviously not far removed from the Court of Spain. He was of a family that might have chosen to remain in the high circles of diplomacy or perhaps the military, but he had chosen the priesthood. Without question, he was a man close to God.

Though he had drunk as much wine as Escobedo and the Alcalde, his tongue was not thick, and his words were patient with forbearance. He spoke softly and with a saintly grace. "The Indian peon is good. The Church has made great progress in his Christianization. He is aware of his burden of sin and of his only deliverance. He attends the masses and rituals. He is simple; but he has a soul." The Priest paused and looked heavenward for his thoughts.

"May I be forgiven, por Dios, if I am wrong." He crossed himself with slow majesty. "But I have come to believe in my heart the Apache is an animal. He has no soul. Either this, or he represents El Diablo upon this earth. He raids even the churches of God, desecrates the sacred images and blasphemes the altars." He spoke more softly. "On two occasions, I have sought to talk with Apache captives, to tell them of love, of the word of God, to reach their souls. In their eyes I find only hate burning at my soul." The priest shuddered at the picture. "Such hate!" His voice trembled. "They have spat in my face and defamed the robe and the Cross with their spittle." He bowed his head at the hopelessness. The indignity.

The Priest, of course, made no review of history in his talk. The history of the bishops, seeing the politicos and the Dons raping the wealth of Mexico and using the slavery of the Indian, while the Church was left standing to take only the tithes of these wealthy. The bishops used their influence with the King to "end the slavery of the Indian."

The King had responded. His proclamation read that all Indians must be paid a "living wage," and he left it up to the Church and the politicos to decide what that living wage should be. The politicos controlled the price of maize and beans, and so the "living wage" fluctuated accordingly.

The Priest did not mention the peon who worked in the mines, carrying three and four hundred pounds of ore on his back up the ladders, hundreds of feet to the surface, fourteen, sixteen hours a day for the "living wage" of a daily peso.

Nor did he mention the Church required three hundred pesos to marry the peon in ceremony, a hundred pesos to christen his newborn, pesos for holy days and confessions, so that the Indian peon worked continually in debt to the Church—and to the seller of the corn, becoming not a slave of one master, but of two, enriching the Dons with the wealth of kings. And the Church now owned millions of acres of land, upon which the peon must work "free" to pay tribute to the Church. The Church, so wealthy even the federal government in Ciudad de Mexico often borrowed from its holy coffers to meet its own haggling budget, at interest, of course.

He did not mention that the average survival time of the Indian mine worker was five years, that the Church urged him to "have children and replenish the earth." He was expected to breed at least five niños before his death.

The Indian of Mexico was dying. Dying in the slow grinding that showed no violence, and wrapped in the black robe of the Church. The steel foot of greed pressed him toward his heavenly reward.

The Priest did not speak of these things. They were material matters having nothing to do with the spiritual; and above all, the Priest concerned himself with the soul of the Indian peon.

The warmth of the wine and the Priest's words and manner made the heart of Capitan Jesus Escobedo go out to this man of God.

He, Escobedo, after all was here to bring hope, safety for the Church, progress for Mexico and civilization. His personal ambition was undoubtedly spurred by these holy and national causes. He could see the destiny, the "manifest destiny" that rested on his shoulders.

He spoke softly, not boastfully, of how he and his fifty Rurales had attacked a hundred Apache, twice their number; had slain thirty-five and put the rest to rout.

One captive he would hang on the western border of Coyamo at dawn as a warning to the Apache, to give encouragement to the Christian peon. The other captive would be hanged at Aldamano, sixty miles to the west.

He recounted how he had fought the pitched battle on the very border at the Rio Grande, and won, and brought back the gringo criminal to face justice at Escalon. If only he had the authority!

He could drive the Apache into the Sierra Madre, follow him where he had never been followed before, wipe him from the face of the earth.

He felt God would be with him, he said, as servant of the holy faith and the advance of civilization.

When Escobedo had finished, the Alcalde was on his feet. "I am in support of such hombres as you, Capitan! You are the life we must have in the north. Tonight—I shall not wait for morning—tonight I shall plead your case for authority to bring about this plan. I shall send it to the state capital—yea! to Ciudad de Mexico itself!" The Alcalde was exuberant and almost danced on the stone of the patio.

The Priest spread his hands before him and studied them. "I am not a man of violence. I have opposed it," he said, "but if the sword must be raised in the cause of the Cross, then it must be raised, as in the Crusades, Capitan! I shall send my support for you to the Bishop immediately."

Escobedo kept his dignity, though the exultation rushed through him, flooding him with excitement. He stood, offering gracias for the hospitality of the Alcalde's hacienda, and kneeling humbly before the Priest for a special blessing.

As he strolled down the dusty street toward his quarters, his spirits soared. He passed the jail where the prisoners were held, and surprised the guardia on duty with a hearty "Buenas noches!"

It was not yet midnight. The Apache girl awaited his pleasures in his quarters.

Somewhere he had read of the fortunes of war, how they turned. Without doubt it was true. The name of Jesus Escobedo would soon be on the lips of all Mexico!

Chapter 7

In the beginning, he had not cared. Slung across the horse, head down, seeing only the ground and hearing the Rurales as they talked and cursed riding beside him, Ten Spot had not cared.

As it had been since Shenandoah. Beautiful, green, mountain-cradled Shenandoah! His parents dead, he had lived alone. A scholar with his books and with his orchard. His apple trees that burst in the spring with delicate pinkness against their white, their fragrance that sweetened the earthy leafing of the mountain oaks and the sharpness of the pine. His apple trees!

Unabashedly they displayed the fetus of life they were bringing, tiny green nubs that took shape and rounded and grew almost to bursting with the exuberance. Often he had walked his orchard, stopping to feel them, to stroke, to rub his hands against the bulging life. He could feel their pulse, hear their breathing.

And in the autumn! The autumn with its melancholy golden light in Shenandoah. How the apples reddened; first the slightest tinge of blush; then deeper and deeper came the redness, signaling to the gods their food purpose; fat and red, and at peace in their knowing they served the cause which gave them birth. He had not loved them for their profit. He had simply loved them.

The War had passed him by. He had his world, separate from the imbeciles who ran up and down the valley, chopping at each other's throats, quarreling, blaspheming the earth with their blood.

His world was apart from the insanities of men and their mean currents of politics blowing over the earth. He could, and did, live without them.

Until Sheridan! Sheridan and his savages with their torches. Like Attila, they burned Shenandoah. Everything, every field, every home, every blade of grass or leaf of tree died in the flames of Shenandoah.

First, he had tried to stop them with words, lecturing to them, as to children. Patiently he explained he was no part of the War. He was above their quarrels. He had no place in their violence.

They had laughed and ridden by him with their torches. He had walked, then run among them, first in rage as the torches licked at his home, then pleading as the flames ate at his books. He had run among the flames, stomping at them, tossing his precious volumes into the yard until he could bear the heat no longer.

He had run after them to his orchard, but the pleading in him had drained. He had watched as the orchard, the trees, the beautiful, life-giving trees, had each become a death torch. He had watched. As the ground grass lit the trees, William Beauregard Francis Willingham had died.

Like all such men proposing to set apart from the world, he entertained not the slightest thought of rebuilding. Impractical in his separate world, he was as impractical at its destruction. He had not even kicked at the ashes, but turned away and stumbled west across the miserable Southland.

No description could fathom his bitterness. He wished for death, but could not bring himself to the technicalities by which he might bring it about.

He became a swamper in saloons, sweeping floors, emptying spittoons to pay for the whiskey. He discovered his deftness with cards, and from New Orleans, he drifted west.

He had begun to feel balm for the bitterness. Deliberately he lived with the scum of the frontier. When men sneeringly referred to him as "tinhorn," he secretly rejoiced in their contempt, as when they called him "pimp," or he woke in the morning beside the body of the coarsest whore. He was these things—all these things—and many more. This is actually what he had been all the time!

Golden Shenandoah had been a shining coin he found in the street, then lost again. It had not really been his from the beginning—he had not deserved Shenandoah! He felt the bitterness leave him.

He proved it each day, earning the contempt of the lowest at the gambling tables. He proved it in his whore-mongering, his drunken revels. This was his world. He thought of Shenandoah no more. Yes, the bitterness was gone. Empty. Emptied of feeling, except the small corner where grew the strange comradeship with Rose—illiterate, a whore with no purpose, empty as Ten Spot.

He had not cared while his head throbbed from the

bullet crease, bumping against the horse. He had not cared until they righted him to ride astride and put the rawhide thong around his neck, tied to the saddle horn of a Rurale.

To be led by the neck like an animal! The resentment rose in Ten Spot. Beside him rode the Apache, bloodied and mangled, looking neither toward nor away from him.

Ahead, the Apache girl had ridden, looped in the same manner about the neck, with the rawhide secured to the wrist of the Capitan, who led them.

When they had camped, Ten Spot and the two Apache were forced to squat, hands tied behind their backs, and watch the Rurales eating. As each finished his meal, he would rise and come over, raking the scraps of food from his tin plate on the ground before them.

Ten Spot refused to eat. The two Apache bent forward, placing their foreheads against the ground; they ate like dogs from the scraps, while the Rurales watched and roared in laughter, pointing first to one and then the other.

"Animal! Bestia! Bruto!" they shouted. The Apache, patiently, stoically, continued their groveling at the scraps. They appeared not to hear.

Now Ten Spot lay against the wall of the Coyamo jail. He was tied, feet together, hands behind his back. It was more a dungeon than a jail.

A single barred window, high in the 'dobe wall, was at ground level on the outside, and heavy stone steps led upward to the single ponderous door through which he and the Apache warrior had been thrown by the Rurales.

They had followed them down, had the Rurales; and had kicked the Apache repeatedly, laughing, crooking their necks in grotesque clownish poses while they held imaginary hanging ropes over their heads. "Muerte, Apache, por la mañana!"

So Ten Spot knew the Apache would hang in the morning.

When they had gone, he stared across at the warrior, who looked at him with unblinking eyes.

Rats began to scurry about in the straw, squeaking, and Ten Spot watched, horror mounting, as two of the huge rodents boldly climbed the chest of the Apache, licking at the blood, and began gnawing at the naked end of a protruding broken rib.

The warrior watched impassively. Suddenly he rolled and caught them beneath him. Ten Spot heard their death-shrieking. He shuddered.

His hands were swollen and numb from the tight leather bindings; but now he worked them, twisting, turning, running a finger up his coat sleeve for the thin shiv knife of the gambler.

He felt it. Slowly, slowly, he worked it downward into the clutch of three fingers. It sliced the leather like butter. He loosed his hands and sat up, rubbing life back into them. He cut the thongs of his feet. Then he crawled to the Apache.

The warrior watched, looked at the knife and back into the eyes of Ten Spot. He expected death. His eyes showed no emotion, only the peculiar glazed glow of hate.

Ten Spot cut the leather from his wrists and from his ankles. The Apache sat up quickly, still unsure.

"Hablo español?" Ten Spot asked.

"Si," the Apache answered softly.

Ten Spot shrugged, pointed at himself. "Well, I no hablo español. Ain't that a hell of a situation!" He laughed weakly.

The Apache smiled. He understood. His front teeth had been kicked out, leaving deep rutted gaps in the gums. His lips were turned outward from puffy swelling. The broken rib stuck a ragged point through his side, and his stomach and breechclout were matted with blood.

He stumbled to his feet and made no sound as his

moccasins paced around the walls. Despite his terrible physical condition, his movements were panther-smooth and graceful in rhythmic body control.

He knelt and dug in a corner. Ten Spot followed and watched him curiously. Down he dug, a foot, perhaps eighteen inches. Stone! The floor was solid stone beneath the hard-packed earth and straw.

The warrior rose and, walking below the window, leaped and grabbed the bars. He pushed with his head; barely the head squeezed through; to get a body through the narrow opening would be an impossibility. Easily, he dropped to the floor. Despite his blood loss, the Apache's strength amazed the weakened Ten Spot. Now he knew why the Apache ate the scraps.

Ten Spot could bear the sight no longer. He pulled off his coat and ripped away his shirt. Motioning the Apache to him, he pushed the splintered rib back into the flesh and tightly wound strips around his chest.

When he had finished, the Apache looked down at the bandage, back at Ten Spot. He pointed to himself. "Na-ko-la," he said simply. And then, "Gracias."

"You're welcome," Ten Spot muttered, "but it'll do you very little good, my friend. They're hanging you in a few hours."

Na-ko-la grinned. He whirled, and his boot moccasins barely slithered on the straw as he glided to the wall beneath the high barred window.

Ten Spot believed he had lost his mind, for suddenly the Apache hit himself in the mouth, hard, viciously. He cupped his hand and blood gushed into it. When his hand was full, he leaped and flung the blood on the iron bars above him and on the 'dobe wall. He repeated the blows to the mouth; this time, when he leaped, he grabbed an iron bar with one hand, drawing himself up; he flung the blood outside the window.

"What the hell!" Ten Spot whispered incredulously.

Na-ko-la came and stood before him. He held out his hand and pointed at the knife. Ten Spot handed it to him.

He moved to the far corner of the cell and knelt. Carefully he moved the knife into the earth, cutting squares. Slowly, with meticulous care, he lifted out the squares, keeping the top soil separated as he set them aside. As he removed more soil, each time in squares, down to the stone floor, he worked faster.

"By God," Ten Spot looked, open-mouthed, "damned if he ain't dug himself a grave." He had, almost perfectly proportioned for his body. He handed the knife back to Ten Spot and smiled again.

Now, untying the breechclout, he squatted, defecating a small pile there, moving and repeating his action close to the head of his grave.

He lay down on the exposed stone surface, fitted himself, and sat up. Legs a-spraddle, with feet laid flat, he carefully picked up the little squares. Laying his breechclout beside himself, he shaved off the excess bottom earth onto the cloth and set the squares over his feet. They fit perfectly. There was no mound or even a lump betraying the resting place of the feet. He moved to the legs, repeating the action; then reaching to the pile of his own waste, he threw it over the ground covering his lower body.

He worked as far as his neck and, breaking a hollow straw, placed it in his mouth and looked at Ten Spot. Ten Spot thumped his chest with the miracle he had seen. "Well, I'm a sonofabitch!" he said.

Na-ko-la, motioning him to place the earth over his arms and head, whispered, "Gracias, Sonofabitch!"

"No, I'm Ten . . . what the hell!" Ten Spot knelt and shaved the earth into the breechclout, carefully placing the squares.

The last square to be placed was over the face of

Na-ko-la. They looked long at each other, and Ten Spot saw not hate, but warmth in the eyes of an Apache.

He placed the square, careful to break the protruding straw even with the ground. Then he lightly rubbed his foot over the grave, pressing together the tiny cut marks, and scattered straw where it had been before.

He took the breechclout and, with infinite care, dribbled its raw earth around the walls of the cell. He dropped his pants to tie the breechclout around him. As he did, a thought occurred.

"Hell," he said to himself casually, "I been having belly cramps for three days. Bet I can drizzle shit enough on that corner to keep a rat from walking in it, much less a Rurale." And he did.

He sat down across the cell, back to the wall, and laughed softly to himself. "It'll be worth a beating—even a hanging, by God, to see the faces of those Rurales when they come."

Perhaps it came from watching the Apache, in the midst of disaster, of hopeless circumstance, of death, change that hopelessness to hope, even to chance for victory over sure death.

Yes, that was it, for in the middle of death, life was flowing back into Ten Spot. Into his brain.

Carefully he slid the shiv knife back into its secret pocket. He picked up the cut thongs of leather and began to chew their ends, disguising the smooth knife cut.

Ten Spot was thinking. Despite his precarious position, he felt better about the whole goddamn thing.

Chapter 8

Three Rurales escaped out of Saucillo ahead of Josey Wales. One had run from the cantina half screaming of the disaster to the two remaining at the station of policia. The three had leaped on horses and ridden west for Coyamo.

Darkness caught them before they had gone ten miles, but they did not slacken the horses' running. Behind them, they could still hear the wild screams of the blood-crazed pistolero, Josey Wales. They fancied hoofbeats in pursuit.

Halfway to Coyamo, two of them, who had unluckily leaped upon lesser horses, found themselves afoot on the plains. One of the horses, heaving for breath, fell and broke its leg. A mile further, the other simply died beneath the rider with a bursted heart.

The two stranded men, hearing the wolf howl and then answered, again and again, from all directions, did not hesitate. They pulled the pistolas from their belts and blew out their brains.

The Apache silently moved in upon them, stripping their bodies of guns and ammunition. On the belt of one they found the scalp of an Apache child. With their knives, they hacked his body to pieces. The horse with the broken leg still lived. They gathered close.

They had been running for seven days and were now without rations. The leader knelt by the horse and seized the jugular vein, as one might squeeze a hose of water. Above his squeezing hand, he cut the vein and placed his mouth to it. He relaxed his grip only briefly, to receive his ration of blood, and motioned for the next warrior to seize the vein. Each stepped forward in his turn, taking of the life ration sparsely, leaving life for his brother warrior next in line.

They had no time to butcher the horse. They cut chunks of meat from it; and as their moccasin feet resumed the muffled, ominous running, they sucked the blood from the meat and chewed its tough rawness.

The remaining Rurale, far ahead, rode a dying horse into the street of Coyamo.

Capitan Escobedo, just returned from his supper with the Alcalde and the Priest, sat on the bunk of his private quarters. At his feet the Apache girl lay. Her eyes were closed.

He was in excellent spirits and reached down, running his hand over the flat muscled stomach of the girl, felt the velvet hardness of tiny breasts.

"Perhaps, querida," he murmured, "despite my tired soul and body, I should question you tonight? Pues y que?

What of that?" He began removing his boots and was delighted that the girl had opened her eyes and was watching. Was it fear?

The pounding came on the door—loud, rude!

"Capitan!" It was the voice of Lieutenant Valdez. "Es urgente!"

Escobedo cursed. "Un momento!" he shouted back at the door. He pulled on his boots, flung open the door, then stepped backward at the mad eyes of the Rurale held between the strong arms of Lieutenant Valdez and Sergeant Martinez.

They crowded immodestly into the room. Escobedo turned away from them. Walking to his desk, he lit two more candles.

"Bring him before the light," he said crisply. The Lieutenant and Sergeant half carried the sagging figure.

The Rurale lifted his face, and his eyes showed rolling and white. Saliva dripped from his mouth. His drooping mustache trembled violently.

"Saucillo!" the Rurale gasped weakly, ignoring the necessity of addressing El Capitan. "Saucillo! Muerte! All dead!"

Escobedo stepped forward and slapped him across the face, open-handed, back-handed, until the Rurale's head fell forward. His sombrero tumbled to the floor.

Lieutenant Valdez seized him by the hair and jerked his head up to face his Capitan. Escobedo slapped him again. Gradually the whites of the eyes rolled down. The Rurale looked at his Capitan. "Josey Wales . . ." He breathed it quietly. His voice trembled and carried a haunting awe of unbelief.

At the name, Escobedo felt a coldness run through him, the coldness he had felt when he had crossed the Rio Grande. His face whitened, and he gripped the Rurale by the throat, "Que? What about Josey Wales? Speak, hombre!"

The story came in snatches: The screams of a madman as he killed! Crazed for blood! Yes, there had been more men. Two besides Josey Wales; the Indian bandido had only one arm, the other they did not see, he had shot from ambush!

Now the Rurale was crying. Tears made ropes of water, wetting his jacket. His nose ran mucus into his mouth and he coughed. Escobedo kicked him in the groin. He vomited, heaving a stenching mess on the floor, on Escobedo's boots.

"Take this perro, this dog. Tie him up, hide him. He must not be seen in Coyamo! Comprendes?" He snapped the orders at Valdez.

The Lieutenant straightened to attention. "Si, Capitan," he said crisply.

They pushed and dragged the Rurale to the door.

"When you have done this," Capitan Escobedo said, "return here, Lieutenant! Rapido!"

"Si, Capitan!"

At the closing of the door, Escobedo rushed to his desk. He jerked a bottle of tequila from a drawer, and his hand shook uncontrollably as he poured half a glass. He downed it in one swallow. He rummaged among the papers of the desk, laying out a map of the area. His hands still trembled. Raising the bottle again, he swallowed more of the tequila.

By the time Valdez returned, he was calmed. Spreading the map between them, he pointed his finger. "Here, to our northwest, no more than ten miles, is the guarida of Pancho Morino, the bandido. Comprende?"

"Si," Valdez answered. His face was puzzled. He had never learned to follow the thinking of his Capitan. He shrugged.

"Morino," Escobedo continued, his voice rising in fever as the plan took shape in his mind, "Marino has fifteen, twenty, bandidos. He is hungry and hunted. This," Escobedo rose from the map, pointing his finger in Valdez' stolid face, "this you must do. You must ride, instante, pronto! When you approach his guarida, fire three shots, that you come in peace. Tell Morino this: I wish to make truce with him. Truce that will profit him mucho. To prove my fidelity, I will meet him in one hour from the time you talk with him, on the road west of Coyamo. I will be alone. He may send his sentinels to prove this. Comprendes?"

"Si, Capitan, but . . ."

"VAMOS!"

Valdez rushed to the door.

"And Lieutenant, you will tell no one of your mission. Have Sergeant Martinez saddle my horse."

"Si, Capitan."

Valdez hurried to the stables and galloped out of sleeping Coyamo.

Escobedo paced the floor, back and forth, in the flickering light of the candles. The panic had left him. He was at his best in a crisis. He knew it, taking pride in his quick cunning.

He had brought fifty Rurales to Coyamo with him; ten were already stationed here. Sixty men. Josey Wales would never attack sixty men. He knew the type. They moved like the coyote. Like the Apache. Wales would strike when he found a weakness—out of the dark, when Escobedo was alone; perhaps in the back. The Capitan had his plan.

He sat on the edge of the desk, swinging his leg easily in a tight circle. He ran his finger along the thin mustache and traced his sensitive chin in thought. Drinking again from the tequila, he smiled down at the Apache girl, a benevolent, even a fatherly, smile. "Perhaps tomorrow night, querida. Business before pleasure, eh?"

Her eyes were closed. Softly he pushed her stomach with his boot, but she did not open her eyes.

He knew she was making the pretense. These Apache! Really children when one with intelligence handled them!

He walked to the stables, mounted his waiting horse, held by Sergeant Martinez. Slowly he trotted the horse out the westward gate. Escobedo would keep his word. He would ride alone. This time.

For nearly an hour, he lazily trotted his mount. Now he began to hear outriders in the brush. These bandidos! They trusted no one.

In the dim light, he could spot Pancho Morino, the silver edging the sombrero, the tint of silver on his saddle. He rode with Lieutenant Valdez, and they halted their horses a few yards from each other.

"You may return to your quarters, Lieutenant," Escobedo said casually to Valdez. The Lieutenant galloped away, glad to leave the encircling riders.

Escobedo waited until the hoofbeats had died in the distance. Then he spoke, "Señor Morino, I have kept my word. I am alone."

The impassive face of the bandido showed nothing. "Si," he said shortly, and sat his horse, waiting.

The wind was rising, and Escobedo slowly walked his horse closer. He halted a few feet from Morino as the bandido's hand fell toward his holster.

"What I have to say is for our ears alone. Comprendes?"

"Si."

Escobedo breathed deeply. How to explain to this subhuman Indian peon who had gone mad?

"A gringo pistolero who calls himself Josey Wales has become a nuisance on my trail. He kills the defenseless, but runs at sight of my troops. He has only two compadres. It would be a beneficio if he was killed . . . beneficio mucho to me."

Morino's horse stomped and skittered in the wind. He brought him under control.

"So?" he said softly.

"Tomorrow," Escobedo continued patiently, "he will ride into Coyamo, but only if I am not there. At dawn this day, I and all my sixty Rurales will leave Coyamo. We will ride sixty miles to the west, to Aldamano. You may place sentinels on the road to guarantee my trust. You are a bandido. You will know how the ambuscade can be made. This is your way."

Escobedo saw the slight lift of Pancho Morino's eyebrows.

"And my profit?" Morino asked softly.

"Your profit shall be this." Escobedo paused for the effect of profit—grande. "The town shall be yours for two days. You may collect your—tribute—in that time. I will not return until two days following a messenger from you to Aldamano that Josey Wales and his compadres are dead."

He waited. The impassive Indian bandido said nothing.

"You may place sentinels on the road at all times, of course, to insure my word," he added, urgency creeping into his voice.

"And how will I know this Joh-seh Wales?" Morino asked.

Escobedo handed a poster across to Morino. "You cannot fail to know. He wears the gray hat of a gringo Rebel. His face is heavy-scarred. One of his compadres has but one arm."

Pancho Morino folded the poster. "It is done," he said.

Escobedo extended his hand. The bandido spat on the

ground. He wheeled his horse, whistled to his outriders, and was gone.

As Morino disappeared into the blackness, Escobedo breathed hard between clenched teeth, "You will pay for that insult, peon bastardo!"

The time was now short until dawn. Back in Coyamo, he ordered Valdez to mount all troops to leave at dawn for Aldamano. Hurrying to the Alcalde's hacienda, he roused the servants to the gate. He met the Alcalde, still sleep-drugged, in the patio.

"My scouts," he announced curtly, "have sighted Apache forty miles to the west. We leave immediately to encircle and destroy them. We shall be back quickly."

The Alcalde came alive. "Bravo! At this hour! I shall commend your diligence to the Governor! Vaya con Dios!" He shouted the last, for the Capitan had bowed stiffly, taking his leave like an officer off to perform his urgent duty.

The Alcalde ran to the iron gate and shouted again to the retreating back of the gallant Capitan. "The Priest will ask a special blessing for you, Capitan, for you and your brave men!"

The Capitan raised his hand in final salute that he heard, but he did not turn.

The troops were mounted. Capitan Escobedo at their head with the Apache girl, neck thonged by his side. Then he sent for the prisoners.

Flinging open the heavy cell door, four Rurales came down the stone steps. They stopped at the sight of Ten Spot sitting against the wall. Dumbly they looked about them. "En donde Apache?" one of them asked stupidly of the others.

Ten Spot laughed and pointed to the window. "He vamoosed, you silly bastards. Through the bars!"

They ran to the window, leaped up to look out, ran around the cell. Ten Spot, already weak, fell over on the floor, laughing. He held his sides. "Vamoosed, bastardos!" He gasped for air between squeals of hysterical laughter.

One of the Rurales stepped into the piles of human waste left by Ten Spot and Na-ko-la. He sniffed, lifted his boot, "Excremento!" he shouted in disgust.

Ten Spot lost his breath. He rolled on the floor, laughing uproariously. They kicked him in the head, the stomach, the face, but could not silence him.

Dragging him up the steps, they flung him, bound, astride a horse. Still his laughter sounded, echoing insanely hollow in the eerie light of dawn.

Escobedo was furious, but his fury had to be suffered in silence. The Alcalde and the Priest would forget all about the Apache when he rode back and rescued their town from the murdering bandido Pancho Morino. Si. Morino would swing just as high on a gallows.

He raised his hand, waving forward, column of twos, west to Aldamano.

And as they rode, the whispers flew down the line of Rurales. No human could have gone through the bars. Only a servant of El Diablo! Truly! The Apache was evilly sainted by El Diablo himself!

Chapter 9

In that same early dawn, the tracker eyes of Chato Olivares found the trail. They had backtracked less than a half hour when he saw the tracks. There was no doubt. "Coyamo, Josey," he said, "they've gone to Coyamo. The tracks are not old. We're getting close!"

Getting close! There in the ghost light of the desert dawn, they sat their horses. Getting close. Then what?

Josey Wales cut a tobacco plug, pushed it into his cheek and thoughtfully chewed. He spat on the flat spoon of a ground cactus and noted, with passing satisfaction, the dead-center hit.

"Well," he drawled as he spurred the big roan, "let's git at it."

They took the trail to Coyamo at a ground-covering gallop. The sun rose behind them, pinking gamma grass and sparkling the cactus spines like silver needles. They kept up the hard pushing of the horses, even as the sun rose higher and raised the heat on the desert floor.

They stopped briefly at the hacked remains of the first Rurale and his horse. The buzzards were already feeding, and boldly hopped but a few paces away, already too glutted to inspire flight.

"Apache," Chato said.

" 'Pears like them fellers want to make shore they do the job," Josey said flatly. Pablo closed his eyes.

They rode on and didn't stop at what was left of the second Rurale. But they were forced to slacken the gait of the horses. For a mile they walked them.

"Wondering," Josey said, "if them was the only two got away, er if there was another un."

"No way to tell, Josey," Chato said, "the tracks are too many."

"Why?" asked Pablo.

"Well," Josey answered drily, "sometimes it makes a difference if ye know company's coming, er if it ain't."

"We being, of course, the company," Chato explained politely to Pablo.

The sun had tipped past noon when they sighted Coyamo, shimmering, flat and white, like a mirage in the desert heat.

Josey pulled up. "Reckin that's her," he said.

"Si," Chato agreed with a fatal solemnity, "that is her."

They sat for a while, blowing the horses. Josey reached back in a saddlebag and drew out the little long-glass. He handed it to Chato.

"Tell ye what ye do, Chato," he said, "ye take this glass and circle around left of that town, up on thet knoll ye see way off yonder." He nodded his head to indicate the yonder. "From there," he continued, "ye look over every-thing ye can, the town. When ye pull thet little glass all way out, she'll give ye twelve, fifteen mile in this country. They cain't hide hosses. Check all around."

"Si," Chato said, and took the glass.

"And Pablo," Josey said, "ye circle right of the town. Ye ride wide, look fer hosses. If ye see more than five er six, ye wave yer hat. Otherwise, both of ye ride in from t'other side of town. We'll meet at the stables. Hosses come first."

"And what will you do, Josey?" Chato asked.

Josey Wales looked surprised. "Me? Why I'm a-going to jest keep walking this hoss right on into town. Onliest way a Missouri brush rider ever learnt to do it. Git!"

They galloped their horses, Chato and Pablo, widening in arcs around the town. As they rode, Josey Wales began to walk the big roan, easy at first, then into a soft Sunday jog, like maybe he was a-going to church or social-calling on a gal. It was the way of Josey Wales.

As he rode, he watched Pablo, riding wide, down a slight dip in the prairie and up again. On his left, he saw Chato reach the knoll and stand his horse for a long time, moving the glass, scanning.

He began to talk casually, to himself and to the horse. "We've rid with some good uns in Missouri, Red. Them two there will do." He came closer and saw Chato come off the knoll and circle still further to the west. Pablo was arcing from the right.

When Josey reached the arched entrance to the town street, he never paused, but trotted in—as any oblivious pilgrim might do, he figgered.

But Josey Wales could not be mistaken for a pilgrim, even by the village idiot. The horse was the kind a man depended on for his life, and pilgrims do not ride about the countryside wearing .44 Colts tied down on their legs, with four additional Colts holstered and showing on the saddle. Pilgrims did not display the scarred grim-looking face that belonged to Josey Wales.

As he came under the archway, a blanketed Indian, leaning against the wall, ran behind the buildings. Two sombreroed peons squatting against the side of a cantina required the slightest of looks to cause their disappearance. The steady clip-clop of the big horse was the only sound.

"Right peaceful 'pearing little village, Red," Josey continued his drawling talk to the horse, "like some of them Kansas towns we used to ride into. Howsoever, I don't see no bank about." What he was saying was what he felt. There was no one on the street. It was peaceful.

He rode past a cantina where three horses were hitch-railed, resting three-footed in the hot sun. The middle horse was a huge dappled black with silver-trimmed saddle and stirrups.

"Now that un," Josey drawled to his horse, "that un there might give ye a run, Red." The big roan pricked his ears and snorted his disgust. Three horses, no more. The town was empty. A storekeeper stood back in the shadows and watched him pass.

He saw the livery barn, wide-aisled, and took the roan in without dismounting. Chato and Pablo were there already.

"Through the glass," Chato said, "es nada, empty as far as I can see."

"Si," agreed Pablo, "nada."

There was no one in the big barn. The stalls showed one mule and a jackass, old and sleeping.

"Reckin we can grain and cool these hosses," Josey said.

They stripped the saddles. Rubbing down the horses, they gave them only a little water. Then from a grain bin they filled nose bags and put them on the horses. They filled their own grain bags, to be slung behind saddles, and had just turned from this when a man walked into the shade of the wide aisle.

Josey quickly motioned Pablo to the back door. The man wore the boots and spurs of a vaquero, but his dress was the poor sackcloth of the peon.

He stopped and politely lifted the straw sombrero, holding his arms wide to show he carried no guns. He was dark-skinned, with a prideful mustache that drooped below his jaws.

He smiled and bowed. "Buenas tardes, señores," he said softly.

"Buenas tardes," Chato answered.

"I reckin," Josey drawled, and squatted on his heels.

"Muy . . . ," the stranger began.

Josey turned to Chato. "Tell him to talk to you. Ye'll tell me, and then we'll all know what in hell he's got on his mind."

Chato spoke rapidly in Spanish. The man smiled and nodded his agreement.

Hesitantly at first, then more rapidly, he talked, continually smiling. Josey figgered he was apologizing for something. When he had finished, Chato turned to Josey. His face was a shade whiter, his lips drawn.

"He say," Chato began, "that his leader is Pancho Morino. He say Pancho Morino is a great pistolero—and he *is*, Josey, *mucho* grande. He has killed many men. He say Pancho Morino is up the street in a cantina, and has heard you are Josey Wales, a pistolero grande. He say Pancho would like the honor of meeting you in the street to contest which is more grande." Chato stared at the ground. Then: "That's all he say—except, if you win, we all ride free of his twenty bandidos; you lose, then we— Pablo and me—we die too."

"Which way is the cantina?" Josey asked.

Chato asked the question and was answered. The man

pointed back toward the east, where the three horses were hitch-railed.

Josey cut a tobacco plug and chewed meditatively. He spat, rolling a confused dung beetle in the manure of the aisle. "Tell this here feller," he said slowly, "that I have heerd of what a great pistolero he is—which I ain't—but tell him that bullshit anyhow. Tell him I know that him being a great hoss man, he understands I got to see to my hoss fust off. Tell him I'll send a messenger up the road there in a few minutes to the cantina, unarmed, to let him know as what is most convenient, all around . . . Reckin that's all."

Chato related the message in fluid Spanish, leaning heavy on the "grande" when he spoke of Pancho Morino. When he had finished, the man bowed politely, turned and walked from the stable.

"Josey," Chato said, "this Pancho Morino is very, *very* fast. He is feared over a great area. He . . ."

"Hesh up," Josey drawled, "I'm thinking." He chewed for an eternity, it seemed to Pablo. Then: "Ye know, thet's a purty hunk of hoss, that dappled black of his'n. Tell ye what—when ye go up there . . ."

"Me?" Chato asked, alarmed.

"Yeah," Josey said, "when ye go up there, tell him all that stuff 'bout me figgerin' that since we're pistoleros and sich, it'd be a sporting proposition if the one come out uppers takes the other's hoss. He's seen mine, riding by the cantina."

"Por Dios, Josey!" Chato pleaded. "Is all you thinking of *horses*?"

"Nooooo," Josey said absently, "I'm thinking something else. When ye go, tell him it'll take me 'bout a hour to git my hoss and sich in good shape." Josey squinted at the sun. "Yep," he said confidently, "hour ort to do it. And Chato, when ye go, study how he hangs his gun. Where he wears it, sich as that . . . Reckin that's all. Shuck yer gun belt and I'll hold it fer ye."

With reluctant slowness, Chato unbuckled his pistol belt. He looked longingly at it for a moment, and with the fatalistic shrug of the vaquero, he walked out of the barn toward the cantina, his jingling spurs dragging in the dust.

Josey turned to Pablo, seated at the back door of the barn.

"Pablo," he called softly.

"Si?"

"Tell ye what ye do, ye git out thet pistol and hold it in yore lap. Takes ye a shade to git it out. If ye let anybody sneak up and kill us from behint—I'll kill ye."

"Si, I will watch closely, Josey." He pulled the big pistol and laid it across his legs. Nothing moved.

The minutes dragged by; half hour. Chato reappeared, flipped his sombrero on the ground, and flopped, his back against a stall. He wiped sweat from his face. Josey squatted patiently. He handed Chato his pistol and belt.

Chato began, "First, Josey, I would never do such as that for anybody else. Remember, next time I want to borrow ahead of the wages. Second, he is the born killer. He cares nada if he dies. He has no fear. He say he has killed eighteen men he know of. He say the hour is all right." Chato paused and wiped his brow.

"Was he drinking?" Josey asked casually.

"Si," Chato answered, "from a bottle of tequila." He looked slyly at Josey. "I had two, maybe three, un poco —just little ones—to learn more, you see . . ."

"Yeah, I see," Josey drawled. "How's he hang his pistol? Sich as that?"

Chato pointed his finger at Josey. "Only once before have I see such a pistol rig—it was fast. He wears a swivel holster."

"Swivel holster? Never heerd tell of sich," Josey said.

"Some pistoleros on the border use them," Chato explained. "The pistol belt has a little knob on it, the holster swings on the knob. The pistola is never pulled from the holster. It is tied into it. The bottom of the holster is open. All he do, Josey . . . ," Chato's voice dropped in doom, "is drop his hand on the handle and thumb the hammer, up come the bottom of the holster, and BAM! She fires. He shoot from the hip, very fast . . . You see, the holster is not tied down . . ."

"Yeah," Josey interrupted, "I see." He scratched the stubble of beard on his jaw. "Is thet there holster tight agin' his hip, er hang loose, kinder?"

Chato frowned, remembering. "It is tight to his hip. It would be a necesidad, you comprendes—the leverage to push down—it could not be loose."

"Figgers," mused Josey Wales.

Chato was nervous. "How do we know when the hour has passed. We have no watch. I could not tell the time if we had one."

Josey squinted through the door at the sun. Where the shade was moving back from the corner of the barn aisle, he drew a line in the dirt with his finger. "When she gits there," he said, "reckin that'll make a good Missouri hour. Ye can wake me up then."

"*Wake you up?*" Chato nearly shouted. "You are going to *sleep?*"

"Well," he said apologetically, "if one of ye is sleepy, I'll split the watch with ye. There ain't but two doors to watch—half and half. How about it?"

"*Sleep?*" Chato exclaimed. "I could not sleep if I was dead!"

"Nor could I sleep, Josey," Pablo agreed.

Head on saddle, hat pulled over his face, Josey spraddled in the aisle of the barn. The restless sleep of the outlaw trail was different. Now he would rest between two friends.

In a moment, Chato exclaimed softly to Pablo, "Sonofa-dog! When Josey *really* sleep, he *snores!*"

And so he did.

The shade crawled quickly for Chato. He watched it, fascinated by the speed of an hour. As it touched the line in the dirt, he shook Josey.

"It is time," he said quietly. Josey stood, yawned, and stretched his body. He flexed his arms, his hands, pulled the big pistols and inspected their loads, then slid them up, down, in the holsters.

He called Pablo and Chato to his side as he stepped to the barn door. "Tell ye what ye do. Chato, ye'll walk agin' the buildings on my right side, four, five steps behind and watch the tops of the buildings, and the alleys *acrost* the street from ye. Pablo, ye'll walk same, agin' the buildings on my left. But ye watch the tops acrost the street, and the alleys. Ye see something looks like it ain't made in Granma's kitchen, ye shoot at it."

"This man," Chato said firmly, "wants a pistol duel. He is not thinking of such."

"Yeah, I know," Josey drawled. "Rec'lect several fellers died of back trouble, thinking the same thing. Ye all watch them buildings. I'll do the acquainting with Mr. Pancho."

They stepped into the street. Josey walked to the middle of the dusty street, before he turned to face east. A three o'clock sun was at his back, broiling hot.

With a pace of excruciating slowness, he strolled toward the cantina. He had measured ten steps when Pancho Morino stepped through the batwing doors, walking to the center of the street.

Turning, he brought his sombrero down to better shade his eyes. Behind him, his two men walked.

All in black he was dressed. Silver trimmed the sombrero, made shining flowers on the tight vest, ran in curling bright loops down the tight britches that flared, vaquero-style, at the boots. The single pistola, he wore high. It was ivory-handled.

Josey calculated the distance as they walked toward one another. He stopped with twenty paces between them. Morino seemed disappointed. He took another step, but Josey would not move. Morino stopped.

His face was thin, angular, dark, with a slim mustache neatly trimmed. The eyes were reckless eyes, black and flippant with their taunting look at death. He was smoking a cigar.

For a full thirty seconds, they stood. Pancho Morino broke the silence. He smiled, good-humoredly, white teeth showing in the sun. "Buenas tardes, Señor Josey Wales." Though polite, his tone was faintly mocking.

"Same to ye, Mr. Pancho Morino," Josey said lazily.

Morino was puzzled by this man. True, he appeared to be an hombre malo, scar-faced, two tied-down pistolas. For a pistola grande, however, he did not stand as all others had stood who had courage; the feet were not placed wide. He was not braced for the grim momento; his feet were almost together, as though he were about to dance. He appeared almost lounging in the street.

Now Josey spoke again, very slow. "Chato," he called softly, not taking his eyes from Morino.

"Si," Chato answered from the building shadow.

"Tell Mr. Pancho Morino that seeing as how he's sich a good feller, sich as thet, I'll leave it to him to call the turn. He can pitch his hat in the air, anytime he gits to feeling thataway. When it touches the ground, we let 'er rip. Remindst him, howsoever, 'bout our hoss trade."

The fluid Spanish of Chato was the only sound; somewhere, someone creaked a door to watch. Morino did not take his eyes from Josey as Chato talked, but he flashed a quick smile. Making a short mocking bow, he said, "Gracias, Señor Wales. I accept."

Now they stood, Morino smoking his cigar. The minute ticked into two. Morino often delayed his killings. It worked the nerves of his opponent, made him unsure, made him think of the death facing him. But he detected no twitch in the languid appearance of the man before him; he was slightly slouched, true, but no movement of the black vicious eyes that stared into his own, no shifting of the feet; only a slow, calculating chewing of the jaws, measured, deliberate slowness of one who, vastly experienced as a professional executioner, might while away his time absently, waiting for the routine to begin. For the first time in his career as a pistolero, Pancho Morino began to feel the chill creep up his spine. A tremor touched the hand he lifted to his cigar. His mind began to race, to search for the last-minute edge; for now he knew if ever he would need the edge, it would be against this man.

As he smoked, he calculated. The gringo expects me to toss my sombrero up in the air. To offer, to casually give me the right of beginning the reach for the pistola. The man is a fool, or a pistolero of extreme confidence. But consider, if the sombrero is *skimmed* at him, waist-high, it will confuse. Quien sabe? Who knows? He shrugged to loosen the unfamiliar tightening of his nerves. In the confusion, the gringo's hand might jerk. Perhaps he could not see the hand of Pancho Morino. He dropped the cigar.

Still the scar-faced pistolero before him did not move, did not even cease the irritating rhythm of the chewing jaws. Slowly Pancho Morino lifted his left hand to his sombrero. His fingers clutched the brim. Suddenly he jerked it, skimming the hat toward Josey.

But when he jerked, the sun hit him square in the eyes. The figure before him dimmed and he hesitated to clear his sight. The edge was lost. The hat sailed, tilted and plunged.

As it flicked the dust, Pancho Morino's hand quick-silvered to push the handle of his pistola; tilting the holster, he got off his shot; but the gringo had moved a full step to Pancho's right!

Like fluid lightning he moved. The puffs ballooned from his barrel.

Pancho Morino felt the hammer blows, one so quick behind the other they were almost one. They knocked him backward into the dust. Pancho knew he had lost. He lay, conscious, staring up at the hot blue sky. How blue it was! There was no pain.

A shadow fell over him. It was Josey Wales. He had holstered his pistol. He had fanned it twice. Josey Wales knew where he hammered home his bullets.

Neither Pablo, Chato, or Morino's men moved a muscle. They stood silent. Josey looked down into the pistolero's eyes.

"Where's Escobedo?" he asked softly.

"Aldamano . . . sixty Rurale trash . . . bestia," Morino whispered. "He waits for my messenger . . . that you are dead. I pray . . . you kill him!"

Life was flowing from him, turning the dust black in the circle, mud beneath his body.

"He have prisoners?" Josey asked.

"Si, uno gringo . . . uno Apache . . ."

He lifted a surprisingly small and delicate hand, fumbling at his jacket. Josey knelt, drew the black cigar and sulphur matches. He struck the match on Morino's silver buckle and lit the cigar. Slowly he placed it between the bandido's lips and stood erect.

"Gracias," Morino whispered. "My horse . . . is yours . . . my guns . . ."

"I'll take the hoss; it was a trade," Josey said, "but I don't take from the body of sich as you."

"Then we share . . . something . . . even in this . . . compadres." Morino's whisper was weakening. "My men are coming. When they see you with the horse . . . they will know who won the game of death. They will let you pass . . . it . . . is . . . my honor."

"Reckin," said Josey, "that's all as sich as you and me has got, thet we can take with us. Adios." He turned to go, his shadow passing from the body of Pancho Morino.

"I was fast . . . eh?" Morino's whisper followed him.

"You was fast," said Josey Wales, and walked away.

Pancho Morino tried to smoke the cigar, it was good; but the life fled quickly. It dropped from his lips and burned a hole in his silvered jacket.

They took the big dapple horse. Chato led it behind Josey as they rode west, past the church. Behind them the two bandidos knelt, hats off, beside their fallen leader.

The Priest stood on the steps of his church. His thin face showed nothing as they passed. He crossed himself and was surprised as the bandido following the scar-faced one doffed his sombrero politely, and the one-armed Indian bandido crossed himself in a pious manner, even managing to pull his sombrero from his head in the passing.

The scar-faced bandido appeared not to notice the Priest. He spat filthy tobacco in the street and seemed to be looking upward at the top of the church. Perhaps he is looking heavenward, thought the Priest, in fear of his lost soul.

But of course, the Priest did not know the way of Josey Wales.

Chapter 10

They galloped west, into the sun. Hangings usually take place at dawn, in the mind of Josey Wales, who had seen many. He'd heard that Ten Spot's would come in the morning, at Aldamano.

For ten miles they set a fast gait, raising the powdery dust behind them, until they saw the first two sentinels.

They sat their horses by the roadside, one to a side; then further on, two more. Josey dropped the horses to slow jog, and looking neither right nor left, rode steadily between them.

Chato, leading the big horse of Pancho Morino, followed. Pablo in the rear. It was like a gauntlet. No word was said. But as they passed, each pair of bandidos lifted their huge sombreros and held them to their chests.

Pancho Morino was dead. He had died in combat of honor; else his killer would not have lived past the guns of Morino's back-up men in Coyamo.

Pablo shyly tipped his sombrero to each in the passing. Chato rode with the proud dauntlessness of the vaquero, roweling his horse and reining him down, to sidle and prance, stepping high by the bandidos. Josey Wales rode casually, almost sidesaddle; his weight on one stirrup, half turned as though resting in the saddle—but his side vision brought in the rear.

The wind mourning in the sage, the slow clip-clop of the horses were the only sounds. Two, four, six, a dozen, sixteen, twenty bandidos sat silently on horseback at their passing.

A hundred yards beyond the last two sentinels, Josey pulled up. They turned to watch. The bandidos were riding hard for Coyamo. The merest hint of sweat rolled down the nose of Josey Wales. He plug-cut the tobacco and chewed as he watched them disappearing in the dust cloud.

"That un," he opined, "was clost—and you, ye crazy Mex," he jabbed a finger at Chato, "didn't help na'ar bit, a-prancin' and a-paradin' around about the whole goddamned situation."

Chato laughed uproariously. "You no comprendes, Josey. It is the right of victor in combat of honor. It was the pride in my bandido chieftain. The bandidos, they comprenden!"

Pablo shook his head at the disappearing dust cloud. "I would not want to live in Coyamo tonight," he said.

"Nor I," Chato answered. "If I was in Coyamo, I would run."

The trail was before them, flat and straight, stretching

endlessly through the plain. They jerked their hats lower against the sun.

Chato pulled beside the jogging gait of Josey's roan. "I watched you, Josey," he said with prideful awe. "I have not seen the quickness before."

Josey spat at a scurrying horned toad, not allowing enough lead, and so only dirtied its tail. He frowned. "The Lord gives to sich as they can do different things. Pablo to make things grow, and live; me, I reckin, to kill."

If there was the hint of bitterness in his voice, he was thinking of Pancho Morino. That man—with a little more of the Code, what he might have become. He hated the thought of Coyamo.

"Why did you move to your left, like the fast water flows, as you drew the pistola?" Chato asked curiously.

The horses, jogging, covered a quarter mile before Josey answered.

"Well," he drawled, "that there swivel gun was tight agin' his hip—had to be, to kick 'er up straight fer his shot; which is fine fer close quarters, saloons and sich, but he couldn't turn it fer 'nough right, at my distance, I figgered. Which he couldn't."

They rode awhile in silence. Then: " 'Course, the sun helped a mite."

"The sun?" Chato asked, surprised.

"Why shore," Josey said, "thet was the reason fer the extry hour—put the sun behind me; thet and allowing Pancho a little more liquoring time."

"Hola!" came from Chato.

"Ain't nothing special 'bout thet," said Josey. "Every town marshal in the west, which has lived long enough, knows. Ye've heerd tell. When a boar coon comes ripping into town, liquoring and shooting and sich, the marshal sends him word to git out of town by sundown, er meet him in the street. 'Course, the marshal makes damn shore he's

at the west end, with the sun behint his back—and the ol'
boar coon, he's done liquored hisself up proper. Thet is to
say, sich is the practice of town marshals which has lived
the longest. Gittin' a little edge ofttimes stretches out his
living by 'most a year er two."

"There is more," Chato said solemnly, "to being a
pistolero than quickness of the hand."

"Ye could say thet, I reckin, fer them that lives longer.
Which ain't exactly to set in a rocking chair, howsoever,"
Josey added drily. "Anyway ye look at it, it ain't much of a
trade to take up, saying a feller has a choicet."

"Why the horse?" came from Pablo, who had pulled up
on Josey's right. "Why must we have Señor Morino's
horse?"

"Thet hoss," answered Josey, "is the onliest one I've
seed thet can stay with ourn on a chase."

"On a chase?" Pablo was bewildered.

"Yep, thet's Ten Spot's hoss. We're going to git right
popular when we yank Ten Spot out'n that hoosegaw
tonight."

It was a thought to bring silence as they rode into the
huge red ball of the setting sun, toward Aldamano,
Capitan Jesus Escobedo and sixty Rurales.

For Pablo, it was a thought bringing stoic resignation to
suicide. And so this way he was to die.

For Chato Olivares, the thought raced reckless excitement through his body, exulting at the prospect, wild as the
plains winds.

For Josey Wales, it was the thought of the guerrilla,
veteran of two hundred fights on the Missouri-Kansas
border. And the thoughts of the guerrilla are the double-
think: How was the other feller thinking? What was his
plan? His character? What did he expect? Necessary
thoughts for a guerrilla; for his was the life of the counter-
punch, flexible, unorthodox, too small of force to initiate

campaigns; and so for him the war was the war of the mind. He must do the unexpected, unexpected by his enemy; or he was dead.

Night swept away the purpling dusk of the plain and brought the stars, among them the Indian-bow sliver of new moon; beginning of the Comanche moon, they called it.

In the winter, the Comanche struck, lightning fast on horseback, deep into Mexico; but in the spring, they rode away to the north, a thousand, two thousand miles, like the wind storming over the plains. Leaving the quietude of finished havoc in its path. But at least there was the respite from Comanche in the spring and summer. The Apache never left.

The Apache was always there. With each birth of morning, in the purple of dusk, in the black of night. The Apache.

An hour into the night, they saw Aldamano. First, a pinprick of flickering light. As they came closer, the lights were brighter, glowing the sky. Aldamano kept the torches burning all night, every night; for looming high, dark and foreboding, close to her western skirts of Spanish civilization, were the Sierra Madre.

As they drew closer to the town, Josey slowed the horses to a walk. They rode single-file on the very edge of the trail, where the soft churned dust muffled sound, where the mesquite waved in the wind at their heads, making them a part of the undulating landscape.

Two miles from Aldamano they stopped; fifteen, thirty minutes they sat their horses, and Josey uttered no word. He kept the long-glass to his eye, sweeping around first one side, then the other of the town.

He clucked the roan into motion. "Ain't no outriders," was his only comment. They walked the horses steadily onward toward the town. Closer; the lighted town loomed larger.

Bringing up the rear, Pablo prepared himself for death. By the Santos! Were they going to ride into the town, down the main street? Sixty savage Rurales!

A half mile from town, Josey led them off the trail into thick bushes. "Grain the hosses with nose bags," he said softly.

"But we grained them not long ago, Josey . . . ," Chato began.

"I know," Josey said, his voice a snarling whisper, "but nose bags stops hosses from snorting and whinneying their damn noses when they smell some more hosses. Which in about half a minute they's going to do, if ye don't move pronto!" The nose bags went on—pronto!

They sat in a tight circle of darkness. The wind rustled the mesquite and sage, and brought sounds of music, laughter and loud voices from the town.

"A fiesta," Chato said longingly. Josey chewed meditatively, listening for more portent sounds.

"Way I figger," he said finally, "Escobedo picked the wrong man, fer him, when he picked Pancho Morino. I could be wrong. But I ain't. Them kind of fellers—Escobedo—thinks anybody Morino's class ain't got no code, no pride, sich. He figgered Morino to jest set up a bushwhack with twenty guns and chop us down."

"This I also believe," Chato said. "He could have found plenty such men, but he believe a peon, a peon bandido is a bestia. Pancho Morino take—took pride in his pistolero reputation—an hombre mucho."

"I also believe this," Pablo said, though he had no idea as to where the "figgerin' " was leading.

"Figgerin' thisaway . . . ," Josey paused, "which is right, because Mr. Escobedo couldn't never believe he was wrong about peons, Indians and sich, it would shake his guts out;

then he'll believe every word of it, when the messenger from Morino tells him Josey Wales is dead. Ain't no other way he can believe. Proves he was right."

"The messenger?" Chato was surprised.

"Yeah," Josey said casually. "Morino told me Escobedo was waiting on him to send a messenger that I was dead."

"Hola!" Chato exclaimed. Then: "But who can we send to . . ." His voice trailed off in the wind.

"Now figgerin' on along," Josey mused, ignoring Chato's question, "Escobedo being, like you said, a politician, he's trying to make hisself a big coon in the holler. He'll double back on Morino's men, chop 'em up. Make hisself might near the biggest boar coon this here part of Mexico. Stands to reason." He chewed slower. "Wonder how many Rurales that'll bring out of Aldamano? Have to be right smart. Morino's got twenty guns . . ." This last he voiced almost to himself, so that Chato and Pablo bent close to listen.

"I am the messenger!" Chato leaped to his feet.

"Right as rain; so ye be," drawled Josey Wales. "Ain't none of 'em seed ye. Onliest thing worries me is yer brain."

"What you mean, my brain?" Chato was indignant. He stood up, hitched his pistol belt and moved to his horse.

"See what I mean?" Josey said. "Ye're ready to stick yer haid in a snake pit and ain't even figgered how to count the snakes. Set down." Chato squatted, excitement dancing in his eyes.

"Fust off, ye ride Morino's horse; thet's proof ye're from Morino. Ye're his lieutenant—some sich Mex name —use yer own. Second. *Try* to act like ye're a little skittish about the whole thing. Third. Look and see where is the jail and how many guards they got around it; how it sets and sich. Fourth. When ye come out'n meeting Escobedo, ye ride *fast* and git out of town pronto!" Josey chewed slowly and thoughtfully for a while. Chato shuffled his feet in irritation, anxious to be gone.

"Reckin ye can git all that crowded in ye haid, without'n it running out'n yer ears?"

"Si, si!" Chato said impatiently. He swung aboard the big dapple horse of Morino's and ran his fingers over the silver-trimmed saddle. "What a saddle!" he exclaimed. "When we get back home, Josey, I will trade for the saddle a . . ."

"Godalmighty!" Josey spat disgustedly. He came close to the mounted Chato, reached up and grabbed his arm, hard.

"Not many men could do it, compadre," he said with steel-softness. "Be careful—Escobedo is a snake thet can see . . ."

The words of the outlaw brought moisture in the eyes of the emotional Chato; beneath the hardness of Josey Wales, Chato knew he was full of care. It meant much to be of brotherhood to such a man.

"Vaya con Dios!" Pablo whispered.

Chato jerked the rein, whirling his horse on back feet, hiding his quick emotion, and galloped down the trail toward the lights and the noise, the streets of Aldamano. In the distance, he lifted his sombrero in jaunty farewell. He did not look back.

Propped on elbows, Josey sprawled full-length on the trail, the long-glass to his eye. Pablo lay beside him.

He watched Chato gallop his horse almost to the open gates of the town and drop to a slow strot. He grunted in satisfaction—Chato made it 'pear like he was a little skittish.

The big torches flickered their lights over Chato as he jogged down the main street. Josey saw him fling up a hand, waving at someone. A woman ran into the street and Chato stopped.

"By God!" Josey breathed, "ye crazy Mex—now he's— godalmighty! He grabbed her—sonofabitch!"

Pablo began a silent prayer for Chato Olivares: that the Santos would bring reason to his thoughts, that God would intervene in his mind, that . . .

When Chato reached the gates of Aldamano, there was indeed a fiesta; unofficial perhaps, but nevertheless, a celebration.

Aldamano had little occasion to celebrate; three times in the last month, Apache had struck in the night, stealing many horses and mules, killing a dozen guardias.

Aldamano lived tense in its dying, hanging on to life like an old man withering past his allotted time. Sixty Rurales in Aldamano! She was letting down her hair.

The better families, if there were any, were not on the street. The peons had disappeared into their hovels. Rurales rolled from the cantinas waving bottles in the air, fondling the tetas of the cantina girls. Laying them openly in the alleys.

True, guardias were about to discipline their actions; no shooting, no rape, strict orders of Capitan Escobedo— but Aldamano was having a fiesta!

Excitement sparkled the eyes of Chato Olivares. The good times! He waved to a cantina girl and she ran drunkenly toward this handsome bandido with the silver saddle and horse grande.

Chato stopped and she ran her hands up his leg. Such temptation! The words of Josey came back to him—keep his head, eh? He asked the girl for the location of the headquarters policia. She pointed drunkenly to the end of the street, where a low 'dobe sprawled, ramada-fronted. The carcel? the jail? he asked politely. She waved to a long building set deep in the ground. It adjoined the headquarters policia.

"Gracias, señorita!" Chato flashed a smile. He could not

resist bending from the saddle and patting her rounded rump. This Josey saw. Ah! the discipline required to be a bandido! It was enough to break the soul of a man! Perhaps this is why bandidos are so mean, so malo!

He moved the horse forward. The cantina girl ran after him pleading, then cursing him as he left her behind. He waved back to her. Veering his horse, he dodged two Rurales staggering across the street. Matted hair, filthy clothes. They stank as bestias. It was a long street.

Reaching the building, he dismounted slowly, flipping the reins around the hitch rack. As he did, he looked back. Yes, it was a very long street!

Jauntily walking beneath the roof of the ramada, he stepped onto the porch. Lieutenant Valdez stood beside the door, and with him, a bearded sergeant. Chato did not wait for their challenge. With flippant grandeur, he remarked arrogantly, "I come from mi Capitan, Pancho Morino."

Lieutenant Valdez snapped to attention. With only a light tap, and waiting for no answer, he flung open the door, motioning Chato to enter. He was anxiously awaited, without doubt!

Chato stepped into the room and came face to face with Capitan Jesus Escobedo. Escobedo had risen, his thin face tense and drawn. Chato needed to act no part in facing Escobedo. He sensed and saw the cruelty; it smelled, stank, emanating from the man like the odor of excremento— but wrapped in silk.

Two candles lit the low-ceilinged room and made shadows across the face of Chato. He did not remove his sombrero. His eyes narrowed with cruelty and arrogance. He was the living figure of the crazy bandido who flirts with El Muerte.

"Well!" Escobedo snapped nervously, then forced a thin smile. "Welcome, amigo! And the news?"

Chato took his time. Valdez stood behind him, and he glanced backward over his shoulder. Impatiently Escobedo motioned Valdez to leave the room.

With the closing of the door, Chato looked coolly into the eyes of Escobedo. "I am Lieutenant Olivares," he announced proudly. "Mi Capitan Pancho Morino send me on *his* horse as faith of his word. Comprendes?"

"Si, SI!" Escobedo's voice strained in his effort at composure before this arrogant bandido.

"It is done," Chato said nonchalantly, brushing dust from his jacket.

"Done? You say done? Josey Wales is dead? Is this what you mean? Say what you mean, hombre—eh, Lieutenant!"

"Si," Chato said, "Josey Wales is dead, he and his two compadres. When you come, forty-eight hours from this moment—you gave your word, eh?—you will find them lying in the stables."

"Ahhhhhhhh!" Escobedo could not contain himself. He rushed from behind the desk and, placing his hands on Chato's shoulders, held him proudly. "And how?" he asked, "how was it done?"

Chato moved away from the hands. He looked around the room. Snapping his fingers, he said, "Es nada. Twenty rifles from the brush. The work of un momento." He remarked meaningfully, "It has been very dusty on the trail from Coyamo."

"Si, si!" Escobedo rushed behind his desk, pulled two bottles of tequila from a drawer and set them before Chato.

"Perdone, por favor," he said more softly, his eyes growing cat-like, losing the blush of excitement. "A drink to bind our word; take the tequila to your Capitan as a token of my fidelity." He uncorked one of the bottles.

Chato turned it up and drank long. Taking it from his mouth, he wiped his lips. "Hola!" he exclaimed with genuine appreciation, "es tequila buena!"

"Si," said Escobedo, his voice smoother now, more condescending, "from Ciudad de Mexico itself it comes."

Chato corked the bottle and smacked his lips with gusto. He greedily picked up both bottles. "For mi Capitan," he explained.

Walking to the door, he turned and his eyes flashed. "The hours are forty-eight? Verdad?"

"True. Forty-eight," answered Escobedo smoothly, "the honor of my word." His mind was already racing ahead.

With a bottle in each hand, Chato kicked the door. It swung open and he swaggered to his horse. Carefully he placed a bottle of tequila in each saddlebag.

"Buenas noches!" he sang out, but the Capitan had already called Valdez and the Sergeant inside. Chato shrugged.

They did not see him casually swing his mount in the half circle by the jail. One guardia walking, stopping to lean against the low building. Another at the end, by the door, in half shadows. A low four-foot wall ran directly behind the jail.

As he rode by, Chato whistled. It was a peculiar whistle, repeated over and over. The Rurale at the wall raised a hand in halfhearted salute. The crazy rider was whistling a greeting, no doubt drunk. He had never heard such a whistle before.

But deep in the dungeon, tied hand and foot, Ten Spot heard, the peculiar whipping call of the mountain whippoorwill. He knew it well from the mountains of Virginia, and Tennessee.

The last place he had heard it was a place called the Crooked River Ranch, the home of Josey Wales. He stiffened and listened hungrily to the sound growing fainter. An unexplainable thrill ran through his body. In the darkness he puzzled in disbelief. Then he smiled.

Chato jogged down the street. The tequila had warmed him and lifted his optimism. There was nothing to it! He even debated pausing and having another drink from the bottle; but no, it could lead him to abandon his judgment, to visit a cantina. Halfway down the street, three-quarters.

He did not see the door of the headquarters policia open behind him. Escobedo, Valdez and the Sergeant stepped out. Escobedo motioned, and the Sergeant raised the rifle, bracing it against a post of the ramada. He took long, long aim . . . CRACK! The rifle split the air with a lightning jolt.

The hammer hit him hard in the back and Chato reeled. Only a life in the saddle, his superb horsemanship, saved him from falling. Without thought, only instinct to guide him, he loosened the reins as his roweled spurs dug the horse's flanks. His hands gripped the saddle horn.

The big horse leaped instantly in a dead run. More rifles cracked. But Chato Olivares, rolling crazily in the saddle, was riding a horse on a death run. They missed.

Josey Wales was watching. He saw Chato slump, the horse leap, long before the rifle crack reached him. He jumped to his feet. "Bring the hosses," he shouted at Pablo.

Snatching the nose bag from the big roan, he hit the saddle, Indian-style, already running.

He did not head the roan for Chato, but away from him, down the trail toward Coyamo. The roan had to match the speed of the big dapple for him to bring it down.

"Git, Red!" he snarled viciously, and the big horse laid back his ears. He sprang like a puma and bellied out, powerful haunches putting him in a frothing dead heat in ten seconds.

The roan could hear the hoofbeats behind him. He had heard them many times before; they were to be outdistanced. His neck straightened out like a deer's. From his great chest, and his heart, he gave all he had.

There was a horse race—but the roan won it. He matched, then surpassed the dapple's speed, until Josey was forced to pull back on the reins, the roan snorting and protesting, until the dapple could catch up. When the teetering Chato came alongside, Josey leaned and snatched the reins, pulling down the two horses, prancing, snorting and heaving. He rode them fifty yards into a clump of thick mesquite and tied them, still stomping, to the branches.

Chato's head was slumped forward, his sombrero dragging the neck of the horse. Blood pumped from his chest and over the saddle. The heart of Josey Wales froze and tightened his breath. He pulled Chato from the horse, yanking at the iron-gripped hands on the saddle horn, and laid the vaquero on his back.

Quickly he pulled away the shirt. The hole was in the lower chest. He turned him on his stomach and struck a sulphur match. The bullet had missed the spine by a half inch.

Pablo came up with the horses. He saw the blood and ran into the bushes. In a moment he returned, his one arm filled with leaves. "These," he panted, "will stop the blood. They will heal."

While Pablo made a mound of leaves on the back wound, Josey jerked a shirt from a saddlebag. He tore it into strips, and he and Pablo turned Chato, mounding the leaves on the chest, pressing until slowly the blood clotted and stopped.

Josey wound the strips of shirt tightly about Chato, rolling him gently on the ground, and tied the wide bandage with hard twisted knots.

Chato opened his eyes. He smiled weakly in the dim light.

"Es malo . . . bad, eh?" he asked calmly.

"It's bad," Josey said. He struck another match. "Cough and spit in my hand."

Chato made a weak effort. "It hurt to cough, Josey," he protested.

"Cough, damn ye, and spit in my hand," Josey commanded. Chato coughed and spat. By the flickering light, Josey examined the spittle. "Ain't no blood, don't believe yer lung-hit."

"Ah . . . ," Chato breathed, "es bueno. I have always said my luck . . ."

"Yer luck," Josey snarled, "ain't wuth a damn. It could be belly er gut; howsoever," he mused, "it missed yer spine."

"God will save you, Chato," Pablo whispered soothingly, "God will not let you die."

They heard it then, sounding first like faraway thunder. Josey knew the sound.

"I'm moving to the trail," he said softly. "If ye hear gunfire, Pablo, ye git Chato on thet horse somehow er 'nother and ride north."

"I will not ride," Chato said stubbornly. "I can shoot good from here."

"I will stay with Chato," Pablo whispered.

Josey Wales glided away from them, silent as a puma in the brush, and back to them floated his whisper, "Ye stupid bastards!"

He lay by the trail under a bush and watched them pass, galloping in columns of twos. Five, ten, fifteen, twenty, they rode toward Coyamo. Twenty times two reckined out to be forty Rurales!

Silently he slipped back and gave the news to Pablo,

squatting by the side of the sprawling Chato. Chato grinned at the number. Forty Rurales riding out of Aldamano!

"I have done my job bueno, eh, Josey?" he asked, weak but boastful.

"I reckin," Josey answered, "thet is, if ye live."

"Live or die, por Dios!" Chato argued in a whisper, "I have done my job well . . . Remember, Josey, next time there is the need I must borrow ahead of the wages, eh?"

"ALL RIGHT!" snarled Josey Wales, "ye're always reminding me about yer damn borrering."

Chato tried to laugh, but the numbness was leaving and the pain cut into his breath.

The sliver of moon dropped further to the west. A coyote raised a tenor voice that carried long on the wind. Josey sat close to Chato and Pablo. He cut his tobacco plug and chewed, looking absently into the waving, wind-whipped mesquite.

"Well?" Chato gasped. The pain was telling. "Is it not now the time to get Ten Spot . . . while the Rurales are gone?" The pain and Josey's unconcerned, methodical chewing made Chato irritable. After all this, were they to sit here like cows?

After a long time, Josey answered, "Figger at the best—thet is, pushing them hosses might near dead—best them Rurales can do is five hours to Coyamo."

"But," Pablo suggested quietly, "if we got Señor Ten Spot now, it would give us many more hours start."

"Reckin not," Josey said. He looked at the moon. "Ye see them military kind of fellers don't never learn. They always change guards at midnight. Saying we went and got Ten Spot now—time I got there and sich, they'd find them dead guards in jest about thirty minute when they come to change their midnight shift. Nope," he chewed thoughtfully, "we'll wait till after midnight; there's yer four-, maybe six-hour start; dependence on how long their guard duty runs, less'n we're unlucky and somebody discovers them dead guards by accident."

"Dead guards?" Pablo asked, bewildered at the "figgerin'."

"Well," Josey said, "it'll either be one way or t'other. I could jest stop by, tip my hat and say as we have come fer Mr. Ten Spot, and would they please turn him loose. But, more'n likely, throat cutting will git the job done. We do the cutting, er they do, take yer pick."

"How will you know . . . the time?" Chato asked weakly.

"I'll know," Josey answered. He lay back on the ground and watched the moon sliver edge downward. After a moment, he lazily called, "Pablo."

"Si?"

"Git some jerky beef from a bag and let thet dribbling loudmouth Chato chew on it. When he swallers, we'll know if he's belly-shot."

Pablo got the beef and handed it to Chato, placing a rolled blanket under his head, and wondered at the mysteries of the mind, and ways of Josey Wales.

Chapter 11

When Chato fell forward at the rifle shot, Escobedo clapped his hands in delight. Dead center. There was no doubt. No, no need to chase the rider. Coyamo was not the horse's home. He would run two, three miles and stop to wander and graze the grass.

The shooting had brought Rurales running from the cantinas into the street. While he had their attention, Escobedo shouted, "To the stables! Alert!"

Whirling back into his room, he motioned Valdez and the Sergeant to follow. "Ahora! Now! This you must do. First you, Lieutenant; pick forty of your best men with the rifle. Ride to Coyamo as fast as the horses can stand. Send twenty into the town shooting every bandido on sight. With the additional twenty, encircle the town. Shoot all who run, and those who surrender. No one, NO ONE! of them must live. Comprendes?"

"Si, Capitan," Valdez snapped.

"Most especial, Pancho Morino must die! Assign five of your best riflemen to concentrate. You know his dress. Get Morino!"

"Si! It's done!" Valdez responded vehemently.

"And when you find the Alcalde, who will be hiding beneath his bed no doubt," Escobedo sneered, "tell him our ever vigilant scouts reported to me the movement of bandidos on his town. That I sent the greater part of my force to rescue Coyamo, leaving a small number for me to fight the Apache. Comprendes?"

"Si, Capitan!"

"This," Escobedo placed his hands on the shoulders of Valdez in a grand manner, "will bring much glory to you. Perhaps a promotion to Capitan!"

The eyes of Valdez shone with the eagerness of a blood-wolf. Capitan Valdez! The words rolled around beneath his breath. His chest rose in pride. He snapped to attention and saluted.

"VAMOS!" Escobedo said, and then softly, "Vaya con Dios."

"Gracias, Capitan," Valdez said. He was on a mission of God, and of course, with it came glory as it should. He rushed through the door.

Escobedo had used the genius of approach to Valdez, first, the promise of glory and promotion; second, softly, the feeling of holy mission. He would not fail.

Already, outside he could hear the crisp shouted orders of Valdez, the running feet, the mounting of horses, the thunder of hoofs as the men swept down the street of Aldamano and faded eastward.

Now he turned to the Sergeant. It required effort, but

he allowed the merest hint of benevolent smile to touch his lips. He considered the bearded brutal features, the matted hair stringing beneath the sombrero. A bestia.

"Sergeant, we are bringing our district into order. We will be recognized by the Governor! When Lieutenant Valdez becomes Capitan, it leaves the open place. That is for you, Sergeant—Lieutenant!"

The low brows of the Sergeant lifted. His grin showed yellow teeth. "Si! Mi Capitan!"

"Now!" Escobedo continued, "you are left with a small force; counting yourself, only nineteen men. I place the safety of Aldamano in your hands. Only five may sleep at each time. The others on guard of four hours. Comprendes?"

"Comprendo, Capitan. It's done!" He saluted and moved to the door.

"And Sergeant," Escobedo called, consulting his timepiece, "it is a little past nine. Go to the hacienda of the Alcalde. Inform him as to the mission of Valdez and his troops. Assure him of our vigilance. Tell him I will dine with him and his family at eleven. Comprendes?"

"Si, Capitan. And El Padre? I must tell him also?"

Escobedo frowned. "Noooo, let us leave the Padre to his peace."

The Sergeant left hastily, filled with the importance of his responsibility. Escobedo opened the door and watched him in the torchlight, rushing on his way to the Alcalde, snapping orders to his men as he strode with the swagger of a general on parade.

Ah! one needed only to understand. That is why Capitan Escobedo got the most from his men. His poor, simple-minded Rurales!

No, he thought, as he closed the door and sat down at his desk, he did not want the Padre despoiling, this time, his plan-making with the Alcalde.

When he had first come into Aldamano, he had met with the Alcalde and the Priest. The Alcalde, a broad, puffish politico, had been even more distressed than the Alcalde of Coyamo.

His town was disappearing before him! It was not his fault; after all, so close to the Sierra Madre. What did the Governor expect? Soon, he wailed, there would be nothing here. He would be an innkeeper, a stable peon, left only for service of the passersby hurrying through. All the mines were shut down. There was no activity. He held his hands outward, upward, beseechingly to El Capitan.

Escobedo had listened with the same silent sympathy, nodding his head in agreement, clucking sympathetically.

When the Priest spoke, rage rose in Escobedo's throat. He had seen his kind before, scattered thinly over Mexico.

He was a wizened little man, his face browned by the sun, spent amongst his peons no doubt. He was old, his white hair stringing and unkempt. He began by speaking softly.

"At one time the Governor of Chihuahua made a treaty with the Apache. That our state would pay a few cattle, a few head of mule each year in tribute to the Apache. The Apache came into our towns. He traded. He kept his word; until . . . ," here the Priest paused and his eyes flashed accusingly at the bowed head of the Alcalde, "ambitious, greedy politicos, seeking to crush the Apache, got them drunk on mescal, and while they were drunk, treacherously murdered them. Slaughter, Capitan! Like pigs!"

His voice had risen, and now he paused and stared at the floor of the stone patio. With pathetic hopelessness, he shook his head. "The Apache will trust us no more. He is a guerrilla trained by centuries. He can, and he will, outmatch the treachery of ourselves. Which we have earned!"

Escobedo was shocked. "But, Padre . . . !" he began.

"Listen to me!" The little priest rose to his feet.

Escobedo noted with disgust that his robe was poor, tattered. Por Dios! He even wore the barefoot sandal of the peon!

"But un momento," Escobedo interrupted, "why should our government pay tribute to a small group of murderous savages? Where is the sense of it?"

"The sense of it?" the Priest answered, "the sense, Capitan; that it is, or *was*, their land, and we took it. We have exacted tribute in gold and blood from every Indian, from Peru to our northern border, except the Apache. Only the Apache has turned about the process and collected tribute from us. I have seen, Capitan—the priests who demand a peon bring in so many chickens a week, a peso, a bushel of maize; that the peon work without pay in the fields owned by the Church, so many days a week as tribute. I have seen his children work for that tribute. I have seen the whipping posts standing by the Church of God, where the peon has been whipped to death for failing to bring in the tribute of a chicken! The stocks I have seen, into which the peon is yoked to die of thirst!"

The little priest's voice rose in fervor. His eyes burned. "I believe," he continued fervently, "as does our new Presidente, Benito Juarez, the Church should own no land, no mines, no holdings. Only the Church! There should be no tributes, except those given by love!"

"Si! Si!" Escobedo said soothingly, "there is much sense to what El Presidente says, but . . . ," Escobedo shrugged his way from the corner, he could not argue against El Presidente, "I am a man of military, Padre; such things are beyond my authority, my influence. My oath and duty is to Mexico. I am sure you comprendes."

The Priest was obviously mad. Escobedo had no wish to antagonize him, though he was sure he had no influence with the bishops and bureaucracy. It was known he collected nothing from his peons. He contributed no wealth. His poverty made him nada. Escobedo worried little at his ravings.

The Priest was obviously a man who had strayed far from God, concerning himself not with the spiritual, but material things, half paganized by the peon Indians with whom he mingled.

The little priest paced the floor. He placed his hands behind his back. Head down, he walked slowly in thought. He sat down at the table opposite Escobedo. The Alcalde was holding his head in his hands and staring at nothing.

The Priest looked across the candlelight at Escobedo and his eyes softened. "Yes, Capitan, you are a man of military. With your permission, while your Rurales are here, I should like to talk with them, en masse."

The request and soft voice startled Escobedo. "Why, most certainly, Padre. The permission is granted."

"I would like to tell them," the Priest continued, as though Escobedo had not spoken, "of love. I know . . . ," he shook his hand at the acquiescent nod of Escobedo, "that love is only a word to them, and . . . ," he looked piercingly at Escobedo, "to others. But I want to show them it is not just a word. It is a law, when broken, one pays extreme penalty.

"God," he said, "gave man sex, and with it, as with all gifts from God, He gave him a choice in its use. The passion of the sex is only the entry to be used, to open into the great mystery of love. Only the intangible binds, Capitan. The bonds of love, not the physical. And so man has his choice. He may smirk, and joke at this instrument. He can become what he calls the 'sophisticate.' He can encourage, make of his women—his women, who would join him in the mystery of love—objects to be flaunted as animal objects. To make sex a simplification, as of the bowel movement, but . . . ," the Priest pointed his finger at

Escobedo, "as he moves from the sunlight of love, he passes into the twilight of the material, and the twilight does not last long. Soon he finds that his passion will no longer be aroused by the coarseness. He is dissatisfied. He is satiated with the coarseness of nada except sex objects. He cannot remain there, and so then he must pass into the night of sadism, of rape, of terror against others. Here he discovers, once again, the material potency he had lost. But this time it comes from inflicting terror and pain, not in sharing love. He has chosen the opposite—the evil choice always given man, with no satisfaction, only emptiness, never satiated, without end. Rape, Capitan, is not a crime of sex, no more than the knife is a crime of murder. The knife can be used to cut the loaf of bread in the love bosom of the family, or used to plunge terror and death from the sadistic soul of the user. The knife is but the instrument, as is the organ of sex.

"God, giving man a soul, also gives him the choice of rising above the animal with love; but if he disdains it, he cannot remain on the material level of the animal. He cannot stop the degeneration, once he begins. He will inevitably embrace the sadism of El Diablo, and so become lower than the animal. Rapaciousness and violence stalk our land, while we grow more 'sophisticated,' and more 'civilized,' with our coarseness we call 'adult.' The intangible of sadism is El Diablo's answer to God's intangible of love. The rapist is not over-sexed, Capitan, he is under-sexed. His is a lost soul. Losing love, he has lost all. For every blessing God offers man, He also offers him the choice of turning that blessing into a curse!"

The voice of the Padre hardened. His eyes looked accusingly at Escobedo, so that Escobedo was forced to drop his own eyes and examine the tips of his boots.

"The rapes must stop, Capitan," the Priest said, "the violence of terror upon people must cease. Man's soul cannot live in a vacuum without love. It must fill that vacuum. And it will embrace the passion of terror. That . . . ," the Priest rose with finality, "is what I would tell your Rurales, and warn them of their flirtation with laws of which they have no comprehension, in their breaking."

He strode from the patio, seeming taller than his height, more majestic than was reasonable for his tattered robe.

For the brief flicker of an instant, fear entered the heart of Capitan Escobedo; but only for an instant. It was the wine.

The Alcalde had raised his head and looked pleadingly at Escobedo. "You see, Capitan, the cooperation I have from the Padre. My authority is impossible in this position; thus you have witnessed."

"I can see," Escobedo murmured; but with more heart, he encouraged the Alcalde. "If you encourage the growth of my own authority, I shall see that the Padre is removed, perhaps to a pueblo, where he can teach the Indians to make baskets. Perhaps, together, we can raise a city from the ashes!"

"You have the whole of my heart in support," the Alcalde answered enthusiastically. "You are the first hombre I have seen in years to bring hope of growth and civilization."

Escobedo departed. He was uncomfortable. Somehow he felt naked, undressed by the Padre. He had noticed the Padre had offered no blessing on him. Neither had he asked.

Now, as he closed the door behind the Sergeant, he shook the thought of the Padre from his mind. The Padre could be dealt with like all such childish men.

A lone candle lit the room, flickering tiny shadows that grew huge, dancing on the walls.

The two Papago Indian women—he had chosen these

servants, because the Papago hated Apache—had bathed the Apache girl, fed her, cleansed and perfumed her. She had, he considered, almost lost the smell of the Apache animal.

She lay in a corner, bound, face to the wall. Escobedo consulted his watch. His hand trembled: nine-thirty. Plenty of time before eleven.

Seating himself on his bunk, he removed his boots, his shirt, pants and underclothing. So he stood, completely naked, gaining control of the tremors that ran up his body.

He knew the girl was a virgin. He knew because she wore no head band. It was the mark of the Apache. He understood nothing else, for he gave no credence to the Apache as having a code.

In truth, the Apache was very strict, his simple reasoning being that the girl who dishonored herself in playing at the great gift of Usen would, of course, not honor the man she married. It was a code seldom broken, for the Apache girl knew to break the code meant a life without a husband. She would be fed by the band to which she belonged. She could work, yes. She could continue as the plaything of loose men; but she would find no husband. A widow—yes, she could remarry with honor.

Escobedo fathomed no such code among the animals called Apache. Now he walked on bare feet to the corner where she lay. In one hand he held the long knife he had pulled from his belt. He cut away the thongs that bound her feet and pulled her upright by the thong about her neck. She looked up at him, black eyes that burned hate. No fear.

"You are not afraid, querida?" Escobedo whispered hoarsely in Spanish. "Then let us see." He led her into the light of the candle, her hands still tied behind her back.

Slowly with the knife, he began between her breasts, cutting downward, the razor sharpness moving smoothly, separating the buckskin. Downward, until the skirt too fell open.

Savagely, by the neck thong, he jerked her about and ran the knife down the back of her clothing. Her dress fell away and she stood before him, naked.

She was tiny, scarcely five feet; the small, hard tetas pointing up; the flat, firm belly and tight-muscled buttocks. She glowed bronze in the candlelight, black hair falling to her shoulders.

The slightest twitch flicked the muscles of the oval face. Her mind could not control the muscle. Escobedo saw the twitch.

"Ahhhhhhhh! Some doubts, querida? Let us see." Laying the knife on his desk, he bent her backward across it. With his knees he held her legs down, toes touching the floor, and bent her back, pushing her face until she was bowed, arching the spine from the surface of the desk. Only her head and shoulders rested on one edge of the desk; her tiny buttocks pressed the opposite edge.

With one hand, Escobedo held the neck thong, and now with the other, he stroked her arched belly, feeling down for the pubic hair. It had only begun its growth. His breathing was heavier at this confirmation of the tenderness of the untouched girl.

Her legs were pulled tightly together. With one knee, he forced them apart and felt the muscles tremble in her legs. He placed himself carefully at the virgin opening and moved into her—slowly—feeling the tightness, the hard contractions, unfamiliar, foreign to the act.

He watched her eyes intently, but they did not change; no flicker. Suddenly he plunged, throwing himself hard into her, so that he grunted with the effort.

Her body arched higher, belly strained and tightening, bridging the space beneath her. The legs jerked out of control. He pulled outward, and the body came down. He plunged again, venomously, and watched the thin body rise in an ecstasy of pain; down—up—still she made no cry, though the legs waved wildly in the air. Still the eyes did not change. Only the body jerked, rising and beating the desk surface. Blood fountained from her. Enough to satiate the most vicious of terrorists; but Escobedo had passed further into the depths of passion by terror. The Priest had sensed—smelled, like Chato—the sadism of the man.

He paused, panting heavily; sweat glistened on his bony body.

He leaned his face close to her small stoic eyes. He was still deep within her; and in slow, clear Spanish, so she would know, he spoke softly. "I am told, querida, that there is a sensation, an exultation, and experience that comes to few men. Do you know what that is, eh? It is the experience of being, as I am now, deep within the virgin. As she dies, the death throes, the contractions, are beyond imagination. Shall we try this experience, little querida?" Madness hoarsened his whisper.

He began to tighten the thong about her throat. Feverishly he watched, as he tightened—tighter—tighter. Her eyes began to bulge. He felt within her a twisting iron that moved in velvet. Her face turned blue. Her tongue popped out. She collapsed.

The passion at last was drained from Escobedo. Her bowels had loosed, flooding him and the desk with excremento. He stepped back, exhausted, disgusted. He was weak as he shoved her from him to the floor, and for only a moment could bear the sight of the wreckage.

He rushed into the washroom behind his office. Cleansing himself, trembling. He dressed in full uniform, careful to polish his boots, flicking the dust from his sleeves.

His legs were weak, and he would not look at the figure on the floor as he passed. Lifting a bottle of tequila, he gulped hungrily. As he opened the door, he consulted his timepiece: ten forty-five. He would be punctual for his appointment with the Alcalde. As he walked down the street, he felt relaxed, warmed by the tequila. Seeing the Sergeant, he stopped him.

"Go to my office, clean up the carnage—of the bestia. Wrap her in blankets. You may hang her outside the western gate of Aldamano, facing the Sierra Madre."

"Si, Capitan," the Sergeant answered impassively. He knew what he would find. He had performed the task many times. He shrugged his brutish shoulders and prepared himself for the stench of the job.

Escobedo, for all his brilliance of maneuver, his cunning in plan, possessed a flaw that cracked the hard solidity of his ambitions. Always, he looked upon those "beneath" him as moronic figures, having no powers of thought, of character, or honor. And like all such men, he never saw the flaw; only cursed the crises that developed, first here, then there, and would of course eventually destroy him.

As the Sergeant had acknowledged to himself, he had performed such an act many times, but never on an Apache.

For an Apache to divine one's thoughts in advance is bad—for the thinker. To tell an Apache one's thoughts is very, very bad. It simplifies the guerrilla art of the double-think.

Escobedo had told the girl in the Spanish she understood. She was to die. He told her how she was to die. He told her what he expected of her at her death.

For generations, the Apache, the guerrilla raised from childhood, accepted the way of riding the thin line between life and death.

Automatically, the girl moved to that line. Not too soon. It would betray the farce. Five seconds before her eyes would have bulged in death, she bulged the eyes. She tensed the neck; and not just before, but within three seconds of death, the tongue shot forward. Inside her, she gave him what he demanded. The pain did not matter. She moved muscle against pain, harder, harder, contracting into a bloody fit, sliding tightening muscles—and so drained the passion from him.

Every Apache was familiar with death, the loosening of the bowels, and so she forced it, disgusting Escobedo. But as he had flung her to the floor, her hand behind her back held the handle of the razor-edge knife, held it in a death grip that would not release.

While Escobedo had washed and cleansed himself, she took bare sips of air, only enough for survival, as she had eaten scraps from the ground on the trail. Discipline against the gulping for life; only enough to hold back the dark line of death.

Now, with the room empty, the knife moved easily through the thongs about her wrists. She reached one hand to her throat and loosened the thong. A huge round welt, blue and thick as a rope, circled her throat and neck. She did not think of it. Her thoughts were on survival and the double-think of the guerrilla. Escobedo would send some one quickly to remove her. She lay back as she was before, hands behind her back.

The Sergeant flung open the door and closed it. He came across the room, around the desk. Seeing the sight, he cursed beneath his breath, "Excremento! Always excremento! I would sooner clean the pens of the hogs." He grumbled to himself as he turned his back on the girl. Taking a blanket, he spread it on the floor and came to drag her onto it.

He bent to grab her hair, close to her face. The hand shot up like the head of a snake. The knife point went home, straight through the throat, so viciously it snapped the spine at the base of the Sergeant's skull. His brain had no time to register the event of death. He only looked blank as he fell over the girl.

Weakly she pushed him from her. She rolled him, crawling and pushing, under the bunk of Escobedo, hiding him from sight.

She tried to stand, but her legs buckled. She crawled, pulling herself up with her hands to the edge of the desk; she blew out the candle and crawled to the rear door of Escobedo's quarters.

Now her knees collapsed. She pulled, desperately up, and lifted the latch, held on as she swung through the door, pulling it shut behind her.

Her knees would no longer support her weight. With her elbows she pulled along the wall, past the rear of the headquarters, along the wall of the jail. It was here that blackness overcame the tenacious Apache will. She sprawled unconscious against the jail wall. The knife, tightly, was in her hand.

Chapter 12

Josey rose from his sprawling consideration of the moon and walked into the brush. He searched here and there, cutting with his kife the heaviest inside growth of the mesquite. In a few minutes he was back and sat down, whittling away the branches and the limbs.

When he was through, he had four sticks, each about five feet long. "A mite limber. They don't grow nothing down hereabouts like the Tennessee mountain country."

"What are they for?" Pablo asked.

"Figgered I might need some walking canes, whenever I'm walking around Aldamano," he said. Pablo puzzled, but did not ask. Walking canes?

Chato had been sleeping, his breath coming in short

gasps moving his chest spasmodically. He had chewed the jerked beef, as much as he could, and drifted off. Now the pain and talk brought him awake.

"How ye feel?" Josey asked, kneeling by his head. "Does yer belly feel paining?"

"I don't know, Josey," Chato said earnestly, "I am hurt all over, my chest, my belly; even my toenails, they are hurting." He rolled his eyes up. "Josey, before I left Escobedo, by the goodness of his heart, he give two bottle of tequila. One for me. One for Pancho. They are in the saddlebag. Maybe, used as medicine, they would help."

Josey went to the horse and brought back the bottles. One he placed in the saddlebag of Chato's gray horse; the other he uncorked and handed to the vaquero.

"Drink a little o' that firewater, by God. We'll know right quick about yer belly; thet is, if it don't numb ye fust from the head down."

Chato raised the bottle and drank. Weakly he smacked his lips and smiled, "Es bueno, good medicine; already I feel it helps me." He raised the bottle again, held it long before lowering it. "Por Dios! It's amazing. I feel I can fork a horse. I am ready for Aldamano."

Enthusiasm rose in the heart of Chato. "You know, Josey, while I ride out of the town, I see the prettiest little señorita; she—when this is over—we must come back to Aldamano." He laid his head back on the blanket and leered crookedly at the sky. "Si! we must come back!"

"We'll come back," Josey said softly.

"Si," Pablo, kneeling at Chato's head, whispered reassuringly, "we will come back."

"Bueno," Chato whispered. His face showed white in the dimness and lines of pain dragged at his jaws. He looked old.

Josey unbuckled and untied the heavy .44's from about his waist. He hung them on the saddle horn of his horse.

Stooping, he picked up the sticks and gathered the reins of the roan and the dapple.

"I reckin," he remarked casually, "I'd better be gittin' along."

"I too am going," came from Chato. He tried to rise, struggled to his elbows and toppled on his side.

"Lay him back on the blanket, Pablo," Josey said grimly. Pablo, pulling and pushing at Chato's shoulders, laid him down.

"I'll be back directly, with Ten Spot," Josey said, "but jest in case ye hear gunfire—I don't mean one shot from some drunk Rurale, I mean business gunfire, rapid fire— Pablo, ye git thet crazy Mex on his hoss someway, and head direct north. Ye hear?"

"Si, I hear, Josey."

Weakly from his blanket, Chato spoke. "Will not run, Josey . . . if you are chased, you lead them this way. We will ambush . . . we will shoot from the brush . . . we will shoot them down like the dog . . ."

"Me too," Pablo said.

Josey whirled on them venomously. "Listen, goddamn ye; if I git in a fight, I'll git out of it. I ain't concerning myself atall about no dribbling cowhand and one-armed farmer! Ye can lay here and rot fer what I give a damn. Ye understand?"

"Si . . . I understand," Chato whispered.

Josey walked, leading the horses, through the brush and disappeared quickly in the darkness.

"Does he mean what he say?" Pablo asked Chato.

Chato grinned. "Josey Wales mean what he do, not what he say. Josey Wales," he continued, a note of pride creeping into his whisper, "he would stand in front of the stampeding cattle if we lie in their path. He like to say he don't care."

"And you—would so stand?" asked Pablo.

"I would stand," Chato said, and drifted into blissful blackness.

There was no mystery to what Chato and Pablo thought was the uncanny "telling of the time" by night as practiced by Josey Wales. For over eight years in the Border War of Missouri, most of his riding, his "work," had been in the night.

And so like the farmer, working by day, who looks at the sun and tells the time within minutes, so Josey Wales could do with the stars and the moon. He knew the night heavens as well as any sailor, and better, for his purpose. He knew the timing of their movements.

He had time to spare. And so he walked, two miles by his figgerin'. The walk would stretch his legs, put him there in plenty of time, and give the edge of not presenting the silhouette of a rider above the bushy tops of mesquite.

He tied the rope of the dapple to the horn of the roan's saddle. They walked single-file, rather than two abreast. It was better for walking in heavier brush, lessened the width of open space and narrowed their target, approaching a man, to a thin black line.

Such care in the smallest detail was second nature, instinct for Josey Wales. In the beginning, he had learned much of it from his Captain, the daring guerrilla, Bloody Bill Anderson. But his Tennessee mountain cunning had added the finesse that Bloody Bill would have longed to possess.

The night wind lessened to a whisper in the mesquite and sage, faintly whining on the cactus spines and the spears of Spanish dagger. Here and there a snake, night hunting, slithered away in the sand.

Josey approached closer to Aldamano, listening to the sounds, for their rhythm, and watching for the familiarity of the way back by which he must come.

He circled wide to the north, around the wall of

Aldamano. The jail was on the western edge of town; and as he circled, he listened for the town noises. There were not any. Good, if they was sleeping off a drunk. Bad, if they wasn't.

He shrugged his shoulders. After midnight was a good time to hit most anything. Everybody was either drunk, half asleep, or sleeping. It was an edge.

Oncet, he remembered, he had jokingly remarked to Bloody Bill thet he wisht the banks which held the Yankee army payrolls, stayed open till after midnight. It would make it a hell of a lot easier than like they had to do, hit 'em in the open sun with every bushy-tailed boar coon around, wide awake and ready. Bill had said thet when they won, he would make hisself governor and he would pass a special law to make the banks stay open till after midnight. Jest fer Josey Wales. Josey chuckled at the remembering.

He must be gittin' on, to commence rec'lectin' sich. Anyhow, Bill went down with two smoking pistols in his hands before the situation was decided one way or t'other —so it didn't matter.

Now he was on the northwest of the town. He had scanned the wall as he walked. No guards on the wall; scared of 'Pache arrows, more'n likely. He began to slant closer to the town in his walk.

'Peared like the torches was burning a mite lower; more shadows. He couldn't see the street. Now he was directly west. He took a deep breath and closed in. Fifty yards from the wall, he spotted the low-slung jail, as Chato had described it. He tied the horses firmly in mesquite. Hanging his hat on the saddle horn, and bending, he half ran, falling lightly, rising to run again in the crouch. He brought himself up beside the wall.

Not even the keen eyes of Josey Wales had seen them. Several times he passed within three feet of Apache. They let him pass. Any hombre moving as he was on the town of Aldamano meant no good for Aldamano, and so this was good for the Apache.

The wall was only four feet high, white 'dobe. Cautiously he raised his head. He was midway on the wall of the jail. He bent and ran farther. Slowly he raised again. He was at the end. He saw the heavy oak door, the guard leaning against the wall, sombrero tilted over his face. Josey sat down and laid his sticks beside him. It was not yet midnight. He would wait, patient as the Indian.

Somewhere in the town, he could hear faint talking; but it was far away and he could make no sense of it.

After a long time, he heard them. "Buenas noches, compadre." That would be the new guard, full of vinegar. The one answering him mumbled tiredly. "Nada" was all Josey heard. That there, according to Chato, meant "nothing." Josey watched them over the wall, the off-duty guard slouching around the corner of the jail and disappearing. Still he waited.

When a guard first came on duty, he was bushy-tailed and went around guarding like hell; but in a little while, just a little while, monotony was the edge. Josey Wales watched as the guard walked about, kicking at the ground. Once he walked almost to the wall, directly at Josey, but turned and repaced his way to the jail door. Now Josey watched him intently, as a scientist watches a bug.

The guard yawned, leaned against the wall, propping his rifle beside him. Josey picked up the sticks and, silent as a shadow, rolled over the wall and lay there, and watched. Five minutes, ten, he watched. The guard did not move.

Silently Josey picked up two of the sticks and slid the Cherokee knife from his boot top. With the sticks under his armpits, he moved, head down, eyes up, watching the guard, closer. He was within five yards when the guard looked up, startled. "Que esta? What is this?" He looked curiously at the stumbling man, unarmed, supporting himself on sticks, obviously wounded.

He came forward, leaving his rifle, to look at this helpless head-down victim, within a yard, and Josey Wales sprang. The knife went upward under the breastbone, buried to the hilt. With the knife plunge, he shoved his open hand into the guard's astounded mouth. They stood thus a moment, silent statues.

The horror in the eyes of the Rurale, staring back at him the vicious eyes of Josey Wales. He died, slumping into Josey without a sound.

Grunting lightly, Josey pushed him to the wall by the door. Using the sticks, he placed one under the pit of each arm and propped the guard against the wall.

Now he crawled in the shadows of the jail. At the corner he could see the main street. There was no one in sight. The Rurales were placing their heaviest guards around the horses and mules, notorious prizes for thieving Apache.

Halfway down the jail wall, he saw the other guard, leaning against the wall. He was about to move on him in the same manner, when his roving eye picked up the figure and he froze.

A Rurale stationed on a rooftop, still as a post, vigilant. Josey began to scan the roofs and saw another farther down the street. He sat back in the shadows. When he got Ten Spot out, time was what he needed—had to have. The guard down the wall was bound to walk up, at anytime, and then raise the alarm. That there guard had to be got— but how? He cut a plug of tobacco with the bloody knife and chewed slowly, squatting in the shadows, meditating the whole damn situation.

"Well," he muttered after an appropriate time of chewing, " 'pears I done fancied out on tricks. Onliest way looks like the simplest."

He rose from his haunches. Yanking the sombrero from the head of the dead guard, he pulled it low over his forehead and eased his head around the corner.

Now, he mused to himself, what, er how, am I a-goin' to call the sonofabitch. I cain't jest say, c'mere, sonofabitch. He remembered the casual, careless Chato; and so, easing his head around the corner, he said, low, "Eh?" and lazily waved his arm, gesturing the guard to him.

The "eh" so casual, the arm lazy, it was obviously no emergency. The guard did not even bring his rifle. He sauntered up the wall. When he reached the corner, Josey Wales simply reached around him with the knife and slit his throat, so deep and brutal the head almost flipped from the neck.

He dragged him beside the door, with the other dead Rurale. Quickly he went through their pockets. There was no key. He felt around them; on the back of the guard propped against the wall, he found the key fastened to his belt. He jerked the key free.

It was a huge key, rusted, and as he turned it in the lock it screeched, opening the door.

The musty smell of damp earth and rotting straw hit his face. He stepped downward on the stone. There was no sound. He chanced a whisper. "Ten Spot! Air ye there?"

From the darkness along the far wall a weak chuckle of laughter answered. "I'm right here, Josey." Josey ran across the straw and found him, hands bound behind his back, feet tied.

He ran the knife through the thongs. "How'd ye know it was me?" he asked the gambler.

Ten Spot answered wryly, "Well, when you asked the question, I said to myself: now Ten Spot, that is a very peculiar Tennessee mountain way of talking for a Rurale, I said; only one fool I know would come . . ."

"Shet up," Josey growled, "we got to git."

As Josey helped him to his feet, Ten Spot stumbled and fell. Josey dragged him up against the wall and carried him to the door. He stopped, looking out cautiously.

"I believe I can stand," Ten Spot whispered.

Gingerly Josey stood him against the wall. He held on for a moment, then turned loose. Ten Spot stood. He watched as Josey brought two more sticks and propped the second dead guard against the wall. He was working quickly, making no sound, except to snarl at Ten Spot, "Make yerself some use; take them pistol belts and pistols off'n them guards. We'll more'n likely have need of 'em."

Ten Spot staggered up to the guards. He shuddered; the throat-cut guard's neck looked like a monstrous mouth. It was smiling broadly and slavering blood. He forced himself to unbuckle the heavy pistol belt, holding the holstered pistol.

Josey stripped the belt from the second guard. "Let's move," he said, and holding Ten Spot by the arm, they moved for the wall. It was then they saw the Apache girl.

Josey dropped to his knees. She was naked, blood-smeared. He felt her heart. "She's alive."

Ten Spot looked down at her. "She was a prisoner too. Escobedo had done this to her. I don't know how she got here."

Josey Wales hesitated for the barest moment; he bent, picking up the girl and slinging her over his shoulder. He pushed Ten Spot toward the low wall. He had to help the gambler get over, surprised at his weakness and skeletal frame. Then he followed with the girl.

They ran for the bushes. Josey laid the girl across his saddle, pushed Ten Spot onto the back of the dapple horse. He jumped astride the roan, but they did not run. Slowly they walked the horses into the shadows of the waving mesquite, away from Aldamano.

Josey guided them, never increasing the pace, through

the winding bushes. Ten Spot reeled in the saddle; black matted beard covered his face, almost a skeleton face. He still wore the black frock coat, but he had no shirt.

Josey whistled, and was answered by Pablo. As they rode into the little circle, Josey motioned for Pablo to take the girl. "The leavings of Capitan Escobedo," was his only explanation.

He eased her down. With his one arm, Pablo tenderly laid her on a blanket. He covered her naked body with another blanket. Josey helped Ten Spot from the saddle, and the gambler sat down suddenly. He looked at Chato, still asleep. "What's the matter with Chato?" he asked.

"Back-shot by Escobedo," Josey said. He stood for a long moment, hat pushed back from the scarred face. "Damned if we ain't set up a horspital, right out here in the middle of nowheres." It was the typical reaction of Josey Wales to disaster.

He was no fool. He knew there was no humor in it. Deep in the heart of enemy territory, riders would be coming, good riders from the east and from the west. Riders who knew the country. Riders who would kill.

The band of Josey Wales was made up of the farmer Pablo, the gambler Ten Spot, Chato badly wounded, and the Apache girl. It was not a band put together for speed in outdistancing pursuers. The odds in a fight would not attract the most reckless of gamblers.

But Josey Wales had learned his guerrilla warfare in the Border War; disastrous situations came as regularly as dinnertime; no quarter asked, no quarter given. He had also learned that the leader lifted those who followed him, lifted them with optimistic lies, or figgerin' plans in the middle of disaster, or vinegar sarcasm in the valley of hopelessness. He was a gut fighter, plain and simple. He meant to gut it out. He knew the fighter traveled on the size of fight and spirit in him; not on mourning his plight, or dwelling on his doom. It was the way of Josey Wales.

He stood over them for a moment, looking down at this camp of weak and wounded. Striding to the saddlebags on the horses, he fixed nose bags of grain for them, and returned with canteens and food.

Pitching a long round of jerky beef and two soured biscuits at Ten Spot's feet, he said, "Start chewing and swallerin'. It'll gripe yer belly, but ye keep at it. Ye've got to git strength. We'll need all ye got in ye."

Ten Spot began to chew. First he gagged and almost vomited, but the hard eye of Josey Wales was on him. He swallowed.

He tossed a canteen at the feet of Pablo, and with it a shirt he had taken from the bags. "Clean 'er up."

"*All* of 'er?" Pablo asked timidly.

"*All* of 'er, toenails to head," Josey said grimly.

With bashful trepidation, Pablo pulled away the covering blanket from the unconscious girl. Wetting the shirt from the canteen, he washed away the blood. As he worked, he spoke to her softly in Spanish, his tone that of the gentle corn raiser, sympathetic, soothing, apologetic, as he cleaned between and down her legs.

She regained consciousness, but as was the way of the Apache, she kept her eyes slit-closed, first to learn into what hands she had fallen, and if necessary to take advantage of the knowledge that her wits were alive, which her enemies would not know. Her hand still gripped the long knife.

She saw the white-eye, Ten Spot, who too had been a prisoner. He appeared free and was eating. She listened to the soft, soothing words of Pablo as he cleaned her body with the tenderness she had not known. She watched, listened, for a long time.

Suddenly she lifted the knife, flipped it expertly, circling in the air, and handed it, handle first, to the startled Pablo. He had not known, and still didn't, how close he had come to death.

He shook his head. "No," he whispered, and smiled. She was to keep the knife.

Standing, Josey Wales watched Aldamano. There was no activity that he could see through the long-glass. He took the chance. At any moment, the guards could be discovered, but he had to put his band in the best shape possible to ride.

He dug the "outlaw oven" in the ground, broke tiny dry sticks and set the fire. From a canteen, he poured water into a tin cup, cut chunks of jerky beef into it and set it to boil. He prepared another cup. When he had boiled the strength of the beef in both cups, he laced them with tequila, handing one to Ten Spot. The other he carried to the sleeping Chato.

Kneeling, he tenderly lifted the vaquero's head and shook him awake. While Chato weakly protested the scalding liquid, he poured it into him. "Swaller! er I'll pistol-whip yer haid!"

Precious minutes were ticking away, fifteen, thirty, but it would do no good to rush wildly away on horseback. His people would collapse in fifteen miles.

He motioned Pablo to take the cups and jerky beef and prepare broth for himself and the girl. But she was already dragging herself, elbow pulling, to the canteens, pouring water and cutting beef into them. She couldn't walk, or crawl. The huge swollen lump in her crotch made her legs splay like stiff crutches. She gave no indication of pain.

Josey watched her briefly. "Saint!" he said quietly.

"Her name," Pablo said, "she have told me, is En-lo-e. She know Escobedo will be coming. She say she will help, and when she cannot, she will roll into the brush, not to slow us." Pablo looked beseechingly up at Josey. "She will not slow us?"

"No," Josey answered softly, "she won't slow us. She'll do."

Josey had raised the quietly cursing Chato to a sitting position, lifting the bloodied bandages and inspecting the raw holes in his chest and back. Ten Spot sat, chewing, gagging, swallowing.

Josey squatted amongst them. "Watch!" he said, "and listen, 'special you, Chato, as was blowing around 'bout you knowed this here country sich as yer hand."

He placed a stick upright in the ground on the eastern side of the circle, another at the west. He drew a line from one to the other.

Pointing at the eastern stick, he said, "Thet there's Coyamo, sixty miles to our east. This here," he pointed to the western stick, "is Aldamano. We're right chere at this west end."

He rose for a moment, took a sweeping look through the long-glass at Aldamano. Without comment on what he had seen, he squatted again. "Them forty Rurales ain't got to Coyamo yit," he said, working his jaws slowly on a tobacco plug. " 'Nother hour fore they git there, riding hard; then they got a hour fight, maybe two—them bandidos is tough. Before they git the story about Pancho Morino, and me killing him." He paused, spat, listened to Pablo whispering in Spanish to En-lo-e what he was saying, "that's two, maybe three hour afore they find out what it's all about."

"Wait!" Chato chortled weakly, "wait until Valdez discover who was the messenger. Por Dios! I would like to see his face."

"Ye'll git to see it, if ye don't shet up," Josey snapped. With studied concentration, he began again. "Then there's

Valdez setting a good five hour from here. He'll ride like hell thisaway to tell Escobedo. Thet figgers—seven, maybe eight hour from Valdez' end—figgerin' thataway . . ."

"Sounds like we're not in bad shape," Ten Spot cut in, between gags of chewing.

"We're in bad shape," Josey said. "Fust trouble ain't coming from Valdez. At best figgerin' we got . . . ," he paused, looking at the sky, "three hour until somebody runs acrost them dead guards. Our fust trouble's coming from this end, right where we got our tails a-settin'." He spat on the hot coals. They hissed and filled the air with rancid tobacco smell.

"Let's say," he contemplated the sky, "thet it takes Escobedo thirty minutes to figger out the whole thing, him being a smart sonofabitch. Then he's a-goin' to send trackers circling the town to cut our trail. Thet's a hour. They'll find it. Thet's four hour, cutting out the thirty minutes. He'll saddle every man he's got and hit our trail. He'll send a man riding to meet Valdez and tell him to turn northwest, trying to cut us off, and meet him follerin' us—thet is . . . ," and he paused ominously, "if he ain't done caught us by then."

"We got to ride north?" Ten Spot asked.

"Well," Josey said, "we damn shore cain't ride east, er west, lessen ye want to go south and take a little sight-seeing of Mexico City, picking up a couple thousand Rurales alongst the way. North it's got to be."

Chato leaned forward, grunted at the pain, and with his finger drew a sloping line in the dust. "Straight north," he said, "the Rio Grande slopes from the north . . . south-east. Straight north . . . we will be forever in Mexico. Somewhere we must turn northeast, so we will hit the bend of the river, as she dips deep into Mexico. It will cut sixty . . . seventy miles off our run to the border."

Josey studied the line. "Fust time," he said quietly, "I

have ever heard a lick o' sense come out'n that cow-trailing head o' yourn. We head north, forty, fifty mile; we find a good place where it's rocky, rough; we switch northeast."

"Remember, Josey," Chato said weakly, "when time comes . . ."

"I remember, about yer goddamned borrerin' aheadst yer wages," Josey snarled.

Chato laughed, and grunted at the pain. "Once more, before we leave, Josey . . . a little of the . . . medicine would help."

Josey uncorked the bottle of tequila. Chato gulped the fiery liquor. As he brought the bottle down, Ten Spot reached and took it from him. "I need a slurp of that. My belly is tied in a knot." He turned up the bottle and drank.

"Remember," Chato said earnestly, his tongue thickening, "that is Pancho's bottle from which we drink; mine is for me, in the saddlebag."

"We'll all be shore and rec'lect thet," Josey said drily, "whilst we set here and drink it up. When Mr. Escobedo rides up, we'll remind him too thet Chato's bottle ain't to be tetched." He stood again with the long-glass and watched Aldamano.

"Time to move," he said tersely. He helped the staggering Chato aboard his big gray, lashing his feet in the stirrups. Ten Spot mounted the dapple unassisted. Color had come back into his face; he felt stronger.

While they had talked, Josey watched curiously while En-lo-e crawled to a mesquite bush. Using the knife, she cut it. Now she spoke to Pablo and he brought the rope from his saddle horn.

She tied one end of the rope to the brush. Pablo clumsily, but tenderly, sat her on his saddle, not astride, but sideways. He mounted behind her on the grulla, and holding her in the crook of his arm while he held the reins, he stood his horse, waiting for Josey to mount.

Josey took a last look at Aldamano. All seemed quiet. He swung aboard the roan and led the way, holding the reins of Chato's horse, the vaquero weaving in the saddle. Behind came Ten Spot, and bringing up the rear was Pablo with the Apache girl. Pablo had dressed her with his peon shirt. It hung on her small figure like a billowy poncho, to her knees.

Josey glanced backward. The girl had taken the reins of Pablo's horse. With his one arm, he held her. Josey noted that she did not drop the brush behind them, to cover the tracks. He knew what she would do. She would wait until they had ridden far to the north, where they would turn northeast, perhaps at a rocky gulch, a slate-side arroyo. Josey Wales would find that spot to turn.

For she knew Escobedo would find this camp. He would know they could not fly away from it, and so would follow the trail; but once they turned in the rocks, if they could reach them, to the northeast, she would drag the brush behind them.

It could take Escobedo's riders an hour, maybe two, riding north, circling to pick up the clear tracks, before they realized the brush had changed the trail.

Josey Wales felt a warmth for this Apache girl. Guerrilla natural-born. She figgered the edge.

And through the deepening darkness before dawn, they rode slowly, walking the horses. A pitiful pace that ticked away the sparing minutes before discovery. The minutes counted now, like drops of blood, for a limping, weakened, wounded band whose chances of reaching the Rio Grande were impossible.

Josey Wales could have made it alone easily; perhaps Pablo. The thought had not entered their minds. The bond of loyalty was stronger than life. Than death.

Chapter 13

How many times the life of a man is determined by the smallest decisions!

When Josey Wales rescued Ten Spot and the Apache girl, En-lo-e, he had pushed Ten Spot over the wall of Aldamano first, and by so doing, saved his own life.

When he had come over the wall with En-lo-e, the Apache warriors, watching, had moved forward to kill him and take the girl. But Na-ko-la touched the arm of their leader. "That is Señor Sonofabitch he has rescued, and so is saving our sister as well." And so they sank back into the darkness of the bush and watched.

When the Rurales had rushed out of Coyamo, Na-ko-la had listened from his grave in the dungeon. All was quiet, and he raised his head. The door was open. It was a simple matter to uncover himself, slip through the door and into the desert.

Naked, he had run in the half circle, and finding the toe marks of his band, had caught them halfway to Aldamano. He told them of Sonofabitch, and how he had helped to save him, even when the Mexicanos had beaten him and kicked him; how he had laughed and would not tell that Na-ko-la lay hidden at their feet.

Friend or enemy, the Apache never forgot. The leader motioned two warriors to follow Josey Wales. In an hour they reported back: the tender care of En-lo-e by Pablo, the plans of the little band led by Josey Wales, the direction north they were taking. Their leader grunted. He said nothing.

They were a large band, for Apache. An Apache band, more often than not, was made up of five. Even two Apache warriors could spread terror through the countryside. This band numbered twenty-two.

They were not a raiding party, a food party. A raiding party sought horses, mules, cattle, and killed only when necessary. This was a blood party. These were the husbands, fathers, sons and brothers of the murdered women and children, butchered and scalped by Escobedo's Rurales. Their mission was not food. Blood for blood. The Code of the Apache.

The Code had been handed down—a hundred, two hundred years, so far in the dim past, they did not know— from father to son, mother to daughter.

The great Spanish nation had moved in on the Americas with their Conquistadores, masters of warfare, born, raised and bathed in two hundred years of war. They smashed the mighty Inca Empire in a matter of months. The Inca, with an economic and judicial system equal to Rome's, with commerce and balanced trade, with stone-paved highways where ten horses could ride abreast for a thousand miles.

The Conquistadores ground it all beneath their steel in months and made peons of the Inca, peons who died by the thousands, the hundreds of thousands.

The Spanish soldiers and priests had piled priceless records and artwork in mounds large as cities and burned them, making a mystery of the Inca's beginning, destroying the knowledge, the temples, the origins, everything.

With them, they brought the advanced stage of barbarism our historians call "civilization." They forced the peons to pay tribute to the god representing pain and death who hung from the cross; and the peon did, feeling sorry for this god, but secretly holding on to his past, the gods who did not promise with the threat of eternal fire and torture.

Northward the steel foot came, crushing the Mayan, the Zapotec, and finally—as climactic, irrefutable proof that the Conquistador was unconquerable—the majestic Aztec Empire.

Raping, pillaging for gold and silver, torturing revelations from the victims for more of the hidden metal; enslaving, setting up the system of politico-priest to create a gigantic bureaucracy of State and Church. And the Indian died.

He died in the mines of silver, enslaved in the fields, at the whipping posts, in the dungeons, at the stocks. The Indians starved on the meager rations, and were ravaged by the thousands as the diseases, attacking the weakened bodies like maggots, cut them down, as the scythe cuts the countless stalks of wheat.

The Indian learned. For survival, he learned to withdraw within himself, to touch his forehead in obedience to his masters, to bend his knee in humble submission, to become the silent, "dumb" peon. He was Christianized, conquered. His heritage and culture, his history and religion, his accomplishments and creativity forever destroyed, crushed beyond resurrection.

The masters of war and civilized barbarism moved north. No Aztec Empire stood in their path, no Inca, no organization. They had conquered even the jungle, here there was no jungle. But their plans became plans on paper. The steel foot stumbled; then it was halted. The masters of war met the Apache. Northward they could move no more.

The Apache invented a new kind of war, a war that made fumbling, frustrated novices of the great Conquistadores and their descendants. Guerrilla.

At first the Apache had met the Spanish, as had all the Indians of Mexico, with open hand. They came to the little towns that were rising in the north. They traded. The priests told them of their god, how they must pay tribute. The politicians gave them mescal, and while they were drunk, butchered them and their wives and children. The captured were tortured and enslaved. The Apache retreated.

No more did he plant his corn field. To come back to it for the harvest was to be ambushed by the Spanish soldier. He moved his mind further toward the mystic of his father, Usen of nature, and he moved his people back, back into the Mother Mountains, the Sierra Madre.

She stretched Her spine far into New Mexico and Arizona. Two thousand miles She plunged into Mexico, a hundred miles wide, thousands of miles of Her children. The Apache trails ran through secret passages where no horse could go. It was said that deep, high, within Her bosom, She nestled beautiful, fertile, hidden valleys of water and grass; but no Spaniard knew. To enter the

Sierra Madre of the west was death. None had ever crossed it. Only the Apache.

The white historian sought to designate the Apache tribes: the Chiricuahua, the Mescalero, the Tonto, the Membreno. But they became confused, for the Apache was the creator of the first rule of guerrilla warfare, later to be studied at the "civilized" war colleges without credit to the Apache. They broke up into small bands within the principal tribes: the Nedni Apache, the Bedonkohe, the Warm Springs—so many. The confusion lasts today.

Small bands came together for war and food objectives, then disseminated after the operation, and reassembled at small rancherias.

If attacked by a superior force, they fled in all directions, confusing the attacker, but always knowing the designated place to reassemble—a secondary, even a third, rendezvous point.

Never the frontal assault. Never the naive heroics of standing to the death; flee—run—hide. Think out the thoughts of the attacker; patience, wait, strike him when he is lulled in his mind, at the disadvantage. Hit his flanks, his rear—run.

The double-think: first your thoughts, then the thoughts of the enemy: what he is thinking, his habits, his way of life, his treacheries; then return to your own planning, based upon the thinking, the plans, of the enemy.

Move. Always move the rancherias. A moving target is hard to plan campaigns against, almost impossible to grasp.

Still they gathered the juniper berries high in the mountains, massaging them into sweetish rolls; gathered the acorns, shelled and made them into meal. But now the principal food must come from the raid. No more could the crops be raised. A field was stationary; it could not be moved. It was a trap of death.

Only the Apache exacted tribute from the Spanish,

who had forced millions of Indians to grind away their lives in payment of tribute to Spanish bureaucracy and the Church. Only the Apache.

And so the generations were raised from the day of each child's first step; the way of life was guerrilla.

The Apache warrior could run seventy miles a day, go five days without food. When he drank from a waterhole and slaked his thirst, he filled his mouth with water, and after four hours of running, he swallowed it. It carried him fifty more miles without the swelling of his tongue.

He never camped by a waterhole, always far away from it; enemies came to waterholes. He never sought the shade of a tree on the plains, or a bush large enough to shade a man. Pick the bush large enough only for the rabbit, talk to the bush, love the bush; become part of the bush, and it will become part of you. The Mexicanos and the white-eyes then will not see you. And they didn't.

When the soldados were sighted, patrolling the plains, send warriors ahead. Within the hour, a frightened Apache would leap and run three hundred yards ahead of the soldados; and they on horseback would run him down, zigzagging, into the open plain where there could be no ambush. But as they almost reached him with their lances, Apache rose from the living graves in the ground and pulled the soldados from their horses and killed them. Ambush where there can be no ambush.

And so the vast lands to the north would remain vacant: Texas, Arizona, New Mexico, Nevada. California could be settled only on the coast, where the ships could bypass the Apache. And the vast territory would fall like ripe fruit into the hands of the United States, the white-eyes who moved in.

The Apache would receive no credit in the United States books of history, for his stopping the Spanish movement northward. He would have no part in writing it.

He welcomed the white-eyes with friendship. He was invited to feasts, and the food was laced with strychnine, killing the Apache in agony. Old Mangus Coloradas, Chief of the Warm Springs Band, would seek peace and be captured under the white flag of truce, tortured with hot irons by United States soldiers and murdered with his hands tied behind his back. The officer-in-charge would receive a promotion.

Now the Apache fought on two fronts. The United States and Mexican governments had agreed: "eliminate" the Apache, man, woman, child, as advocated by the Sheridans, the Shermans. But now, one of those fronts was at the back of the Apache. The United States Army.

The U.S. Army, as treacherous as the ambitious officers who thirsted for victories and promotions; the politicians who fevered to embellish their records by advancing "civilization." As treacherous as the newspaper editors who screamed for more troops at the behest of men who hungered for the yellow gold. As treacherous as the men who sold the ammunition and supplies to the Army and must have the "war." The Apache had experienced it all before.

Though orators sounded in the "civilized" halls of their parliaments with speeches on the holy cause of "freedom"; though the scribes, with deep and moving phrases, wrote of this cause for mankind—it was the Apache, for generations, who had lived on the thin line of death, running, hiding, fighting, raiding, moving; who had fought for, and only for, this "freedom." Freedom from government! Freedom from the tributes, the taxes, the regulations, the parasite bureaucrats—the inevitable bureaucracy that sucked man dry of his spiritual self and ground him, rotting his soul with ambition for money, prestige, power; all the currents of storm and hell that man moves above the Mother Earth.

The Apache would receive no footnote on history's page

for this cause. He would be written as the "murderous renegade." The Apache would have no pen to touch the page of history.

Now the Apache band outside Aldamano moved closer to their leader. They asked him nothing. They simply waited for his decision. His wife and child had escaped the butchery; still he had been chosen to lead.

For nearly ten years, he had been the principal war leader. Ten years ago, he had returned to a butchery at his band's rancheria. There he had found his first wife, his slender, beautiful, frail Alope, raped so repeatedly that the female organ was unrecognizable, a huge lump pushing outward. Her tiny breasts had been cut from her and stuffed in her mouth. He had found his three children who, bellies sliced open by the Spanish soldados' sabers, had dragged themselves over the ground, snagging their entrails on the rocks. Dying as they had reached the body of their mother.

He had loved them deeply, as the Apache loves, without fault. He had burned all that had belonged to them. He had walked down to the river and he had stood, and the mysticism he had felt in his childhood grew in him.

He had walked into the desert and grown with the spirits—into the mountains—and it was said he was seen dancing with the mountain "gans," the spirits.

His flawless love had become the flawless diamond of hard hatred, pure as the love that gave it birth.

It was known he could talk to the wolf and the coyote. That the mesquite whined its secrets to him on the wind. More than once he had saved war parties from soldados.

One time, caught on the open plain, he and ten warriors were surrounded by two hundred soldados. He had turned to face the light breeze that sang in the bush. Softly he had sung his wind song. The breeze lifted to a wind; more he sang. The wind grew stronger; its temper became furious, whipping the desert into a storm, blinding the soldados. Every Apache had escaped. More than once he had done this. They knew. They had seen. His word was never questioned on the trail of blood.

Now he retreated from his warriors. He knew they wanted to strike Aldamano. It lay like a juniper nut before them, ready to be gathered. He went back into the brush and sat down alone.

He faced first to the east and softly sang, then to the south, the west, the north. He sat a long time. Slowly he rose and came back.

They would not hit Aldamano. He saw ahead, two, three days. He would lead them to that rendezvous. He yawned, and again, and again.

White men would misspell his Apache name. They would not be able to catch the soft, liquid talk of the Apache. Some would write he was called Go-klah-ye; others, Go-yak-la. The name meant "One Who Yawns." He had learned it long ago—the yawn that helped his mind to the alertness, to prepare it for the visions.

He motioned three warriors to him and gave them instructions. Quietly they slipped away. He squatted alone and waited, a short, powerfully built man, with black eyes that burned.

History would not know how to "classify" his Apache standing. He was not a chief. He held no official position. He was not a medicine shaman. But the white man's history makes no allowance for the mystic, the spiritual. They would write him off as a murderous renegade. They would wonder at his power and be confused. But they would not misspell the name given him by the Mexicanos. He was Geronimo.

Quietly the Apaches crouched. They were out of rations and waited for the three warriors. They came, leading the mule.

As ghosts, they had slid among the Rurales. With rawhide strips, they tied the mule's legs together, leaving him only a short stride. With another strip, they pulled down his head.

A shuffling head-down mule is obviously grazing. As he moves clumsily along, stopping here and there, he attracts no attention. Patiently he was moved into the shadows, and away from the Rurales as easily as a riverboat gambler slides a card from the bottom of a deck.

They led the mule a mile to the northward, where they butchered him, each cutting the pieces he desired into strips for his food sack. They ate. Then rising without a word, they followed their leader, Geronimo, in the rhythmic, shuffling stride toward the northeast, the same direction as the little band of Josey Wales.

Their soft shuffling moccasins, the light grunting of their throats, brought a rise in the wind. Some range riders would have recognized the sound. It was sometimes heard, and called viento de muerte, the "death wind."

Chapter 14

The pace was slow. In the darkness, Josey turned his head to watch the stride of the gray, carrying Chato. The stride was long, smooth. He stepped up, by the slightest gait, the smooth, long walk of his roan. Just under the trot. A jolting trot would jar the jagged wound that ran through the body of Chato. He would bleed inside. And he would die.

Josey judged the walk, four, maybe five miles an hour. He watched the sky and counted away the time. One hour, two, three hours, and the wind rose in the blackness, morning wind that breathed harder before birthing the day. Soon it would be sunrise.

The light shot upward on their right, wiping away the

stars, and the sun burst, exploding over the rim of the plain. Ahead of him Josey could see waves of flat, endless mesquite. The plain.

He turned, not halting, and tried to look backward toward Aldamano, but could not see it on the flat surface. At best, an hour before Escobedo's Rurales, circling the town, would cut their trail. Escobedo would send the messenger to meet Valdez, instructing Valdez to turn northwest and meet him on the trail north.

He cut a tobacco plug and chewed slowly. Figgerin' high, it would give 'em twenty-five miles before Escobedo would take the trail after them. He'd be crazy mad, messing up his plans. He'd ride his Rurales like hell was on their tail. Josey Wales chewed and figgered. It was a tight corner they was in. He spat, topping a lizard's head resting in the shade of cactus.

Once he turned and snarled at Chato, "By God, it's a pleasing thing, jest to ride along without'n yore big mouth running off."

Chato, his head sagging, sombrero dragging the neck of the horse, raised his head. It was an effort. His head waggled, but white teeth flashed in a weak smile. "Si," he whispered, "don't worry for me, Josey. I can ride." The sombrero dropped; head down again.

"I ain't worrying none about ye," Josey said. "Yore damn belly-shot condition is improving of yer ways, is all I was remarking."

The sun rose, hotter. Ten Spot weaved only slightly in the saddle. His colorless eyes stayed steadily on the back of Chato.

Three hours, Josey figgered. Three hours and Escobedo would be on their backs. His eyes scanned the plain ahead—flat, not even a damn place to hole up. Without slackening the pace, he pulled the long-glass from his bag, looking ahead now for anything, a butte, even a good-sized rock, by God. There was nothing. The mesquite waving in the wind, the cactus, the ocotillo and gamma grass.

The sun had tilted past noon. Every fifteen minutes, Josey raised the glass and scanned the prairie ahead. For an hour. And then he picked it up—a thin wavering line off to their right, a shallow arroyo running from the north that petered out on the plain. He slanted the horses toward the arroyo.

Now with the glass he looked back. First he saw nothing, then the cloud of dust, a big cloud growing larger, moving fast.

"Escobedo," he muttered beneath his breath. The sun slanted another hour toward the west when they reached the arroyo. He stopped the horses. It was a disappointment.

Narrow, its sides gravel and small rocks, so shallow it would barely hide a man's head on horseback, standing on the sandy bottom. It wavered and twisted northward, a runoff for the water of rare cloudbursts. Josey led them down into the ditch, for it was only a ditch, sliced in the prairie. With their horses standing on the bottom, they could not see the prairie.

"We can hold them here, Josey," Chato said.

"Hold 'em, hell," Josey said. "They'll lay back and pot-shot, circle us and wait on Valdez. With sixty Rurales, they'll splatter us all over these here rocks."

Pablo and the girl started to dismount.

"Everybody stay on yer hoss," Josey said. "Git out the jerky and be eating while I'm telling ye . . ."

"And Pancho's bottle," Chato interrupted, "it is still half filled. My bottle . . ."

"I know," Josey snapped, "your'n ye're saving."

Ten Spot took the bottle, Pancho's, from his saddlebag. It was half full. He raised it and swallowed long, passing it to Chato. The vaquero swallowed great gulps, lowered the bottle and smacked his lips, "Bueno." Pablo shook his

head. He had tried the tequila before and found nothing
bueno in it. They ate on the jerky.

" 'Pears," Josey chewed slowly, "this here is the way it
is. The hosses need water bad, and graining."

Chato, briefly revived by the tequila, pointed to the
northeast.

"Twenty, maybe thirty mile, there is a hacienda grande.
We . . ."

"All right," Josey said, "here's what ye do. Pablo, give
me yore sombrero." Pablo took off the hat and passed it to
Josey. "I want all the blankets; and I'll need yore coat, Ten
Spot." The gambler asked no question. He shucked the
coat, leaving him half naked in the sun.

"Now," Josey said, dismounting and rolling the blankets
behind his saddle, "ye all wait right here. When ye hear
Escobedo and his men riding by, ye wait fifteen, twenty
minutes; then ye head northeast. Pablo, ye tell the girl
everything I'm saying. Let her lead; 'Pache knows how.
Ten Spot, ye mind after Chato; lead his hoss; no trot, er
Chato will die."

"There will be no trot, Josey," Ten Spot said flatly,
"even if they're on our tail."

"Now . . . ," Josey cut tobacco and chewed, "tie the
rope to Chato's hoss. Let it drag the bresh behint ye, might
be it'll help; but drag slow, no dust. When ye git to the
hayseenda," he cocked his eye at the sun, "it'll be after
dark. Ye wait in the bresh, maybe three hour. If I ain't
there in four hour, I won't be coming more'n likely. Go in,
take yer chances."

He walked to the side of the arroyo and with the long
knife slashed three heavy mesquite branches. Walking to
the roan, he lifted the rope from his saddle horn. One
end of the rope he tied to the pile of mesquite he had cut;
the other he wrapped securely around his saddle horn.
When he had finished, he walked beside Chato, lifting his

shirt, inspecting the bandages and wounds. They were bleeding.

"What you do, Josey?" Chato asked.

Josey spat on a rock. "Me and Big Red is aiming to take a little ride." He checked the sun. "We're going to ride hour, two hour, straight north. Me and Big Red is going to ride so hard the dust cloud will look like we're all skeered out'n our head, and breaking fer a last run. Mr. Escobedo, he's going to figger he's jest about got us proper. After that," Josey sighed, "well, it'll git dark. They cain't track in the dark. Me and Big Red will meet ye sometime tonight at the hayceenda."

He didn't mention what they all knew. Pulling the heavy mesquite, could the roan last an hour? Two hours? If he stepped in a hole, broke a leg, stumbled, it would be over for Josey Wales.

It was a death ride. Every one of them knew it. Even the girl; for softly in Spanish, Pablo had told her.

They were receiving new life, a night of non-pursuit. A chance for this little band of weak and wounded, where there had been no chance.

Josey shook the hand of Chato. The tequila and the emotional nature of the vaquero made tears run unashamedly down his face. "This," he whispered brokenly, "this . . . Josey . . . should not be, we should not part, we . . ."

"Shet up, ye cow-trailing drunk. I'm glad to git shet of ye."

Ten Spot said nothing. He gripped Josey's hand hard. Pablo held his hand long and prayed silently. En-lo-e leaned from the saddle to touch him as he passed.

He leaped on the roan and rode out of the arroyo. At the top, he pulled the long-glass, and now could plainly see the Rurales. He figgered them to be thirty, maybe twenty minutes away.

He slid the glass back into the saddlebag, cut a chew of tobacco into his cheek.

"Vaya con Dios!" The voice of Pablo floated up from the arroyo.

"Same to ye," said Josey Wales. He pulled his hat low. "All right, Big Red," he growled, "Let's see if'n ye still got it in ye!"

The big roan jumped, jerking at the huge roll of mesquite. He strained, leaping into a run, and his ears came backward until they lay flat. Big Red, like Josey Wales, did not cotton to sich as figgered he couldn't do.

Ten Spot had crawled to the top of the arroyo. "By God!" he exclaimed, "that dust cloud looks like an army running for the border." He looked back and could see the Rurales coming, shouting now, triumphant; they had jumped the rabbits in the open brush!

As he rode, Josey guided the roan with his knees, trying to keep him in the open. He shortened the rope, pulling the mesquite almost to the heels of the horse; it gave him better control to keep from snagging on the brush.

Now, at intervals, he lifted the mesquite entirely off the ground, creating puffs of dust instead of the steady roll. Each time he lifted, it gave a few seconds respite from the pulling to the roan—a very small edge.

The Rurales' horses drummed closer to the arroyo, and they thundered past where the little band couched over their horses. Some of them had drawn their rifles and were shooting at Josey. Then, as thunder rolling over the prairie, disappearing in a fading rumble, the sound of their horses was gone.

Pablo and the girl led; Ten Spot, leading Chato, followed; out of the arroyo, northeast away from the pursuit, walking slowly, quietly in the wind. Their thoughts were on the desperate chase to the north. Each knew that ride was giving them their lives.

Pablo prayed for the scar-faced bandido, Josey Wales. Even if it was, as said by the priests, that the bandido had no soul, he asked the Santos and God to guide the feet of the roan so he would not stumble, he would not fall.

Eyes narrowed against the sunlight, Josey Wales picked the ground ahead for the big horse, pressing first with the left knee, then the right. The roan responded cat-quick.

For thirty minutes it was a horse race, the roan slowly losing. The Rurales, excited over jumping their quarry, were charging at dead heat. Slowly they gained ground. But they could not hold it. Big Red had been walking all day. The horses of the Rurales and Escobedo had already been driven hard. There was, too, the matter of the roan's big heart and will. The Rurales began to fade.

At the end of an hour they were far behind, forced to slow the horses or kill them. Josey pulled down the roan into a low gallop. He did not want to move too far ahead, neither did he want to exhaust the big horse under him. Already froth blew back from the bits and sweat was ringing the saddle blanket. He dropped the pace slower. Always he kept the arroyo to his right, as it wound snake-like to the north.

The sun fell, losing heat, turning the prairie a bloody red through the dust haze, and then dropping behind the jagged rim of the Sierra Madre. Twilight came. With it came the evening wind. Josey brought the roan to a stop.

Far behind, still they came, dragging at a slow pace; but Escobedo, he knew, would bring them on. He hooked a leg loosely around the horn of the saddle. He was covered with dust. Plug-cutting his tobacco, he commenced his slow chewing. "Let's see, Red," he told the heaving horse, "they'll figger us to be run out, 'cause they are too. They got to figger we'll try to stop and hide in the dark—only chanct we got, hosses dead under us, and sich. Time they git to where we're setting at, it'll be total dark."

Settling his foot in the stirrup, he dropped the horse down into the shallow arroyo and up the other side. Ten yards back, he tied him to a mesquite, filled a nose bag with grain and set it over the horse's mouth. "Might's well be stuffing up, last we got," he reminded the horse.

He moved quickly, pulling the blankets, the sombrero, Ten Spot's coat that he had rolled behind the saddle. He walked down into the arroyo. He draped the coat around a mesquite bush and set the sombrero atop. Stepping back, he admired his handiwork. "Right as rain," he opined softly.

Taking the blankets, he cut, and rolled in each of them, a small mesquite: lumpy, blanketed figures that slept on the ground. He cut a long stick and leaning it in the mesquite that held the sombrero and coat, he stepped back admiringly. "Damned if'n ye don't look jest like ye was guarding, though 'pears like ye've hunkered down and gone to sleep, ye sorry bastard."

He knelt and built a small fire and dropped jerky beef into it, filling the air with the smell of burnt meant. He stomped the fire out. "The smell'll bring 'em, fire looks liken to be a trap . . ." He talked conversationally with himself as he worked.

The twilight deepened. The brightest star came out. He ran to his horse. Reeling in the mesquite brush, he untied it and rolled his rope around the saddle horn. Mounting the roan, he recrossed the arroyo and rode back in the direction of Escobedo's troops, turned after a hundred yards and came back, down into the camp he had made; round and round, he rode the horse, stomping the ground, then up the opposite side, and disappeared into the bush.

For the common outlaw, this would have been enough. Chances were that the Rurales, unable to track in the night, would simply encamp until morning, waiting to pick up the trail. But Josey Wales was no common outlaw, he was a warrior-guerrilla. There was the slightest chance they might circle, carefully looking; might have an Indian to determine the tracks of the roan going east. Josey Wales meant to take the edge off the chance.

He walked, leading the horse a hundred yards south, toward the direction the Rurales would come, but opposite them on the bank of the arroyo.

Tying the roan back in the bush, he lifted two '44's from the holsters on his saddle and came back to the arroyo. He picked a spot at the very edge beneath a small bush and lay forward, propped on elbows, the .44's already cocked.

Ye could figger the military bastards. When they spotted the camp, they would send out flankers to encircle it. They would cross the arroyo a hundred yards to the north of the camp, and figgerin' from here, a hundred yards to the south. If Josey had lain directly opposite the camp, he would have been caught in the circle, first-grade stuff for Josey Wales.

Now he listened. The moon sliver had broadened, dropping a ghost light on the prairie, making a dim white strip of the sand on the bottom of the arroyo. Wind brought the faraway howl of the wolf and the yelp of the coyote.

He heard them. Tired horses, dragging their feet in the dust, the creak of leather. They were riding the very rim of the arroyo. They figgered, that being the only place to hide, there was a chance of their quarry trying to double back. On they came, the heaviness of the horse hoofs increasing.

Almost opposite him, across the arroyo, Josey heard a soft exclamation in Spanish. He grinned evilly. It was no coincidence that he lay at the very edge of the burnt-beef smell. All sound stopped.

Straining his ears, he listened for the whispered conference, men dismounting to sneak forward along the arroyo.

Ten minutes passed, a horse stomped, fifteen minutes. The scouts came back.

Softly they were whispering. He heard a large number of them scurrying alongside the bank of the arroyo, that would be the ones to go beyond the camp and cross the arroyo above it, and the ones to charge it from that side.

These across from him would give them time before they moved. Another fifteen minutes, twenty, and Josey strained his eyes. A figure came down the opposite bank, bent low, walking cautiously, followed by another and another.

They were coming almost directly to him. Still he waited, noting another and another. The first one was already scrambling up the bank in front of him. Couldn't wait too long, the sonofabitch would be stepping on his haid. Six in a line, he counted.

The first figure rose before him not five feet away. BOOM! The deep throat of the .44 echoed and knocked the Rurale backward. Before he hit the ground, the Colt hammer fell in Josey's right hand and had killed the second. The left-hand Colt boomed again; the third fell like a sack in the sand at the bottom. The figures behind them turned to run back up the bank; methodically, Josey thumbed the hammers, one, two, between the shoulder blades, and they pitched sprawling on the rocks. The last of them made it into the brush on the other side.

"Goddamn!" Josey spat in disgust.

He came to his knees, shoving the emptied Colts into his belt, and drew the two from his holsters. He fired, rapid fire, spacing his shots, walking them along the rim of the arroyo, until the guns were emptied. Bending, he ran, and taking the reins of the roan, walked slowly away to the east.

Behind him, bedlam was breaking loose. Rifles and pistols cracked and boomed, echoing in the arroyo, spitting fire first one way and the other. After walking a hundred yards, Josey mounted the roan and headed him east.

The shooting was dying down; now only an occasional shot. He heard shouted orders in Spanish coming faintly on the wind. Then all was quiet.

He kept the roan pointed east. After thirty minutes of easy trotting, he turned in the saddle; huge fires lit the night sky behind him. "Now thet," he reckined to the roan, "would be the signal set fer Mr. Valdez to make haste his tail-to."

In the silver moonlight, he slowly reloaded the pistols, and allowed himself a satisfied chuckle. "Why hell, Red," he drawled, "that there Escobedo wouldn't had lasted past breakfast in Missouri."

Josey figgered the way. He had ridden north. Chato had said they would ride northeast. He trotted the roan, figgerin' to double their slow gait, directly east. Though still deep in the enemy's territory, sure to be trailed come dawn, Josey Wales was feeling better about the whole damn thing. He permitted himself some light entertainment.

> *"I got a gal on Flywood Mountain*
> *Purtiest gal in Tennessee*
> *Reckin come Sunday, I'll go a-courtin'*
> *Up thet mountain, m'hound and me."*

The roan gave a disgusted snort. There was one thing Josey Wales could not do. He couldn't carry a tune in a bucket.

The Apache, leaving Aldamano, had run northeast too, but the tangent of their run carried them further north. Seldom did an Apache cross the plains in the light of day, and so at daybreak they had rested, crouched beneath the small bushes near the arroyo into which Josey Wales would ride.

They had watched the dust clouds coming with growing interest, moving farther back into the brush. Then they recognized the scar-faced white-eye who had rescued their sister.

In the purple of desert twilight, they had moved close, curiously watching him set up the false camp. They had moved back, behind him, to watch. They were bolder now. Usen had brought the night and dimmed the vision of the enemy.

They had watched it all. The staccato gunfire of Josey Wales, the confusion and firing of the Rurales as they moved in on the false camp. Then they faded away into the bush.

Admiration for the scar-face rose in the breast of Geronimo. How many times had the Apache tethered the useless pony, set the false camp, scattered the cooking utensils.

When the soldados had surrounded the camp for the ambush, the Apache had moved in to ambush the ambushers. The scar-face thought as the Apache.

Geronimo had no way of knowing: Josey Wales' raids in guerrilla warfare matched the number of his own.

Now the Apache did not follow Josey Wales. They set out toward the east, but running slightly toward the north. Geronimo had the vision of events to come. An edge of which Josey Wales knew nothing.

Chapter 15

Two hours he lazily trotted Big Red. Chato had said there was fresh water at the hacienda. The roan wanted water, bad. Josey loosened the reins and let the roan have his head. The horse kept the same direction for a while, then his nose came up, his ears. He smelled the water, and altered their course, turning slightly to the north. Another hour. The roan picked up speed, falling into a rolling lope.

Josey scanned the landscape ahead. The white 'dobe of a big hacienda would show right smart in the moonlight. He didn't see it, and so with the increasing gait of the roan, he sent a piercing whistle, "SKEEEeeeeee!" the scream of the Tennessee nighthawk.

He stopped the roan and listened. There was only the wind. For another thirty minutes he let the roan have his head; and halted, whistling the same piercing sound, again, and again.

Faintly, from far away, he heard the whipping call of the whippoorwill, directly ahead.

The little band was not far; the whipping whistle had come from Chato, the weakness giving it the sound of distance.

They were camped in heavy bushes of mesquite as he rode among them. It was not much of a camp. There was no food, no blankets, no fire for warmth. Chato lay spraddled on the ground and around him sat Pablo, En-lo-e and Ten Spot.

Their horses were tied tightly together, held from the water smell by the tight grip of Pablo and En-lo-e. They stomped and snorted. Ten Spot was blistered; his face, shoulders, chest and back showed red, even in the moonlight.

As Josey swung from the roan, Ten Spot said sourly, "By God, I'll die 'fore I give away my coat again in the middle of the goddamn desert. And," he thumbed angrily at the sprawling Chato, "this crazy bastard thinks it's funny if he gets the chance to slap me on the back."

Pablo and the girl said nothing. It required nothing to be said. They were done. Another mile and they would drop in the desert, food for the buzzards.

Except Chato. He had placed his sombrero under his head, in lieu of a blanket, and his teeth flashed white. "It was an accident, I swear Josey . . . both times. Señor Ten Spot, how he jump!" The vaquero laughed weakly and coughed.

Josey cut a tobacco plug. With methodical, nerve-screaming slowness, he chewed. Ten Spot stood impatiently, feeling his chest and stomach. Josey spat and nodded toward the gigantic white lump rising two hundred yards to the north, "That there hayceenda—seen anybody abouts, coming er going?" he asked.

"No, Josey," Pablo said, "I have watch. Nobody. No guardia on the walls. But there is a light at the back, a candle. Part of the roof behind has been burned and fallen in . . . ," he shrugged, "the War."

Josey watched the hacienda for a long time. It was two-storied white adobe with a high wall fronting it that held a patio. He squatted on his boot heels and looked at Pablo. "Ye still got them peon sandals and britches in yer saddlebag?"

"Si," Pablo said.

"Tell ye what ye do," Josey said, "pull off them vaquero britches and boots and put them sandals and peon britches on. Let the girl keep the shirt, ye'll look more ragged without a shirt."

"I will?" Pablo asked. But he rose, went into the bushes and changed the clothes.

"How you figuring, Josey?" Ten Spot was becoming interested. Josey made no answer. He was watching the hacienda. Pablo came from the bushes, sandals on his feet, the white ragged pants he had worn as the beggar in Santo Rio. With no shirt, the stump of his arm hung pathetically. He was a sorry-looking figure.

"Good!" exulted Josey, "ye look jest right. Now tell ye what ye do. Ye go around to the back of that hayceenda. Ye knock politely on the door, like'n ye're scared . . ."

"I am scared, Josey," Pablo said humbly.

"Good," Josey continued, "ye jest keep knocking, polite, but keep at it—that way, ye more than likely won't git shot, as if'n ye was banging away at it." He paused, sorting out the thinking. "Then," he drawled, "when somebody opens the door, er winder, ye move into the light so's they kin see what a sorry-looking thing ye look like—which ye do. This will," Josey added emphatically, "more'n likely keep ye from gittin' shot agin."

Pablo shuffled his feet nervously and nodded.

"Ye tell 'em ye was with a mule train coming out of Coyamo, thet 'Paches jumped ye, ye're the onliest one got away. Tell 'em ye want to warn the bigshot there."

"The Don," Chato interrupted.

"All right, Mr. Don," Josey said, "so's he kin wake up his men and sich, as they 'pear to be coming thisaway." Josey was silent for a while. "This here will bring out whatever is hiding around in them rooms and bunch 'em up fer me. I'll be clost by."

Pablo crossed himself and a shudder ran over his body.

"Ye got it in yore mind now, how to knock, stand in the light, the story?" Josey looked hard at Pablo.

"Si," Pablo said softly, "but . . ."

"And tell 'em ye're hongry and sich. That'll sound natural," Josey added.

"I am hungry," Pablo said simply.

"Good," Josey said, "then ye're might near everything ye're making out to be. Won't be no trouble atall."

"But . . ." Pablo said.

"Git," Josey snapped softly, "vamoose!"

The Apache girl rose and fell, trying to follow Pablo. He turned; holding her hand, he explained in rapid Spanish. Still she tried to crawl after him.

Josey grabbed her arm brutally. "SET!" he snarled. She sat.

As Pablo walked hesitantly away, Chato called softly, "You are now, official, in the Josey Wales Messenger Service. Vaya con Dios!"

The half-joking words of Chato brought added weight to the heavy doom Pablo felt in his mind. So this was the way he was to die! He faltered, but then, stubbornly, he continued his slow walk, circling the hacienda to reach the door at the rear.

Josey knelt and watched intently the retreating back of Pablo. He was counting the steps to the hacienda.

"Josey?" came from Chato.

"Yeah?"

"How did you do . . . how did you manage to escape Escobedo?"

"I couldn't git but five of 'em," Josey spat. "Might near got another un, but . . ."

"*You* couldn't kill *but five!*" Ten Spot exclaimed. He jumped back to his feet. "How in hell did you kill . . ."

"Shet up," Josey drawled, "I'm a-countin' the ground to cover fer that hayceenda."

En-lo-e watched Pablo intently until he disappeared around the white wall.

Josey sat down. "Escobedo cain't foller the tracks now. He's set big fires, guiding Valdez to 'em. Come daylight, that's . . . ," he looked at the stars, "six hour, they'll be coming, sixty, er fifty-five, I put now, Rurales. Escobedo, he'll be madder'n a coon dog which treed a possum."

"Can we stand them off here, Josey?" Chato asked softly. "So many . . ."

"Ain't aiming to," Josey said. He rose in a half crouch. "I'll be sending Pablo back fer all of ye, er if I don't, shoot whatever comes thisaway."

With this terse advice, he left, running crouched, falling, rising to run again. Chato raised on his elbows; Ten Spot stood to watch. They could see, only dimly, the head rising, then falling, appearing as a bush that waves down, then rights itself in the wind. He disappeared into the shadow of the high wall.

Josey lay there. He heard no sound, the prairie wind, the tenor call of a coyote. Flat on the ground, he pulled himself slowly to the big open gate and cautiously looked inside.

A second-story veranda, with steps leading up from the patio, ran round the building. The patio was stone, unkept, weeds growing between the stone. Thick doors indicated rooms on the ground floor and second story.

He stood against the wall, and silently, quickly, he slid into the shadow of the veranda. Inching his way along the wall, he came to the back. The door was open and inside he heard voices—Spanish; he couldn't understand.

He edged away from the wall, backing further from the door where candlelight spilled out on the stone. Now a voice was raised in furious anger, and Josey heard the hard pounding of flesh on flesh. He moved again, and brought into view a small white-haired man, old, dressed in a silken night robe. He was standing, impassively watching something before him.

Josey stepped easily to his right. A big man, bull-shouldered, with long black hair, had his back to Josey. He was vaquero-dressed with high-heeled boots, and a white-handled pistol hung on his belt. It was he who was shouting. He held Pablo by the throat with one hand, and as Josey watched, brought a brutal fist down on Pablo's face, knocking him to his knees.

Pablo was trying to answer some question. His face was swelling from the blows. One eye was almost closed.

Then the vaquero felt the slight pressure on his spine; the click of the cocking .44 was unmistakable. He froze, fist in the air.

Josey Wales did not even look at him. With the cocked .44 in the vaquero's back, his eyes scanned the room. The old man stood as in shock. His eyes widened. Against the wall, two fat Indian women, servants, covered their faces.

As if inquiring of the weather, Josey casually addressed Pablo, struggling to his feet, "What they say, Pablo?"

Pablo spoke through swelling lips; blood ran from his mouth. "They say, Josey, their ladies are in Ciudad de Mexico, for safety. They say their riders are on the range, gathering up the cattle scattered by the—the Indian son-of-a-dog, Juarez. They are all who are here." Pablo wiped the blood from his mouth with his hand. One eye now was completely closed.

Josey eased the gun barrel away from the vaquero's back; as he did, the big man dropped his arm and turned to face Josey.

Josey's hand moved so fast he had no time to raise his arm in protection. The gun barrel of the heavy Colt flashed in a downward stroke. The vaquero fell like a log. The split in his hair showed white skull, and blood ran over the floor.

"That'll learn ye," Josey drawled, "what a Missouri slapping is liken to." The two servant women screamed and sat down, trembling against the wall.

Josey turned to the old man, who had not moved a muscle. "Ye speak English?" he asked conversationally.

The old man drew himself up proudly. "Much better than you, bandido! And French, and Spanish, and Ger . . ."

"All right," Josey drawled, "ye're eddicated. Set down in that there chair." The old man stood. With a boot, Josey kicked him sprawling into the chair. "SET!"

"Ye done right good there, Pablo," Josey praised, holstering the Colts. "Tell ye what ye do. Tell them two women to stoke up a fire in that big fancy stove they got there; fill them three wood tubs full of hot water. Tell 'em to put on plenty of vittles, and sich fer eating. Tell 'em pronto, er I'll shoot 'em in the haid."

Pablo spoke to the women softly; at the end of his talk, when he reached "the haid" part, they leaped to their feet and began to open the stove, setting a fire. Repeatedly they crossed themselves for the bandido who had no soul.

"Pablo," Josey spoke softly, "reckin ye can bring the others in. Be careful with Chato; too much jolting will bust him inside."

"Si." Pablo padded through the door and across the patio.

They were there in a matter of minutes. Chato unconscious from the pain of movement. Josey had him stretched on the table, and En-lo-e unwrapped the dirty bandages. The ugly wounds were not closing, but still, there was no fester, no infection.

At the appearance of En-lo-e, the servant women shrank back. "Apache!" they breathed; but Pablo instructed them, and they filled the tubs with hot water, brought clean bandages and salves for the wounds.

Pablo and Ten Spot stabled the horses in the barn at the rear, watering, graining them, and rubbing them down. They reported only two other horses in the barn.

Pablo spoke to En-lo-e. She stripped the long shirt from her body, and naked, stepped into the hot tub of water. She sat, luxuriating in its warmth, and slowly her head tilted backward, resting on the edge of the tub. She slept. The warmth of the water washed away the weariness, the aches, the pain, and the blood.

Josey sat down in a chair, facing the Don, while the women bathed Chato and dressed his wounds.

Ten Spot, washing, shaving away the beard, stepped back from the mirror. "By God! I feel more like a human again!"

"Since ye're feeling human," Josey said, "ye might sashay yore tail through Mr. Don's rooms and round up all the guns and ammunition."

"A good thought, for a human," Ten Spot smiled, bowing to the Don as he passed. He could be heard in the rooms, banging doors, pulling open closets.

The Don could stand it no longer. He stood erect. "This

—you disgrace my hacienda—plundering my belongings—it—it . . ." He could find no words to express the indignity. He sat down and held his head in his hands.

Pablo was slicing beef and rolling it into big chunks of bread. He handed a roll to Josey. As he chewed, Josey watched the Don narrowly.

"Mr. Don," he drawled.

The Don's head snapped up. "The *name*, bandido, is Don Francisco de Garcia. Don is a title, not a name!"

"No need to git tetchy about it," Josey said soothingly. "Like I was a-goin' to say," he took a large bite from his beefed bread and chewed for a moment, "what ye got so hell fixed agin' this here feller Juarez?"

Fire shot from the eyes of the Don. "Juarez," he said, "is a pagan. A Zapotec Indian—El Presidente, indeed! He will take all the land from the churches, the mines; he says he will bring about land reform, as he calls it, which means stealing part of my land and giving it to the Indians. My land!"

Josey accepted another huge sandwich from Pablo and began chewing again. "How much land ye got?"

"My land," the Don replied proudly, "would require five days for a fast horseman to ride across."

Josey sat up in genuine amazement. "Lord Almighty, ye don't say—and ye say, it's all yourn?"

"It is all mine," the Don announced.

After a long silence, Josey said, "Reckin with that much land ye ain't never seed all of it."

"No, I haven't," the Don said, "but it is there."

"How'd ye manage to git all sich land?" Josey asked curiously.

"The land, bandido," the Don answered, "was handed down to me from my father, and his father before him, and his before him."

"Where'd he git it? I mean the fust un?" Josey asked.

The Don looked puzzled. "Why, he conquered it, of course," he said.

"Never heerd tell of conquering land," Josey said around a mouthful of beef. "Plowing land, grazing it, sich . . ."

"The Indians," the Don said impatiently, brushing a thin hand through his white hair, "he conquered it from the Indians."

"Oh," said Josey Wales. "I see: he reformed it from the Indians, and this here Juarez feller is aiming to reform some of it back. Sounds reasonable."

The Don stared at this ignorant, murderous fool. "You are stupid apparently of all civilized procedure. It is useless to discuss it further." He dropped his head again into his hands.

"Well, reckin I am some ignorant, not gittin' schooling to speak of, but don't feel so bad about it, Mr. Don," he said comfortingly. "You'll have enough land which ye can ride around and see, git to like it, git taken to it. You and the Indians liable to git on jest fine, it ain't all that bad. My motto," he said, propping a boot heel on the belly of the brute lying before him and crossing his other boot comfortably over it, "is live and let live."

The Don, looking down at the figure on the floor, said sarcastically, "Yes, I can see it is your motto."

Ten Spot stepped into the room, a different man. He wore shined boots, a ruffled shirt with laced cuffs, and the black coat had velvet on the collar. "Almost," he said, "a perfect fit. When I am in, ah, better circumstances, Don Francisco, be assured I shall reimburse you for this generosity."

Josey looked coolly at the gambler. "Ye look exactly like a Kansas City pimp. How 'bout the guns?"

Ten Spot reached outside the door and brought forth a carbine. "It is the latest model," he said. "Cartridges . . ." He handed over a long belt of cartridges.

Josey felt the gun, smoothing his hands down the stock. A fine rifle.

"This here," he said, "put in the boot of Chato's saddle, and hang the cartridge belt on it. He's the best rifle shot."

Chato had awakened. Lying on the table, he raised himself on elbows. "You have never admitted so before this, Josey . . . always you have said, I was not . . . Remember?"

"I know," Josey snarled. "I jest said thet to keep Pablo from shooting hisself with it."

To Ten Spot, he said, "See if ye can cram something down that big mouth of his'n besides tequila. Like beef and bread, fer instance. I got a sneaking notion the reason he cain't stand up is his legs is full o' liquor."

It was Pablo that Josey assigned the first watch on the outside wall. The stoic Indian, strapping on the pistol belt, looked long at En-lo-e, still asleep in the tub.

"She's healing, son, and resting well," Josey said, almost tenderly. Pablo nodded. "Ten Spot will relieve ye in two hour," Josey said. "Take, and watch with care."

"I will watch," said Pablo, and faded into the darkness.

The candle burned lower. Ten Spot lay on the floor, Chato on the table. The two Indian servant women slept, crouched against the wall of the kitchen.

Slowly the old man raised his head a mere trifle. He looked cannily at the bandido seated across from him. There was a derringer upstairs, if he could reach it. For a long time he studied Josey Wales, chair propped against the wall, feet crossed on the belly of the foreman sprawled on the floor. The gray hat shaded the bandido's eyes. Were they open or closed? Beneath the shaded brim the deep scar jagged through the stubble of black beard. He seemed to be breathing easily, regularly.

With painful slowness, the old man raised himself from the chair. Once standing, he stood for a long time, gaining reassurance the bandido slept. Softly he took the first step toward the door. He merely blinked his eye, and the big hole was staring at his face; the .44 had moved magically, hammer clicking in the cock. He stood petrified. How had it moved so quickly!

The bandido said nothing, but the hole of the barrel followed the Don back to his seat, and as magically disappeared when he sat down. He was resigned.

Quietly he addressed the bandido. "Do you never sleep?" He sniffed. "Or bathe?"

The drawl came lazily from beneath the hat brim. "Reckin I sleep practical most of my waking time, so to speak. As fer warshin', well, I never could cotton to tub warshin', being from Tennessee original. Creek warshin' more er less being the style there, ain't never shook it, I reckin." He spoke softly, conversationally. A strange bandido!

The candle weakened. The old man fell asleep, sagging in the chair. Josey Wales lifted his feet, unstrapped the pistol belt from the ranch foreman at his feet and laid it on the table beside Chato. He stepped to the door and studied the heavens.

In a moment, he turned and shook Ten Spot. "Time to relieve Pablo," he said.

The gambler rose, strapped on his pistol and stepped through the door without a word. Pablo came in. He walked to En-lo-e, and kneeling beside her, stroked her hair, listened to her breathing. Then he too stretched on the floor and slept.

In the deepest black of night, there is a breath of wind, different, that tells of the coming birth of dawn, as the rhythmic pangs warn the woman of the coming of her child. Josey Wales knew that breath, back there in Missouri.

He felt it; and rousing from his curious half sleep, he walked to Chato, lying on the table. He shook the vaquero gently. "Chato," he whispered.

"Si, Josey."

"How far ye reckin from here, going north, is thet big deep canyon we come through on the way down?"

Chato shook the sleep from his head. "It will be twenty-five, maybe thirty miles, Josey. Why?"

"Jest figgerin'," the outlaw answered. He walked to the door, and whistled Ten Spot in. Toeing Pablo awake, and then En-lo-e, he said, "We're moving. Git the guns, pack grub, fill grain sacks fer the hosses. Chato, ye lay where ye're at, till we're ready. Ye can have thet white-handled pistol there."

"Gracias, Josey," Chato said, surprised at this uncharacteristic generosity of Josey Wales.

"It's more in the way of a loan," Josey said drily. "Ye got but one pistol. Ye'll be needing two after a while."

They were saddled now, Chato's feet again tied in the stirrups. They took the two horses from the hacienda. En-lo-e sitting astride one, Ten Spot leading the other.

The old man stood in the candlelight of the kitchen door. "So," he said indignantly, "you are horse thieves as well. A hanging offense, I warn you."

From the back of the roan, Josey looked down at the old man. "Jest borrerin' the hosses, so to speak. We ain't leaving no fresh hosses fer Escobedo."

"Escobedo!" the old man exclaimed. "So it is Capitan Jesus Escobedo who pursues you. He is my friend. I warn you, when he arrives, I shall tell him the direction in which you have fled." He stuck out his little chest. "Unless, of course, you murder me now."

"You do thet, old man," drawled Josey, "and if Escobedo is yore friend, watch yer back whilst he's around."

He clucked the roan into motion, leading Chato's horse; En-lo-e followed, and Pablo. Ten Spot brought up the rear. Into the black before dawn they walked, slowly north. A pitifully slow gait. A long way from the Rio Grande.

Chapter 16

The wind freshened. It was new from the coming dawn. Later it would grow tired, and mean, and hot.

The single file walked north; the horses' gait, set by Josey in the lead, was a long stride that sometimes caused the shorter-legged horse of En-lo-e to break into a brief trot, but not Chato's.

Gray in the east, and the light daggers shot their arrows into the spaceless sky. Sun broke the rim on their right and made changing colors of the brush, the cactus, the spiny plants. The wind was cold.

The ground elevated gradually. When the sun was an hour high, Josey halted his horse, pulling Chato beside him. The vaquero still slumped in the saddle, but he was conscious. Looking at the bandages, Josey saw fresh blood, only a little, but fresh blood, soaking through. He grunted in disappointment.

Ten Spot came up from the rear, and with him, Pablo and En-lo-e. Ten Spot turned his blistered face backward, then up at the sun. "How you figuring, Josey? The chances?"

Josey plug-cut tobacoo and cheeked it. His jaws worked slowly as he judged the sun. He hooked a lazy leg over his saddle horn, while the horses blew their sides and rested.

"I figger Escobedo is might near a hour on the trail," he said.

"But it will take him time, will it not, to trail you?" Pablo asked.

"Nope. Na'ar bit," Josey said grimly. "Ye all made that ride to the hayceenda in six hour, walking. I made it in four, trotting easy." He chewed some more, frowning at the figgerin'. A horned toad, in the westward shade of a rock, received a dead hit splat on his head and staggered beneath the rock.

"Escobedo—his riders will cut my trail from the arroyo in fifteen minute of fust light. They'll trail fer a while, till they see the tracks heading dead east. Escobedo knows this country. He's 'quainted that water is at the hayceenda. After thet, he won't trail. He'll tail-whup them hosses straight in. I figger three hour fer Escobedo to make the hayceenda."

"Three hours!" The shocking realization made Chato almost shout. "Why, at our gait, Josey, in three hours we will be but halfway to the canyon. He will catch us in an additional three. He will catch us at the canyon. The canyon is a death trap!"

"They's death traps scattered all over creation," Josey drawled. "Good Lord made more briers than He did flowers."

He clucked the roan into motion and led them on. But Chato would not be satisfied. He was alarmed, feverish. "Listen," he called to Josey, "listen to me, you idiota! Lope the horse, ride faster, I can stand it! I swear on my father's head!"

The words of Josey Wales drifted back to him. "Ye ain't got no pa, ye damned bastard, shet up!"

"All right, then," Chato said indignantly, "then let me drift off into the brush. They will not follow one track. I know this country. I can make it. You, then, can easily outrun him for the border. Allow me this honor!"

Chato watched the impassive back of Josey before him. There was no answer; only the back, swaying in the saddle. He cursed Josey Wales, calling him obscenities that would have brought death to other men; he cursed him with the passionate abandonment only a loving brother who had shared the brush of death could do. The impassive back swayed on. Chato spent his strength and slumped forward again.

From behind him, the cool voice of Ten Spot floated to his ears. "After you riding in, after you and Josey coming two hundred miles to pull a worthless saloon bum from a dungeon. Chato, I will shoot you in the back before I will see you ride into the brush."

Pablo wondered at these men, cursing each other. Risking their lives, one for the other, then threatening. And the cold voice of Ten Spot meant what he said, threatening to shoot him in the back. It was a wonderment beyond the comprehension.

The prairie sprouted more rocks. The ground rose steeper. Weakly now, Chato said, "When we go into the canyon, Josey, Escobedo will send riders along the rim. They will shoot us like pigs in a pen. You comprendes, this, of course," he added bitterly.

Josey spat at a side bush. "Reckin he will if'n we don't make it past the fust quarter mile."

"The first quarter mile?" puzzled Chato.

"The fust quarter mile," Josey repeated. " 'Bout a quarter mile in, they's canyons running east and west, seven, maybe ten miles splitting out from the sides of the canyon. They's cliff canyons he cain't jump ner ride into. If he sends his riders around 'em, cost 'em three, maybe four hours."

"I had not noticed, when we came," Chato said.

" 'Taint yore business to notice," Josey drawled. "Ye're a wuthless cow-trailer thet misses half yer rope throws at a steer. Boar coon, coming down the mountains, if'n he don't take notice of the brier patches and trees he might need in a hurry coming back up thet mountain, he's a damn fool boar coon. My pa didn't raise no damn fool boar coons."

By the sun time, Josey figgered three hours. They halted in the climb, while he pulled the long-glass and searched backward. He guessed they had made fifteen miles from the hacienda. From his higher elevation, he swept the prairie below. The glass was not strong enough to bring out the details; but he could reason the lump on the prairie—the hacienda. And coming close, maybe a mile from the east, a huge dust cloud—many horses, coming fast.

He grunted. "Called it might near on the nose," he said with satisfaction. He called to those behind him. "Escobedo is mighty near the hayceenda. Seed his dust." He clucked the roan into motion, but doggedly refused to increase the walking gait.

The old man would tell Escobedo of the badly wounded vaquero, the Apache girl. He would tell Escobedo that the band of Josey Wales could not put up a hard ride. He would tell.

The telling would cost Escobedo thirty minutes, while he blew his horses, watered them. Thirty minutes.

Josey had known the brute foreman was not dead. Propping his boot heels on the belly, he had felt the tensed muscles as the foreman had tried to hide his breathing. From beneath his hat, he had watched; the eyes slit, looking. So he had taken the gun belt. He had taken the two horses—not for the reason he had told the old man. Two horses, fresh, would mean nothing to Escobedo. He'd have to bring his whole crew. But had he left the horses, the foreman would have ridden out to round up the riders of the hacienda and join the chase. The old man would have ridden to intercept Escobedo, and turned him northeast.

Josey had lied to the old man why he took the horses. No sense giving any idears to sich as them. It added a little edge.

The horses were laboring now, the climb steeper, the sun hotter. But the mind of Josey Wales was not on the sun. Valdez would tell Escobedo that he found no dead Josey Wales in Coyamo. Escobedo would guess the arroyo ambush as that of Josey Wales. The old man would confirm it: Josey Wales was alive.

Josey Wales! With a mestizo vaquero, a one-armed, stupid peon! Josey figgered as he rode. Sich would be the outrage of a uppity feller, figgerin' he was better than sich trash, it would might near make him lose his entire sense of reasonableness. Sounded reasonable.

Josey, reading the sign of Escobedo, he was sich a man. And as a few years later the crafty Sitting Bull would figure the thinking of the egotistical Custer, and feed that egotism, and slaughter him, so the mind of Josey Wales worked on the character of the leader chasing him.

Another thought, a small awareness that had rattled

about in his head, began to grow. Everywhere they had been on the trail of Escobedo—the Apache tracks! Always. Now, slitting his eyes with narrow intentness, he watched the side of the trail.

Another hour, and he halted the horses. With the long-glass he looked backward and saw the dust cloud coming north.

"They're coming," he announced laconically, and moved the horses into motion again. Head down, he watched the edge of the trail. Faintly he saw the tracks, but he frowned, puzzled. They were headed away from the trail, southwest. He motioned Pablo forward. "Ask En-lo-e 'bout them tracks." He pointed.

Pablo spoke to the girl. She swung from her horse and knelt in the dirt. She squatted, studying them. She crawled along their path, twenty, thirty yards toward the southwest. Then she rose and came back. She spoke softly to Pablo, and with her hand motioned north.

"She say," Pablo interpreted, "that the tracks point to the southwest, but they are not going that way. Sometime the Apache run backward ten, twenty miles. The earth-deep is on the toe, not the heel. The sand that flip outward is from the toe, forward, not the heel. The Apache —they are men of her band—they are running backward, for the canyon."

The revelation brought a surprised grunt from Josey Wales. The wind was hot, baking the ground red and yellow, loosing its sand on the upward slope. Josey pushed the horses, blowing froth from their bits, heaving their sides. An hour of such riding brought them to the crest, the plateau. Here they halted, and every head turned backward to look. Far down the long, bouldered slope, they could see them. They were strung out in a long line, just beginning the climb from the desert floor.

" 'Pears we're powerful important," Josey drawled, chewing, and watching the troops.

"Looks like the whole army of Mexico," Ten Spot said. "This Escobedo must be crazy."

"Figgers," Josey nodded in satisfaction, "jest half crazy will do."

They rested the horses a quarter hour. Pablo looked nervously at the oncoming riders. They were beginning to mount the slope.

"Let's move," Josey said. He needn't have urged them.

They crowded their horses close behind. Chato had said nothing. Though conscious, he hung his head down, holding to the saddle horn.

It was easier riding across the plateau, a tableland of patched grass, saguaro cactus and stunted mesquite. The horses' stride was easier and stronger.

Though it was still morning, the sun was high when they saw the mouth of the canyon, a shallow cavern at first, teethed with barren rocks. In less than an hour they had entered it, and almost immediately the trail slanted downward, and the walls on either side rose higher.

The path narrowed and beneath the horses' hoofs was almost solid stone, so that sometimes they slipped on the smoothness. Deeper they plunged along the path, always leading down; and when there seemed no end to its descent, it suddenly leveled out. Three hundred feet above them they could see the rim of the plateau.

Josey picked up the stride of the horses, and though none of them spoke their relief, each felt the exultation as they passed the canyons, splitting east and west, of which Josey had spoken.

Deep canyons. Escobedo's riders at least would not be riding the rims above them.

Josey led them on. The mystic vision that was

Geronimo's did not belong to Josey Wales; but their minds were the minds of guerrillas, and so their channels of thought would run alike on the choice of timing, of terrain. So it was, as Josey rode.

He watched the narrowing sides of the canyon. His eyes recognized the place as they rode into it. Scarcely room for two horses to ride abreast; the sides too steep for a horse to climb, rocked and bouldered. Such terrain lasted for perhaps a hundred yards, before the trail widened slightly, the walls gave more slope. Josey led his little band through the hundred yards of narrowed canyon, the horses' hoofs echoing on the hard stone. Any whisper carried in the canyon, and echoed.

At the end of this stretch, Josey halted the horses and dismounted. Pulling his rope from the saddle horn, he tied the reins of all the horses to it, except the roan. He led them into a narrow clump of mesquite, securing them to the bushes.

Chato sagged, held up by Ten Spot and Pablo. En-lo-e watched Josey closely, her eyes unnaturally bright.

Josey chewed and watched the sun almost directly overhead. There was not a breeze in the canyon. High above, the wind, as though playing a flute over the narrow canyon, sounded distant, agonizing a high-pitched note of monotony. They listened. Far away, there was the rapid clatter of horses.

"They're coming, Josey!" Ten Spot exclaimed. Josey spat on a hot rock.

"Nope," he said softly, "them's two hosses. Escobedo sent 'em ahead, see if we made it past the canyons. Listen!"

The horses' hoofs stopped for a moment, then echoed back, going farther and farther away.

"They're going back now," Josey said casually. "Ten Spot, ye climb near to the rim in them rock on the west side, not high 'nough to skyline ye, but high. Pablo, ye and

En-lo-e, ye climb, same wall, twenty feet below Ten Spot. Find ye some good rock to git behint. I'll put Chato a little uppards along the rocks to git his spot. He'll handle the rifle. Give En-lo-e one of them Rurales pistols. Pass out the ammunition. Remember, nobody shoots till I do."

Ten Spot stepped close to Josey. "If we're bushwhacking, Josey, seems to me some of us should be on the eastern wall. Catch them in a cross-fire."

Josey looked patiently at him, as one looks at the unknowing child. "Fust place, they ain't got nowheres to go, nobody kin git up thet wall. Second," he looked at the sun, "minute er two that sun'll be bringing a shade down our western side; they'll be in the sun, looking inter it, our shooting'll come from the shadows. Understand?"

"I would not have thought of it," Ten Spot murmured.

They passed out the guns, the belts, the ammunition; and clambered up the rocks, almost perpendicular. Gently Josey pulled Chato's arm around his neck, and slowly with ginger steps they moved up the wall. Halfway up, he found the rock, and laid Chato behind it.

Beside him he laid the carbine and the cartridge belt. The vaquero lay flat on his stomach, head down toward the canyon. He struggled to his elbows and lifted the carbine.

"She's seven-shot, Chato," Josey said. "I'm depending on ye to shave the ones down around Escobedo so I git to him fust. Remember, Escobedo is mine."

Chato looked up at Josey. "And you, Josey . . ." Tears ran down the face of Chato. "You . . . ," he choked, "you mean to die down there . . . in the canyon."

Josey Wales looked hard on the vaquero. "I ain't never aimed to die nowheres. I aim to kill Escobedo, which I set out as obliged to do in the fust place." His eyes softened, and his voice, as he turned. "Ye'll do, Chato; rec'lect ye're a better man than ye think."

Chato watched, eyes blearing, as Josey picked his way carefully down the wall.

They watched him from the canyon wall. The sun tilted more, and the shadow crossed over Ten Spot. Josey Wales was on the floor of the canyon. He was rubbing down the legs of the roan, picking up his hoofs, removing pebbles. They watched as he slid the big pistols up and down in his holsters; only then did he swing aboard. He didn't move the horse. The roan seemed to know. He stood, still as a rock. Josey swung a leg lazily over the saddle horn and pulled the long knife.

Ten Spot, watching, breathed to himself, "Cutting his tobacco, by heaven!"

Josey did, and chewed slowly, slowly, checking the shadow inch down the western rim, and listening.

Far away, at the beginning, the sound came, like the distant patter of rain. Then closer. Now the clip-clops of the horses sounded plainly, echoing and re-echoing until they filled the canyon with sound. The sound rose from a grumble into a roar. So many horses! deafening! They came in sight. The army officer at their head, saber swinging; behind him in column of twos, the Rurales. On and on they came, an endless stream. A formidable sight.

The shadow had moved farther down the western wall, but Josey Wales, now both feet in the stirrups, sat stolidly in the path, brilliant in the sunlight as it picked the fire-red from the magnificent roan beneath him.

The army officer was fifty yards from Josey before he saw him. The still, stolid horseman had not caught his eyes. He held up his hand in a halt. He peered beneath his cap brim at the figure, sitting like stone.

Josey Wales tied his reins together, hanging them loosely around the saddle horn. He needed no rein control over the roan; Big Red had made too many charges, faced too many such men on horseback. He knew, and his muscles trembled beneath Josey's legs in anticipation.

They sat silently for a long moment. A whispering line of sound ran back down the ranks of Rurales. Suddenly the shout came; it was filled with rage, mad as a madman, and it came from the throat of Josey Wales. "ESCOBEDO!" And it echoed, "ESCOBEDO! ESCObedo! Escobedo! escobedo!" Far down the canyon, the echo carried the name and the rage.

The army officer pulled a saber and raised it, glinting in the sun. "I am Capitan Jesus Escobedo!" "JESUS Escobedo! jesus escobedo!"—the echo carried the tone of arrogance with it.

The echo died, and for a full minute there was silence, and the voice came flat, hard, taunting, snarling: "I be JOSEY WALES!" "JOSEY Wales! josey wales!" The echo rang away, and a quiver of motion ran the rank of Rurales; the whispering of their voices echoed also, "Josey Wales!"

When Josey shouted again, the voice was not loud, but flat and murderously vicious. "Git something in yer hand, ye yeller-livered slime. I'm going to kill ye!" And the echo carried "kill ye . . . kill ye . . ."

Lieutenant Valdez moved his horse to come beside his Capitan. Chato wiped the sweat from his eyes. He didn't even use a chest shot; he was that good. He blew the side of Valdez' head off. The Lieutenant toppled from the saddle. The crack of the rifle sent ominous sounds through the Rurales. They slid rifles from their scabbards.

The Sergeant moved his horse forward, and the rifle cracked again, knocking him, almost headless, to the ground.

Escobedo sat alone. "You will face him alone!" Chato panted beneath his breath, "you will face him alone . . . as long as I live."

Escobedo dropped the saber. His face was white, either crazed or frightened. He reached and pulled the rifle from its scabbard.

As he did, Josey Wales leaned forward. "GIT, RED!"

The roan leaped in a half rear, front feet coming off the ground. The horse before him was his enemy, he knew from so many times before. The .44's were in both hands of Josey Wales.

Escobedo was slow with the rifle, he sunk spurs to his horse, but he had already lost the edge.

The roan was in a dead run. Josey raised the pistols. One boomed like cannon from the walls of the canyon, then the other. Escobedo flipped backward from his horse, his chest blown out. Still the roan plunged, knocking the horse of Escobedo sprawling in the trail.

Josey whirled him with his knees in a rearing turn and with deliberate methodical action fired into the body on the ground; once, twice, three times. He paid no attention to the line of Rurales so close. He spat on Capitan Jesus Escobedo.

The Rurales were frozen in this instant of brutal action; now they charged. If they expected the lone horseman to flee, they were badly surprised. With his knees, he whirled the roan to face them, and charged into them hammering the pistols, booming from his hands.

From the western wall the rifle cracked, again and again. The pistols began to fire from the rocks. And out of it all, began—low, then rising higher, higher into a scream of inhuman exultation—the blood-fight lusting yell of the rebel, Josey Wales. It tingled the spine of Chato. Pablo shivered at the sound. The Rurales ceased their shouting curses. The scream broke, echoing down the canyon over and over.

Ten Spot was no gunfighter. There was really no violence in Ten Spot, the derringer he had carried was a pretense.

He had gambled, but before that, it had been his apple trees and his books.

And so from his books, the gallant picture of the sixteenth-century duelists was all he knew. He rose, standing erect; one hand on hip, he raised the pistol and cocked; with deliberate aim he fired, knocking a Rurale from the saddle. His ruffled shirt fluttered in the wind. The fine black frock coat gave him the picture of himself in his mind. Again, he raised the pistol. He was no longer Ten Spot. He was William Francis Beauregard Willingham.

Rurales spotting the tall figure raised their rifles and fired. Two of them hit, knocking Ten Spot down. It was undignified. He struggled back to his feet, weaving, blood running from his chest. He deliberated his aim, careful to place his left hand on his hip. Five rifle slugs riddled his body. His gun, already cocked, fired. He stood, swaying, and plunged stiffly through the air, like the statue of a statesman toppled by vandals. He plunged, turning in the air, and smashed against the rocks at the bottom. At last. William Francis Beauregard Willingham was dead.

The Rurales, finding only two abreast could charge the madman, feeling the killing fire from the wall, turned to run. As they did, the figures came out of the rocks on either side. APACHE!

With bows and arrows, lances and guns, they fell on the Rurales. The first horseman to escape was galloping headlong, when the squat figure leaped behind him on the horse and split open his skull like a melon with a hatchet. The powerful Apache then whirled the horse, and with lance leveled, raced back down the path. If the scar-faced would plug the neck of the bottle, Geronimo would hold the bottom!

The screams of dying men were cut short by the sogging sound of the lances striking home. Wounded horses whickered and tried to rise. The Apache moved among them. Where they found men with the scalps of their women, their children, they butchered their bodies.

Josey Wales had dismounted. Sweat covered the blood running from his side, the saber slash on his shoulder.

Slowly he walked to the battered body of Ten Spot, lying almost in the trail. Pablo and En-lo-e stumbled down the rocks, supporting Chato between them. They stood in a little circle, exhausted, and looked at Ten Spot. His body was broken, bloodied beyond recognition.

Tiredly Josey Wales bent and began to remove the rocks, deep enough and long enough to bury Ten Spot among them. He moved slowly, rolling the body into the hole. Chato stood, swaying, while Pablo and En-lo-e helped pile the rocks, making the mound. They paid no attention to the Apache warriors fifty yards up the canyon, stripping the bodies of guns, ammunition, rounding up the horses. Now the trail was in shadow.

Josey pulled his hat from his head. His face looked vacant. Pablo and Chato pulled their sombreros, holding them over their breasts.

"Well," Josey said, and his voice was hollow, "reckin we got to say something."

"Si," Pablo said, "we must give Señor Ten Spot the burial."

"Lord . . . ," Josey began.

"Si," Pablo said.

"Shet up!" Josey snarled, "cain't ye see I'm a-prayin'? Lord," he began again, "Ten Spot wa'ant his name, but I cain't rec'lect off-hand what it was. It was a long un, and Ye'll know it, I reckin." Josey paused and frowned. "Ten Spot never meant nothing by stacking a deck, er bottom-sliding a card. It was jest didn't mean thet much to him. He obliged me, Lord, as I come to pay thet obligation. Reckin he died without a speck o' yeller. We'd 'preciate Ye considering Ten Spot." Josey paused again. "Ashes to ashes, dust to dust, Lord gives and takes away—and sich. Amen!" He placed his hat on his head.

"Amen!" said Chato. "Adios, Ten Spot."

"Amen," Pablo said, and crossed himself. He had not known prayers were said in such a manner.

"Does he not—Señor Ten Spot," Pablo asked quietly, "does he not need something to mark his grave?"

Josey cut a tobacco plug and chewed on the question for a long minute. "Noooooo," he said, "I rec'lect Rose telling me oncet thet Ten Spot when he was drunk talked continual about a place called Shenandoah, a valley which was green, and about some apple trees of his'n." He paused. "No, I reckin that's where Ten Spot's gone, not here. Could be," and the scarred face brightened, "could be he's taken Rose along with him. No," he seemed satisfied, "Ten Spot ain't here."

Pablo and Josey, supporting the stumbling Chato between them, walked to where the horses were tied, and mounted. Josey leading Chato, Pablo following. En-lo-e hesitated. She looked back. The Apache were standing, silent, watching. She waved, and leaped astride the horse, following Pablo down the shadowed trail.

The Apache returned to their work, hanging the guns and ammunition across the horses, stringing the extra horses together, the captured prizes of war. "Loot" the white man would call it—unless he took it himself.

They rode in a long line, Geronimo at their head, down the same trail taken by Josey Wales. They passed the grave of Ten Spot. They did not stop or look at the small bandaged Apache standing by the mound.

It was unbecoming to display emotion. Anything felt by the Apache could be, and was, translated into action; but sometimes, sorrow—there was no way. And so they did not look, for they would not embarrass their brother Na-ko-la.

Na-ko-la stood by the grave as the shadows lengthened.

He squatted, and sang the death song for the hero, which sounds as a savage, meaningless chant to the ear of the white man, but he sang:

"You have helped the helpless who could not help you
You have befriended the friendless who could not be your
     friend
You have died the death of bravery and courage
You will come back in the great circle
You will be born again, Brother, higher in the great
     circle, for your deeds have earned you this place
I, Na-ko-la, have sung, so the spirits of the circle of life
     will hear my humble song for you."

Na-ko-la stood. The song was finished. Tears came into his eyes. The Apache feels deeply. Na-ko-la cried. He stumbled away down the trail. Turning, he called back, "Adios, Sonofabitch!"

Fifty yards down the trail, he found the horse tied to a bush, left for him by his comrades. He mounted and followed their tracks. They would wait.

Chapter 17

Far down the trail, the canyon wall sloped gently upward to the plateau. It was here that Josey led them, until they came again to the plains.

The sun was low and firing the prairie with a crimson haze, scattering the red paint of dust in the air and on the cactus and the brush. They continued north over a slight roll and felt the cooling breath of the evening come, spreading the death shroud on the day.

Pablo eased his horse beside Chato. "Chato, what good has come of it all? The killing—Señor Ten Spot is dead."

Chato shrugged his shoulders. "Must good come of it, niño? It was the obligation. It is paid." Chato softened his voice. "Perhaps good comes sometimes. Quien sabe? Who know? Maybe the wiping out of Escobedo's Rurales will bring El Presidente Juarez north to investigate. I comprendes he love his people and travel about in a plain carriage and will not have even one guardia. Maybe," Chato shrugged again, "the zapotas, the buzzard politicos who fly around him, will confuse him. Quien sabe?" Then Chato said quietly, "Josey?"

"Yeah?"

"Look, back there behind us."

Josey stopped the horses. Lined up on the knoll over which they had come were the Apache. They sat their horses silently and did not move. They were watching Josey Wales, and his little band. Below the knoll, halfway between the Apache and Josey Wales, a mule was tied to a bush. On its back were heavy sacks, sacks loaded with something.

En-lo-e broke her horse into a run, riding to the knoll. She talked with the squat, powerful leader who sat his horse in the center of the line. Now she came back, but only as far as the mule. She motioned to Pablo. Pablo rode to meet her. He dismounted and he and En-lo-e talked, and talked.

Josey crooked a leg around his saddle horn and pushed his hat back from the hard face. "Shore hope we ain't got to tussle them none. I'm mighty near tuckered out."

"I too," Chato said, "am heavily tuckered."

Pablo rode back. He got down from the horse. He still wore the sandals and ragged pants of the peon. He stood and looked at the ground and finally up at Josey.

"She say," Pablo began hesitantly, "she say there is a valley high in the Mother Mountains where the soldado cannot come, where the político cannot reach. She say there is a stream of water that . . ." Pablo paused. "The sacks have kernels of maize, bigger than the thumb,

Josey," his voice rose in excitement, "and the bean, the squash, she say . . ."

"I know what she say," Josey said tiredly.

Pablo hung his head. He looked up at Josey with the humble yet stubborn will that Josey Wales first recognized in him. He took Josey's hand in his own. "I am sorry, Josey. I cannot be a vaquero, a bandido. I—I cannot."

"What," Josey Wales asked sternly, "makes ye think I give a damn what ye are?" But then, with the closest emotion to kindliness that could touch the eyes of Josey Wales, he said softly, "Don't be sorry, son, take your woman to the valley. Raise yore corn, feel good in the honest sweat, lay by the side of yore woman in the evening without listening fer a foot er a hoss. Sleep the good sleep. Be happy, Pablo!"

If there was sadness in the voice of Josey Wales— perhaps there was—then it was of a little mountain farm far away, and too long ago, for the man, now made, to go back.

Tears filled the eyes of Pablo. He shook Chato's hand, and gave the reins of his horse to the vaquero. He walked to the mule. He helped En-lo-e astride the mule. He climbed aboard her horse. He felt he must say something in farewell, and so he waved the stump of his arm. "The first niño," he shouted, "will be name Chato Josey!"

Chato laughed and shouted, "Gracias!"

"Go to hell," said Josey Wales. Pablo grinned, for he knew. Josey Wales only rarely would say the words he felt. He rode, leading the mule and En-lo-e, and the sacks of corn.

Ahead of him the Apache turned their horses toward the mountain, guiding him to the Mother. Only one remained on the knoll. He watched the retreating Chato and the scar-face fading to the north for a long time.

He would fight, nearly twenty years more. He would strike and run and strike again. In one year, with only nineteen warriors, and with Mexican soldados harassing his flanks and his rear, he would fight a United States general with five thousand troops, he would fight him to a standstill. During that time, he would lose only one warrior.

If it is so, as the militarists say, that guerrilla warfare is a warfare of the mind, then the most brilliant mind in the history of guerrilla action must belong to Geronimo. But history would record him as the murderous renegade. He cared nothing for the written pages of the white men. Pages of paper mold and rot and wither away.

Only the spirit grows and lives—lives forever.

Geronimo turned his horse and followed the warriors, and En-lo-e and Pablo.

But first, like Josey Wales, he scanned the horizon, noted the wind that waved the bush, listened to the sounds and read the track in the sand.

Chapter 18

They rode far into the night toward the Rio Grande, as far as Josey dared, until Chato swayed so violently in the saddle, his horse stumbled. Only then did Josey pull off into thick brush. He pulled Chato from his horse. From the canteens, he poured water into his hat and watered the horses and fixed nose bags of grain to their bridles.

Pulling Chato's saddle to him, he laid the vaquero's head on it and covered him with a blanket against the cold wind. Only then did he open his shirt and inspect the ugly bullet gash along his own side. He stripped a shirt and bound himself tightly. Pulling down the fringed jacket, he checked the slash of the saber. It was not deep, and using his teeth, he knotted another bandage around it.

Chato was awake as he finished. "Es malo? Is it bad, Josey?"

"It ain't bad," Josey said quietly.

Digging a shallow hole, he set a fire, where he suspended the can of water and jerky beef to boil.

Chato reached into his saddlebag and brought forth the bottle of tequila. He held it aloft. "Mine!" he announced proudly, "and is all full." He pulled the cork and swallowed long. Wiping his mouth with the back of his hand, he said, "I will say this, Josey, for Señor Escobedo, he keep the best tequila everywhere I have tasted it." To verify this truth, he took a long pull from the bottle again.

Josey watched the fire. "Go ahaid," he drawled, "git drunk. Ye'll make good bait by the fire fer any passing throat-cutter, whilst I sleep in the bresh."

Chato was feeling the warmth of the tequila. "You know, Josey," he said philosophically, "if it was, that I was not Chato Olivares, you know who I would want to be?"

"Let me guess," Josey said drily, poking at the tiny flame. "Ye'd want to run a whorehouse in San Antone?"

Chato took no offense. He smiled. Drunkenly, but carefully, he corked the bottle and laid it by his side with a comforting pat. "No, Josey," he said dreamily, "if it was that I was not Chato Olivares, I would want to be Pablo." He closed his eyes, smiling, and slept.

Josey pulled the can from the flames and wolfed down the stew. Pulling his saddle and blanket into the darkness of the brush, he lay down, rolling the blanket around him against the wind; but first, he laid the .44 across his belly.

Chato lay, as he had been promised, near the fire.

They were up before dawn, Josey pouring stew down Chato and tying his feet in his stirrups. Sun broke the eastern rim as they splashed their horses across the Rio Grande at Santo Rio. The town was asleep.

They did not ride the street, but crossed behind the Lost Lady Saloon, behind the hotel, near the barn where Pablo had hid. Josey stopped the horses at the side of the three square boards, already bent and weathering. The lettering on each was simple: MELINA—KILLED 1868; KELLY—KILLED 1868; ROSE—KILLED 1868. As sparse perhaps as their lives had been.

Josey pulled their horses close to the graves. The wind was cold, and the roan sidestepped against it. He pulled his hat lower against the blowing dust, and from his pocket he pulled an object and dropped it on the grave of Rose. It was the glass earring. The wind rolled it, pushing it against the board, and sand began to cover its glitter.

"It's done, Rose," Josey said quietly. The roan stomped and sidled. He turned him into the wind.

"Si," Chato said, as he passed the leaning board, "it is done."

They rode northwest, quartering the horses into a blue norther wind. They did not stop at noon; and late, as the sun touched the jagged teeth of the buttes to the west, they saw the Crooked River mountains.

A line of horsemen were to the west, silhouetted against the sun high on a ridge. "Comanch," Josey said. He pulled the long-glass and watched. A huge fat cloud of smoke rose in the air, followed by a smaller cloud, and then a third that was waved toward Crooked River.

Josey swung the long-glass to the mountains of the ranch. A thin ash smoke rose, followed by another, another and another. It was the thin smoke of the Cherokee.

"Well," he grinned at Chato, "Comanch sent the word. Big cloud, big chief, meaning me—little cloud, which means a hombre wuth next to nuthin', thet's you— waving it north, means we're coming in. T'other smoke," he added with a satisfied air, "that was Lone, thanking 'em fer the message."

Chato raised his bottle of tequila. The wound was hurting. "To hell with it," he said, referring to the little cloud.

Dusk had fallen when they rounded the mountain, into the warmth and the grass of Crooked River Ranch. "By God," Josey said, "even from here I kin smell Granma's cooking. She'll have a big un fixed up fer us." He quickened the gait of the horses, who were bending, snatching at the long grass, as they walked.

"Josey," Chato said.

"Yeah?"

"You will not tell Granma of the puta and me in Saucillo, eh?" They rode on, and Josey Wales made no answer.

"Josey?"

"Yeah, I heerd ye," Josey said.

"You know the belt I have, the one with silver concho for a buckle. You have always wanted it. Once you tried to trade with me, eh? If you will not tell Granma of the puta, the belt is yours. What you say, Josey?" Chato's voice was anxious.

They rode further in silence. Josey was chewing and considering. A longhorn snorted and trotted away. After a long time, the words floated back to Chato. "I reckin," said Josey.

The soul of Chato Olivares was now at peace. Granma would keep him resting, maybe even a month, while he sat beneath the big cottonwood and watched the others work. The belt, it was nada. He could always borrow ahead on the wages for another. Peace—for even the Comanche knew: the word of Josey Wales was true.

Afterword

by Lawrence Clayton

The very best recently created hero of Western fiction and film is Josey Wales, the battle-hardened Confederate guerrilla fighter who kills Yankee soldiers to avenge the brutal murder of his wife and young son by Kansas Red Legs in Missouri in the early stages of the Civil War. Wales refuses to stop his vendetta when the war ends and simply transfers the hard riding and fast shooting guerrilla tactics at which he excels to robbing banks. Then he becomes a hunted outlaw forced to kill in order to live because of the reward offered for his capture or death.

The creator of this character was Forrest Carter, who chronicled the adventures of his outlaw hero in two novels, *Gone to Texas* (1973) and *The Vengeance Trail of*

Josey Wales (1976). Orphaned at five, as he tells the story in his 1976 autobiographical account of his boyhood, *The Education of Little Tree* (his Indian name was Gunyi Usdi, or Little Tree), Carter lived with his Cherokee grandmother and his half-Cherokee grandfather until their death when he was ten. With no formal schooling, he worked on his own as a cowhand, wrangler, farmer, and at other odd jobs around the South and Southwest until he attained success with the publication of *Gone to Texas*. His fourth and last book was *Watch for Me on the Mountain* (1978), a superb novel depicting the Apache leader Geronimo as a mystic warrior of unsurpassed ferocity.[1]

Carter's brief but highly successful literary career began in 1972 when he wrote a novel privately printed as *The Rebel Outlaw Josey Wales*. A major step came when through his agent, Rhoda Weyr, he placed the book with Delacorte/Eleanor Friede of New York, which issued the book under the title *Gone to Texas*. The book sold well. Carter made several personal appearances to promote this and his succeeding books. He appeared live for a very successful interview by a supportive Barbara Walters on the *Today Show* on July 29, 1975. He made a later appearance at the Wellesley Book and Author Patron Party in Dallas in 1978, where he shared the platform with Lon Tinkle, Elizabeth Forsythe Hailey, and Barbara Tuchman, all prestigious literary personalities.[2]

His career made a meteoric step when his first book was made into a film. Carter had sent copies of *Gone to Texas* to various people including Hal Wallace of Universal Studios. Another was director/actor Clint Eastwood, who quickly bought the rights, directed the film, and starred in the title role. When the film version of the novel, *The Outlaw Josey Wales*, appeared in 1976, Carter's success as a writer seemed certain. The film was the first Western in years to show a profit at the box office. The screenplay by Sonja Chernus and Phillip Kaufman alters the novel in several ways—especially by adding the characters of Captain Terril and Fletcher—to provide unity that would not have been present had the novel been directly made into a film, but the strength of both works is in the outlaw hero, Josey Wales.

Eastwood also planned to make the second book, *The Vengeance Trail of Josey Wales*, into a film, but that plan was aborted. A film version of the second book was made starring Michael Parks, but the project was never released.[3] Audiences may hope to see the project resurrected by Eastwood, whose portrayal of Josey epitomizes the character that Carter created.

As a novelist, Carter knew his material thoroughly. He frequented libraries and was a voracious reader as well as an astute researcher of geography, history, and folklife. For example, one can easily trace landmarks cited in Wales's trip to Indian territory and then on into Texas. Carter's knowledge of the Southern guerrilla leaders and tactics, of Indian legend and lore, of weapons and horses, and of the evil men inflict on others was remarkable and became grist for his fictional mill, especially the creation of his outlaw hero.

In developing the figure of Josey Wales, Carter relied heavily on the established historical and mythic traditions of the Western outlaw. Wales's background in Missouri, the "cradle of outlawry," is an excellent choice, for men like William Clarke Quantrill, Bloody Bill Anderson, and Fletcher Taylor, all acknowledged masters of guerrilla ferocity, emerged from this setting. The Missouri people's hatred of the Union, its institutions, and its leaders permeate the personality of Wales. Several of the activities credited to Wales are commonly associated with the Missouri outlaw Jesse James, whose life parallels the fictional existence of Josey Wales to a remarkable degree. Several conflicts with authorities prompted James to join the rebels, and he began his training as a guerrilla under the direct influence of Bloody Bill Anderson, one of Quantrill's best lieutenants. Carl Breihan says that Jesse James "fought with the fury that even the guerrillas had to admit was inhuman." According to Anderson himself, James was "the best fighter in the group" and was "not afraid of the devil himself."[4] During the war, James is known to have visited Indian Territory on at least one occasion as one of the guerrillas. After the war had ended and the James-Younger gang took to the outlaw trail, their first robbery was that of the Clay County Savings Bank in Liberty, Missouri, in February of 1866, the same event that Carter uses to launch Wales's career. Fewer resemblances to Josey Wales are found in the life of Cole Younger, but his home was burned by Red Legs in 1862, and his mother and sister were harassed by Unionists. These and other details are incorporated into the background of Wales.

Gone to Texas and *The Vengeance Trail of Josey Wales*, like Machiavelli's *The Prince*, may well embody Carter's fantasy of the ideal leader, one willing to resort to any end, even to violence, in order to thwart evil politicians and institutions and to protect his followers. The activities of Conn Tolley and his Texas Regulators and the comments in the conversation of Wales and Ten Bears that highlight the irresponsibility of government, the evils of the Catholic church in Mexico, and the brutal behavior of the Mexican Rurales of Captain Jesus Escobedo show Carter's concerns.

The same attitudes are apparent in his other work. In *The Education of Little Tree*, Carter criticizes institutionalized religion and politics. For example, when Little Tree is sold the dying calf by the man who claims to be a good Christian, Little Tree tells his grandmother that he has learned not to trust Christians. When the Methodist minister who runs the orphanage to which the boy is sent denies that Little Tree has a soul because his parents were not married in a Christian ceremony, Little Tree experiences racial intolerance and bigotry. When the politician makes his speech to the people of the small mountain hamlet, Little Tree sees political sham and deceit. The native boy, like Twain's Huckleberry Finn, guides the reader through the sham to reality, and Carter's criticism of government and religion is apparent.

Just as he seemed ready to achieve fortune and fame, Carter died suddenly in his mid-fifties on June 7, 1979. At the time of his death, Carter was reportedly working on a screenplay of *Watch for Me on the Mountain,* and to do so he had put aside a projected Little Tree book entitled *The Wanderings of Little Tree.* This volume would involve various latter-day outlaws in Oklahoma—Pretty Boy Floyd, for example. He had planned another Josey Wales novel. Neither, however, has surfaced in the years since his death. Carter also was preparing for publication a volume of his poetry, the kind, he said, that "New York editors don't call poetry." With Carter's death, this project, to be illustrated by Austin artist Bruce Marshall, an ardent fan of the Confederacy, failed along with the film versions of the other books.

I had met Carter at a Southwestern Writers Showcase in Abilene in 1974 and liked him immediately. I used his book in my course in life and literature of the Southwest that fall and found his work well received by students. Since he was in Abilene at the time, he agreed to speak to the class and captivated the students. During the years that I knew Carter he was a cordial, amiable man whose stories about his life and experiences fit the mold he sought to project. We enjoyed many a casual lunch whenever he was in town.

On the surface, Carter's work is exciting Western romance. Below the surface, however, one finds a serious bent toward social and religious criticism, for these two factors strongly influenced Carter's view of the world. The second level more than suggests that Carter went beyond the bounds of a writer of popular or formula Western fiction. True, he was an outstanding storyteller but he ably used the formula as the vehicle for his campaign against social and religious disorder and injustice.

Whatever his past, some things about Carter are certain. First, he was an excellent storyteller. The action depicted is often brutal; perhaps Carter is at his best when depicting the violent action he could bring to life in a remarkable way. But he could express tenderness and humor as well, as readers who have laughed and cried over *The Education of Little Tree* can testify.

Another certainty is that Carter had in him a streak of outlawry in the Confederate guerrilla sense. He stood outside the circle of polite and conventional politics and fought instead for what he thought was right. He had the strength to follow his convictions, just as Wales does in following his convictions with the fervor of the blood feud that drives him for revenge. Carter's small but important body of fiction entitles him to a place in the halls of honor of the genre, to rank with Louis L'Amour, Zane Grey, Luke Short, and others who depicted brutal, exciting human drama of the Western frontier and who peopled it with heroes in a time when heroism was sorely lacking in fact and fiction.

Lawrence Clayton
Hardin-Simmons
University
Abilene, Texas

NOTES

1. All four books were issued in hardback by Delacorte Press/Eleanor Friede of New York. References are cited in the text.

2. *Dallas Times Herald.* Monday, October 2, 1978, p. B-3.

3. Letter from Mrs. India Carter, 7 December 1983.

4. Carl W. Breihan, *The Day Jesse James Was Killed* (1961; rpt. New York: New American Library, 1979), pp. 25–26. Breihan quotes Anderson but cites no source.